A DEATH OF DIVINITY

Also by Maddie Jensen

Legacy of the Lost Trilogy
Blood of Queens
Heir of Kings
Fall of Empires

Smoke & Mirrors Trilogy
Book One

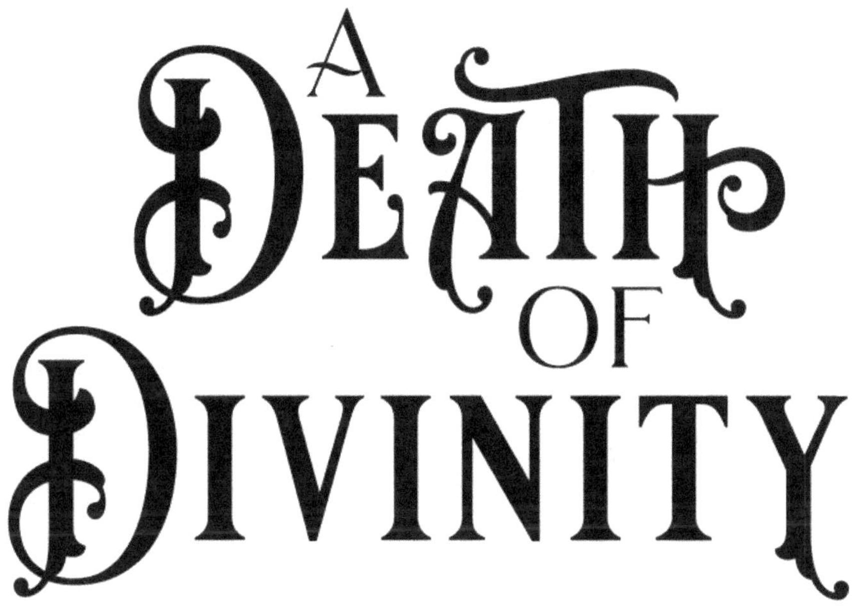

MADDIE JENSEN

A DEATH OF DIVINITY
Smoke & Mirrors Trilogy: Book One

The text of this book is set in 12-point Adobe Garamond Pro
Interior Design by Fox & Rabbit Press, LLC

ISBN:
978-1-7641074-0-2
978-1-7641074-1-9 (ebook)

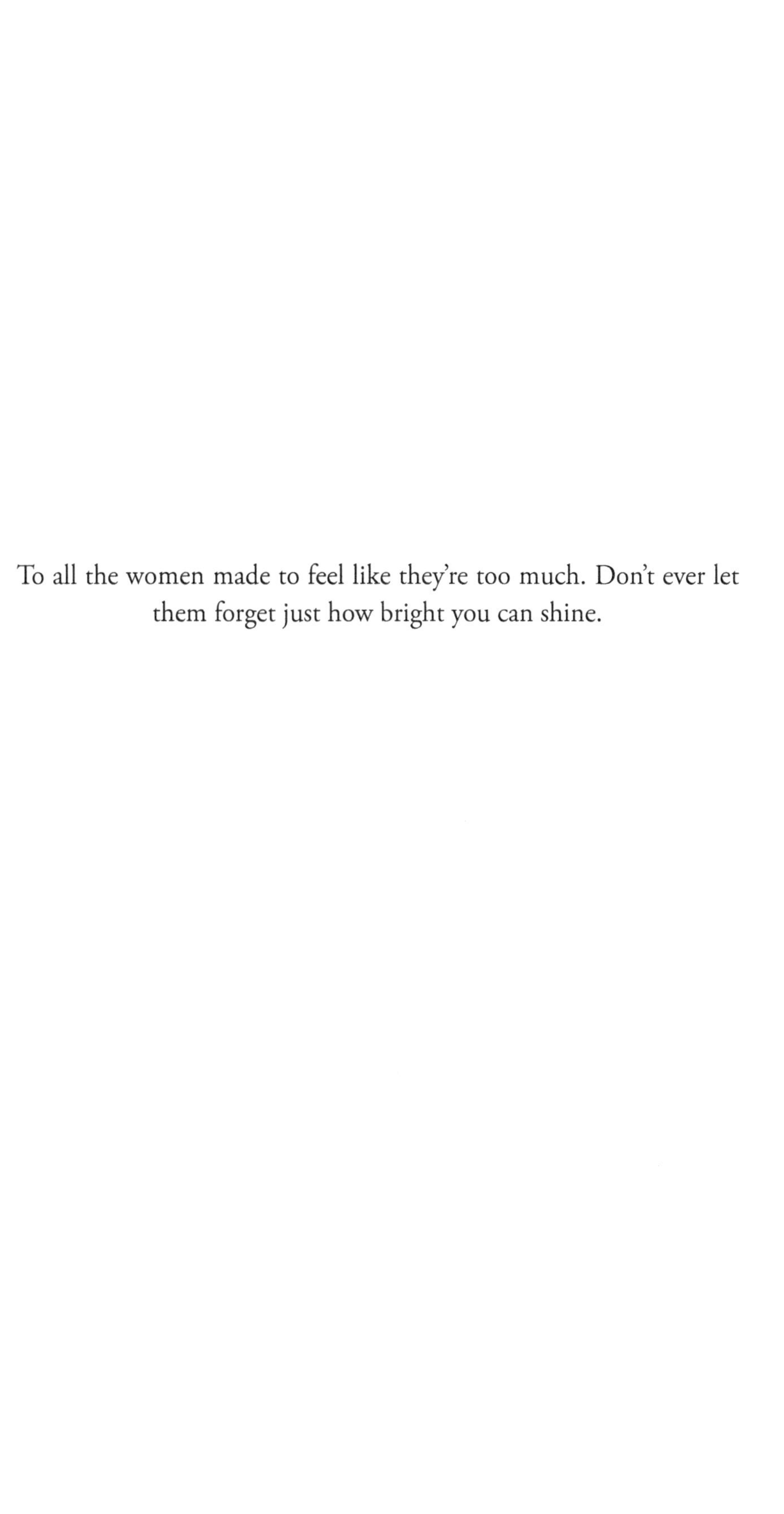

To all the women made to feel like they're too much. Don't ever let them forget just how bright you can shine.

TRIGGER WARNINGS:
some suicidal ideation, domestic abuse, toxic relationship, pregnancy,
PTSD, physical violence, attempted murder, sexual situations

TABLE OF CONTENTS

PART THREE

PART ONE
QUEEN OF SWORDS

CHAPTER ONE
Andie Fairley

THE WINTER NIGHT'S AIR WAS WARMED by the heat of two dozen braziers and the promise of power as Andie Fairley strode toward the carnival's crimson and ivory tents. Her polished black Mary Janes clicked against the wooden walkway, one of many winding through the trees of Central Park. Even the magic that was cast to keep the carnival comfortable in the dark of winter was no match for nature. Her teeth chattered as she wrapped her black velvet coat tighter around her body. The warmth of the fires caressed her cheeks, a welcome respite from the icy breeze that whirled through the park on a whim.

Beneath the thick coat, the glittering gold of her costume was a nod to the carnival sector that she performed for: Sun Carnival. As the sector associated with summer, the audience's rapt attention was hinged on light and laughter and warmth. Andie had performed in the Carnival of the Seasons for the past year. The cold did not bother her; winter's bite prodded away with a cheerful indifference and the vigour of her performances, leaving her warm enough to endure.

Tonight's performance, though, would be more marvellous than any before. Many eager to attend the city's anticipated Times Square ball drop were certain to flock to Central Park either before or after, taking in the Carnival's wonders as if they were parlour tricks and not genuine magic.

As the clock ticked down the minutes until 1920 dawned over New York City, Andie had delved deeper into her spellbooks than ever before. It embarrassed her to utilise verbal magic, her incantations proving her capable of only the most basic of the magical arts. Unless Lord Summer deigned to give her some of his own magic, she had little choice.

"You'll catch your death in that."

Andie's heart thundered in her chest as she spun to face a familiar grinning face. Patrick Rhodes had been friends with both Andie and her older brother, Syl, since they'd been children. These days he worked at the Carnival as a stagehand, predominantly in the Sun Carnival. Andie liked to think it was to be close to her, though certainly such a thought might be rooted in vanity.

"I'm wearing a coat, thank you."

"Still." Patrick indicated her long, brown legs, bare to the night's encroaching chill. "Doesn't Lord Summer know that winter exists, too?"

Patrick brought with him a sense of ease that helped Andie's rigid posture relax, that coaxed a playful smile to her lips. With Patrick, she didn't have to bother with the masquerade of the bold showgirl. She could just be Andie Fairley, and it was enough. She had spent years pushing aside the truth of what that meant, and why her steely confidence dissolved into giddy butterflies every time he grinned at her.

Over the years, somewhere between ten-year-old Andie weaving him a friendship bracelet out of the silk strands of a dress she had outgrown, and the horrific night when her and Syl's fierce sibling bond had torn at the seams, Andie's feelings for Patrick had shifted. They had spent a night together when she had been sixteen, fuelled by desire and desperation and dread. He had probably pushed it behind him, a flight of fantasy, just as he'd probably discarded the bracelet to gather dust in a drawer.

"Are you going to watch my show tonight, Pat?" Andie asked coyly, though she did not need to guess at the answer. Syl might view her performances with disinterest bordering on disdain, but Patrick's face was always there in the crowd, warm brown eyes sparkling with delight.

"Wouldn't miss it." Patrick caught her hand and spun her in a circle, her heels catching in the grass as she stumbled. He rested a hand on her waist to steady her, and she tilted her chin up, ignoring the heat burning in her cheeks. His dark eyes were so deep she could melt into them, brow creasing as he examined her. "Hey now, Larkin doesn't have you working too hard, does he?"

Larkin. Lord Summer was the name that everyone referred to him by, but since he and Andie had become close, he'd insisted that she call him Larkin. He'd taken a shine to her, and Andie was counting on that now to further her career. Not just her career—her access to higher magic. Only the inner circle of the Carnival had access, and it was something that Andie wanted desperately.

Larkin was the only one who understood just how hungry Andie was, how far she'd go to succeed. She had never dreamed she might become a glamorous showgirl in the Carnival of the Seasons, but even that wasn't enough. She was more than just something lovely to be looked at, and that was where she and Larkin agreed.

Andie was well aware that Larkin's interest was what had initiated her abrupt rocket upwards to become one of the Carnival's most renowned performers. She owed him a lot, and part of her regretted wanting more. But she was restless; being a beloved attraction wasn't enough. She wanted to be a puppeteer. She wanted to pull the strings.

Andie liked Larkin, but she didn't want to sleep with him—at least not yet. She doubted that Ursula Delavane, Larkin's mother, needed to utilise sex as a weapon to get her way. Andie didn't think she should have to either. She wanted Larkin's respect and trust, things she felt she was close to earning.

"Of course he doesn't have me working too hard." A bright smile flashed across her lips, mischief dancing in her eyes as she tilted her chin up to examine Patrick, the way strands of light brown hair fell across his face, the strong set of his square jaw. "He's just not as easy to be around as you are."

What Andie felt for Larkin was different from her bond with Patrick. Her stomach squirmed with a strange guilt when she flirted with Larkin, every calculated time she rested a hand lightly on his shoulder or arm, every time she kissed him. She ruthlessly pushed any such shame aside. Andie did what she had to in order to get ahead, as she had always done.

Larkin was a means to an end. Patrick was something unattainable. It was laughably odd, that she trusted her chances more with a powerful member of the elite than with a mere stagehand, but Andie was haunted by the words Patrick had whispered in the mid-winter mist after they had caught their breath.

"We shouldn't have done that. It was wrong."

Wrong. Patrick saw their dalliance as a mistake, and five years later, recalling the guilt and regret in his tone was a knife twist to the gut. Andie had come to him with tears streaming down her face and a hollow heart, seeking comfort in the one place she had known she could find it. Patrick had kissed her until the jagged edges of her pain had softened, touched her in ways that had stolen the breath from her lungs.

To her, it had been magic and mourning all at once. To Patrick… well. He had made his opinion quite clear.

"Andie?" Concern laced Patrick's voice as he used a finger to gently tip her chin up. She playfully batted him away, looking up at him through her lashes. She did not need to wear the mask of the carefree showgirl with Patrick, and yet she found herself doing it regardless, like it had become second nature.

"I'm fine." The glitter that adorned Andie's eyelids sparkled in the corners of her vision as she planted a hand on her hip. "Really, Patrick. You should be more concerned with making sure the braziers stay lit rather than if I'm cold or well."

Hurt flashed through his eyes, so brief that Andie would have missed it if she hadn't been watching him so intently. It made her confident smile falter, her hand slip from her hip. She stepped back, heel sinking into the damned grass once again. Before she could speak, someone else sauntered into the light of the braziers, golden-haired and luminescent as the sun.

"There's my best girl." Larkin Delavane's pearly white smile coaxed a dazzling one from Andie in return, an impulse reaction to echo his mood. "You look stunning tonight, sweetheart. Are you ready for the performance?"

"Of course." Andie let Larkin rest an arm loosely around her waist, his blue eyes fixed on Patrick. Everyone in the Sun Carnival in particular whispered about Larkin and Andie. He flirted with the showgirls, but any fool could tell his interest in Andie was different. Deeper, more genuine perhaps. She had him under her spell, and she knew it.

"Maybe I'll see you later." The smile painted across Patrick's lips was forced, and familiar guilt seared through Andie as she gave a carefree shrug of her shoulders. The guilt made a home inside her more often than not where Patrick was concerned.

"Well, maybe."

Patrick nodded curtly and stuck his hands in the pockets of his brown trousers, whistling as he headed toward Bloom Carnival. When Andie chanced a look at Larkin, there was a hard gleam in his blue eyes and a wickedness in his smile. He stepped in front of her, resting his hands on her hips as he pulled her close.

"Larkin!" Andie giggled, teasing out the syllables of his name, resting her hands on his chest to steady herself. "I just did my makeup. If you kiss me, you're going to get lipstick everywhere."

"So what?" Larkin tilted his head to the side, a few loose strands of blonde hair falling across his forehead. That was typical of Larkin, not wanting to play by the rules. It had not been long since he'd come to power, but he had taken every opportunity to revel in it.

Andie enjoyed the benefits that came with it that extended to her. Higher forms of magic could be gifted, poured out of the user and into the hands of someone else. Though she itched with impatience to generate her own, the ability to already do so did not override the fear that came with revealing something fundamental about herself.

Verbal magic, or Larkin's gifted magic, were safe. No one asked about her using them, but questions would arise once Andie displayed her proficiency for mind magic, and that was only scratching the surface. The volumes spoke of mind magic with casual cruelty: "a form of magic unlocked with those of unsound mind".

Andie had almost thrown the book out of sheer anger when she'd first read it upon arriving at the Carnival a few years ago, though the volumes were centuries old and did not come to the conclusion that magical society had today: mind magic was generated by those whose minds operated differently. Andie, who found it hard to breathe in stressful situations and collapsed in the corner of her trailer after performances, certainly fit into that category.

"Come see me after the performance." Larkin's voice was husky as he caressed her cheek, but Andie utilised her typical saccharine smile and caught his wrist.

"It's a late night. I'm certain I'll be tired."

"You know I don't mean anything untoward," he drawled, his eyes lingering on her lips. Though he had never said as much, the desire that glowed in his eyes and the familiarity of his touch of late indicated the direction he saw their relationship going. "I just enjoy spending time with you. I have some matters to attend to, but then I can come and see you."

'Matters' indicated that it was something far above Andie's station. She had stashed a bottle of expensive champagne among her costumes back in the trailer. Her hopes of taking it over to Patrick's trailer to share a drink were dashed by Larkin's invitation. Lord Summer would not take kindly to being rejected for a stagehand. Andie was tempted to pop the cork of the champagne and drain the whole bottle herself.

"No promises." Andie pressed a quick kiss to Larkin's lips, drawing back to look up at him through her lashes. "I have to make sure this is a new year celebration to remember first."

Chapter Two

Prue Clermont

WATCH WHERE YOU'RE GOING, TOMATO!"

A horn blared through the cacophony as Prue Clermont skirted around the car's hood, stammering profuse apologies. She had been so focused on her goal that she hadn't looked twice whilst crossing the street, and ended up nearly flattened by a taxi. The driver threw up his hands in exasperation.

"Sorry!" Prue shouted for the third time above the hubbub, her heels clicking a staccato beat as she stepped up onto the pavement and wrapped her coat more tightly around her slim form. Even through the thicket of trees, she could see the Carnival. A delighted smile spreading briefly across her lips, she hurried toward the bright lights, drawn in like a moth to the flame.

The Carnival of the Seasons had existed for decades, or perhaps longer, though Prue had only become involved with it during her husband's absence. Searching for an escape while Mark was on the front lines, an acquaintance of Prue's had introduced her to the magic and marvel of the Carnival. It was not an open event by any means—but Prue's friend knew the ins and outs.

Prue clutched tonight's ticket in a tight fist, crumpling the red paper between her fingers. She felt guilty for lying to Mark and saying that she was visiting her aunt, but if she had told him about her real plans, he'd have forbidden her from attending. Mark was not a man for extravagance, and the Carnival was precisely that.

A few months ago, Prue would never have ventured into such a scandalous place, but the Carnival was addictive. It had an allure to it, and she didn't see the harm. It wasn't as though they checked for escorts at the gate. Besides, tonight was special; it was the new year, the turn of a decade. Mark had mumbled something about working late at the coal factory, and Prue felt a hot lick of shame at the relief that washed over her at the realisation she could spend her time elsewhere.

Her heart started to beat faster as she approached the admittance gate. Prue could see the bright lights and colourful tents begin to shimmer into view. You didn't see the Carnival unless you wanted to. If you didn't know about it, it didn't exist. That was one of the hundreds of magical things about the Carnival—*real* magic, the sort of thing Prue hadn't believed in until she had seen it with her own eyes.

"Prue!" A familiar head of sleek, dark auburn hair bobbed toward her. Prue's heart fluttered in her chest as Sadie Crawford embraced her tightly. The two had become friends through a chance meeting at a fundraiser during the war, and it had been Sadie that introduced Prue to the glitz and glamour of the Carnival.

As the ticket taker checked Prue's sweaty, crumpled ticket and nodded his approval, it was like stepping into another realm, a dizziness washing over her as she moved through a pair of white stone pillars. The trailers were painted in bold colours and sweet-smelling smoke wafted up from an unknown source. A man on stilts ambled from one tent to another while showgirls in glittery costumes giggled and flirted with several businessmen standing by the candy stall.

"How have you been?" Sadie asked as she linked her arm through Prue's. Her scent of citrus and honey mingled with the others, the warmth of her fur coat rubbing softly against Prue's skin.

"Well enough." Prue did her best to keep her tone neutral. Sadie was unwed, and though Prue's closest friend, could not understand the difficulties of marriage. Mark had returned from war a different person, one who screamed in his sleep and stared into his morning coffee with blank eyes. It wasn't something to mention in polite conversation, and she found that when she was with Sadie, Mark wasn't what, or who, she wanted at the forefront of her mind.

Prue did her best to understand, but her patience stretched thin. This was not the Mark Clermont she had married, and it unsettled her to be living with a stranger. The pair had been married for a decade, and they had experienced their share of trials and tribulations, lack of children and money troubles chief among them. This though...it was something Prue could not comprehend, and she distanced herself from it at every available opportunity.

She wished that their marriage could have been the whirlwind romances she heard women gossiping about, but there had never been a spark between Prue and Mark. Their marriage had been convenient for both of them, and try as Prue might to get through to the shell-shocked stranger her husband had become, the silences between them had grown painful.

"I see." Sympathy laced Sadie's voice, but one of the best things about her was that she did not ask questions or pry when Prue closed herself off. Instead, she steered them toward the food stalls, the scent of buttered popcorn making Prue's mouth water.

Prue purchased a toffee apple from the stall, her stomach squirming with discomfort at handing over some of Mark's hard-earned money. She was typically a frugal woman. Even at the Carnival, she did her utmost to keep a tight grip on her purchases. She would only buy herself one treat, she promised herself.

"How come more people don't talk about the Carnival?" Prue asked, casting a look around at the throng gathered around the attractions.

Sadie scoffed. "Who is going to believe you if you come into work rambling about how magic is real? Part of the mystery hinges on whether they think it's really magic, or an illusion made to *look* like magic."

At first, Prue had believed the latter. She was a respectable woman, and not one to fall for cheap tricks. Yet over time, and more sessions at the Carnival, she had realised that what she saw was real. Not everyone was as perceptive, with most of the women in Prue's sewing group claiming the Carnival was a charlatan's ploy to obtain money that the wealthy elite didn't even need.

"Besides, there are wards," Sadie said as she licked thoughtfully at her own toffee apple, the dart of her tongue momentarily distracting Prue. "Invisible barriers that separate the magical world from the normal one. I have no idea what that powers them, but they say the barriers have existed as long as magic has."

Prue didn't quite know what to make of that. To her, the air was fraught with magic. She struggled to reason how others simply wouldn't know or see that. Perhaps all it took was a discerning set of eyes to perceive the magic for what it was. What, precisely, did the barriers keep out? Prue shuddered and wondered if she was better off not knowing.

"So, which of the carnivals did you want to visit tonight?" Sadie asked, grey eyes glimmering with the promise of adventure.

A colourful signpost gave Prue pause. The Carnival of the Seasons was so large that it was composed of four smaller carnivals, each with their own attractions. The Frost Carnival was representative of winter, with its faux snow and glittery white appearance. It was the first of the carnivals that Prue had experienced. The huge carousel in the Bloom Carnival was tempting, as was the Ferris wheel of the Dusk Carnival. However it was the Sun Carnival and its gaudy moving performances that drew Prue in tonight.

"The Sun Carnival."

Delight glimmered in Sadie's expression as she followed the bright yellow sign, Prue licking at her toffee apple as she glided along in her wake. In truth, Prue knew little about Sadie, but perhaps it was the enigma that made her friend so enticing. Sadie was unwed and lived alone—much to the consternation of people like Mark who could not understand how a woman in her thirties was happy that way.

The sound of applause and loud cheering snared Prue's attention, and she craned her neck to see what was happening. Tonight's performance consisted of jazz music, acrobats, and showgirls. They always fascinated Prue, tumbling around in the air, even seeming to float at times. That was when she'd known the magic was real, when she had seen performances that defied logic.

One of the girls boasted tawny brown skin, piercing blue eyes, and cocoa-coloured corkscrew curls, and she drew the most attention, especially among the other pale and fair-haired performers. Her golden costume glittered like a thousand stars in the bright lights, and the way she swayed her hips was almost as hypnotic as the sparkling butterflies she blew out from her hand like a kiss.

The crowd gasped as the butterflies fluttered about them, some of them settling on people's shoulders and in their hair. The girl did several flips backwards, landing in a split. As soon as she hit the ground, miniature fireworks burst out around her like a ring of colour. She pushed herself to her feet, spreading her arms wide above her head to indicate a grand finale.

"Ladies and gentlemen, Andie Fairley!"

It was a man in his mid-twenties with a golden crown of stars in his fair hair. She had seen him around the Sun Carnival before and knew who he was—Lord Summer, the pinnacle of authority in this particular carnival. He strode over to the curly-haired girl and kissed her cheek, causing a wide smile to bloom across her mouth.

Rumour had it that the previous Lord Summer had died during the war, leading to this young man taking his place. He was a charismatic figure, and his presence was like sunlight wherever he went. The same could be said for Andie, who was clearly a favourite performer. Someone collided with Prue's shoulder, a rich floral scent tickling under her nose, but within the bustling crowd, she couldn't have said who had jostled her.

Finishing her toffee apple, Prue checked her watch to realise with alarm that it was getting close to midnight. She didn't know where the time went, but it just seemed to fly when she was at the Carnival. Mark would be over in Times Square by now for the ball drop. If she wasn't home by the time he returned, he would begin to get concerned, and if he called her aunt to check in on her, he would realise she had lied to him.

"I should head home," Prue said, turning an apologetic look onto Sadie, who lifted a nonchalant shoulder.

"I'll come with you!"

Warmth flooded through her, the sort of warmth she only experienced with Sadie. Though she cared about Mark and loved him in her own way, it was never the sort of way that other women gossiped about over lunch. She had never felt that heat with him, and it both excited and alarmed her that she did with Sadie.

Sadie was the sort of woman you would see in the clothing catalogues, with an auburn bob and piercing eyes. She carried herself with her head held high, as though nothing in the world could quash her spirit. It also didn't hurt that she had the cutest button nose and plump lips often carved in crimson lipstick.

As Prue walked away from the lights, music, and laughter of the Carnival, it filled her with a sense of sorrow. It was almost like leaving a part of herself behind in a way she couldn't quite explain.

A cool chill raced up Prue's arms, a sudden change to the wind that whispered of danger.

Prue staggered, the toe of her pumps knocking against something in the darkness. Sadie quickly caught her arm and straightened her up, but the trees hissed in the wind, shifting so that moonlight shone down on the glassy, brown eyes of a young man. Her sharp gasp ripped through the quiet, and she put a hand over her mouth.

No longer a man, but a corpse, a blood-red gash carved across his pale throat.

Prue's stomach turned, bile burning its way up her throat. She'd only ever seen a body in a funeral home, never something like this that wasn't a grainy, black and white photo on the front page of the paper. A loud wail and a sharp snap came from overhead, Prue flinching at the noise before looking up as colour exploded in the night sky above them, fireworks bathing them in bright pink. In the distance, a bell tolled as the clock struck midnight. The cry of 'Happy New Year' was audible over Sadie's choked sob.

"We should do something." Prue cast around. She had yet to see a police officer at the Carnival, but certainly there must be someone who could help them. "We need to report this."

"No." Sadie's fingers clamped tight on Prue's shoulder, grip hard enough and voice firm enough to make her wince. "We…we can't be here. We need to leave, and pretend that this never happened."

"Never happened?" Prue asked incredulously, nausea rolling in the pit of her stomach as she looked down at the body again. "A man is *dead*, Sadie."

"I'm aware of that," Sadie snapped, tears shining in her eyes as another snap sounded overhead and fireworks bathed her in an eerie green. It was in that light when Prue realised her friend recognised the man.

"Was he someone you knew?"

"No." The single syllable was sharp as a knife and twice as cutting, for Prue could see in the horror of Sadie's expression that it wasn't true. "Look, Prue…I thought the Carnival would be fun. I thought it would be an experience you'd enjoy, but there is more going on here."

Prue's brow furrowed in confusion. "I don't understand."

"I don't want you to understand." The bite in Sadie's tone gnawed its way beneath Prue's skin. Her grief morphing into determination, she caught Prue's hand in a vice-like grip. "I want us to leave, *now*."

Prue's protests had so far gone unheard, so she didn't think another attempt would be taken well. She stumbled as Sadie dragged her off, knees trembling. The Carnival had been her escape from a marriage she no longer felt a part of, from a life she was struggling to continue living. Now it seemed even her escape was tainted, the memory of glazed brown eyes and a slashed throat burning in the back of Prue's mind.

The Carnival was many things, but it was only at that moment Prue began to realise that it was dangerous.

25

CHAPTER THREE

Ursula Delavane

LARKIN ARRIVED HOME IN THE EARLY hours of the morning. Ursula heard the door to their upper Manhattan brownstone manor click closed from where she sat on the aubergine velvet couch in the living room, taking a drag of her cigar. The champagne silk of her pyjamas whispered against her skin as she crossed her legs in irritation. She blew out a plume of smoke as Larkin froze at the threshold, startled to realise that she was still awake.

Ursula was well aware of where her son had been. The revelries at the Carnival for the New Year had continued well into the darkest hours of the night. It was not where her son had been that irked her, but rather who he decided to spend his time with. She arched an eyebrow as Larkin dusted his shoes on the mat before removing them.

"You were with that girl again."

"Her name is Andie." Larkin shot her an irritated look, sweeping his blonde hair from his eyes. "You can call her by her name, Mother."

Andie. That was her name. She was a beautiful young woman. Ursula could see why Larkin was so taken by her. Once upon a time, she wouldn't have batted an eyelid at such a distraction, but her son was Lord Summer now. He had responsibilities, and he couldn't afford to shirk them because of *Andie*.

Ursula supposed that a harmless flirtation with a Sun Carnival showgirl was better than becoming absorbed in the politics of the other Seasonal Lords. She respected them, as did all associated with the Carnival. That didn't mean she agreed with them.

Cyril Fordyce was the worst. Ursula's lip curled at the thought of Lord Autumn, who had been a treasured friend of her late husband's. He'd taken Larkin under his wing and introduced him to decadence he'd never beheld. Franklin had never much cared for his son's induction into the magical world, holding Larkin at arm's length as he always had, much to Cyril's delight when her boy had come to power. Unfortunately for Ursula, Cyril's magic was also the strongest of all the Seasonal Lords; to plot against Cyril was to beg for death.

"You missed a meeting with the others," Ursula reminded him as she tapped out her cigar into a glass ashtray, pushing herself to her feet.

"So?" Larkin rolled his eyes, his nonchalance bleeding into the relaxed slump of his posture. "They're boring. All they discuss is politics, how they want to expand the Carnival, how they're always looking for more. I don't need to be at a meeting to know what they talk about."

The meetings with the Lords were one thing, but there were others he should have a standing with, men who had involved themselves in the magical world, and from whose influence they could stand to benefit. The Alderidge brothers, for a start, were precisely the sort of people they wanted to be rubbing shoulders with. A healthy investment from Garrett Alderidge would be rewarded with support for his next campaign.

"It's important you attend, Larkin," Ursula said sharply as he hung his coat on the stand. "Don't you realise that? With your father gone…"

"Yes, I'm in charge," Larkin snapped back, spinning around to loom over her. He clearly resented the conversation they'd had for months since his father had died during the war, tearing a hole in the centre of their lives that throbbed with each mention of 'responsibility' or 'duty'. "I know that. I know we need to make good impressions to keep the Sun Carnival afloat. I *know* how it works, Mother."

Ursula wondered if she had been so petulant when she had been twenty-five years old, though she'd never been as spoiled as her son. No, her life had been different when she had been his age—Larkin had been four by then, and already restless. He'd inherited that from his father, who could never understand Ursula's patience.

Franklin had been tempestuous, but he had been steady, a constant force of nature that Ursula found she could rely upon. She had been the dutiful wife throughout their entire marriage, understanding and accepting that her role was to be subservient.

"No, you don't," she responded with quiet firmness. Larkin was a child when his father had become Lord Summer. He'd grown up knowing about the Carnival, learning magic. That didn't mean he was suddenly equipped for a role that had been thrust upon him. Franklin had not particularly cared to educate their son on what it would mean to become Lord Summer, and Ursula's partial insight following his death was all that Larkin had.

Larkin shrugged, and Ursula noted scarlet lipstick streaked on his neck. "We're making a profit. Business is booming. Our magic is stronger than ever."

Ursula thought that if Larkin was so interested in 'business', he should be interacting more with their investors. The Lords were mostly from old-blood wealthy families but the investors were a different calibre. Many of them were new money, hungry to spend their top dollar on the benefits that magic could buy them. Did Larkin truly care what they thought, or was he too busy fooling around with showgirls?

Ursula was torn between horror and fascination at the mercurial nature of magic. As the former Lord Summer's wife, she knew magic's true face. She performed it where and when she pleased, as did most associated with the Carnival's inner circle, though as a woman she was only entitled to perform verbal magic. It had never much perturbed

Ursula, for she had seen what befell women who were granted a greater power.

The higher forms of magic were a vicious beast, only sated when something was given back. This year, they'd used more magic than ever before. Mind magic, heart magic, soul magic. The three forms that required you to give more of yourself than many would dare, an exchange for power.

Magic was a thing of beautiful violence. The end result was pretty as a picture, but the cost wasn't always worth it. Verbal magic was learned through books, but performing it took more than just an education. Those with the higher forms of magic may as well have been gods for the way they were worshipped. Once, Ursula had looked at magic with wonder. Then she married Franklin Delavane.

"We are also taking more risks, Larkin." She held in a deep breath, attempting to centre herself in a bid to not lash out at her son. "Your father was always careful. I know you had low opinions of him…"

"They were more than opinions, Mother," he bit out. "They were my reality."

A cloud of tension thickened over them, weighing heavy over her at the hurt and anger in Larkin's pale eyes. Franklin was a sensitive subject even now, with him buried in the ground. She reached for Larkin, but he brushed her off.

"Go to bed, Mother."

Ursula bristled with indignation. She thought it was high time Larkin found himself a wife. The inheritance of lordship depended on a legacy, and Larkin had no one to pass the mantle onto. It was time he turned his back on revelries and made a man of himself. Not that lordship and age were the making of a man—Cyril Fordyce had been married three times, and conducted numerous affairs with Carnival performers.

Perhaps she had become an overbearing mother to an adult son, but Larkin was all she had left. With Frankie dead, all she could do was ensure Larkin lived up to everything his father had been. He looked like an angel with his fair hair and light blue eyes, but there was a darkness in him.

If Larkin did not pass on his legacy to his own kin, it would go to someone else, as had been the case with the current Lord Winter. If that mantle left them, Ursula would be nothing more than dust. She refused to fade into the shadows. She hadn't when Franklin died, and Larkin was the only tether to power she had left.

She had wanted more children, but Larkin's birth had been complicated to say the least, and Franklin had little interest in a large family, dismissing her distress at the idea she may not be able to have more children. His indifference to the matter had made things clear cut: Larkin would be their only child.

"This dalliance with Andie needs to end." Ursula gripped the polished oak bannister as Larkin ascended the stairs. "Larkin, I mean it."

Most of the showgirls were pretty little airheads with no ambition other than to perform and look good doing it. Andie was different. There was a certain zeal about her, a hard determination to be something more than just Larkin's favourite, despite her humble Hell's Kitchen origins. Perhaps that was what he liked about her. Her son never backed away from a challenge.

There were women of far better breeding who would suit Larkin more, women who would accept their role with a gracious smile as Ursula had. Andie was, quite simply, not suitable. A curly-haired hellion from the harshest streets in the city was not an appropriate match.

"We have bigger concerns." Larkin swivelled halfway up the staircase to face her, fingers resting on the bannister and his jaw clenching. "I don't have to go to meetings to know about the rebellion going on. What are they calling themselves now? The Magical Freedoms Brigade?"

Not everyone was happy that magic was carefully regulated amongst the elite, and those disgruntled people—mostly former Carnival employees and those who had never quite made it to the top—had started a resistance group to campaign for magical knowledge to be freely accessible. Ursula had not thought much of it, as magic had been regulated for many centuries. Unfortunately, those voices had grown louder post-war, demanding magic become a resource rather than something for the upper class to gatekeep.

"It will die down." Ursula drummed her fingers against the bannister. "It always does. These little grumblings come up from time to time. Once we learn who's behind it, we can silence it. God only knows what the masses would do if magic was just there for anyone who wanted it."

The general populace had no idea of the sacrifices that the higher forms of magic entailed. They could not know how much work went into learning even from just the spellbooks. Verbal magic was nowhere near as powerful, yet it was cumbersome in its own way. It would be like handing everyone a loaded gun and expecting they wouldn't be stupid enough to pull the trigger.

"Yet you insist on focusing on a girl I'm seeing." Larkin's lip curled derisively. "Do get some perspective, Mother."

His feet thudded up the remainder of the stairs. One of the floorboards outside his room creaked, and the door to his bedroom clicked shut.

Exhaling deeply, Ursula returned to the couch and lit up another cigar. She had not slept well, not since she'd received the telegram about Frankie's death. It seemed so cold and impersonal, letters neatly printed across a folded-up page, and sometimes she still believed he might come walking back in through the door. She had more power and influence than she'd ever possessed when he'd been alive, but she would give it all up just to have Frankie back.

She remembered how she had sank to her knees, the iciness of the kitchen tiles biting into her skin. Her marriage to Franklin had not always been sunshine and rainbows, but the treasured moments remained embedded in her memory. The sly wink he'd tipped her when she reached the end of the aisle on their wedding day, the marvel in his eyes as he'd beheld Larkin for the first time. He would never live to see grandchildren, to see the sort of potential their son might have.

Under the guise of a spoiled young man, there was something else in Larkin, something Ursula was afraid to look at. She knew the darkness of the Carnival, and just how horrific it could be, what it cost to keep it going. But that was nothing compared to the savagery that Ursula suspected lingered in her son, concealed beneath a charming exterior.

Magic could corrupt. Ursula had read up on the old legends, the days of ancient magic in the time of King Arthur Pendragon. Arthur, who had been driven mad after obtaining all forms of higher magic, leading to his fatal fight with Mordred. It was rare, but not unheard of, to possess all three. For some though, the cost of magic was too high a price to pay. Whether fact or fiction, Arthur's fate remained a cautionary tale.

Was it corruption eating away at Larkin? Was it the impact of lordship? Or was it something else entirely?

Chapter Four

Andie Fairley

There was a deep ache in Andie's joints as she made her way through the Sun Carnival toward her trailer. It was the good kind of ache, the sort that told her tonight's performance had been a success. A satisfied smile crossed her lips as the door to the trailer squeaked closed behind her and she shrugged off her coat, draping it over the back of one of rickety chairs circling a small dining table.

The trailer always smelled saccharine sweet, thanks to all the perfumes that had been sprayed in there over the years. The sweetness mixed pleasantly with the milder lavender of the candles that Andie liked to burn before she went to sleep. It wasn't much as space went, but it was safe enough that Andie kept her Colt Derringer in the top drawer of the dresser instead of under her pillow.

A few ardent fans, men she didn't recognise, had attempted to waylay her with promises of cotton candy and cherry pies after her performance. Andie's practised smile had never faltered as she'd politely declined, though there had been steel in her spine and a stiff set to her shoulders as she returned to the trailer.

"You'd think after months with you as the star of the show, it'd be someone else's turn." Flo Rafferty, a fellow showgirl who she shared the trailer with, lowered the *Vogue* magazine she'd been flicking through.

A rivalry had developed between Flo and Andie the moment that Andie had skyrocketed into Carnival success. Flo had been with the Carnival longer, despite being a few years younger than Andie. She looked like the sort of doll that Andie had played with as a child—glossy blonde hair, dark blue eyes and a flawless porcelain complexion. Underneath the pretty exterior, there was bitterness and jealousy.

"Oh, don't worry, I'm sure your turn will come," Andie said in a cloyingly sweet tone, sitting down in front of the mirror and removing the golden clips from her hair. She was used to Flo's hostility by now, and took every care to throw her position as Larkin's favourite in her face.

"He will get bored of you." Flo pushed herself up off the bed and padded over to Andie, her grin cruel as she toyed with Andie's curls, fingers mimicking talons as they played with her hair. "You aren't the first girl he's shown an interest in. You aren't special."

Andie gripped Flo's wrist, twisting hard, and the younger girl gasped sharply. In the foggy reflection of the mirror, she saw Flo's eyes widen. A cold smile curved Andie's lips as she yanked Flo's wrist, making her cry out. She was tired of vicious little bitches like Flo, girls who thought they could have anything they wanted if they just pouted and batted their eyelashes and who spat venom when they were passed over.

When she released Flo, Andie eased herself out of the chair with languid grace, leaning against the dressing table and folded her arms over her chest. She was filled with a surge of satisfaction as Flo nursed her wrist, glaring at Andie.

"If I'm not special, what the hell does that make you? He doesn't even look at you."

"Fuck you, Alexandra." Flo stomped back over to her bed, flopping amidst her myriad blankets and pillows to sulk.

Andie rolled her eyes, striding over to the wardrobe she and Flo shared. She tilted her head to the side, making a show of going through the dresses before she removed Flo's favourite from the hanger. It was one of the only things Flo owned that wasn't glittery, as most of their costumes tended to be. Andie held it up to the light.

"Do you mind if I borrow this?" She took Flo's sullen silence as affirmation, a smug smile crossing her lips. "Didn't think so."

Andie changed into the dress, feeling Flo's heated gaze boring into her back. When she spun back around, tying her hair up into an updo, Flo's expression was like sour milk. She clearly guessed where Andie was going, and who she was meeting with.

"Do you really think if you have sex with him, he's going to share the secrets of higher magic with you? You would really sink that low?"

Andie gripped Flo's chin, digging her nails into her skin. The younger girl glowered but didn't tug away. Making Flo uncomfortable gave her a thrill of power. It wasn't nice, but Flo was such a bitch that she made it easy.

In truth, Andie wanted to see Patrick. Perhaps some of her animosity toward Flo stemmed from feeling as though she had little choice in seeing Larkin instead. A thumping at the trailer door made Andie release Flo, nudging past her with a furrow in her brow. Larkin knocked like a gentleman, not hammering upon the door like a savage.

Wrenching the door open, a scowl crossed Andie's lips. Neither Larkin nor Patrick stood outside; instead Andie was greeted with glittering green eyes, a wide smile, and a stumble that spoke to an overconsumption of alcohol.

"Hey, baby sister." Syl Fairley leaned against the side of the trailer with a mild slur to his speech that made Andie huff irritably. Upon hearing Syl's voice, Flo poked her head around the corner with a shy smile.

"Hi, Syl."

"Oh, fuck off." Andie grabbed her coat and stepped outside, closing the door in Flo's hopeful face. The other showgirls had a tendency to flirt with Syl, always gushing about how *different* he was. Three years older than Andie, the siblings shared the same brown skin and coiled hair, but Syl's eyes were green instead of Andie's blue. Several inches taller than Andie even in her highest heels, Syl's easy smile was enough to make the other girls swoon.

The others may find him charming, but Andie was constantly vexed by him. Syl lapsed easily into vices like alcohol and drugs, slithering comfortably into such decadence like a snake through the long grass. Though he was typically security at the Carnival, everyone had noticed he wasn't quite stable. A surge of guilt washed over Andie along with the prickle of annoyance, because when it came down to it, *she* was the reason he had fallen so far in the first place.

"What do you want, Syl?" Andie asked, toying with the ends of her unruly curls.

"I can't check in on my family?" His tone remained buoyant, but there was a twist to his lips and a hard gleam in his eyes. He was the blade of a knife waiting to slice, and he always cut the deepest when his breath was sweet with mead. "I suppose it's something that doesn't come to mind for you, does it?"

A nerve ticked in Andie's jaw. "Come on."

If this was to devolve into an argument, as it often did with Syl, she didn't want the curious ears and prying eyes of the other showgirls to catch wind of it. Folding her arms over her chest, she prowled toward the trees that encircled the clearing where the living quarters trailers were set up in Central Park.

The braziers surrounding the trailers emanated a soft glow, the only sign of the magic that warmed the Carnival within the colder months. The neon hues of the fireworks no longer lit up the skies, and the cheers from the Carnival had dulled down into quiet chatter in the distance. Once the shade from the trees filtered out the starlight, Andie whirled to face her brother.

"I asked you what you wanted. If you've come to throw some verbal barbs, I'm not in the mood for it."

"But you always have some of your own to retaliate with." A mocking note edged Syl's tone, before he leaned against the trunk of a tree, swaying slightly on his feet. "Fine. Dad's been asking about you. Says you haven't come to visit in weeks."

A cold chill whistled through the leaves, making Andie rub at the goosebumps that rose on her arms. For the past year, she had embraced the glittering image of the Carnival showgirl, all too pleased to don the bubbly mask that won the hearts of revellers everywhere. She convinced herself she belonged among the elite, but the Carnival employees were not of the same stock as their benefactors.

Flo had grown up in the streets, a two-year stint in a brothel in The Bronx preceding her time as a showgirl. Patrick was an orphan, working in the smoke and steam of local factories before he'd been employed as a stagehand. Like them, Andie had a gritty past she would prefer to forget, and though she loved her father, he was the harshest reminder of all. She and Syl had escaped the mould-spotted, cracked windows, and the damp mildew of Hell's Kitchen, but its ghost breathed down her neck.

Warren Fairley had done his best to raise two young children after their mother, Sarah, had abandoned them. He and Sarah had never been officially married, though he had been gutted when she had fled back to her family in Harlem. It was difficult, a second-generation Irish American man raising two mixed children, in an apartment block building where there was constant chaos and cacophony.

He was a tarot mage, what the Carnival elite would have sneered at as a cheap charlatan. He had nothing but love for Syl and Andie, even if he had warned them against working at the Carnival. Even if Andie could never shake the horror in her father's eyes the night he realised what she had done.

Why is there blood all over you, Andie? What's happened? What have you done?

"I've been busy in the leadup to the New Year's show." Andie tilted her chin up, flaring with indignation at Syl's interference. Why did he even bother working at the Carnival? Why did he stay so close to her, if he could hardly stand the sight of her? "Not that it's any of your business, Sylvester."

"Cold and dismissive, as usual," Syl snorted, the hard breath coming out as mist from his nostrils. His skin was a shade or two darker than Andie's. He had the same strong jaw and high cheekbones as their father, paired with pale green eyes and full lips often curved into a condescending smile. "Don't know what I expected, really."

"Fuck off," Andie snapped, heat searing through her despite the cold that had settled over Central Park. There were times when she and Syl were amicable. Those times were when her brother possessed a clear head. Syl drank to take the edge off his own pain, but instead he added to Andie's.

"Just thought you might care about your family." A cruel twist of Syl's lips made her stomach drop, certain of what was coming next. "Oh wait…"

Bitterness coated Andie's tongue even as angry tears blurred her vision. Syl's teasing had never possessed a malicious bite to it, not until a few years ago. Not until Andie had torn apart their sibling bond the moment she'd first fired a gun. Could she blame him for lashing out at her in retaliation?

Andie's hands balled into fists and her knees trembled. The magic surged within her, as it always did in her most vulnerable moments, greedily pushing at the boundaries of her stability and composure. She ignored the deep ache, the gnawing, as she always did. It was a temptation to use her mind magic, to prove what she was capable of, if only to distract from the fact that she could do far more.

Syl almost tripped over something, and his eyes flicked down and widened in horror, and he stumbled over his own feet as he backed away. Andie turned her head to follow his gaze, and all the noise of the Carnival was sucked into a void. The only sound was that of her own breath rattling against her ribcage as she stared down at the corpse on the ground, half-bathed in moonlight.

Patrick was pale in death, skin white as snow against the deep red wound across his throat. His brown eyes, warm in life, were cold and glassy. There was none of the mirth and merriment that she had known since childhood, only agony frozen across his face, burning its image in Andie's mind. With shaking hands, she reached for his face, for any trace of the man she had loved and lost before she could ever have him.

Andie had seen death before, held out her hand to brush against it, but this was different. She wanted to scream. She wanted to cry. Instead she fell to her knees, the damp grass soaking into her skin. But she did not feel the cold; she didn't feel anything.

A flash of colour against the pallor of Patrick's fingers caught Andie's gaze. Gently prising open his bloodstained fingers, Andie's body stiffened. Behind her, Syl's choked sobs grazed against the edge of her awareness. Andie's slender form trembled as she lifted her discovery up to the crisp night air.

The friendship bracelet she'd made him, the silk strands worn and discoloured from frequent use.

The loss stabbed through into her gut and twisted hard, the shock and grief threatening to tear her apart piece by piece. Another part of her heart, ripped free from her chest and discarded. A gaping hole where Patrick had once been. Where he never would be again. Where she would never be able to tell him that she loved him.

* * *

Hell's Kitchen had a scent, like overripe fruit masking the pungent odour of mould. The buildings were in a constant state of disrepair, tin roofs studded with holes and cracked windows. The streets that Andie had once called home were lined with rubbish and rubble, and the shouts of neighbours as children ran across the road from one hovel to another.

Nonetheless, there was a vibrancy to them, a splash of colour across the brick houses. It was a defiant spark of personality that Andie had never appreciated as a young girl, but she admired and took note as she strode down the cobblestones in Mary Jane heels instead of flats with battered soles. Hope was etched in every stroke of the paintbrush, joy in the crackle of jazz music on the record player.

Once, she had been a creature of those streets, a child of shadows and secrets. Now, she tugged her fur-lined coat tighter around herself as she stomped up the apartment stairwell and rapped her knuckles against her father's front door.

Syl's presence was a silent one, a ghost trailing in her wake. His eyes were red-rimmed and his jaw had been set the entire journey. She was not the only one who grieved for Patrick. Silence was preferable to the venom that Syl spat when they set out, vowing vengeance upon whoever had killed Patrick. There was no doubt in Andie's mind either: it had been a murder.

Who would want to kill Patrick? His mischievous smile was infectious, and he was not the sort to hold a grudge. Andie couldn't think of him having any enemies. Every time she thought of the silk friendship bracelet clutched between his fingers, her eyes brimmed with tears and a lump itched in her throat.

The door creaked open, the scent of Warren's rose potpourri wafting under Andie's nose. It reminded her of telling tales late at night under worn sheets, reminded her of how strongly she associated this place with Patrick, with how much she associated Patrick with the feeling of home.

Though Andie had wanted to be resolute and poised when she visited her father, she pressed her hands over her mouth to muffle a sob. Warren Fairley moved forward to wrap his arms around his daughter. She buried her face in his chest and cried, furious and heartbroken over all the tender moments with Patrick that had been ripped from her, and how she would never have any more of them.

"Oh, sweetheart." Warren's deep voice rumbled against Andie's frame as she sniffed back tears. "Come inside. Seems we have a lot to talk about."

Andie glanced over her shoulder at Syl, hands stuffed in the pockets of his threadbare brown coat. Her brother's grief did not manifest as tears, but an awkward, silent intensity. He didn't utter a word as he brushed through the front door past Warren and Andie, boots slapping against the old hardwood floor as he marched into the kitchen. Andie trudged in after him, clicking the front door closed behind her.

The kitchen hadn't changed. An old stove with a stained kettle perched atop it, ready for tea. The teal wallpaper was peeling and discoloured, and the chairs at the dining table still wobbled when Andie sank into one. Warren bustled about the room, humming quietly under his breath as he brought the kettle to a shrill whistle. A strained silence encompassed Andie and Syl. She wanted to bait him with barbed words to elicit a response.

"I was so sorry to hear about Patrick." Warren strode over to the table with a mug of tea for each of them. He was as tall as his son, but his pale skin and blue eyes spoke to his Irish heritage. In his late forties, his dark hair had begun to streak with silver at the temples.

Andie stared down into the murky brown depths of the tea, dashed with milk today. A privilege, since in their youth, they'd barely been able to afford food, let alone the luxury of milk for their tea.

Their past of poverty lingered all too close, a gnawing hunger in Andie's stomach throughout her childhood that had only been sated once she'd joined the Carnival. They had all done their best to make ends meet. Andie recalled her part clearly, the jazz performances that Warren adored making her mouth hurt from smiling and her toes hurt from dancing. She shifted uncomfortably in her expensive coat and wriggled her feet in her brand-new shoes.

Syl had his choice of jobs, a wealth of opportunity that had never been extended to Andie. With Prohibition looming, an array of less savoury positions were also available to Syl. Her career choices were limited, though all possessed a prerequisite for a sweet smile, an art that she had perfected.

A handful of tarot cards were strewn face-down across the table. Andie wondered if Warren had a client earlier. Tarot cards held no magic in themselves, but Warren's mind magic could seek out even the most evasive of answers. The cost was moments of melancholy, mornings when Syl and Patrick had taken Andie out to get a loaf of bread because Warren couldn't bring himself to get out of bed.

"He was murdered." It was the first time Syl had spoken in perhaps an hour, words loaded with venom. When he raised his green eyes to look at their father, they burned with a sheen of tears and a rare steel. Andie was mildly astonished that he had come along sober, though she didn't put it past him to have a flask of moonshine hidden in his pocket, bartered or bought from one of the many bootleggers who were drawn to the Carnival like moths to the flame.

"Well, no one thought he cut his own throat, Syl," Andie responded coolly, the heat of the tea scalding her tongue as she raised it to her lips.

Syl's livid gaze flicked across the table and he rose magnificently to the bait just as she had suspected he would. It would not do to have her brother silent and sour. If she could not dig her way out of the hollowness of her grief, she would elicit rage in another. Someone needed to be enraged about Patrick's death if she could not find the willpower to light that match within herself.

"He was in love with you, you know."

If there had been malice in Syl's tone, Andie would've loaded on a bitter smile in return, a withering look through the steam that steadily rose from her mug. Instead, the brittle china seeped cold beneath her fingertips, chilling her to the bone. A stone dropped through the pit of her stomach, awakening something in the dark abyss that Patrick's death had excavated inside her.

"What?" The word was half-whisper, half-threat. She had been so focused on the Carnival, on her performances, on what that could get her. She hadn't stopped to consider the possibility that perhaps her feelings were reciprocated, that the glances Patrick snuck her were more than just those of a friend.

"You heard what I said, Andie." Syl slammed his palm down on the table, tea sloshing over the edge of his mug, one of the tarot cards fluttering down to the floor. "I know what happened between you two. I know he thought you deserved better than him, so he told you it was a mistake. He loved you. Why else do you think he kept that stupid bracelet after all these years?"

As Andie had lit the fire within Syl, so did he ignite something dangerous within her. The bitterness of an unrequited love sharpened, tearing apart a 'nothing' and digging mercilessly into the 'something' that she and Patrick could have been. Tears blurred her eyes, knees trembling and hands shaking. There had been no spite in Syl's words, yet the cruelty of the situation cut deeper than a knife, deeper than how far the body she had once dumped in Harlem River had sunk.

On the stovetop, the kettle shrieked as flame burst to life beneath it. Andie gritted her teeth and tempered her magic, pushing it back down into the box she kept it in. She reached down to pick up the fallen tarot card, turning it over to reveal the Ten of Swords. She slapped it face-down on the table with the other cards.

"Andie." Warren rested a gentle hand on her shoulder. "You need to rein it in. If those at the Carnival knew about your heart magic…"

"They wouldn't care." Andie shook her head fervently, though the lie tasted of ash on her tongue. Of course they would care, or else she'd have displayed it by now. "It's fine. I control it, it doesn't control me."

Magic was treacherous, as Andie had learned the hard way. It both enthralled and terrified her, and she had risen *and* fallen by its savage grace. It had not been magic that had ripped Patrick from her, from this world. Simply a knife, crude and efficient. A knife was nothing when it came to the power that surged through Andie's veins, a power she kept secret for fear of what the others, what *Larkin*, would think of her if they knew the truth.

Magic was neither blessing nor curse, but a weapon, and Andie was fully loaded.

Chapter Five
Prue Clermont

THE KETTLE SHRIEKED TO A BOIL, rocking violently on its stovetop perch as steam filled the tiny kitchenette in Prue's apartment. The shrill whistle pounded against Prue's throbbing headache as she sat hunched over the scratched wooden dining table, and she groaned, raising her fingers to massage her temples in the hope of alleviating the dull ache. She brought her toast, slathered with butter and a cheap apricot jam, to her mouth and crunched.

The one-bedroom apartment that Mark and Prue had lived in for the past seven years was modest and bare. Most of their furniture was secondhand or gifted from members of their families over the years. The walls were painted a patchy cream, and Prue had hung some old art she'd inherited from her family around the place. Nonetheless, she could never help the claustrophobic way the apartment made her feel, the walls encroaching in on her, a heaviness settling on her chest.

The beige couch had splitting seams and the fabric was rubbed raw, but they certainly couldn't afford a new one. The refrigerator's loud hum was audible all throughout the night, so they closed the bedroom door to ward it off. The odour of expired vegetables permeated the apartment even when the kitchen had been thoroughly cleaned. The neighbours were loud and the ones above them argued often, but it had not been the neighbours that had kept Prue awake last night.

Prue hardly slept after the incident at the Carnival. She tossed and turned, waking in a cold sweat despite it being winter. Memories of the young man's glassy eyes and the gory cut across his throat burned behind her eyelids. She had risen before the sun crested over New York City in pale yellow and orange, busied herself tidying the kitchen and preparing Mark's lunch.

At the sudden thump of footsteps Prue raised her head from her half-eaten toast, remembering the boiled water on the stovetop. Easing herself to her feet, she mixed the hot water and ground coffee, pouring it into each of the chipped cream mugs on the bench. Beside her, Mark raked his fingers through his unruly sandy hair as he opened the refrigerator and squinted inside.

"You were back late last night."

Prue reached around him for the milk, wrinkling her nose at the sour scent but pouring it into the coffee nonetheless.

"I was at my aunt's."

Mark raised his eyebrows, suspicion etched across his features. "You wear your best shoes and nicest dress to your Aunt Ethel's now?"

Hot guilt seared through Prue, piercing as broken glass. She and Mark had been married a decade and though they'd had their share of issues, it was not often that they lied to one another. Prue remained silent and dipped her head in quiet shame as she slid Mark a plate of toast and handed him a mug of coffee. She was not accustomed to lying, and with something that did not come naturally to her, she fumbled it.

"You went to the Carnival, didn't you?" The question was as bitter as Prue's first sip of coffee, lacking the sugar they had struck off the latest shopping list. Typically, Mark would instead cut the bitterness with something alcoholic, but the crutch he had relied upon since his return had been kicked from underneath him with the introduction of Prohibition.

"I didn't think you would be happy about it." The words were soft on Prue's lips, masking the unpleasant surprise that left an acidic aftertaste on her tongue. The Carnival was a frivolity, a luxury. A working man like Mark, a man with deep purple crescents underlining his eyes and blackened fingernails, was not the sort of man who sought out its magic.

"I'm not." His moustache bristled with barely concealed anger. In the early days of their marriage, he had never possessed a temper. Though their union was more a proposition of convenience than one of romance, Mark had been steadfast and sweet. He picked her daffodils from the local parks on his walk home. He had not forced her to give up her work as a seamstress, allowing Prue the freedom to take up a handful of regular clients.

The Great War had ruined him. It had ruined *them*. They had seen their share of misfortune and difficulties, from the onset of poverty to the revelation that Prue was unable to have children—the latter of which was a secret relief rather than a distress to Prue. Nonetheless, they had weathered the worst storms together. Until the war, until Mark came home and flinched at the sound of a car backfiring in the streets and battled demons Prue couldn't even fathom, shouting at her when she closed a cupboard too loudly.

"Mark, I…"

"You were with Sadie, weren't you?" Mark blew out a long breath, sinking his lanky frame into one of the chairs with a creak. "I've told you, Prue. I don't like her, and I don't think she's a good influence on you."

Prue leaned against the bench, folding her arms over her chest. "So you'd dictate my friends now?"

"Of course not," Mark retorted, the forcefulness of his tone causing Prue to grit her teeth. "But she's strange. She's thirty, isn't she? Unwed, and none too displeased about that."

Prue's Aunt Ethel had never married. She lived a few blocks away, in an apartment that reeked of mildew and cat piss. She thought it best she did not point this out, since Ethel was the example of the sort of woman that Mark believed Sadie would become. Prue had once asked why Sadie had never married, and the other woman had simply shrugged and replied that no one had caught her interest. A simple response, free from the burdens of societal expectation. Prue had admired her for it, the way she cared nothing for the judgement of others.

"It was just nice to have a break," Prue murmured.

"Breaks don't exist for people like us." Mark pushed himself to his feet, dumping his empty mug in the sink. "I have work to do, and you have to maintain the place here. Maybe bring on a few more clients, though I'm sure the denizens of the Carnival don't need their socks darned."

"Mark." The syllable was riddled with exasperation.

He pressed a quick kiss to her lips. "I'll be home late again. The boys have been unruly with Prohibition setting in soon, so there's more work to do in the factory, but it means some more money for us."

Prue rubbed her arms as Mark grabbed his coat from the rack behind the door. Relief washed over her like a cool balm as the door slammed closed behind him, and she heard his boots thudding down the staircase.

Mark had his demons, and now Prue had hers. Just as he couldn't discuss the things he had seen in France, neither did she know how to talk about the grisly murder she had come across at the Carnival. There was a chasm that yawned between them, without a bridge for either to cross.

The awful truth that both Prue and Mark knew but could never confess aloud was that they were both aware Prue had never loved Mark. The pair had attended school together, Mark in the year ahead. Their families had been friendly, and that had been enough for Prue's mother to nudge Prue toward a relationship. One by one, each of Prue's four older siblings had left home and after an accident in the workplace, her father had no longer been able to work. It was the final straw that pushed her into a marriage that, while amicable, held no love.

She cared for Mark, of course. She did not think there was anyone she was closer to, and yet there were secrets she kept from him. She suspected the same of him, though she was not certain if the thought brought her peace or chagrin. Their life, their marriage, had faded into a colourless grey that paled in comparison with the rainbow hues of the Carnival. The way she cared for Mark was not the same as how her palms went clammy every time Sadie's fingers brushed her arm.

A rap on the door jolted Prue from her reverie and made her waning headache pulse once more. Putting her own mug in the sink, she stumbled across to the door, wrapping her thick brown dressing gown more firmly around her form. When she slid the lock across and jerked the handle to open it, her heart thundered in her chest at the familiar sight of sleek auburn hair and sparkling eyes.

"Sorry. It is a bit early." Sadie tucked a strand of hair behind her ear as she raked her gaze over Prue, warmth flooding Prue's cheeks at her friend's boldness. "I've disturbed you."

"No, I…" Prue was painfully aware of her bedraggled appearance in comparison with Sadie's easy composure. "I hadn't dressed yet. Did you want to come in?"

It had taken a few visits to the apartment before Prue was comfortable inviting Sadie in for tea. It wasn't even the idea of having someone new in her home; she was embarrassed by the meagre nature of her existence, especially revealing it to a woman who was always dressed in such a fashionable and glamorous manner. It was rude to pry about one's financial affairs, though Prue had often wondered about the source of Sadie's income, since the auburn-haired woman was clearly well-off.

"Of course." Sadie pranced into the apartment, grey eyes flicking about the modest furnishings with curiosity rather than judgement. It had been some months since she had come inside, and Prue could not recall if Sadie had ventured inside at all since Mark's return from war. "You best get dressed. We have things to do today."

Unease prickled up Prue's spine. "Oh. You see, about the Carnival…"

"We aren't going to the Carnival." Sadie shook her head, her hair swishing across her shoulders from side to side. "I need to call on a friend of mine, and I was hoping you might come with me. I could use the company. If you aren't too busy, that is."

Doubt swirled in the pit of Prue's stomach. Just the night before, they had stumbled across a dead body, a man that Sadie had deceitfully claimed she did not know. Today there was no mention of what they had seen, merely an invitation to see a friend. Prue could not help but suspect that the two were connected, though she could not have said how. It occurred to her, with a mixture of excitement and terror, that she was being dragged deeper into the mystery of the murdered man.

Prue was tired of holding her tongue and making herself small and scarce for the comfort of others. Sadie saw something in her that no one else did, even if she knew the dead man despite her claims otherwise. Picking apart a mystery, unravelling the threads to determine the truth, was a far cry from tending to the dying plants in the apartment and waiting until Mark returned home to begin preparing the evening meal.

"Alright," Prue said warily, fingers picking absently at the split ends of her dark brown hair.

"Perfect." Sadie's satisfied smile filled Prue with a sense of warmth, a weight easing from her shoulders. "Come, I'll help you find something to wear."

Chapter Six

Ursula Delavane

Beneath the vast expanse of Central Park, in the shadow of an ancient magic, The Vault was silent as a crypt. Ursula clasped her velvet-gloved hands demurely in front of her, grateful for a respite from the frost, even if she had forsaken one form of cold for another. Around the circular layout of the stone basement, gas-lit lamps illuminated the space in a golden glow, the flames licking Larkin's blonde hair as he cast a look around The Vault.

It was a dark and airy place, accessible only through a magical barrier and situated beneath Belvedere Castle. It was as wide as Sterling Templeton's greenhouse, though lacking any such warmth. There were no windows, and only the magically-protected double doors granted entry. It was like stepping into the past, and a grim one at that.

Neither of them had been in this place since before Frankie's death, but by the way Larkin's throat bobbed, they could both feel the power that thrummed through the stone beneath their feet. The source was illuminated by the lamps, dazzling even in the low light. The hilt of a sword with its blade buried in a large rock, the centrepiece of The Vault's collection. Even underground, hidden away from the public, Clarent was capable of commanding an awe-inspired silence.

Clarent was the most well-known of the sword's many names. The Sword in the Stone, the Traitor's Blade. The sword with which, centuries before, Mordred had slain Arthur Pendragon. None could tell precisely how long it had been encased back within the stone, but many had tried and failed to draw it, Frankie included.

"I'm not doing this again, Mother." Larkin swivelled on his heel to face Ursula with his hands balled into fists, boots squeaking against the polished floor as his disapproval settled upon her. "I've tried twice to pull Clarent from the rock. I'm not the Born Again, no matter how much you want me to be."

An old prophecy, one spoken from father to son for centuries. One day there would come a mage with a power like never before who could draw the sword from the stone, and they would be known as the Born Again. Perhaps not quite a reincarnation of Arthur, but as close to the Once and Future King that would ever exist.

Many dwelled upon the promise of such words with wonder, but it had always made Ursula shudder with dread. They divided power amongst themselves, and she disliked the implications of what a rogue element such as the Born Again could do to disrupt that balance. She had hoped with fervour that her son would be the one. Not because she believed Larkin was any more special than any mother who doted upon her only son, but because at least it would rest in the hands of one who already belonged among them.

"You agreed to come down here," Ursula reminded her son, causing him to wave his hand dismissively.

"Because I wished to speak in private, not because I wanted to humiliate myself by wrestling with a sword that isn't meant for me."

"Then speak." Ursula spread her arms, casting around the dimly-lit basement. They were alone, their only witnesses the lamps and a still-slumbering sword.

"The Carnival serves its purpose, but we need to be doing more," Larkin said. "We could use magic for more than simply entertainment."

He folded his arms over his chest, striding over to inspect Clarent despite himself. Magic had a pull, a dark allure that even Larkin could not resist. He would, in the end, put his hands on the hilt of the sword. The magic that flowed from Clarent in palpable waves was wild and untamed, a magic unlike any of the forms that existed within their society. Verbal magic was tame and malleable, the only sort Ursula had ever used. She wondered if the other forms felt more like Clarent.

"What do you suggest?" Ursula's surprise was too great to mask. Her son had little interest in the internal politics of the Carnival, so the idea that he hungered for something more was news to her.

"This absurd Prohibition, for a start." Larkin's blue eyes shone and his teeth gleamed in the darkness as he smiled. "Imagine how we could use magic to create alcohol, or even new substances. We could transport it, use it in the speakeasies…"

"So use magic to accomplish the tasks of common bootleggers." Disappointment welled within Ursula, and her tone did little to disguise her contempt. "I had hoped you wanted magic for more than petty crime."

"What do you understand, Mother?" Larkin sneered as he rested his hand atop Clarent's pommel, fingers drumming against the ruby-encrusted hilt. "You only use the magic that the Lords approve of. What say do you have in what's done with it?"

"Of course." Ursula bowed her head, though anger pulsed through her at her son's derision of her. Her fury was only ever a simmering thing, like water beneath the lid of a pot as it came to boil. What point was there in loosing it, when she could never occupy the same sort of space as her son? "I just thought you had bigger goals, Larkin."

"I want to expand beyond simply performing. It's become about parlour tricks, but I see use for magic beyond that."

"It's about control." Ursula stepped forward, her black fur coat caressing her shoes. "If everyone could simply use magic as they pleased, where would we be? The Magical Freedoms Brigade has similar ideals."

A tense silence clogged the space, and Ursula could have sworn that The Vault grew colder, a chill racing down her spine. Larkin's jaw set and in the dim light, his blue eyes looked to be aflame. A fury burned just beneath the surface, but when Larkin spoke again, his words were dangerously soft.

"I am not the Magical Freedoms Brigade. I am Lord Summer."

It would be folly to forget that. Larkin may be her son, but he exerted a greater power than Ursula could hope to hold. As a woman, her power lay within her influence, her years as Frankie's wife and having rubbed shoulders with all of those of note within the magical community. Yet one word from her son, and those decades of building up her image, her power, could come crumbling down.

"We could use magic to ensure things as terrible as the Great War never occur again." Larkin's fingers tightened around Clarent's hilt. "With some leverage, the others wouldn't even question it."

"Leverage?" The word was an ominous one, leaving Ursula to wonder precisely what her son had in mind.

"You brought me down here for a reason." Larkin tugged hard at the hilt, jaw clenching with the effort. When both sword and stone remained unmoved, he released it, though disappointment flashed briefly across his face. "Not because you think I'm the Born Again. You want to remind me of a more ancient power. Clarent was not the only sword capable of wielding by one with great magic, even if the other was lost to the ravages of time."

Excalibur. The thought sent ripples of horror through Ursula. If one loose cannon was not a terrifying enough idea, what of two? Clarent may be real, one of the few concrete pieces of evidence that the legends of Arthur were fact instead of fiction, but over the years, Excalibur had become a fantasy. It was a fairytale told to children at bedtime, a hope dangled over their heads they could never reach.

"Excalibur has been lost for centuries. No one knows if it's even real, except for rumours that it's held by…"

"The Lady of the Lake," Larkin finished impatiently, carding his fingers through his golden hair. "Another tall tale to you, no doubt. What matters isn't whether the Lady or even Excalibur are real. It matters that many of the magical old guard think they *are.*"

"So you want to lie to them? To claim you have Excalibur, or know where it is?" Irritation surged through Ursula. Why could her son not accept the way things were? Larkin was at the pinnacle of power and still he wanted more. They had control of magic, of the rabble who pushed for change. If Larkin began to alter how things were done, what then?

"I want more than to throw parties and perform circus tricks!" he exclaimed, hands clenching into tight fists. "We show everyone that we alone own magic, that we have control they can never dream of. What's the point of the show if none of it is real? What's the point if we can't use magic to do things in the world around us?"

"We do." Ursula's voice dropped to barely above a whisper. "You know we do, and we have to be careful."

Larkin scoffed. "Influencing political agendas like that of Garrett Alderidge isn't what I'm talking about, Mother."

The Alderidge brothers were prominent within the magical community. Garrett, the eldest, was the Governor of New York. Coming upon for re-election, having the backing of the elite would be of great benefit to his campaign.

Noel, a few years younger, was more of a wild card, mired by tragedy. He had been married once, to a wife who'd died of disease when their daughter was young. The daughter had died a few years ago, allegedly a tragic suicide. Noel was a knife in the darkness, a silent shadow who was always by Garrett's side, and who most of the community was smart enough to fear.

Magic was shown at the Carnival, but it lived elsewhere. In dark spaces, in the corners where no one thought to look. Larkin knew that as well as Ursula, and yet he still insisted on publicity, for reasons she could not fathom.

"If the world knew of the true power of magic, beyond what they perceived as clever tricks, what then?" Ursula demanded, hands planted on her hips. "It's a powder keg waiting to erupt."

Larkin smiled humourlessly. "The Magical Freedoms Brigade would agree with you on that, at least."

The mention of the Brigade made knots twist in Ursula's stomach, a cold shiver traversing down her arms.

"This is best discussed with the other Lords, not your mother."

Larkin gave a soft hum that could have been either approval or dismissal. Casting one last look at Clarent, he turned on his heel and marched from The Vault, the click of his boots echoing across the stone. In the quiet that ensued, Ursula examined Clarent with mild interest. She had never touched the sword herself, for it was not a woman's place to seek magical glory.

She knew that she was not the Born Again, and even in the darkness where there was no one to bear witness, she had no intention of embarrassing herself by stooping to a common curiosity she did not possess.

Chapter Seven

Andie Fairley

Although most performances occurred within the confines of the Carnival of the Seasons, it was becoming more common that Andie was whisked away to parties in other settings, such as fancy bars in upper Manhattan that would lose business during Prohibition and the clubs of Brooklyn. Her cold certainty of her status as Larkin's favourite likely helped, along with the onset of Prohibition, which this particular performance marked the dawn of. At midnight, alcohol would become illegal in the United States of America. Dazzling though magic may be, Andie did not know if it would be a worthy substitute in the gambling dens and speakeasies of New York City.

Tonight's venue was perhaps the most glamorous establishment that Andie had ever set foot inside, though she would never say so, would never allude to her gritty Hell's Kitchen roots. *Camelot* was owned by Lord Spring, a thinly veiled reference to the magical elite's odd obsession with Arthurian legend. Nonetheless, it had all the decadence that one might associate with a mythical castle.

Crystal chandeliers sparkled overhead, their lights reflecting off walls embedded with mirror shards. Rich crimson carpet, the same colour as Andie's sparkling heels, was broken only by the white marble of restrooms and the bar. The stools adorning the bar itself along the left were black and gold, the same statement colours that splashed over all of the booths. At the back was a large, polished stage, bordered by a deep red curtain to match the carpet. The opulence was smothering, and Andie took a long breath to ground herself.

"How do you like it?" Larkin asked as he put an arm around Andie's waist, fingers catching in the tassels on her glittering ruby-red dress. The motion reminded her of something Patrick might have done, how easily he had caught her and spun her around, but she quickly disguised her flinch with a giggle. Patrick was gone. Someone had taken him from her, perhaps even someone in *Camelot* right now. Andie would dwell on his murder at another time, for she would not even let the most personal of tragedies detract from her performance.

"Careful, Larkin, you don't want to pull any of the tassels off," she demurred, her skin crawling beneath the heat of his hand.

Larkin released his grip on the fabric and linked his fingers through hers, tugging her along to one of the booths near the stage. "Come on, I'll introduce you to the other Lords."

Andie had seen a handful of them in passing, had heard Larkin make mention of them in the past. Excitement seared through her at the idea of an introduction to the most prominent men in the magical community, and she quickly tucked a stray curl behind her ear. She had let her hair fall in its natural ringlets and painted her lips a rich red to match her outfit and shoes, her eyes lined with black, her cheeks liberally rouged. She had to make a lasting impression on these people if she ever hoped to obtain the rarest and most powerful form of magic: soul magic.

Larkin had spoken little of the ritual one underwent to obtain such magic, save that not everyone survived it. Perhaps soul magic was so powerful due to the high danger in obtaining it. High risk, high reward. Only those amongst the elite had access to the ritual, and therefore to soul magic itself. One day, Andie was determined that despite being a woman, she would have it herself instead of having to borrow Larkin's.

There was a distinct difference in the feeling of owned magic and gifted magic, tangible to Andie each time she used either. Owned magic was like controlling a current of water, the steady flow of a strong tide. Gifted magic was sharper, a crackle of electricity between her fingertips. The difference between a throbbing bruise and a fresh cut. Andie borrowed at Larkin's whim; she planned for that to change, to never have to borrow at all.

"Gentlemen." Larkin stopped at the booth, Andie coming to a halt beside him. He reached up to affectionately tilt up her chin. "This is Alexandra Fairley. She's one of the Sun Carnival's best showgirls, and extremely talented with magic."

"I think your mother might have mentioned her as your latest plaything." It was the oldest of the three men who spoke, his tone disdainful, lip curling derisively as he examined Andie. He was in his late fifties, with thinning grey hair, sharp grey eyes and a paunch. He wore a tweed suit that, with its fine detailing, must be worth more than what Andie made in a year. He must be Lord Spring, and though she burned with indignation at his dismissive comment, Andie smiled politely in response.

Lord Spring, or rather Sterling Templeton, was of old magical blood. His family's magic traced back hundreds of years, and the Templeton Scale that measured one's raw magical potential was named after them. He owned several speakeasies across New York City, and Andie vaguely recalled that he had several children and grandchildren. She could already tell that he was an arrogant piece of shit.

How *dare* he call her a plaything. The idea that it was Larkin's mother Ursula who had prompted such talk only served to further cement her dislike of the woman. She'd met Ursula in passing, a beautiful blonde woman in her mid-forties with nothing but coldness behind her blue eyes.

"Now, Sterling, don't be crude." Another of the men shook his head in disapproval. There was grey just beginning to pepper his brown hair, and he appeared to be of a similar age to Ursula. He took Andie's hand

and kissed the back of it, though his eyes roamed over her figure in a way that made her stomach squirm uncomfortably.

Lord Autumn, or Cyril Fordyce. He had been a close friend of Larkin's father, Franklin. Cyril was something of a playboy, a man who enjoyed indulging in parties and women. He was on his third wife now, a pretty young thing Andie had seen about the place, perhaps fifteen to twenty years Cyril's junior.

Under the facade of debauchery, Cyril was not someone to cross. His magic ranked at a seven out of ten on the Templeton Scale, by far the strongest of the Lords. In some ways, perhaps that was worse, that the most powerful among them was a man who merely existed to indulge his own impulses.

"Are you performing tonight, Alexandra?" the youngest of the three asked, leaning forward with a pleasant smile.

"It's just Andie, and yes I am," she piped up, cheeks warming when she realised they were the first words she'd spoken to the Lords. So much for leaving a lasting impression.

The man chuckled. "Well then, if it's just Andie, I insist that I'm just Desmond."

Lord Winter, also known as Desmond Bellisario. He was handsome, with dark hair and brown eyes and a friendly countenance. In his early thirties, Desmond was the only one of the Lords who was not of a wealthy background. Once a Carnival employee, he had worked his way up the ranks before being noticed by the elite. It was Desmond's story of success that gave Andie hope she could one day follow in his footsteps.

"I should escort Andie backstage so she can get ready." Larkin caught hold of Andie's hand once again, inclining his head to the others. Andie managed a small wave before she followed Larkin around the back of the bar to the walkway leading behind the stage. Irritation at Sterling's contemptuous remark rendered her bold, and she tugged her hand from Larkin's.

"Why didn't you say anything when Sterling called me your plaything?" she snapped.

The laughter and chatter from the other side of the thick black curtains masked her words, and the darkness obscured most of Larkin's face. A sliver of light cast across his cheek, and he stepped toward her, looping his arms around her waist and pulling her close against him. He swept her hair behind her ear and pressed a kiss to her forehead.

"Sweetheart, don't be cross with me. You know what old men are like. Sterling just can't fathom that I might have a genuine interest in a showgirl."

"I'm more than a showgirl." Despite Larkin's attempts to placate her, Andie's words remained venomous. "You said it yourself, I'm a talented mage."

"You are." He released her, the wooden planks beneath the walkway creaking as he strode backstage. With a huff, Andie followed, her heels clicking angrily. Once they were in the warm glow of the backstage lights, Larkin rested his hands on her shoulders, rubbing his thumbs on her skin in soothing circles.

"I want to be more than that." Andie's voice was a fierce whisper, her blue eyes flicking up to meet his and finding a familiar fire there. She and Larkin both blazed bright, true embodiments of the Sun Carnival. They were an inferno that couldn't be doused.

"I know you do." Larkin's eyes flicked to her lips. "I want more, too."

Andie inhaled his peppermint breath as he leaned in to kiss her. There was always a hunger in his kiss, as though he was holding himself back. Perhaps it wasn't just magic and power that Larkin wanted more of. Andie wrapped her arms around him and drew him closer, her soft curves pressing against him, pulling a groan from him. His hands dropped from her shoulders to skim up her sides, resting on her hips, fingers digging in hard enough to bruise.

"Sorry if we're interrupting something."

An unfamiliar male voice made Andie wrench away from Larkin, wiping her mouth on the back of her hand. Larkin likewise stepped back, straightening out the creases in his shirt. Andie looked over toward the source of the intrusion and found a jolt of familiarity surge through her. Though she had never seen this man before in person, anyone would recognise Garrett Alderidge, Governor of New York. His picture was always plastered all over the newspaper, a man of close to fifty with a plain but personable appearance.

"Garrett." A grin spread across Larkin's lips, a boyish mischief in his expression. "It seems you caught me in a compromised position."

"I'm actually here to see your lady friend." Garrett held up a bouquet of daffodils with a bashful smile. "These are for you, Miss Fairley. Hopefully they inspire a spectacular performance tonight, though from what Larkin says, you won't need these to help."

"Thank you, Governor," Andie said, accepting the flowers from him with a sweet smile. She was a little astonished at the familiar exchange between Larkin and Garrett, though she made note of it. She'd heard talk of the Alderidge brothers before. She had not known how enmeshed they were within the magical community.

"Might I steal Larkin away for a word?"

"But of course." Andie wanted to believe that Garrett's courteous nature was genuine, though it was far more likely to be a farce considering what she knew of the Alderidge brothers.

As Larkin and Garrett's footsteps receded down the walkway, Andie examined the surroundings of the unfamiliar backstage environment. A halo of light from the dressing room off to the side with a thick curtain for privacy, a mirror adorned with lightbulbs so she could fix her makeup. Andie set the flowers down on the table. She could find a vase and water for them after the performance.

A few stagehands bustled about backstage, frantic with last-minute preparations and checking that the stage was ready for a promising performance. Their footsteps and the low creak of the wooden boards was background noise as Andie's fingers traversed the soft petals of the roses.

"How high you have risen, Andie."

This time, it was a man's voice that was all too recognisable to Andie, brittle and baritone. She lurched away from the table, the flowers dropping to the ground with a wet thud that matched the sound of her heart beat against her chest. Her knees trembled as the man who spoke stepped into the light.

Noel Alderidge was more handsome than his older brother, though the sharp features of his face possessed all the cruelty that Garrett lacked. His mouth twisted into a cruel smile at Andie's shocked expression, hazel eyes piercing as knives as they latched onto her. He was one of the very few people whose mere presence was enough to make Andie lose her composure entirely, though she regained it quickly, hands balling so tight her nails cut into her palms.

"Why are you here?" she demanded, emphasising each word, her own mouth curling into a snarl.

"None of the pretty courtesies you have for my brother, then." Noel's tone was dismissive. "Well, hardly a surprise there, since he's the Governor. I often go where Garrett does, but I'd not expected to see *you* in a place like this."

Andie lifted her chin. "Too far above my station, is it?"

"Why are you cosying up to the Lords?" Noel strode toward her as he asked, his menacing presence casting a dark shadow over her that made her fight the urge to shrink back.

"I'm a performer," Andie responded coldly, her posture rigid as Noel stepped right up into her space. Though he was not that much taller than her, it filled her with anger and self-loathing to suddenly feel so tiny. "It's my job to entertain. Larkin and I have just become close."

"Close enough to know what you are?" He leaned in, his voice a vicious whisper. "Does he know what you've done?"

Memories surged to the forefront of Andie's mind, burned forever into her like a brand. A dilapidated old warehouse falling apart in front of her. Her arms burning with exertion as she dragged an immobile form from rubble.

"Please don't leave me, Andie!"

A gunshot, tearing through a quiet evening with the force of ripping through paper into a Christmas gift. A wheelbarrow carrying a bloodied body. The white froth of settling water as a corpse disappeared beneath Harlem River's surface.

"You left me. You left me, Andie."

Tears stung Andie's eyes, blurring her vision. She choked out a gasp at the sudden onslaught of a night she had pushed to the back of her mind. She had to forget, or it would tear her apart. She had to forget, or she could never move forward with the person she wanted to become.

"Oh, don't start that." Rage coloured Noel's tone. She wished she could hate him, but the only person she had to blame was herself. "Fortunately for you, my brother is up for re-election. While uncovering the truth of what you did might be satisfying, it would ruin him, and I care about him more than I hate you."

"I didn't mean it." Andie's voice trembled. Suddenly, she was sixteen again, with blood on her hands and no idea where to turn. She was sixteen, with no way to mend the hole she had torn open in her own heart. "It was…it wasn't…"

"Let me guess: it was an accident." Noel seized her by the arms and shook hard. Andie bleated out another jagged sob. "You're a fucking liar. One day, they're all going to know what you did, Andie. I'm going to watch them rip you apart."

He released her unceremoniously, and Andie wobbled on her heels before toppling to the ground. One of the stagehands gasped, but none of them stepped in to help her. She gritted her teeth against skinned knees and wiped away her tears. If she dug into the gaping pit of the loss she had endured, she would bury herself alive. If she started crying to pour out her grief, she would never stop.

Patrick was just the latest heartbreak. It had started with Claire.

"Fortunately, fate offers mercy of its own." Noel mused as Andie pushed herself to her feet, dusting off her dress. "No punishment I could deliver is as righteous as the fact that Syl will never forgive you either."

Truth was always a much sharper knife than any hurtful lie, and this one cut to the bone. Syl had been damaged by that evening in his own way, both physically and mentally. Noel was right though: Andie and Syl's dynamic had its complexities now, there was no forgiveness in store for her. Not from Noel, not from Syl.

"Miss Fairley." The stage manager strode over, concern illuminating his expression, his white-gloved hands twisting together. His worried eyes flicked between Andie and Noel. "If you please, it's time for you to take the stage."

The first notes of a jazz band's piece emanated from the stage. Alarm coursed through Andie as she recognised this as her cue. She straightened up, smoothing out her dress and making sure no evidence of her fall was visible. Noel smiled mockingly, though his eyes remained empty.

"Go on then, Andie. Give them a show."

Her heels clicked in a flurry as she positioned herself behind the thick velvet curtains. When they rose, she was not the grieving girl with scars on her heart mourning a loss she had been wholly responsible for. She banished the tears from her eyes and pasted on a dazzling smile under the bright lights, for the mask was all she had left.

CHAPTER EIGHT

Prue Clermont

THEY HAD VISITED SADIE'S FRIEND THREE times in the span of just over a week, and Prue's patience with their purpose was beginning to wear thin. Initially, she had quelled her excitement under a polite demeanour, eyes eagerly assessing the man's humble residence. Despite his imposing stature, Warren Fairley was a gently-spoken man with kind eyes and a ready smile.

The Hell's Kitchen apartment was reminiscent of Prue's, though the raucous laughter and music from the neighbours, along with rubbish strewn through the stairwells, made her glad of the quiet and cleanliness of her own. The curtains within were faded and moth-bitten, the furniture well-worn and faded. Each time Prue visited with Sadie, she noted the stack of tarot cards on the dining room table, red ink on white cards glaring at her through civilised conversation with Sadie and Warren.

Sadie asked questions about how Warren was keeping. About his two children, who worked at the Carnival. There was no mention of a wife, and so Prue did not bring it up. Sadie asked after the welfare of people Prue had never heard of. Brimming with frustration at why she was even present for these discussions, all Prue had learned was the name of the deceased young man: Patrick Rhodes, who had known Warren's children, Syl and Andie.

It was on their third visit that Prue reached out for the tarot cards with curiosity. Typically she would not be so rude as to rummage through someone else's belongings, but the cards had a pull that she could not explain. Her attention had been consistently drawn to them, and when she rested her fingers atop the deck, ice surged through her veins. She shivered and drew her hand back. A strange yearning tugged at the pit of her stomach.

"Would you like me to do a reading?" Warren asked.

"I mean…" Doubt clouded Prue's ability to make a decision, combined with embarrassment at being caught prodding at the cards. "I wouldn't really know what that entails."

"Warren has magic, Prue," Sadie said softly, resting a hand on her arm, a jolt of warmth replacing the previous cold sensation. "Mind magic. His gifts lie within reading tarot cards. You interpret your own meaning from the cards he draws."

When Prue had been perhaps ten, she and her older sisters had conducted a seance in the attic among the dust and spiders. They had whispered in the midnight darkness, as though the volume of their voices would raise the spirits. Their hands moved across the board, nervous giggles bubbling from their lips as they asked silly questions. Her oldest sister, Charlotte, had screamed when a spider skittered across her leg, and they'd been discovered by their mother. They had been reprimanded as faithless heathens.

Was Prue faithless? What did she believe in? These days, she thought the greatest power of all was magic.

Mark would also have disapproved of the cards. He would call it a charlatan's trick, used to coax suspicious minds into parting with coins. Yet Warren had not asked for payment, just Prue's permission. Licking her lips, she settled further back into her seat and nodded. Warren shuffled the cards as the wind howled and rattled the windows like a hungry dog begging for scraps.

Warren set three cards down in a line in front of Prue. Across from them, Sadie drummed her fingers against her mug, a contemplative expression slackening her face. Prue picked at her nails as Warren turned over the first card.

"Seven of Cups." He slid it across the scratched surface of the wooden table so that Prue could see it. "This first card represents your past. Seven of Cups indicates your opportunities and wishes. You have been faced with choices, but the promise of these choices may have been an illusion."

Prue's brow furrowed as she tried to think what choice Warren meant. The only choice she had made recently was befriending Sadie, accompanying her to the Carnival. Surely that could not be what Warren meant. Before she could consider further, Warren turned over the second card.

"Five of Pentacles. This card represents your present." Warren grimaced, reaching up a hand to his temple as if struck with a headache. He blinked rapidly, before clearing his throat and continuing. "It indicates poverty and lack of finances. There is much isolation and worry here, most likely in relation to hard times."

A rueful smile curved Prue's lips. Well, that was one card she certainly understood, for she and Mark had experienced nothing but hardship since his return from war. Warren flipped over the last of the three cards.

"The Tower. This card…"

Warren gripped the edge of the table, leaning forward with a pained groan. Prue levelled a concerned look at Sadie, whose face was etched with worry.

"Warren?"

"I can't…my magic…" Warren rasped like nails grating down a chalkboard. "My magic isn't right. There's something erratic about it." He choked down a shuddering breath. "It's like it's become unstable."

"What?" Sadie reached across to grip Warren's arm. Prue was frozen in her chair, unable to comprehend what was happening as Warren panted, struggling to breathe. She knew little of how magic was used, though she had never seen anyone react like this to using it. When Warren's head shot up, his blue eyes gleamed with horror as they fixated on Prue.

"Something is wrong." His voice was ragged and hoarse as he jabbed an accusing finger at Prue. "Something is wrong with *you*."

An ache yawned open within Prue, both foreign and familiar, ageless and ancient. The ache begged to be soothed, though she could not perceive how. A craving she could not satisfy lay bare, reaching out for something Prue didn't know how to offer. Terrified and trembling, Prue screwed her eyes shut and willed it away. The ache persisted, pulsating within her, a starving creature screaming to be fed.

"Prue." Sadie's fingers grasping her wrist tore her away from the battle that raged within her. Her eyes snapped open and she staggered to her feet. "Come on. We should leave."

Warren would not meet Prue's gaze as Sadie dragged her out of the dining room. Her knees buckled, gripping onto Sadie's coat to stop her falling over. She had seen magic performed various times at the Carnival, but never questioned whether she might have it. The idea seemed absurd, but what else could the strange ache be? What else could Warren have meant?

"I'll take you back to my apartment." Sadie put an arm around Prue, rubbing her lower back in smooth circles. "Perhaps we can have something a bit stronger than tea and have a talk."

* * *

Sadie's apartment was as opulent as Prue had anticipated. Situated across town in Brooklyn, there was even a concierge to allow them through the front door. The apartment itself was one of only six on the same floor, and Prue's breath caught in her throat when she examined the dark wooden surroundings with golden art deco flourishes. The curtains were either satin or a glossy silk, and deep blue in colour. There were no marks nor moth holes on them.

Perhaps in the future she would pluck up the courage to ask where the woman's wealth came from. Now she sat by the hearth with a glass of brandy, taking slow sips of the taboo beverage. Prue's gaze slid over Sadie's velvet lounge, the plush rugs adorning the cream carpet. The scent of citrus and honey that lingered on Sadie's skin was more prominent here, and it gave Prue warm comfort to inhale it.

"Tell me about magic." Prue set down her glass on a wooden coaster. "Tell me why Warren reacted like that to me."

Sadie's pale eyes rested on the flickering flames, a vacancy slackening her expression. She inhaled deeply through her nostrils, pinching the bridge of her nose. Leaning back against the plump cushions, Sadie plucked up her own glass of brandy and tilted her head to consume it all. Prue swallowed as she watched the graceful movement of Sadie's neck.

"There are several forms of magic. Many of the ancient ones have been lost to time, but we have three higher forms and one basic form. The basic form is accessible to anyone who has a spark of magic, or rather, an essence…"

"Wait, hold on." Prue held up a hand. Things were starting to become pleasantly warm, though she could not have known whether to attribute it to the fire in the hearth or the brandy she'd consumed. "What is an essence?"

"Ah." Sadie smiled ruefully. "The bare basics, then. For someone to use magic, they need an essence. It's as I said, the spark of magic. If one does not possess an essence, they cannot use magic, no matter how much they try, not even if they meet the qualifications of the various kinds of magic."

"Alright." Prue could tell that this was going to take some time to wrap her head around. "So, anyone with an essence can use the basic sort, there aren't any other sorts of qualifications?"

"No." Sadie raked her fingers through her auburn hair, busying herself toying with the ends. "It's verbal magic. Learned through spellbooks. You recite an incantation, and the magic does most of the work.

It's also the only type of magic that the elite amongst the community typically approve of women accessing."

Prue examined Sadie, the way the firelight threw her angular features into sharp relief, shadows dancing across her pale face. She could not help but wonder if Sadie possessed magic, since she knew so much about it.

"What are the other forms?"

Sadie shuddered, rubbing her arms as though a sudden cold caressed her.

"Mind magic is the first. The qualification is that those who use it…they are often in possession of some sort of malady of the mind. This magic yields telepaths and clairvoyants, among other cerebral forms of magic."

Prue picked at the tassels on the edge of a black cushion. She was aware that magic came with sacrifice, and she could imagine the sort of people who would use mind magic. Prue's mind drifted to Mark, waking in the night screaming of terrors only he could see. If he had an essence…

"Heart magic is the second. It requires a betrayal of the highest order. A betrayal of someone you love. The nature varies, but the result is the same: the betrayal must break your heart. Only then can you access heart magic, which favours elemental power."

Prue's stomach twisted and curled in on itself, a rope tying somewhere deep in the pit of her being. How horrific did the betrayal have to be to break someone's heart like that? The more she learned of magic, the more terrible it seemed. One would inherit great power, yes, but was the cost worth it?

"The third form is soul magic." Sadie's expression hardened along with her voice, jaw tightening and a nerve ticking in her cheek as she stared into her empty brandy glass, the reflection of the firelight burning in her pale eyes. "It's the rarest of the three. One may only access it after completing a ritual which essentially splits the soul open. Not everyone who endeavours to accomplish this ritual survives it, but the power it gives those who do…"

Despite all that she had shared, Sadie remained an enigma to Prue. A wealthy, unwed woman who knew all about magic. As far as Prue was aware, only the elite among the Carnival and their selective society had such knowledge, and yet it was clear Sadie stood apart from them.

"Most magic is controlled by the elite of our secret society. However, there are always cracks where magic seems to…seep out. Much of it originated from the days of King Arthur, and it's said some relics of that age exist in secret."

"King Arthur?" Prue arched an eyebrow, stifling a giggle at the fact that after all Sadie had shared with her, things that should be impossible, it was the existence of a mythical king that flooded her with disbelief.

"So they say," Sadie mused as she offered a nonchalant shrug. But then her slim frame tightened and tensed. "Warren…he has mind magic. He's a telepath, and he reaches out to the minds of those he does readings for. I assume that's what he did with you, and yet…"

Hot guilt stabbed through Prue. "Did I hurt him?"

"I don't know," Sadie admitted, reaching out to rest a gentle hand on Prue's shoulder, "The truth is…I think you *do* have magic. I just don't know what kind yet. It certainly isn't soul magic, and heart magic…"

Prue recoiled, the idea burning at the back of her throat like she'd washed it down with brandy. "No. I haven't betrayed anyone."

"Then it leaves only mind magic, but why touching your mind was painful to Warren, I couldn't say."

Distress clawed its way up within her. Whatever magic she had, she had hurt someone with it, despite it being unintentional. The thought of her magic causing harm to Mark, or Sadie…fear thrashed in her ribcage, hastening her heartbeat and making her tremble. She had known magic existed for some time, but the idea that it existed *within her*…bile rose in her throat, and she grimaced and swallowed it down. It was meant to be something she observed as a bystander, not something she possessed.

"Is there a way to get rid of it? Magic, I mean."

Sadie's brow creased, a confused expression contorting her face. "You want to get rid of your magic?"

Prue bobbed her head vigorously. "I don't want to run the risk of it causing someone else pain as it did Warren."

"There is only the Scourge Ritual, and it must be sanctioned by the Lords themselves." Sadie chewed at her lip, and alarm buzzed through Prue at the idea of the elite knowing what she was, and that she had an ability that even she didn't understand.

"There's no other way?" Prue was aghast. Sadie did not appear perturbed by the revelation of her abilities, and while that was as calming as seeing a lighthouse during a storm on the sea, it was obvious that Sadie believed magic to be a gift, not a curse.

Sadie paused to examine her curiously, before she laughed mirthlessly. "I mean, if you can find a Scourge, be my guest. I'm afraid you may be out of luck there."

"What is a Scourge?" Prue asked wearily, wondering if Sadie found her ignorance to the magical world as exhausting as she did.

"There hasn't been one in…centuries, at least." Sadie drummed her fingers on the arm of the couch. "A Scourge is where the name of the ritual comes from. It's a mage with a rare and dangerous power, the ability to remove someone's essence entirely. The ritual does the same thing, but it's the difference between cutting meat with a butcher's knife or a bread knife. The ritual is…imperfect. It's not used often."

Uneasy chills slithered up Prue's spine at the idea that someone could be so powerful that they could simply reach in and rip out a mage's essence. She didn't ask Sadie whether one could still do magic with an essence torn out, for she was certain that the answer would only further horrify her.

"Prue." Sadie shifted, fabric rustling as she turned to take Prue's hands in her own. The silver rings across her fingers were a cool balm against Prue's skin, a welcome respite from the burning heat of the fire and the blossoming warmth in her cheeks. "Isn't this something you want to understand? Magic takes time to learn, and I know that you're scared because of what happened to Warren. But we could explore this. I could help you."

Sadie was certainly knowledgeable about magic. Along with the other burning questions Prue had about the woman, she resolved to enquire further at some point. Now, with her fingers linked through Sadie's, she could hardly think of more than the softness of Sadie's pale skin brushing hers.

"I'll try. But if it turns out all my magic can do is hurt people, I do want it gone."

"We can do this." Sadie leaned forward to press a kiss to Prue's forehead, grey eyes sparkling with delight. "You and I."

* * *

Prue had not discerned which would anger Mark most: that she had been out with Sadie, that she had consumed brandy, or that she possessed magic. The gulf between them had widened once more, and now Prue found it difficult to see across to the other side. The scent of spiced vegetables and rice filled the apartment as Prue set the evening meal down on the table, sinking into one of the chairs. She'd heard Mark's keys jingling in the door and quickly prepared the knives and forks. As he hung his coat on the rack, she summoned a hollow smile.

"How was work?"

"The usual." Mark flopped into the chair across from Prue, eyes lighting up as they latched onto the plate of food. "This looks delicious."

"I thought we might speak." Prue nudged her food around her plate with her fork, shoulders going rigid as she focused her attention on a particular piece of broccoli. "Something happened today. I went with Sadie to see a friend of hers…"

Mark made a disparaging noise, his knife falling to the plate with a clatter. "Prudence, honestly, what have I said about that woman?"

"I have magic." She blurted out the words, the confession as freeing as ripping off a bandage from an itching wound. She had intended to prolong the conversation, to carefully get to the issue, but somehow she decided in the moment this was the best course of action. When Prue finally raised her head, Mark was leaning back in his chair with a slack jaw.

"Is this some sort of prank?" he asked, eyes round as saucers and arms folded over his chest. He looked as horrified as Prue had felt in the moment she'd recognised the truth about herself.

"No." Prue's leg jiggled under the table. "I don't know what sort of magic yet, but Sadie is going to help me."

"I see." It was the disappointment in Mark's tone that stung the most, searing like salt on a fresh cut. "Was it Sadie who told you that you had magic?"

"I discovered it myself, and…" Prue's vision blurred as tears crept into her eyes. "It frightens me, Mark. I have to learn to control it, before someone else gets hurt because of it."

"Someone *else?*" Mark stared at her in abject horror, and she could feel the chasm between them widening further. Whoever they had once been, the two people at this table were strangers to one another.

Mark had his demons, and Prue had hers. Neither could comfort the other, for neither could understand their spouse's situation. Prue remembered their wedding day, daisies threaded through her hair and a secondhand dress she had borrowed from Charlotte for the occasion. She had been nervous then, though not the same way she was nervous about Sadie. She was nervous because she knew then the expectations of marriage, and when she pictured having sex with someone, it was not Mark that had come to mind.

"Would you have me ignore this?" she demanded, her voice trembling in despair. She and Mark had been together for a decade and while the war had changed them, she had hoped he might stand by her.

"You have been obsessed with that bloody Carnival of the Seasons since before I came back from war." Mark's chair screeched in protest as it scraped back from the table. "With the idea of magic. This is reality,

Prue. You and I, this apartment, me going off to work and you keeping the house in fit shape."

Either he did not believe her, or he chose to turn a blind eye, and she did not know which hurt more. Swallowing the lump scratching at her throat, Prue eased herself to her feet.

"I think I might go and stay with Aunt Ethel for a while." When Mark opened his mouth, she raised a hand to silence him. They had only been apart during the war, and the idea of being alone opened a pit of anxiety in her stomach, but she had the sinking sensation it would be better than living a lie. "You can call on us if you don't believe that's where I'll be staying. I need space, Mark. I had hoped to count on your support, but I see now that would be a fool's wish."

He flinched, though Prue could not take back the bite to her words. She held no malice toward Mark, only a desperate desire to be seen in a way in which he could not comprehend. The world of magic may frighten her, but it was true that it also enthralled her. Mark was a man of practicality, of long work days and weary nights. He would never see there was beauty existing on the horizon, when all he could focus on was the mundane.

They were worlds apart. They were not only no longer on the same page, but they lived within entirely different books. Mark was a constant in Prue's life, something steady that kept her anchored, but she didn't believe it was enough. She trudged into their room and picked up a small bag, stuffing some clothes into it and picking out two pairs of shoes.

When Prue thought of freedom, she didn't think of Mark, of the way he'd kiss her cheek on his way in and out of the door, or the way she'd endure passionless sex once a fortnight to try and feel something for him. She thought of Sadie's smile, of the soft brush of her skin when she and Prue's fingers had intertwined.

To associate freedom with Sadie was dangerous, and yet more intoxicating than any illegal alcohol a bootlegger might sell her.

Chapter Nine

Ursula Delavane

As a woman accustomed to luxury, Ursula was still enthralled by Garrett Alderidge's uptown apartment. Though married, the man had no children, and as such the place was kept in a pristine manner with old magical relics adorning the public areas. Ancient books with cracked spines and gold lettering adorned the wooden shelves. Tarnished jewellery was framed up on the pale blue walls. The flooring throughout the apartment was polished parquet.

The Alderidge brothers were new blood, not of families steeped in magical history like the Templetons. Their presence within the tight-knit community ruffled some feathers, but Ursula found she rather liked Garrett, at least.

Ursula sipped a chamomile tea as she perched on the edge of the cream couch, observing a metal contraption behind Garrett by the shimmering silver-blue curtains, one of many relics within the Governor's possession.

It did not matter whether money was old or new, for it still spoke volumes.

"Do you like it?" Garrett cast a glance behind him, setting down his own porcelain mug. "It's an iron maiden from the late 1600s. I admit I don't know the history of magic as well as the rest of you, though I'm aware that particular time was a difficult one. They used contraptions like this iron maiden to drown mages. Being sealed in metal can, I hear, have a dulling effect on magic."

Ursula wasn't certain on that front, but the idea of being tossed into a metal prison and thrown into the water to drown made her tea scald her throat on its way down.

"The inventions designed to dampen magic are often more cruel than magic itself," she admitted.

"Indeed." Garrett leaned back in his chair, regarding her with intrigue sparkling in his eyes. "I must confess, I don't like how the Lords keep you out of their business, Ursula. You are an intelligent woman. Once Larkin replaced his father, he worked even harder to shut you out."

Garrett was not wrong, though a tolerant smile from Ursula warned it was not a topic she wished to broach. For centuries, women had only been able to use verbal magic, or borrowed magic from men. Using their own was strictly forbidden, though of course these rules only existed amongst the elite. The idea of someone like Andie flaunting her own power was a disagreeable notion to Ursula. The Lords knew Ursula well enough that if she needed to be party to something, they would inform her. Larkin had power, but he was practically a boy still.

"I am a woman, Mr Alderidge. We are not meant for leadership."

"I wished to speak to you about something that is troubling me." Garrett selected a cracker and cream cheese from a silver platter on the coffee table between them, dismissing notions of women and the positions they were allowed to hold. "You and the others are not as familiar with my younger brother Noel as you are with me."

Unease settled over Ursula like a damp blanket she couldn't shrug off. Garrett was friendly and easygoing. Noel lingered like a shadow, a quiet and menacing presence who rarely spoke. Whispers circulated that he possessed magic, though none could pinpoint what sort. Ursula had the grace to attribute Noel's strange behaviour to his tragic past, but not everyone was as accommodating.

"He does not make an effort to ingratiate himself with the Lords," Ursula said, setting down her empty mug, "It has been noticed."

"Noel is...strange," Garrett hedged, nodding slowly as a shadow passed over his face. "Something changed in him after his daughter's suicide. Fourteen years old, and already so promising. It was a hard time for our family. Lately though, he has become—well, volatile, and it seems in relation to a particular person who keeps company with your son."

"Andie." Ursula had not witnessed such behaviour from Noel, though she immediately knew it was the young woman of which Garrett spoke. Beautiful and proud, yet an enigma. Her older brother also worked for the Carnival, but it was disturbing to know so little of their history, other than that they were the children of Warren Fairley.

"She is a lovely girl, to be sure." Garrett smiled thinly, the compliment to Andie not quite registering in the dullness of his eyes. "Something about her vexes Noel, and the fact that he will not even tell me is troubling, to put it lightly."

A darkness lingered about Andie Fairley, a murky past she clearly did not want others knowing about. Was Noel somehow involved in it? What had happened between Noel and Andie to make the man despise her so? Chaos dogged the girl's steps, and Ursula would not have her involving Larkin in her discord.

Most women would be content with holding Larkin's attention. Perhaps one day he would even marry someone, make Ursula a grand-mother. The thought of marriage caused turbulence to spin within her, a bittersweet mixture of joy and fury. Her second wedding, to Franklin, had been perfect. Her first...well, the less said about it, the better. It was a wedding that had never really happened at all, a wedding that dispelled Ursula's blissful notions of romance and pushed her toward practicality.

Ursula could not condemn it too thoroughly, for her path had taken her where she needed to be. To Franklin, a man with wealth and influence. To her son, and how precious he was to her.

Ursula had only one child, and though Larkin could often be at odds with her, she loved him dearly. There was nothing she would not do to protect her son, no boundary she would not cross, no crime she would not commit. What was power compared to the strength of a mother's love? She would always save Larkin, even if it meant saving him from himself.

She drummed her fingers on the arm of her chair as she considered Noel's predicament, mysterious though it may be. It would rip her to shreds to lose Larkin, so she could only imagine how deep it must cut to lose his daughter. Loss was a wound that did not fully heal, a scab picked off to bleed afresh when one least expected it.

Garrett's eyes brimmed with the pain of loss, a hurt that had not yet gone away and never would. Ursula understood all too well, for despite the complexities of her relationship with Frankie, she missed her husband and cursed the war for ripping him from her.

"Noel's daughter. What was her name?"

"Claire."

CHAPTER TEN

Andie Fairley

WHEN LARKIN CAME TO SEE ANDIE, his arrival was heralded by the unmistakable scent of flowers. The exact floral smell depended on which variety he chose to bring her, but today it happened to be daisies. Andie's smile was as sweet as the aroma that wafted through her trailer, filled with all the bouquets Larkin had brought her. Flo complained about the smell, but knew better than to toss out any of the flowers.

Andie reacted with carefully staged awe each time Larkin presented her with flowers, but she saw what they came with: terms and conditions. Men didn't simply present women with gifts unless they wanted something in return, and though Larkin's attention emboldened her, it did not come without cost. A price she knew that she was not yet aware of, and yet one she would have to pay.

"Is this payment for my performance?" Andie teased, flicking a sly look at the tense set of Flo's jaw as the blonde girl lingered by the doorway of the trailer.

"I hoped we could speak in private." Larkin offered his hand. "Perhaps at my apartment."

Andie beamed and accepted his proffered hand, stepping down from the trailer and toward the promise of luxury.

She would pay the price of his attention in her own way: with secrets, pieces of her fractured past that she had yet to share with him. As she sat with Larkin in the lounge room of the glamorous apartment he shared with his mother, marvelling over luxuries she would never own in a lifetime, she knew she had to give something of herself back. Larkin's favour came with expectations.

"Are you still angry with me about what Sterling said when we met the Lords?" Larkin asked over a glass of champagne that made Andie's head buzz pleasantly.

"No," she responded honestly, setting her crystal glass down. She had given the other Lords no reason to believe she was not the plaything they expected her to be, and gave Larkin no reason to take her side over that of such powerful men. Despite the delightful tingle of the champagne, Andie's focus was razor-sharp. She chose which parts of herself to give away and which to keep.

"You must attend more performances like *Camelot*." Larkin grinned, draining the last of his glass. "You were utterly dazzling, sweetheart. They all loved you."

Not all of them. Andie shivered as she recalled a cold smile sharp as glass, hazel eyes burning with utter loathing.

"Can I tell you something, Larkin?" Her voice was soft as she asked, and the tremble in it not altogether feigned. "Something that I'd like to stay between us."

"Of course." His expression softened and he leaned forward to catch her hands in his, thumbs running over the back of her hands. "Anything."

"I have more than just verbal magic." Andie drew in a deep breath, gathering her courage as she tried to anticipate his reaction. "I have mind magic."

The silence was excruciating, broken only by the gentle patter of rain against the diamond lattice Tudor-style windows. Would he judge her, as she had once resented her father's late morning lie-ins, his inability to rise even when his children needed him? Larkin's eyes searched her face, before a bright smile adorned his lips. Utter relief slackened Andie's shoulders, and an answering smile dawned on her own mouth.

"Of course you do." Larkin shook his head slowly, as though he should have known better. "You've always been brilliant. I should have known you were capable of more than just verbal magic."

Andie eagerly latched onto the compliment like a fish catching the bait on a hook.

"Exactly. It would be much easier to use my own magic, rather than having to pester you for yours, or even using verbal magic…"

Larkin's sudden raised hand brought Andie's words to an abrupt halt, the excitement dying on her lips at the furrow in his brow. Frustration punctured her enthusiasm. Hadn't this been what Larkin wanted?

"I can't have you doing mind magic, Andie. It's simply not done. Women either use verbal magic, or one of the higher forms gifted to them."

"*You* make the Sun Carnival rules," Andie reminded Larkin in a seductive purr, resting her fingers on his arm and tracing patterns on the fabric of his shirt. There were some roles that he gravitated toward more than others. When she lapsed into the temptress, it was the role he seemed to enjoy most of all. "You could make an exception."

"We'll see." The noncommittal answer made Andie's impatience surge, but she quelled her annoyance beneath an adoring smile. Larkin's eyes latched onto her lips. "You are talented, I can't deny that. I want more for you. More for both of us."

How could he possibly have more? Larkin possessed all of the power and privilege that Andie had to drag herself up the social ladder for. She stifled her contempt, the bitter undercurrent of derision that Larkin was nothing more than a spoiled young man handed the world on a platter.

Women like Andie danced until their heels cracked and bled. They smiled until their jaws ached. They endured the derogatory remarks, the lecherous stares, the wandering hands. All of that work, unnoticed, hidden beneath a sparkling dress and the magic that they rarely got a taste of.

Larkin shifted closer across the couch, pressing his lips to Andie's with a ravenous hunger.

'*It's my turn to make you dance,*' she thought triumphantly.

She slid her arms around his neck, leaning back against the velvet armrest so that his weight rested atop her. She tilted her head back, curls catching on the pillow tassels, as his lips descended down her neck.

She could feel what he wanted. She wasn't a fool.

Part of her revelled in it. Larkin Delavane, Lord Summer, was wrapped around her little finger. The idea of having control over him elicited a sharp gasp from her lips as his mouth reached her collarbone. His wicked smile pressed against her skin, fingers roaming her slender body. His hands caressed her breasts through the thick cream wool of her knitted shirt.

A heat rose up within Andie, but she pushed it back down. A wildfire could do nothing but burn out of control. She had to be ice, cold and collected. As warm as Larkin's touch made her, no matter how much she might fight to catch her breath, she was the one who was pulling the strings.

"Larkin." Andie's voice was soft but firm as she caught hold of his wrist as he made to tug up her skirt, fingers curled in the rich cotton fabric.

Larkin drew back, a mischievous smile crossing his lips as he carded a hand through his dishevelled blonde hair.

"It's alright, Andie. I know it might make you nervous…"

"Why would it make me nervous?" Irritation seared red-hot through Andie as she sat up, arching an eyebrow. Where was he getting the assumption that she shied away from intimacy? Larkin's silence shed light on a suspicion lingering in the back of her mind, and a laugh bubbled from her lips. "Wait, do you think that I haven't had sex before?"

"I assumed you hadn't." Larkin admitted stiffly, and Andie wondered if her value had just disintegrated in front of him. Some of the men talked about Flo in ways that made her blood boil, as though her worth was simply in her purity, as though she had none because of her past in the brothel. Andie begrudgingly respected Flo for it, a working girl through and through who would never rely on a man to support her.

"Does it matter?" Andie asked, voice sharp as a knife's edge.

"Was it Patrick?"

The air in the room thickened, gripping Andie by the throat and making her choke. The grief she had pushed aside came fighting back to life with teeth and claws, shredding into her and cutting away any patience she had left.

"Is that really what you want to know?" Andie pushed herself to her feet, staring down at him with her heart thundering in her chest. "Is that what really matters? Whether it was my dead best friend?"

"Andie…" Larkin realised his mistake, his eyes pleading as he rose to touch her arm. She wrenched away from him as though his skin scalded her.

"Don't." The single syllable was acidic, a serpent spitting venom. Picking up her coat, Andie marched from the grandiose apartment, slamming the door on the way out.

It was the fury she held onto the tightest. The rage that Larkin had the sheer audacity to ask such a question, simple though it may be. There was always that lingering, heavy expectation, one women were burdened with and men were not: the idea that women alone were to value sex as sacred. Her value lay in more than what parts of herself she chose to give away, and what parts she chose to keep.

The frustration bit at her with needle-sharp heat, but she welcomed it. She didn't want to dig below the anger. If she did, she would be faced with the ache of her loss, and she was terrified she didn't have the strength to stop it swallowing her whole.

* * *

Dusk threw deep hues of orange and purple across the sky as Andie strode through Central Park, past the Carnival and to the trailer she shared with Flo. The irritation within her had quieted, a throbbing cut dulling to a nuisance of a scratch. When she pushed the door open with a creak, Flo spun around and started at her appearance, fingers pausing where they had been rifling through Andie's clothes.

"Oh, be my guest." Andie cast off her jacket onto the chair by the mirror, flopping onto her bed. She didn't know who Flo was intending to impress, but she had apparently been stepping out with someone from the Carnival lately. "Most of my dresses are nicer than yours, in any case."

"Really?" Flo hesitated as though uncertain whether she believed Andie's consent was genuine. After a moment, she turned back to Andie's wardrobe, the white rail of which was beginning to tilt, humming under her breath as she flicked from hanger to hanger.

In the dying light of the dusk, something glittered like starlight amidst Flo's blonde waves, making Andie bolt upright. The recognition of the sparkling silver ribbon in Flo's hair and the anger at Larkin's insensitive line of questioning collided, mashing together into something violent and bitter, terribly bright and burning.

Lurching to her feet, Andie seized hold of Flo's hair, fingers twisting in the blonde tresses and making the younger girl cry out.

"You are *never* to wear that ribbon again," Andie hissed as she tugged it harshly from Flo's hair, curling it up safely in a closed fist. At Flo's stubborn silence, Andie's fingers tightened. "Do you fucking hear me? I don't care what else you touch but this ribbon is *not yours*."

"It's just a ribbon, Andie!" Flo wrenched away from her with fury and confusion glimmering in her pale eyes. Something about Andie's expression made her hard ire soften, and Andie despised the pity that replaced it. "Oh. It's from someone who was important to you. Was it your mother's…?"

"No, it didn't belong to my mother," Andie responded coldly, folding her arms over her chest and wishing she could slap the regretful look off Flo's flushed face. "It's none of your business, actually. Whoever you're off to see tonight, just get out and go meet him now."

"Andie…" There was compassion in Flo's tone, and she reached out a hand toward the older girl. Her desperation to bridge the gap between them made Andie's fury flare. She did not want to be pitied. She wanted to be envied, admired, desired. If Flo could not give her any of that in this moment, Andie couldn't stand the sight of her.

"I said get out!"

Flo scuttled from the trailer, the door banging shut on its hinges behind her. Andie leaned against the wall, pinching the bridge of her nose to stave off the rising tightness in her chest. She clutched the ribbon, *Claire's* ribbon, close to her chest as tears stung in the corners of her eyes.

"*Please don't leave me, Andie!*"

The panicked words, five years gone, continued to burn a hole in her heart, leaving a wound that wrenched open and knit itself closed, but never truly healed. She had done this. To Claire, to Syl, to herself. She could not blame Noel for hating her, but it would never compare to how much she hated herself.

Andie sank down on her bed with a wail building in her throat. First Claire, then Patrick. Perhaps she was cursed to lose people she loved. Tears spilled hot and fast down her cheeks, choked sobs catching in her mouth. She opened her fist to examine the silver ribbon, the way it sparkled in the waning light.

Andie wanted success because she had nothing else. She had insatiable ambition, she wanted to master soul magic, wanted to be pulling the strings. How could she do anything else? The scant handful of people in her life who still loved her deserved for her to be something, to be more than the shattered pieces of a woman who destroyed everything she touched.

She was a living performance, one mask constantly replacing another. To the Carnival, she was the bubbly showgirl. To Larkin, she was both the fragile girl who needed saving and the beguiling temptress who enjoyed being chased. To Syl…she wasn't certain what she was to her brother anymore, for they had grown too far apart.

What about her was *real*? What about her was enthralling, behind the masks? She didn't think anyone would find the angry, grieving young woman as appealing. She had constructed so many elaborate facades that she no longer knew who she was deep down, or perhaps she didn't *want* to know.

Maybe Noel was right about her. Maybe she was just a monster, a murderer.

Andie rubbed at her aching temples. The secrets and lies of the past five years felt like they were knocking against her head, trying to push their way out. She had to hold it all at bay, no matter how much it hurt. The truth wouldn't just destroy her, but it would ruin other lives, too.

Noel knew that better than anyone. Noel might loathe Andie more than anyone else on the planet, yet he was aware of what the truth would cost. It was why, however begrudgingly, he had agreed to lie for her.

CHAPTER ELEVEN

Prue Clermont

PRUE HAD NEVER MUCH LIKED VISITING Ethel's apartment. As a girl, the cloying scent of cat piss had left her breathless with excuses to go outside. As a woman, she stayed a polite amount of time, suffering the discomfort with a smile and her fingers twisting in the hem of her skirt until her face ached and her fingers twinged. So it was strange then that she found herself preferring the odorous apartment to the dreaded thought of going back to Mark.

One of Ethel's nine cats twined itself around Prue's legs as she held her knitting up to the lamplight, scowling at her progress. Though she had always been adept at stitching up clothing, knitting had never been a strength of hers. She had indulged in whatever hobby Ethel insisted upon since her arrival, hoping it would fend off any of her aunt's questions. Prue had mentioned a quarrel with Mark, nothing more.

A sharp rap at the door made Prue set down her knitting, dusting cat hair off herself. No matter how she tried to shake off the cat hair throughout the apartment, it seemed to get everywhere.

Ethel heaved a sigh and turned away from the stove where she had been preparing tea. She ambled over to the door, grimacing at the stiffness in her knees. She was a small woman with a tidy brown bob, watery blue eyes and wrinkles lining her forehead and around her thin lips. Perfectly capable of taking care of herself, Ethel had admitted that Prue's presence helped her with household chores due to the tightness that crept into her limbs, particularly in the winter. She opened the door to a man in a three-piece navy blue suit that looked like it cost more than Mark's annual salary.

"Good evening, ma'am." He removed his hat, affording Ethel a pleasant smile. "Sorry to disrupt you. We're looking for Prue Clermont."

"Oh, yes." Ethel bobbed her head in affirmation, turning to smile fondly over her shoulder. "My niece. She's staying here with me at the moment."

"Are you a friend of Mark's?" Prue asked, though she could guess he certainly was not. Unease rippled up her spine, but Ethel had opened her mouth and it was too late to undo the damage. Whoever the man was, he was dressed in a too polished and expensive manner for Prue to believe he was anyone associated with her husband. A shining brass pocket watch adorned his breast pocket, his moustache slick with a subtle curl at each end.

"Not quite." The man's smile didn't reach his eyes, cold as the frost adorning window panes during the winter. "May I come in?"

"I'm not sure that's a good idea." Prue's hands clenched into fists by her sides.

"Oh, don't be ridiculous, Prudence." Ethel waved her hand, beckoning him inside. "Of course you can. Would you like tea or coffee, perhaps?"

"That won't be necessary." The man stepped inside, kicking the door closed behind him. He strode over to Ethel and pressed a hand over her mouth as he took out a gun and shot her in the shin.

As Ethel toppled to the ground, clutching her leg and yowling like one of her cats against the pain, Prue staggered away from the man, terror causing her heart to beat like a sledgehammer against her ribcage. She had no idea what this man's purpose was, but his attention was fixated on her. She had no way to defend herself, and she had never felt more weak and helpless and *angry.*

"Scream and the next bullet goes in her head." The man pointed the gun at Prue, who flinched but pressed her lips together in a firm line.

That ache within her, both foreign and familiar, yawned open with a vengeance. It wanted to be fed. It needed to be sated. The ravenous sensation clawed its way up Prue's throat and as the man aimed his gun at her head, she reached out with curled fingers. She didn't know what she was hungering for, only that somehow, something in him could sate it.

The front door slammed open, ricocheting off the wall. A halo of light burned its way through the open space, making Prue wince and raise her hand to shield her eyes. When her vision adjusted to the brightness, she drank in the sight of a familiar head of red hair, contrasted with the unfamiliar fire that burned in each of Sadie's hands. Sadie's pale eyes gleamed with raw fury as she hurled a fistful of flame at the man, bowling him off his feet.

Prue scurried over to Ethel, who was groaning in pain, stomach lurching at the sight of the bullet wound. The wound didn't appear too deep, no bright shine of white to indicate bone. Prue had never been confronted with violence, never had to deal with more than a cut finger from a blunt kitchen knife. Picking up a blanket from the couch, Prue brushed as much cat hair as she could from it before tying it tightly around the wound.

Sadie advanced on the man, who crawled across the carpet toward the front door with a hand above his head as if to plead for mercy. She held her hands high, a dark smile twisting her lips as the fire licked at her fingertips, its burning glory reflected in her eyes.

"You know who I am." Her voice was cold as ice and sharp as steel, cutting through flesh and bone and making the man cower before her. "You know what I could do. *Tell* me who sent you."

He grinned and Prue found the smile at odds with his earlier show of fear. "Not a chance."

The man clicked his fingers and vanished, disappearing from the spot as immediately as if he'd turned invisible. Perhaps he had. Prue gaped at the empty space he had once occupied. Sadie cursed under her breath, dropping her arms as the fire extinguished from her fingers. She turned to face Prue, striding over to kneel by Ethel's side.

"Here," she said softly. Sadie untied the blanket from around Ethel's leg, ignoring both Prue's questioning look and Ethel's wild stare. "This will hurt a lot, but just for a moment."

Before Ethel could so much as nod, Sadie's fingers dug into the wound for the bullet. Ethel cried out, and Prue took her hand and gave it a reassuring squeeze in an attempt to distract her from it. Sadie's fingers came away covered in scarlet with a sliver of metal between them, and Prue's stomach heaved. She swallowed back the bile that surged up her throat as Sadie dropped the bullet on the carpet.

Sadie reached across to place her hand back over Ethel's wound, eyes screwing shut in concentration. Prue watched with fascination as the flesh knitted itself back together beneath Sadie's splayed fingers, until all that was left was an angry pink strip of skin. Wiping her bloodied hands on her skirt, Sadie pushed herself to her feet.

"We have to go."

"What?" Prue shook her head fervently, a thousand questions bouncing around her skull. "I can't just leave my aunt here, not after what happened."

"I'm not a talented healer, but I've done the best I can."

In the moment of her using magic, she had looked like an otherworldly goddess, glowing with firelight, radiating power and confidence. Now Prue could see the dark circles under her eyes, the limpness of her hair. Sadie told her that magic was give and take, that its energy must come from somewhere. In this instance, it had come from Sadie herself.

"You want us to leave?" Prue asked, brow furrowing.

"Don't you understand?" Sadie's voice prickled with impatience. "That man was here for *you*, Prue."

"Something is wrong with you." Warren's words echoed in her mind. There was magic that simmered beneath her skin. She could feel it, though she didn't have the slightest clue in how to control it. The type of magic might be uncertain, but it was strong enough to have Warren spooked. Perhaps there were others who realised there was a wrongness about her, too. Perhaps they wanted her gone.

"Let me put Ethel to bed first," Prue insisted, helping her aunt to her feet. Ethel's knees trembled as she led her into her bedroom, nudging aside several cats to tuck her in. Her aunt was disconcertingly silent, as though processing what she had just endured. Red-hot guilt surged through Prue, but Sadie was right. Ethel would be safer if she wasn't there. Perhaps they all would.

* * *

A grim silence lingered over the lounge of Sadie's apartment, broken only by the snap of logs in the hearth as the fire consumed them. The same fire that had burned in Sadie's hands only hours before, the fire she had wielded as a weapon. Combined with the way she had healed Ethel's bullet wound, that was at least two different kinds of magic that she possessed. Prue had her suspicions about Sadie, but seeing them confirmed brought her unease instead of comfort.

"So, you can do magic and you simply…never told me."

"I didn't want you to think I was part of the Carnival." Sadie raised her glass of champagne to her lips, staring into the flames. They were reflected in her eyes, burning bright and terrible.

"Aren't you?" Prue persisted, her tolerance hanging on a needle-thin thread.

"No." Sadie's gaze shifted to her. "I'm a mage, yes. But there is magic outside of the elite, as you've seen in Warren. He's one of many mages who agree with what I represent. Magic is controlled by the Lords and their families, dating back centuries. But those with a raw aptitude for it deserve to learn its history and its intricacies. That's how the Magical Freedoms Brigade was born."

Prue remained silent, folding her hands in her lap. She had never heard of the Brigade, and had no comprehension of the scope of Sadie's involvement. She had only seen the wonders of the Carnival and Warren's own magic, though she supposed she had never questioned why it was only amongst the rich that this magic was treated as an exhibition. The wealthy had always flaunted their power, why should magic be any different?

"The Magical Freedoms Brigade came about because mages outside of the elite are often persecuted. They're mostly forced to join the Lords, or sent to asylums where their word on magic would be seen as madness. Some are even quietly dealt with, so that control remains within the grasp of the Lords and their elite circle."

The fire snapped sharply, making Prue jump. A cold shiver sliced its way up her spine, icy horror at the idea of what happened to those who didn't conform. Mages like Warren would always exist, but even Warren was an ex-Carnival employee. What deal had he made, she wondered, in exchange for his small piece of freedom?

"The young man we came upon…" Sadie swallowed, her eyes glistening with unshed tears. It was yet another indication that she was closer to the murder victim they'd stumbled upon than she'd previously admitted. "His name is Patrick Rhodes. He was a fundamental part of the Brigade, and he'd infiltrated the inner circle as an employee. He had a mission, a dangerous one, and his fate tells me someone found him out."

Prue wriggled with impatience at learning where she fit in, a missing piece of the puzzle still unsure where she was to be slotted. Patrick had been a firm piece, an integral part of the unravelling web, but now she was dead. She had seen his body, the gash carved across his throat. She wasn't even part of the Brigade, and people wanted her dead. Was it because she was a mage outside of inner circle control? Was it because of something more nefarious still?

"I think someone believes that we saw who killed Patrick." The vulnerability was eviscerated from Sadie's tone, replaced by a hardness that matched the tight clench of her jaw and the sharp gleam in her eyes. "I think they want to silence us."

"Is that why they want to kill me?" Prue's brow furrowed in confusion.

"No." Sadie drained the last of her champagne from her glass. "You're different, Prue. I don't exactly know how, but your magic isn't the same as most."

"Then how do we determine what magic I have?" Irritation tugged a sourness out of Prue. "People are after me either because of this magic, because of Patrick, or both. I need to know what I'm working with if I'm ever to defend myself."

"There's someone who can help." Sadie reached across and rested a hand over Prue's. Her touch was light and cool against Prue's warm, flushed skin. It was comforting, and yet suspicions ran riot within Prue's mind. There was a lot that Sadie had kept from her. Could she truly trust this woman? Did she have any alternative?

Prue dragged in a deep breath and withdrew her hand from Sadie's. She could not afford to be reliant on anyone, not even the woman she was so infatuated with. Warmth and comfort were alluring, but they were treacherous.

Chapter Twelve

Ursula Delavane

The Delavane residence was accosted by cigar smoke and copious glasses of brandy. Such was the way, when a meeting of the Lords was convened. They tended to rotate through the residences, but Ursula was always invited. Though not a Lord herself, her knowledge and experience within their matters could prove invaluable for Larkin, should he actually choose to take her advice.

"How was your meeting with Garrett, Ursula?" Sterling's cheeks were reddened from an overabundance of brandy, though he insisted on refilling his glass. The man tended to be insufferable when he was drunk, bellowing out his opinions like he thought the world wished to hear them, though he had not quite reached that stage yet. Ursula plastered a practiced smile across her lips.

"Well. He is in possession of a great deal of arcane artefacts."

"New money," Cyril scoffed derisively, raising his cigar to his lips and blowing out a plume of smoke. "They always feel the need to flaunt their wealth."

Ursula arched an eyebrow but said nothing. She had once seen Cyril purchase a bottle of champagne infused with pure gold. She did not believe it was purely 'new money' who tended toward extravagance.

The Lords did not fully trust the Alderidges. It was true that both parties benefited one another. The power of the Lords and the families of the inner circle. The influence of the Alderidges within the everyday world. Garrett praised the wonders of the Carnival, though like Larkin, he believed magic could be expanded upon. It seemed both the young and the inexperienced lacked nuance and subtlety. Magic was more prevalent than they thought.

"Garrett is concerned for Noel and fears his brother may be some-what unstable," Ursula said as she poured more glasses of brandy. "He thinks it has to do with Larkin's companion, Andie Fairley."

Perched in a chair by the window, Larkin leaned forward, annoy-ance pinching at his brows as his fingers tightened around his cigar.

"Precisely what are you implying, Mother?"

Ursula lapsed into silence. The Lords, as usual, underestimated the threat that Andie posed. She knew better. She recognised how danger-ous women could be, the peril that lay behind that well-practised smile. She would tear off Andie's mask, no matter how daunting. She would plunge her fingers into the dirt beneath and dig deep until she found the truth.

Had it not been a woman who had once brought about the fall of the Arthurian age? It was Guinevere the Scourge who had ripped the magic from Arthur, Lancelot and Mordred. Legend had it that the essences had been given to Merlin, though no one knew for sure, the essences lost to time. Some claimed Guinevere had done it to prevent further warfare and bloodshed, but Ursula always suspected it was motivated by greed and a desire for power.

"She is ambitious, Larkin."

Larkin sneered. "Were you not ambitious once in marrying my father? This is a meeting of the Lords. If you insist on spinning tales born from your own dislike of Andie, there is no place for you here."

Ursula could not deny her own ambition, though she had settled in the role society had expected of her. Her marriage had been made based on advantage, but had she not stepped into the shadows, existing in the thankless role of wife and mother? Franklin was not always an easy husband, and Larkin certainly was not an easy son. Yet she had persevered through the years, finding it easy to be amongst the elite with the privilege that entailed. Life always had difficulties, why should she expect marriage and motherhood to be any different?

Ursula made sacrifices that Larkin could never understand, though she bit down on her tongue rather than chastise his ignorance.

"The boy has a point, Ursula," Sterling remarked, his tone of false sympathy stinging a bitterness within her that she quickly buried deep.

Larkin's eyes narrowed. "I am twenty-five years old, Sterling. If you wish to infantilise me, prepare to get 'old man' in response."

Over by the fire, Desmond snickered.

"Forgive me." Ursula swept her hair behind her ear, offering the Lords an apologetic smile. "I forget myself. By all means, please continue with business."

She sank into the velvet couch and took up her proper place; out of the way and with her mouth closed. Many of these modern women may disagree with her, but she found a great joy in listening and learning rather than speaking. Though she may chafe against Larkin's lack of judgement, particularly when they concerned a woman he was enamoured with, it was not her position to question his choices, merely offer a gentle hand to guide him.

"We need to discuss the Magical Freedoms Brigade." Cyril folded his arms over his chest, brow furrowed in thought. "The boy they found dead, with his throat slit, he was one of them."

"How do we know that for certain?" Larkin asked, scepticism colouring his tone.

"Wasn't he a Carnival employee?" Sterling frowned in consideration as he asked. "How did he keep his involvement with the Brigade secret?"

If Patrick was involved in the Magical Freedoms Brigade, what was to say that Larkin's shining star wasn't as well? There was a serpent slithering beneath the sweet facade, coiled, waiting for a chance to sink in its fangs.

"We've done some investigating." Cyril's airy tone was at odds with his steely smile. "While we've no idea who actually murdered him, it's clear that Rhodes had ties to this growing resistance. His actual role is unclear, but his death makes it a lot more difficult to pin down some of the others."

Ursula's gaze flicked to Larkin, assessing his expression. Did he know more than he was letting on? Her son's countenance remained stony, a step above boredom. If Larkin had information on Patrick, then he was keeping his cards close to his chest. When his face was closed off, his jaw set and his eyes sharp as flint, his resemblance to his father was striking.

On Frankie, that look had been a warning, the alarm bells sounding in Ursula's mind when his pale eyes flared with danger. It was the split second head start she and Larkin had before Frankie's fist flew. Ursula entwined her fingers, clasping them together and squeezing her own hands hard. She and Frankie had spent many years together, but the rose-tinted memories sometimes bled crimson, like her lip or cheek when Frankie raised a hand to her.

Larkin never understood. He had boiled with hatred for Frankie since he'd been a child, the loathing settling down into him like a stone. With every blow, the threads that tied Frankie and Larkin together had loosened a little more, until Larkin cut them loose completely, with nothing but contempt for the man he felt forced to call his father.

Larkin had suffered beneath the yoke of Frankie's overbearing authority, and if there was anything Ursula could change, it was that her son had not been the victim of such violence.

For her, it was more complicated. She had not married Frankie for love, but to secure her place in a world where she struggled to find meaning for herself. After her former fiance abandoned her at the altar, the cold truth seeped into Ursula's bones. Love was not enough. Love would not give her what she wanted: stability, a family, influence. Frankie had given her that, despite his violent tendencies. The bruises were a fair trade for the beauty of magic.

"Well, then." Larkin steepled his fingers together. "Perhaps we should actually look into who Rhodes' associates were."

"You already know the answer to that, Larkin." Softness caressed the sharp barb beneath Ursula's words. "Everyone knows that Patrick spent a lot of time with Andie. The two were such close friends, practically inseparable."

Larkin inhaled sharply through his nostrils. "Yet another transparent attempt to discredit Andie due to your own dislike of her. Tell me, Mother, is it resentment that causes you to constantly pin any crime you can think of on her? Or is it jealousy?"

Larkin's cold smile, combined with Cyril's quiet snicker, made fury flare beneath Ursula's graceful composure. Why in the name of Merlin would she envy Andie Fairley? The girl was from an impoverished background, with little to her name and only Larkin's obsession to keep her afloat. Ursula was secure in her position.

Men, as shallow as they were, might paint her natural suspicion of an envy for Andie's youth and beauty. Such things were inconsequential to Ursula. Her youth was far behind her, and though she still retained her beauty, it too would one day fade. Power was what mattered. Power was what Ursula had, what Andie never would. Perhaps not as much as the smug men surrounding her now, but power enough to forever silence someone like Andie should the girl prove more trouble than she was worth.

"Resentment?" Ursula scoffed the word, lapsing into a bored drawl. "Larkin, my darling, you are blinded by your own infatuation. You refuse to see the bad in her."

"I think we all know what Larkin wants to see *in* her," Cyril remarked slyly, earning an irritated look from the younger man.

"It's what Rhodes saw in her too." Desmond's words lacked the crudeness that oozed from Cyril's. "Anyone with eyes could see that he was in love with her. That does not mean she had a part in the rebellion, but neither should we completely disregard the potential for her involvement."

A triumphant smile snaked across Ursula's lips. She quite liked Desmond, despite his lower-class background. He spoke with neither Sterling's grumbling or Cyril's smarm, instead armed with practicality. It was an unusual quality in a man who had clawed his way to power by his own means with no family name or money to back him. However, Ursula knew better than to underestimate him; such men were always hungry, prepared to do whatever it took to sate the appetite of their ambition.

"So you want to investigate her now?" Disdain dripped from every syllable as Larkin folded his arms over his chest.

"Nothing so intense." Desmond waved a hand as if the motion would dispel Larkin's doubts. "It's simply worth keeping an eye on her."

Larkin's silence was sweet as honey on Ursula's tongue, for if he had reservations, he would certainly voice them. She wished, for her son's benefit, that her suspicions had no merit and that Andie was trustworthy. But with Noel's antagonism toward her, Patrick's involvement in the Magical Freedoms Brigade, and a wicked smile that flashed sharp as a knife, Andie Fairley was definitely trouble.

* * *

The mouth-watering aroma of rosemary pork wafted through the kitchen. Ursula still sometimes dreamed of the early days, before she had married Frankie, when she had taken on cooking herself. It quieted her mind to keep her hands busy, but after her marriage, Frankie made it clear they had servants and a cook for such endeavours. Ursula did not mind having food cooked for her, but a small shard of her missed preparing meals.

Larkin swaggered into the dining room as the cook, Jane, removed the roasted pork from the oven. His pupils were blown wide and his nostrils were lined with white powder. Ursula frowned in disapproval, though she could not claim surprise. Larkin had a tendency to indulge himself in cocaine following the Lords' meeting. It often gave his tongue that same blunt cruelty that had lain within Frankie's fist.

"Dinner is ready, Larkin." Ursula seated herself at the head of the table, gesturing for her son to sit. "Why don't you take a seat?"

Larkin was disturbingly silent as he sank into a chair beside his mother, fingers combing through unkempt blonde hair. Regret seared through Ursula at the dark circles beneath his eyes. Responsibility weighed upon his shoulders like a heavy cloak, the mighty mantle of Lord Summer settling over a young man who, despite his own protests, had not been ready for it.

"I think we need to talk about your presence at meetings, Mother." His voice was laced with an undercurrent of venom as Jane entered the dining room, serving the pork, roasted vegetables, and a good dollop of homemade gravy onto their plates. The warmth of the food was negated by the cool chill that tickled up Ursula's arms.

"Whatever do you mean?"

The neatly-set silverware across the mahogany dining table shimmered in the warm glow of light from the crystal chandelier dangling above. The plates set on ruby-red velvet placements were made of the finest porcelain. Everything in the Delavanes' apartment boasted wealth and excess. It had taken Ursula's breath away when she had first married Frankie, but it caught her breath for another reason tonight.

"I don't think it's necessary." Larkin's knife flashed in the light as he cut up his pork. "You pry into matters that are none of your concern."

Frustration held Ursula in its rigid grasp. "If this is about Andie…"

Larkin's blue eyes flicked up to meet hers, cutting deep as broken glass. The tense set of his jaw made her stomach twist at her misstep. Danger dined at the table tonight, and it wore the face of Ursula's cocaine-addled son.

"This is precisely the problem. Everything comes back to her. How you disapprove of her, how you think she's a distraction or worse, a spy for the Magical Freedoms Brigade."

"Are you so certain she is not?" Ursula coated her words in sugary sweetness, but soothing words had never prevented the fist that followed. From Frankie, it had been to the face, the stomach, wherever he gauged it would hurt the most. From Larkin, the table jostled and the silverware clinked as his fist met wood.

"You never sat in on the meetings with Father. You always waited for him to debrief you after, if he felt like it. So tell me, why do you insist on doing so with me?"

The truth would be a hard pill to swallow, but it seemed that Larkin was done devouring candy-coated lies, so he would have honesty even if he choked on it.

"Because you're not ready. You can't handle it all. It's expected, since you are young. I accompany you so that I may help you."

The laugh that pulled free of Larkin's lips was a dark, mirthless thing that bathed in bitterness and danced with disdain.

"You think I am some naive boy who needs coddling? I am stronger than you give me credit for, *Mother*, and I see clearly. You want to manipulate me, to push your own agenda through me."

Ursula's fingers fisted in her silk skirt as her heart rose to beat against the hollow of her throat. "Larkin, that's not…"

"You have no idea," Larkin hissed, lurching to his feet with cold fury, a mask of composure barely held together with the strings of begrudging restraint. "You have *no idea* who I am."

Ursula had always seen Franklin in her son, in the rage smouldering in his eyes, in the nerve that ticked in his cheek when he was angry. Yet looking at him now, pushing past the gauzy curtains of what she wanted to see, her own stubbornness glared back at her. Her own unshakeable confidence and certainty, her own determination.

Dread clawed a burrow within her at the vehement shine to Larkin's eyes. She had long suspected a savagery to him, but despite Frankie's violence, he had been a man of purpose and precision. No, the wildness within Larkin, the urge to bare fangs and lash out like a snake, that came from Ursula herself.

Larkin was *her* son. He was her only child. In many ways, he was as bright and warm as the summer sun. Yet it would never do to forget that for all its light, the sun could burn and blind. The sun could be unforgiving and cruel.

In Larkin, Ursula recognised not only the best and worst of her husband, but the best and worst of herself. In that ice-cold realisation came the unsettling knowledge that her son would do whatever it took to prove himself, whatever it took to establish himself as Franklin's worthy successor.

Did those traits make him blessed, she wondered, or doomed?

Chapter Thirteen

Andie Fairley

The Carnival was a haze of dreamy pink and vibrant red in preparation for the Valentine's Day performance. Excitement thrummed to life in Andie's chest as she swiped scarlet lipstick across her full lips, but the feeling was tainted by the ache deeper down, the grief that maintained its sharp sting as she gnawed on it like a dog with a bone. She stared into the mirror, familiar features reflected back at her; the oval shape of her face framed by tight curls, the constellation of freckles across her nose, the blue eyes that seemed out of place against her darker skin. When the reflection offered no answers, no comfort, she looked away.

Usually, she would have spent the day with Patrick. Not even in a romantic sense, but simply enjoying one another's company. Instead she was in her trailer, suffocating on the scent of Flo's rose perfume, her glittering red dress digging tight into her ribcage. Andie allowed the sensation of drowning to wash over her, closing her eyes to the panic that dragged her under. She had to sit with it, to hold her breath through it, before surging to the surface and breaking free of its tyrannical grasp.

Her fingers, curled into a fist in the sequined fabric of her dress, loosened. She blinked away the useless tears that stung in her eyes. She pushed aside memories of Patrick's easy smile, the warmth of his embrace, the laughter that bubbled up from his chest. She would never have any of those things again.

Vengeance burned hot as Andie leaned over her dresser, gripping the edges as she examined her reflection, the brightness of her eyes and the clench of her jaw. 'Be the bigger person' would be the advice Warren would give her and once, she may have heeded it. But the years had grown cruel, and kindness was often met with malice. Andie had no intention of being the bigger person, not where Patrick's death was concerned. She would sink low, dragging her stomach through filth until she carved up the truth.

She let her jaw relax, let her lips fall into that charming smile she was so practised in. Her eyes were sparkling with pink glitter, rimmed with kohl.

She was dressed to kill. Perhaps that was precisely what she would do.

Pushing herself away from the dresser, Andie stepped out of her trailer, inhaling the heady scent of campfire smoke that billowed through the evening air. She had to focus on the performance. She had to be *perfect*. Things between her and Larkin were laced with unmistakable tension since their argument, and if she still intended to progress her magic, she could not afford to hold a grudge or sulk.

Breathing deeply, she drew her confidence around her like a cloak, the dress shimmering in the pale orange light of dusk as she sauntered toward Sun Carnival. Her own magic simmered in her veins, but she would have to content herself with the electric touch of Larkin's. A sour taste danced across her tongue at the notion of being unable to use her own magic, though she ignored it.

Between shows, Andie would lose herself in the Carnival, the bright lights of the ferris wheel and merry-go-round spinning through the darkness, the candy-coloured tents and stalls offering tempting aromas of various sweets and warm food. Dominating it all was a large stage, boasting the same pink and red as the rest of the Carnival.

Striding past the pink tents selling heart-shaped candy, Andie was invigorated with a sense of purpose as she approached the stage. She was so close to achieving what she wanted, the taste of victory honeying her tongue. The power she wanted was dangling above her, almost within arm's reach. She just had to be bold enough to reach out and take it.

"Andie!" Larkin, exuberant as ever, strode over in a glittering red jacket that matched Andie's dress. He snaked an arm around her waist and kissed her cheek, and she beamed brightly at the attention.

When he clasped his fingers through hers, the familiar jolt of his magic surged through her, making the hairs on her arms stand on end. Magic could be gifted directly or indirectly, but Larkin preferred to let her absorb the power he offered, their hands intertwined as she breathed through the sharpness of the transferral. It didn't hurt, but it could be an overwhelming sensation, like lightning crackling beneath her skin.

"Thank you." Andie gave his hand a light squeeze, dropping her gaze to her shoes. "I know things have been strained between us recently. If I offended you, I'm sorry."

"You have nothing to apologise for." Larkin took both of Andie's hands in his, stepping so close she could smell the rum on his warm breath. "I was insensitive. I just hope that you can forgive me."

"Of course." She tilted her head back to press a light kiss to his lips, allowing a slow smile to grace her own. "Tonight will be a performance to remember, I promise. You'll see just how proficient I really am."

She let the playful insinuations sink in, watched the way his throat bobbed and pupils dilated with barely concealed desire. Smirking, Andie drew her hands from Larkin's and blew him a kiss as she walked over to the stage. She would be the opening act, despite how heavily she had campaigned to be the finale. No matter; by the time she was done, she would blow them all away. They would *remember* her.

If she was a spectacle, a shining star, then Larkin would have to see her worth clear as day. It would not take much convincing for her to ease her way into using her own magic, and then gaining soul magic. She had him wrapped around her little finger, a puppet operating at her whim, and she just needed to tug the strings in the right direction.

Andie's gaze raked over the crowd assembling in front of the stage, nudging each other forward. The familiar weight of pre-performance anxiety niggled at her as she took her place behind the thick velvet curtains, a feeling she ruthlessly crushed beneath her burgeoning ambition.

Closing her eyes, she let herself listen to the sounds of the Carnival. The murmurs of the crowd just beyond the curtain. The excited exclamations of those on the rides. The calls of the vendors at their stands. The scent of butter popcorn and cotton candy, sweet in the air. Larkin's magic tingling at her fingertips, begging to be used. The gentle flow of her magic beneath, like waves lapping against the shore.

Andie's heels clicked across the polished wood of the stage as she took her place in the centre, the curtains creaking as they rose like the sun heralding a new dawn. By the time the evening's waning light washed over Andie, her trademark dazzling smile was set in stone, arms raised above her head.

Like Larkin, she believed that magic could be used for more. She suspected that, behind closed doors, it certainly was. For now, she would make do with it being a spectacle for the amusement of the crowds. Something pretty and shiny, the horrors and dangers of which the casual onlooker would never perceive.

Throwing her arms wide, Andie strode across the stage, one exaggerated step after another. At a click of her fingers, fire blossomed at her fingertips, and a cold jolt raced up Andie's spine. She had never questioned what magic Larkin possessed, or what magic he might give her, but she hadn't suspected that he had heart magic. Whether intentionally or not, he had gifted it to her, bestowing upon her not only the power of the elements but also a horrific truth: he had betrayed someone dear to him in order to gain this power.

Just like she had.

Locking in her smile with steely resolve, Andie let the flame turn pink, turning it over in her hands and watching it caress her skin without burning it. The crowd gave the polite 'oohs' and 'aahs', but they had seen tricks like this before. Andie brought her hands together and in a single clap, the fire consumed her entirely. It washed over her like a trickle of water, tickling against her arms and legs, crawling over her sparkly red dress.

Concentrating, the buzz of magical control soothed Andie like someone stroking her hair, as she allowed the fire to eat away at her dress. The crowd whooped in delight as the red garment burned away to reveal a pale pink one beneath it. Andie swivelled on her heel, tossing them a conspiratorial wink over her shoulder, before ripping the red dress off her body completely. When she raised it in the air above her head, a warm thrill raced up her spine as she transformed it, red and pink fireworks thrown up from her fingers.

The crowd cheered as the fireworks came down as confetti, drifting over them and the stage. The familiar fatigue following magic use tugged at Andie's muscles, but she wasn't done. She couldn't be until they were chanting her name, begging for her to continue. Breathing deeply and ignoring the way her pulse pounded against her temple, Andie reached deep down beneath the sharp current of Larkin's magic into the comforting warmth of her own.

She would decide what was forbidden. *She* would decide whose magic she used.

Her mind magic nudged at her like a dog nosing at its owner's hand for affection. Brow furrowing in concentration, Andie gripped onto her power like she was a drowning woman and it was a rope. Then she tugged at it, feeling it yield to her as the stage beneath her feet groaned and pushed off the ground, floating upwards until it was levitating a few feet off the grass.

The crowd yelled and clapped, a frenzy of noise that beat against Andie's concentration. Every muscle in her body screamed at her to stop, but she was nothing if not stubborn. A feral smile adorning her lips, Andie held the stage with every magical fibre of her being, dipping a cheeky curtsy to the crowd. She drowned out the cacophony as she released her hold on her magic, slowly, lowering the stage back down onto the ground.

The applause was enough to appease the twinging of the muscles in her arms and leg, the way her lungs burned when she drew in a breath, the sweat that beaded on her brow. Andie basked in it, not simply the adoration, but the sheer thrill of the magic that whispered promises of power.

When the applause died down, someone in the middle rows was clapping aggressively, the noise making Andie pause on her stage exit. Murmurs took up residence within the audience as Noel Alderidge swaggered toward the stage, the slight sway in his step an indication that he'd overindulged in alcohol.

"Pretty performance, for a *murderer*."

Cold dread dropped in the pit of Andie's stomach. Noel could sneer whatever he wanted in private, but this was a public display, and the quiet unease that washed over the crowd was palpable. Her hands balled into fists, carefully manicured nails biting beneath the skin of her palms and drawing blood.

"Noel." There was a harried smile on Larkin's face as he strode over to throw an arm around Noel's shoulders, steering the man behind the stage. "Let's take care of this privately."

Garrett elbowed his way through the crowd to pursue his brother, concern pinching at his brow. Andie's breathing quickened, panic replacing the euphoria she'd felt moments before. The anxiety caught her like a net, though she took care to steady her steps as she retreated from the stage, knees trembling as she descended the stairs.

Out the back of the stage, New York City was awash in a glow of pale pink and purple light, the dying embers of the day surrendering to the embrace of the night. The beauty of the city was undercut by the argument occurring by the painted wooden panelling of the stage's borders.

"...what the fuck you're talking about, Noel." Garrett's tone was one of stern disapproval, fingers tugging through thinning hair as he took a drag of his cigar. "This behaviour, it has to stop. You're unstable."

"Because you don't know the truth!" Noel was a man deranged, his hair falling across his face and his eyes bright with malice as he turned to jab an accusatory finger at Andie. "You don't know what *she did*."

"It's not as though you've told me anything." Garrett arched an eyebrow. "So if you're about to start, you need to get to it. Otherwise this emotional outburst is going to be all over the papers with no explanation…"

Noel sneered. "Oh, anything but the papers. Anything but your reputation. Has it never occurred to you, Garrett, that I am the one who has lost the most in ensuring your *reputation* was nothing more than golden?"

Garrett tossed his head back in exasperation. "Noel, what are you talking about?"

"Claire!" Noel shouted, the single word shocking everyone into silence as effectively as a gunshot. Andie paused at Larkin's side, feeling him tense beside her at the mention of Noel's late daughter.

"I am trying to understand here." Garrett's tone was one of patience worn down to a tired thread.

"I am not the one you should be asking questions." Noel fixed Andie with a look of pure loathing. "Ask her. Ask why she has heart magic. Ask her about Claire."

"You have heart magic?" Larkin glanced at Andie, but the shock in his eyes paled to what was coming. A storm that had always lingered on the horizon, a secret Andie and Noel had buried and laid to rest, only for him to unearth it now. Her whole body started to shake, tears pricking behind her eyes.

"Claire committed suicide five years ago." Garrett said the words slowly, reciting the well-rehearsed story that he had swallowed the moment Noel offered it on a platter.

"I told you that because the truth would have destroyed you." Tears spilled down Noel's cheeks, fingers reaching out to grip Garrett's shoulder. "You were coming up for election. The truth about my daughter would have ruined us."

"Noel…" Andie's voice trembled over the single syllable, a desperate plea to spare both of them the pain that this confession would lead to. Instead he whirled on her, teeth gritted in fury as he grabbed her by the neck and slammed her against the wooden panelling. His fingers tightened around her throat, and Andie's struggle to breathe was no longer purely anxiety, but a physical lack of air.

"You killed my *only child*, you fucking bitch!" Noel screamed in her face, spittle landing on Andie's cheeks as she shook like a leaf, sobs grating against her throat. His handsome face was mottled with red, veins bulging in his forehead as he attempted to crush the delicate bones of her neck. "You shot her and threw her body into the Harlem River!"

Garrett tugged Noel away from Andie, and her knees gave out from underneath her. She collapsed onto the grass, dissolving into tears as the memories of that horrific night all came flooding back. Claire, vibrant and sweet. Claire, who had trusted her. Claire, who she had failed in ways there was no forgiveness for.

"Please don't leave me, Andie!"

"I had to," Andie choked out, staring up at Noel's burning hatred and Garrett's blatant horror through errant curls. "I had to end her suffering."

Noel lurched toward her, restrained by his brother. "It should have…"

"Been me?" Her laugh teetered on the last vestige of sanity. "You have no idea how long I spent wishing that it was."

"That's enough." Garrett's voice was cold and commanding, a stark difference to the typical warmth he presented. "Noel, we can discuss this at home. When you're sober."

Larkin strode over to Andie with hesitant steps, offering a hand. Against her better judgement, she took it. When he tugged her to her feet, there was hurt and accusation in his expression. Resentment coiled deep within her. How could he feel hurt about not knowing about

Claire, about her heart magic, when he should surely understand why it cut so deep for her to possess it in the first place?

"You didn't trust me with any of this. You hid your power from me." There was no mistaking the anger in Larkin's tone, and Andie gritted her teeth at having to do damage control while still reeling in her own emotional turmoil.

"I would have thought you'd be more horrified that I killed my own sister."

Larkin drew back as though she'd struck him. "What?"

A bitter laugh bubbled free from Andie's lips. She was surprised Noel had not brought up their relation, to cut even deeper beneath her skin, to cement the guilt further. Taking Larkin's hand in her own, Andie sat down on the grass, overlooking the city. Larkin's anger and confusion faded, his brow softening at the silent tears that spilled down Andie's cheeks as she tore down the final barrier between them, all the regret and self-loathing of her past flowing free.

"When I was a baby, my mother, Sarah, left the family. I suppose life in poverty wasn't what she imagined for herself. She remarried within the year, and when I was two years old, Claire was born. My mother's second husband was Noel Alderidge."

For so many years, young Andie had been hurt and resentful toward her mother. When Sarah had died from tuberculosis, the year before Claire's death, Andie felt nothing. What was she meant to feel, for the mother who had turned her back and never given her a chance? What was so wrong with her and Syl, that they deserved to be abandoned, cold without their mother's love?

"Despite tensions, Noel hoped that having us play with Claire as we grew up would result in a sibling bond developing between us all. He was right. Claire and I were possibly even closer than I was with Syl. Things I couldn't share with my brother, I would speak about with her."

Late nights giggling under the sheets, far past their bedtime. Andie running a brush through Claire's smooth blonde hair, so different from her own wild curls. Whispers about Patrick, things she would never confess to Syl. Bittersweet memories, overshadowed by the knowledge of what came after.

"We were messing about in a warehouse. Syl, Claire and I. We all had our own brands of magic, and we wanted to demonstrate them. I…I went too far, and a telekinetic blast I produced destroyed the support beams in the warehouse. I was the furthest away, when the initial debris fell, I found myself with a choice to make. I could manage to get one of them out in time, but not both. I chose Syl. When the beams fell, Syl got hit, knocked out cold. But I dragged him out of the wreckage. The whole time I could hear Claire screaming out for me as she was buried in the falling rubble. She said…she said *please don't leave me, Andie!'* but I did."

The words were difficult to choke up, razor blades cutting the inside of her mouth as they sliced their way free and left her choking on the blood of the past. An admission of guilt, of her own role and her responsibility. It might have been an accident, but what followed her was deliberate, even if it had been the only mercy Andie could have bestowed upon her younger sister. She stared up at the sky, spangled with stars, as isolated and uncaring as they had been on that horrific night five years before.

Syl had loathed her ever since. Syl hated her for choosing him, and had reminded her as often as he could that she had made the wrong decision.

"You left me, Andie." Her final words. An accusation that would haunt Andie until her own dying day. A cruel but deserved twist to the gut every time she thought about them.

"I went back for her once I'd managed to drag Syl clear, but it was too late. Claire had been impaled with metal shards and I wasn't a doctor, but I knew I couldn't save her. I stroked back her hair and soothed her the best I could. Then I took out the Colt Derringer that Syl had got me for my birthday, and shot her in the head. When it was dark, I loaded her body into a wheelbarrow and snuck down to the bridge. It was quiet. Almost peaceful. When I threw Claire's body into the water, it felt peaceful, too. I watched her slip under the water."

Larkin gripped Andie's hand in his own, and Andie allowed the gesture, though she was too caught up in her own traumatic memories. They had played mermaids as children in that river, diving under the water and holding their breath. Only this time, Claire had never come back up.

"Noel met Syl and I on the bridge not long after. I told him what had happened, the cold truth of it. The silence…it went on for so long. I genuinely thought maybe he would kill me then and there. I still don't know why he didn't. He probably wishes that he had. But he was the one to suggest we frame Claire's death as a suicide. Not to protect me, he assured me, to make sure Garrett's campaign went smoothly."

Fact and fiction began to mingle together, as Andie held the last cards she had to her chest. There were some things Larkin didn't need to know. What had happened on the bridge that night was between Syl, Andie and Noel. She tapped her fingers against Larkin's hand.

"That was the night Patrick and I spent together, because I was mourning and he comforted me. That was when my heart magic flared to life."

Again, not the whole truth, but enough of it. When she glanced over at Larkin to ascertain his reaction, any animosity had dissolved into pity. She would have preferred the anger. She did not need or deserve sympathy. Her sins ran deeper than any river, and she could still feel the blood on her hands.

Yet, in the cogs of her mind that were still cold and calculating, perhaps his sympathy could be of benefit to her. Perhaps this was something she could utilise to get what she wanted. Larkin was soft for her at this moment, his negative feelings about her secrets banished in lieu of his pity.

Andie leaned in and pressed her lips to Larkin's with desperation, wondering if he could taste the salt of her tears rather than her vicious triumph.

Chapter Fourteen

Prue Clermont

Sadie's apartment was no warmer than Prue's, yet more often than not, she found herself waking in a sweat. Sadie had politely offered the lounge, which was more than comfortable. As Prue's nightmares of the attack persisted, Sadie grew more and more concerned and finally suggested that Prue share the bed with her, which she had accepted. She had to begrudgingly admit that her sleep had been better since, though she often felt the brush of Sadie's skin against her beneath silk sheets, which led to other reasons for her dwindling rest.

Prue's absence would protect Mark and Ethel. It was a reassurance she'd first heard from Sadie, one she repeated like a mantra as she stared blankly at the ceiling, watching the sliver of light where the moon peered in through the curtains. She could not shake the unsettling feeling that there was something terribly amiss with her. The magical hunger within her had quietened as though sated, though perhaps she'd found a way to suppress it. It was a foolish hope, and she reprimanded herself for entertaining it.

Prue sighed and kicked her legs free of the tangled sheet. Sadie stirred beside her, rolling over to face her. She couldn't see her friend's face in the darkness, and it was growing dangerous to think about Sadie's eyes, and her lips, without feeling a hot flush wash over her and a pleasant tingle race up her spine.

"Can't sleep?" Sadie murmured, the words a soft caress against Prue's skin.

Prue missed Mark. Not in the longing sense, but in a manner of familiarity. She had spent so much of her life with him that it felt like a lost limb to be away from him. It frightened her, to realise she had been so reliant on him, on *them*. But 'them' had changed after the war, until Prue was no longer sure of how much of 'them' was left.

Then there was the matter of her magic. Sadie had her calm explanations for the forms of magic, but only confusion when it came to Prue's. It shocked and scared her in equal measure, the idea that there was something inherently wrong with her, a sickness that dwelled beneath the surface.

Fortunately, they would be visiting Sadie's friend tomorrow morning. Not Warren, in whose blue eyes the horror still reverberated through Prue's being. His son actually, Syl Fairley. According to Sadie, Syl had a rare gift: the ability to 'read' magic. Warren might have had a sense of what Prue was, but Syl would be able to confirm it. Occasionally involved with the Magical Freedoms Brigade and a friend of Patrick's, Syl was renowned for his love of drink and drugs. Unreliable, but gifted.

"What if Syl doesn't have the answer?" Desperation tinged Prue's tone, making her wince at the whine of it. "What if it's just another question mark? I'm afraid I'm a problem that cannot be solved."

Sadie was silent for a long moment, but her fingers reached out to brush against Prue's. Fireworks erupted in Prue's chest, something bursting to life within her, something that only Sadie had the ability to awaken. She tightened her fingers through Sadie's.

"I was a question mark once." The words were soft, trembling enough that though Prue wanted to ask how someone as vibrant as Sadie could ever be a question mark, the other woman's vulnerability lulled her into silence. Sadie was opening up to her, a rarity. "My parents…were not married. My father ensured that I lived a comfortable life, so that he never had to hear from my mother and I. Because to him, I was a reminder of his shame and his betrayal."

Prue had assumed Sadie came from a wealthy background, considering her obvious life of luxury, though she would never have imagined that the other woman was born out of wedlock. The velvet cloak of the night's darkness hid Sadie's face, but not the sting of bitterness from her tone. The circumstances of her birth had, more likely than not, been weaponised against her in the past.

"I decided that wasn't who I wanted to be." Sadie's voice grew harder, like she had drawn a stone wall around herself. "I wasn't my father's shame. I was my own person, and I made my own life outside of that. I no longer tell people who he is, because my relation to him doesn't matter. I am more than that."

There had been a boy that Prue attended school with, who had nasty whispers about his parentage. The older children had thrown sand in his eyes, etched crude drawings on his belongings. Every time Prue saw him, his mouth was downturned, eyes burning with misery and accusation as they searched everywhere for the next attack. She wondered if it had been like that for Sadie growing up, and realised for the first time how desperately *lonely* the other woman must be.

"You will have the chance to decide who you are." Sadie reached out to tuck a strand of Prue's hair behind her ear, the whisper of skin against skin making warm pins and needles reverberate through her body. "Once we talk to Syl, no matter what he says, you are no longer just Mark's wife. You're Prue Clermont, and it's up to you to choose who that is now."

Who *did* she want to be? She wished she could be effortlessly charming like Sadie, but when Prue paused, she realised that was something she admired about her friend, not a quality she expected in herself. Anxiety gnawed at her from the inside. She didn't quite know who she wanted to be, which felt rather embarrassing.

Yet…why did she owe it to anyone, let alone herself, to have it all figured out? She had learned about magic, that she had magic. Her life had been thrown into a tumultuous spin that she was reeling from. She had to let things stop and settle before she could see the path forward clearly.

When Prue tucked herself back beneath the silk sheets, perhaps a bit closer to Sadie than she'd been before, she was nestled in a cocoon of security that she had not felt since she and Ethel were attacked. The pieces would fall together. They had to, before she fell apart.

* * *

Syl's caravan was on the edge of the Carnival, a distant planet in orbit around the brightness and wealth of those it served. The caravan was more rust than metal, in a similar state to the streets where Prue had met Syl's father Warren. Did it remind him of home, or had he simply allowed it to fall into a state of disrepair? As the moon crested over a cloud above them, Sadie cursed and kicked a pair of boots away from the front mat before rapping her knuckles against the wire door.

There was a thump somewhere inside, before a dishevelled young man nudged open the door with a mischievous grin. Prue remembered seeing Warren's daughter Andie performing and thought she must have been the most beautiful woman alive. Syl was as handsome as his sister was stunning, bright green eyes in contrast with his brown skin and dark hair. Where Andie was all glitter and grace, he was roguish charm. He doffed his hat to them, a plume of smoke billowing out through his nostrils as he let them both inside.

The inside of the caravan was in about the same state as the outside. Disorganised, overrun by old newspapers, empty glass bottles and used cigarettes. Prue was too polite to wrinkle her nose, especially when it wasn't all that much better than her aunt Ethel's overcrowded apartment. The scent of stale beer and cigarette smoke invaded her nostrils as Syl sprawled on the couch and batted away an empty food tin.

"Been a while, Sadie. Are you keeping busy?"

"Not as busy as you, it seems." Sadie pointedly looked around the caravan with a prim sniff. The abrupt honesty made Prue certain that Sadie and Syl knew each other fairly well. She picked at the sleeve of the woollen jacket Sadie had lent her as it itched against her skin.

"So. You're a mage, but don't quite know what you are." Syl's gaze locked onto Prue as he asked, and at her hesitant nod, his smile warmed. "No need to be nervous, love. It's not a painful process, and it's very quick."

Syl's lean form slid forward, and he reached out to pick up a book from underneath the scattered newspapers. There was no title along the cracked spine, but the aged black velvet and faded golden accents sent an unpleasant shiver down Prue's arms. Was this one of the books of verbal magic, the form most commonly used amongst those who didn't have the means to access other power? Syl pored over the volume, fingers tracing over barely legible text before coming to rest on a page near the end of the book.

"Here we are. I can't say that I use this ritual often, but it hones my magic in. Makes it focus on yours. Not a lot of people can do the Sense ritual successfully." A note of pride coloured his tone. Though Syl lacked the stillness of his father, instead emanating a youthful exuberance, they possessed the same genuine warmth. Taking a deep breath, Prue steeled herself.

The truth, at last. Answers, for once. The first step forward in the path of finding who she was meant to become.

"Let's do it."

"Perfect." Syl patted the spot beside him. Prue sank onto the couch, less concerned about the ash stains than the way her heart thundered in her chest. Staring into Syl's earnest green eyes, the hunger in Prue stirred, as if her magic was reaching out to his when she placed her palms down in his outstretched hands. Syl closed his eyes and took a deep breath, and when he opened them once again, they were full of steely determination, the friendly look on his face closing off.

"We ask for insight." When Syl read the words off the page, a deep authority leant to his cadence. His speech was imbued with magic,

Prue realised with a certainty that tingled up her spine. "We ask for revelation. In this person, we seek understanding of the magic that inhabits them. In reverence, we ask for answers. In doubt, we ask for certainty."

Prue could make little sense of Syl's words, or to whom exactly they were addressed. The hunger within her swelled, a ravenous appetite that roiled and squirmed at Syl's words, setting her teeth on edge. Whatever magic was inside her felt like it was fighting her and feeding her at the same time. It reached out for Syl with a harsh tug, her fingers tightening on his.

Syl snatched his hands from Prue's, staggering to his feet with the same horror in his eyes that Prue recalled in Warren's. The magical tome fell to the floor with a dull thump. Prue stared down at her hands with frustration, the craving subsiding. It left an emptiness behind, a guilt that swirled in the pit of her stomach.

"A Scourge." Syl's voice was hoarse, accusatory eyes turning sharp on Sadie. "You brought me a fucking *Scourge*."

"No." Sadie pressed her hands over her mouth, shock contorting her expression.

Scourge. The word settled over Prue with a bone-deep terror. A Scourge was a mage with the ability to remove someone's magical essence. With the ability to, brutally and permanently, rip a person's magic from them.

The hunger that lurked within her, yawning open and demanding to be fed…it was the desire to *take* magic, not use it.

No wonder Sadie and Syl looked at her like she was a beast waiting to strike. There was no erasing the fear in their eyes, and it made Prue certain of her path forward: she could do nothing but destroy. Lurching to her feet, she fled the caravan, the wire door banging open in her haste. The night air burned her lungs, and she heard Sadie call her name as she ran, away from the bright lights of the Carnival, into the darkness where she belonged.

PART TWO
QUEEN OF CUPS

Chapter Fifteen

Ursula Delavane

The incident of the Valentine's Day performance did not go unnoticed, least of all by Ursula. Though she lacked the specifics of what had happened after Larkin escorted the Alderidges backstage, everyone had heard the drunken accusation Noel had thrown at Andie: murderer. Larkin would not speak of the matter when pressed, though his unkempt hair and use of cocaine when he'd returned home were answer enough.

Ursula was right. Something dangerous lingered beneath Andie's pretty smile, and Larkin knew what it was.

Larkin's suggestion of hosting a dinner and inviting Andie came immediately after the event, a bizarre one on his part since he seemed to prefer not having his mother and his lover in the same room. Ursula insisted upon including Desmond Bellisario as another guest, if only because the man was observant and altogether far too charming. If anyone would see the truth of what Andie was hiding, Ursula was certain it would be him.

She fastened her sapphire earrings, smoothing her hands down her deep navy dress. Her blonde hair was neatly slicked back, silver heels lending an elegance to her appearance. She would be stone, unmoved and inscrutable. She would not allow some *girl* to ruffle her, no matter how vexing her presence may become.

"Mother." Larkin's voice rang out as he appeared with Andie on his arm, and Ursula's critical gaze swept over the young woman. In contrast to Ursula's rich dress, expensive heels, and perfectly curated makeup, Andie wore minimal makeup, a plain green dress and modest pumps. Ursula smiled brightly, pushing aside how vexing Andie's natural beauty was, and leaned in to kiss each of Andie's cheeks, inhaling the abundant scent of wild flowers.

"Alexandra. It's such a pleasure to spend this time with you. Larkin talks about you constantly."

"The pleasure is all mine." Andie clasped Ursula's hand in her own. "Please, call me Andie."

Larkin's sharp gaze passed over the pair of them, and Ursula held her warm smile with all her might. She would offer her son no reason for pause, no cause for criticism. Linking her arm through Andie's, she led the young woman into the dining room, where Desmond reclined in his seat with a glass of chardonnay. At their entrance, his face brightened and he eased himself up, crossing over to kiss each of their cheeks.

"Ladies. You are both looking positively radiant. Thank you, Ursula, for organising such a wonderful dinner."

Ursula racked her mind thinking of Andie's family. Her father, Warren, had worked at the Carnival in his youth. Andie had an older brother, Sylvester, who was a current Carnival employee, though Larkin uttered his name with disdain, leading Ursula to believe that the siblings were not close. They took their seats as Jane served more chardonnay, promising to return with the meal in a few minutes.

"How is your father, Andie?" Ursula raised her crystal glass to her lips, scarlet smearing the rim as she took a sip. "He lives in Hell's Kitchen now, doesn't he?"

The thought of the dilapidated streets made contempt swirl through Ursula, but she schooled her features in a curious expression so as not to show it. Desmond had come from humble origins as well, though unlike Andie, he had never made an attempt to hide it. Was she ashamed, Ursula wondered, or was there more about her past she hadn't told Larkin?

"He is well." Andie's fingers tapped against the stem of the glass. "He keeps to himself, for the most part, dealing in his tarot cards." The reply was soft and dismissive, Andie's blue eyes glazing over as she stared down at the table. Ursula had tweaked at a bond that strained and frayed, and the smile on her lips spread wider.

"I am glad to hear he's well."

Jane bustled out with plates of food, setting them in front of each guest. Larkin helped himself to his herbed potatoes dishes before Jane was even finished serving their plates. Desmond waited patiently for everyone to receive their food before he started eating. Andie's gaze raked over the dishes, raw hunger adorning her expression for just a moment before it dissipated.

Ursula recognised that hunger. She had seen it in Desmond, though now it was more polished and contained. It wasn't a hunger for the delicious aroma of the food that covered the table. No, this gnawing went deeper still, the gnawing that only someone who had seen days without a meal could understand.

"I've seen some of your shows, Andie. You are a spectacular performer."

An unguarded smile crossed the girl's lips. That, at least, was genuine.

"Thank you. It's my greatest dream to become one of the best, and Larkin has been a treasure in aiding me to achieve it."

Dreams. What a ridiculous notion. Women were not made for the cold, hard ambitions of men. Their place was behind the curtain, pulling the strings like a puppeteer, not in the bright lights of the stage that Andie enjoyed so much.

At Andie's age, Ursula had been married with a baby. A thought took root in the depths of her mind, an insidious weed that refused to be pulled.

"Larkin certainly talks about you a lot." She cut into her spiced chicken, keeping her eyes firmly on her plate. "He is quite taken with you."

"Mother." Larkin muttered in exasperation.

"I did wonder when he would begin to settle down." Ursula raised her gaze from her meal, fixing it firmly upon Andie. "He's had affairs with several showgirls, but you are the one he seems serious about."

There was a bitter truth to the words, even if there was an ulterior motive behind them. If Larkin knew what was good for him, for Andie, he would see Ursula's meaning clearly. Andie could be an asset to them, but only if utilised properly. Her fire needed to be stamped out, contained within a ring on her finger. Besides, Ursula was ready to be a grandmother.

Andie's bright blue eyes studied Ursula, attempting to discern what lay behind the words. An indolent smile spread across her lips and she leaned back in her chair, crossing one leg over the other. Ursula didn't miss how Larkin's gaze caught the movement, desire flashing across his face.

"I'm so grateful," Andie simpered as she set her wine glass down. "I value Larkin more than words can say."

She *should* say it. She should be down on her knees in gratitude for all that Larkin had done for her. Yet, interfering in Larkin's business had earned his ire more often than not, so Ursula said nothing. Instead, she turned her attention on her son, whose narrowed eyes bored into her.

Desmond and Andie were well practised in courteous smiles and disguising the meaning of their words. They needed to be, for their own survival. They did not have the same resources as many of the old blood families, and as such, they dug their claws in and refused to let go, all while hiding their knives behind pleasant facades. Larkin had no such necessity, a spoiled child who had only known privilege, and so his emotions were worn on his sleeve.

Foolish boy.

"Can we speak in private, Mother?" The irritation to Larkin's words made Desmond arch an eyebrow, but Ursula simply set her knife and fork down.

"Of course."

Put on edge by her son's inexplicable annoyance, Ursula refilled her wine glass, heels clicking across the tiles as she followed Larkin into the kitchen. Upon seeing him marching in and loosening his tie, Jane scuttled away without a word to some unseen corner, the dishes once more left to soak in soapy water. Larkin spun on his heel to face Ursula, arms folded over his chest.

"You're like a wasp, you know that? You always feel compelled to sting."

Ursula sighed deeply, annoyance beating at her temples. "Larkin, I don't know what…"

"Yes, you do," Larkin snarled, arms dropping to his side and hands balling into fists. "I see you prodding away at Andie, wanting a reaction. What is your aim here, Mother? I invited her to dinner so that you might learn to get along, not so you could be aggravating."

"I think you should marry her."

The words settled between them for a moment, marinating like one of Jane's delicious steak sauces. In the dining room, Ursula could hear Desmond regaling Andie with some sordid story involving *Camelot*. Larkin blinked in astonishment, while Ursula remained silent, letting the seed plant itself. He claimed that Andie was different, that she was special. If that was what he really believed, what was to stop him from marrying her?

"I didn't even think you liked her." Larkin's confusion was palpable, the taste of it ripe on Ursula's tongue.

"It isn't about my feelings. You are my only child, and you deserve to be happy."

She cast her gaze down upon the checkered black and white kitchen tiles, before raising her glass to her lips to take another sip, letting the golden liquid trickle down her throat. Her words were a concoction of lies and truth. She did want what was best for Larkin, and she could see how enamoured he was with Andie. Yet she also wanted the young woman to realise that her place was not beside Larkin, but beneath him.

"So I have your blessing, if that's what I decide?" Larkin carded his fingers through his blonde hair, frustration stiffening his movements. How could she blame him? She had spent more breath on her suspicions regarding Andie than she had on the merits of marriage, after all.

Everything Ursula had done, all she had been since Larkin had been born, was for him. He may not understand or even appreciate it, but Ursula did not have to be liked by her son. She simply needed to do what was best for him. Andie on her own was a loose cannon. Andie as a wife could be more…malleable.

"Of course you do." Ursula reached out to caress his cheek. There was so much potential in him to be something better, something more. "If you put your mind to it, you could become even more powerful and influential than your father. You just need to make smart choices, especially when it comes to women."

Striding past him and back into the dining room, Ursula paused when she noticed Desmond and Andie laughing together, the girl's fingers resting on his bicep. It was oddly familiar, and Ursula could not help but wonder if Andie was typically so liberal with physical touch. When the pair noticed Ursula, the laughter ceased like a faucet being turned off. Andie held Ursula's gaze, a smugness tugging her full lips upwards, head tilted to the side as if in anticipation of a question or comment.

Ursula resumed her seat without breathing a word. Andie wanted a reaction, and Ursula would simply not provide one. Instead she offered the girl a warm smile and raised her glass to her lips. Whatever challenge Andie thought she presented, Ursula had seen it all before. Though certainly a force, Andie could be controlled if Larkin put his foot down once in a while instead of indulging her every whim.

Even hurricanes blew out after a time, despite the destruction they left in their wake, and Andie Fairley was no hurricane, merely a strong wind rattling at the windows, begging to be let in.

* * *

Ursula waited until Larkin shuffled upstairs to bed, drunk on champagne and his lover's intoxicating company, before she spoke to Desmond. He stood by the hearth twirling his empty crystal glass, the flames setting off warm hues in his dark hair. When he heard Ursula's heels clicking across the floor, he drew himself from his reverie and offered her a tired smile. She held up the bottle of champagne.

"A refill?"

"No, thank you." A soft smile crossed Desmond's lips and he shook his head slowly, eyes raking over the bottle. "It's funny. A decade ago, I would probably have needed to sever a limb for a taste of Dom Perignon champagne, and now I drink it by the glass. Strange how the world works, isn't it?"

Ursula had no response, for she had been drinking the brand since she had been a teenager, though she and Desmond came from vastly different backgrounds.

"So, what do you think of her?"

"Andie?" Desmond arched an eyebrow, and a gleam entered his brown eyes that gave Ursula pause. Perhaps her son was not the only man enamoured with the girl. Perhaps she had been a fool to summon Desmond, whose lowly background was so similar to Andie's. "I can see why Larkin is so besotted with her. There's a magnetism about her. She isn't what I would say is easy to get on with, but there's a charm to her."

"Don't tell me you're spellbound by her act, too." Ursula shook her head in disappointment, filling her glass with champagne and watching as it fizzed its way to the rim before settling.

"I think there's an honesty to it." Desmond sank onto the couch, draping an arm over the back of it. "An absent mother, a dead sister… underneath it all, there's a vulnerability to her."

"Dead sister?" Ursula's brow furrowed. Whispers circulated that Warren's wife had left him with their two young children, but there had only been *two* of them. Syl and Andie. Whatever sister Desmond referred to, this was a revelation, and bitterness burned in Ursula's gut at being excluded from this knowledge.

"Ah." Desmond smiled tightly at her reaction, setting down his empty glass. "Larkin didn't tell you, then."

Larkin most certainly had not told her, which was to Ursula's chagrin but not her surprise. When it came to Andie, Larkin was vexingly secretive.

"Perhaps you'd care to enlighten me."

"It's no secret that Noel has…a strong dislike for Andie." Desmond drummed his fingers on the arm of the couch, his brown eyes distant as he stared into the fire. "As it turns out, Noel's late wife was Andie's mother, Sarah. You've no doubt heard the tragic tale of their daughter, Claire. A lie, concocted to conceal an even harsher truth. Andie killed Claire, five years ago. It was framed as suicide, as Garrett was up for election and it would have been a scandal."

Ursula's breath was sucked out of her until there was nothing left but a hollow chasm in her lungs, a tightness that made her head spin. Andie had killed her own sister? She had guessed the young woman to be dangerous, but this was something more extreme than even Ursula's suspicions could have concocted.

"It appears that an accident left Claire in…a bad way. Andie felt a quick death was a mercy, but Noel disagrees. When he met with Andie and Syl after they had tossed Claire's body into Harlem River, there was a confrontation. Noel wanted to kill Andie with his bare hands, but she blackmailed him, threatening to destroy him and Garrett, saying that lying about what happened was the easiest solution and would protect the Alderidges from a disgrace greater than suicide."

"Larkin *knows* all of this?" Ursula asked incredulously. Her son could be blind when it came to Andie, but surely not so blind as to support such a violent crime, and such a cruel manipulation. It was no wonder that Noel loathed Andie, when she had added insult to injury following Claire's death.

Desmond's smile grew sharp and wicked. "I believe he's been told her version of events, which is…slightly different to Noel's."

If Andie could murder her sister and then twist the knife even further between Noel's ribs when he confronted her, what else was she capable of? What if she intended something as ominous for Larkin? Ursula shook off the unwelcome thought, prying it away like cobwebs. Andie was nothing without Larkin, and she was clever enough to know that. Without Larkin, she became expendable.

Ursula surveyed Desmond's expression. There was a cool calm that lingered still, unperturbed by Andie's crimes. Ursula wondered what, exactly, Desmond had done to end up in the prestigious position he held today. Did she even want to know the answer? She was familiar with deception and brutality, but wielding a murder as a playing card held a malice that was beyond even Franklin's deeds.

"You don't seem too shocked," Ursula noted, sipping the last of her champagne. "Do you admire her handiwork, perhaps?"

Desmond laughed, teeth gleaming sharply in the warm glow of the lamps. Danger danced in his dark eyes. He was a snake in a den of wolves, his fangs bared and prime for the bite. What venom would he sink into them? Or was he harmless now, his fangs long since sharpened on the corpses he'd slithered over to be sipping Dom Perignon in the Delavane residence?

"Oh, I have done worse than her, but I believe that's a story for another time. It's late."

"Of course." Ursula hoisted an empty smile across her lips. "Thank you for your company tonight, Desmond, and for what you've shared."

"A lady should never be unprepared." Desmond took her hand and pressed a soft kiss to the back of it. When he raised his head, he was grinning. "Information is either a sword or a sword or a ba shield, Ursula. You decide which."

Chapter Sixteen

Andie Fairley

Dinner by candlelight at Warren Fairley's residence was often a stark reminder of how many times Andie had stared down at this table, devoid of food as her stomach grumbled. The times where Syl had come back battered and bruised because he'd gotten into a scuffle to steal something. The times when Andie had gone out onto the streets to spin like a top until the cobblestones made her feet bleed, a bright smile and a flash of her leg earning enough coin for a loaf of bread or wheel of cheese.

Andie tugged her mind from the murky depths of the past. There was never anything but shame and regret colouring any of those memories, just as with her memories of Claire. Her spoon clinked against the side of her plate as she scraped through the soup that Warren had cooked over the stove.

"I hear you went to visit the Delavanes for dinner the other night," Syl stated, breaking the silence as he rocked back in his chair so the front legs rose from the floor. "Look at you, Andie. Aren't you something special now?"

There was a time when his teasing had made her flush or swat playfully at him, but that was before the teasing was edged with a hint of steel, a constant promise of the ability to cut beneath her skin.

"The Delavane family?" Warren's brow furrowed as he set down his mug of tea. "You can't trust the magical elite, I hope you know that."

"She trusts Larkin." Syl's smile grew wicked. "Or maybe it's power you want from him. Is that why you're fucking him?"

There it was, the barb digging into her, pressing for a reaction. Andie ignored Syl, scooping up more soup and shovelling it into her mouth.

"Not that it's any of your damn business, but I haven't slept with him. You have no idea what I want, Syl."

What she wanted, what she *really* wanted, had been dead and buried since they'd found him on New Year's Day. A girlish fantasy, a romantic illusion of a future that had been torn from her grasp. Now she would have power, and Larkin's obsession with her would give her precisely that. She had shown him her most vulnerable face, let him have a glimpse of a side no one else saw.

"I know you have more ambition than sense." Syl's chair thudded back down on all fours. "You think that Larkin Delavane will give you freedom? He wants to own you."

"I'm not an object, Sylvester," Andie snapped, her temper rising despite her best attempts to quell it. "I'm not stupid either. I don't blindly trust Larkin, or any of them. He's a means to an end."

"Power, then." Syl's voice was flat and unimpressed, a scoff escaping his lips as he rolled his eyes. "The only thing you care about."

"That isn't fair, Syl," Warren said, easing his broad frame up and collecting the empty soup bowls. He stared down at his son with disappointment etched across his face, and Andie smirked as Syl squirmed uncomfortably in his seat. He might be a grown man now, but when faced with his father's disapproval, his guilt was palpable and he looked like a boy once more.

"Is this about Claire again?" Andie gripped the edge of the table, staring hard at her brother. Once, she would have given anything to avoid their sister as a topic of conversation, but she held the knife now, and she twisted it between Syl's ribs. It was *his* turn to feel its sting. "If so, I would much prefer you stop beating about the bush and come clean. After all, isn't that always what it boils down to? Claire, and the fact that you will never let me forget what happened?"

"Why the fuck should I?" Syl lurched up suddenly, making Andie flinch at the rage burning in his green eyes. "You made a choice. You called the shots that night. I don't owe you forgiveness. In fact, I hope it keeps you awake. I hope you never find peace with it."

The cruelty of the words ripped open the thousand half-healed wounds inside her, and she was bleeding all over again. It was a pain beyond tears, beyond fury. She sat rigid in her chair, while her mind was thrown into the torturous loop of that horrific night on repeat. She forgot how to breathe, the oxygen rattling against her lungs, beating against it like the bars of a cage as her body shook.

She couldn't breathe. She couldn't move. Every time she tried to suck in more air, she spasmed, panic contorting her limbs as her traitorous brain replayed Claire's final words, her pleas. Syl was right. She didn't deserve mercy let alone forgiveness. It was her own mistakes that had gotten them here.

"Sylvester, you apologise to her right now!" Warren's voice thundered through the small room, making the floor reverberate beneath them. Andie could count on one hand the amount of times her father had ever raised his voice. "You have no idea what it is to live with that kind of regret. The weight of it, knowing a single choice could have changed everything."

Warren did. Even in the haze of her own hyperventilation, Andie recalled the heaviness in her father's expression when she had told him everything. Warren had never said anything more, nor had she asked. Some secrets were meant to stay buried, for unearthing them would only bring more pain.

Andie focused on her breathing, on bringing herself back down into her own body instead of feeling like a prisoner within it. She wriggled her fingers and toes, her eyes flicking to Syl. She expected to see his righteous ire, but it had been replaced by something harder to swallow. Bitter sorrow, brimming in the form of tears.

"You sound so much like Noel when you talk like that." Her voice was hoarse as she managed the words with a wry half-smile. The words made Syl wince as though she'd struck him. Whatever his feelings toward her, he had always despised Noel Alderidge. "Both of you, so eager for me to live with it, when I would have preferred to die with it."

The hard, unflinching truth, unearthed beneath layers of confidence and shoved even further down than Andie's own self-loathing, something she had only just begun to recover from after years of hating what she had done. Patrick had anchored her to reality, to the fact that someone still wanted her there. She was not as fragile now as she had been then, and yet it was another punch to the gut, a reminder of how hard the loss of him hit.

"Andie, listen to me." Warren rested a hand on her shoulder, desperation to his grip. "What happened was a tragic mistake. You could have done things differently, but so could Claire, so could Syl. We can never know what the outcome might have been, only what happened. You were faced with a choice, and an ugly one at that, but you need to understand that there was no *wrong* choice."

The gentleness of her father's words, the compassion that warmed his blue eyes, made tears cloud Andie's vision. She had spent years becoming respected, admired, wanted, even envied. The one thing she had forgotten was that she was allowed to be loved as well, something she had closed herself off to after Patrick. How could she have forgotten that despite battling his own demons, her father always made her feel seen.

"Come here." Warren pulled Andie close, her tears seeping into the thin fabric of his shirt. She clung to him like he was the last thing keeping her afloat, sobs wracking her frame as she stopped pushing aside the grief and let it consume her. She had spent too long making herself all sharp edges that she forgot she was allowed softness.

"Andie…" Regret dulled Syl's fire, and he reached out a hand to her, but she wasn't quite soft enough to accept it. She brushed him away, tugging free from Warren's grasp.

"You meant those words, Syl. Don't take them back now."

He had spoken from a place of anger and agony, a place that Andie was all too familiar with. Unlike Syl, she had honed herself to be better, to let all but the harshest of insults glide off her skin. If she flared up every time she was offended, she didn't think she would ever have a moment where she wasn't simmering with rage. She let those feelings wash over her, though perhaps more of it took root within her than she was comfortable with.

In the darkest hour, she had chosen Syl. It had been a choice that rent her apart inside, a jagged wound that Syl insisted upon continually prodding.

He would never understand her choices. Not with Claire, not with Larkin. Syl was a man of ready fists and brutal words, unencumbered by the constraints that Andie experienced by virtue of her status—whether that was her status as Black to some, as mixed race to others, as a woman to all. Simply by being born a man, her brother had something she never would. Syl's indulgence in alcohol and drugs was an amusement to others, but if it were Andie who partook, she would be a disgrace. He did not have to walk the same tightrope, perform the same careful balancing act with ambition in one hand and caution in the other.

* * *

With the prestigious Midsummer Ball rapidly approaching, most of Andie's time was spent in Larkin's company, discussing the mechanics of the event and the magic she'd be performing on the night. Occasionally, Ursula would glide in and out of the apartment, exchanging a sparse few words with Andie before sauntering off to whatever social event took her fancy.

Curled on the lounge with a cool glass of fresh lemonade in her hands, Andie was touched by a cool certainty that this was what she wanted. The wealth, the power, the privilege. It may be considered uncouth by some to say as much, but she had always been bold about what she wanted. She twirled a loose curl around her finger as Larkin examined the seating plan he'd strewn across the coffee table.

"Tell me more about soul magic."

The words made Larkin's eyes flick to her, startled. Though they often spoke about magic, Andie had respected that Larkin did not go into detail about the rarest form…until now. She craved knowledge, and he was the only member of the magical elite who would give it to her.

"It's the most dangerous to acquire, by far." Larkin leaned back against the cushions, fingers slicking back his blonde hair. "There is a ritual to obtain it which not everyone survives. It's why not everyone is interested in trying to get it, in case they fail."

Andie shifted forward, eyes gleaming with excitement, resting a hand on his leg. "Explain the ritual."

Larkin's face slackened, and she wondered if he was reminiscing on his own experience, knowing that he possessed soul magic. She tapped her fingers lightly on his leg, quietly coaxing him into sharing the story.

"The ritual involves plunging into an ice-cold bath, slowing down the heart rate until you reach the brink of death. Only there can you find the spark of soul magic. Only then does it activate. Some people don't come back from the brink."

The idea of a brush with death both horrified and enthralled Andie. It was truly a heavy question: did she value magic more than her own life? Did she value power enough to risk dying for it? The answer screamed back with steely surety: *yes*.

"It splits your soul." Larkin's pale eyes bored into her, void of any hint of flirtation or mischief. "That is what the ritual does, Andie. When you reach the brink of death, your soul splits open permanently. That's how you gain access to soul magic."

"What does that mean?" Her brow furrowed. It sounded unpleasant, to say the least. But the word 'permanent' made her think there were repercussions no one had mentioned. Perhaps no one had told Larkin either when he took the plunge. "To split your soul, I mean."

"Think of it as a magical wound." Larkin slipped his fingers through Andie's, strands of hair sweeping across his forehead and falling into his eyes. "No two people have the exact same side effects, but there *are* side effects. It's a wound that doesn't heal. You might have gained great power from it, but that doesn't stop it from bleeding. King Arthur Pendragon had soul magic, and it's claimed in the histories that was what drove him mad in the end."

Andie was admittedly behind on her studies of the Arthurian legends from which magic was born, though the hairs raised on the back of her neck. She'd heard that, at least. Mad King Arthur, Guinevere the Scourge who had stolen magic from several of the others and fled with it. Wounds that never quite healed…well, those she was most certainly familiar with.

"Are you hoping to scare me off getting soul magic?" Andie's playful tone disguised the burning desire within her. She swung a leg over Larkin and straddled his lap, tracing a finger down his prominent cheekbone. "I'm not afraid, Larkin. This is what I want."

"I thought you might." A wry smile turned up the corners of his lips. "I wanted you to know what it meant, to gain that sort of power. What it costs."

There was a cost to all magic. She'd learned that the hard way. The idea that it was her life and soul in the balance was of little consequence to her considering everything else she had sacrificed.

"It's a price I'm willing to pay."

Gripping his chin between her thumb and forefinger, she pressed her lips to his in a hungry kiss. Larkin reciprocated with fervent passion, fingers sliding up to tangle in her curls. A wicked smile spread across Andie's lips as she pressed closer. Larkin's free hand rested on her hip, his skin warm through the thin fabric of her dress. His power and his influence enthralled her, the idea that she could be his equal as arousing as his hot touch.

Andie rolled her hips forward again, the motion sending heat through her core as she felt his erection rub against her. A hiss escaped from Larkin's mouth, his pale eyes shining with lust as he tugged at her hair to tilt her head back, examining her smirk.

"You're a wicked woman."

The huskiness in his voice only made Andie bolder, unbuttoning the front of his shirt to trace her fingers down the smooth planes and subtle muscles of his chest. When Larkin's lips descended to her neck, her eyes fluttered closed and she succumbed to the warmth pooling in the pit of her stomach. Maybe this was about more than power. Maybe there was desire in this on her part, too. Maybe she wanted him almost as much as he wanted her.

Larkin gripped both of her hips, rocking up against her and making her gasp as his hardness elicited a surge of pleasure. Her heart was thrumming a fast-paced beat in her chest, her breathing coming in quickened bursts. Her body yearned to surrender to the delight his roaming hands promised, but her mind rebelled against it. She hadn't gotten what she *really* wanted. Not yet.

"Larkin." Andie caught his hands in her own, linking her fingers through his. His head tilted up and he examined her with confusion. "I want you. I do. Just…not now."

With his blonde hair a mess, his shirt half-unbuttoned and his lips red from their fervent kisses, she was almost tempted to kiss him again. Pushing down the impulse, Andie smoothed out her dress and slid off his lap. Larkin let his head fall back against the couch, Adam's apple bobbing in his throat.

"I'll ask them for you. The other Lords. About the soul magic ritual."

Frustration coursed through Andie's veins. Why did she need permission? If she was willing to undergo the process, wasn't that enough? She loathed the outdated views on magic, that women could only use gifted or verbal magic. Why would they even agree to hand a woman over such magic, unless…

Andie sat bolt upright, shoulders rigid.

"Larkin. Who was the last woman granted permission to undergo the soul magic ritual?"

His brow furrowed in thought. "Sterling's late wife, from memory. My mother was offered the opportunity, but refused it."

"What did she do with that magic?" Andie imagined that the rules would have been even more strict if it had been decades.

"Well, she obviously didn't use it herself." Larkin drummed his fingers on the back of the couch. "I believe she would often gift it to Sterling. As much as the man prattles on about being part of an old-blood family, his magic is…lacking. Hers was not."

A dead woman, her life's sole purpose being to gift magic to her weaker husband. Andie started to connect dots that she didn't know if she was meant to see. Powerful women as magical conduits, never allowed to harness the power that they were granted. If she was allowed to gain soul magic, it would be on the basis that there was a man whose own magic she could strengthen. Larkin's magic was strong, though not as strong as Cyril's, and perhaps others.

Andie bit down on her tongue, bit back all the words she wanted to unleash and all the questions she wanted to ask. If she spoke up, she could ruin any chance she had at gaining soul magic. If the Lords thought to offer it to her, believing she would gift her magic to Larkin, then she would allow them to steep themselves in that false notion.

Andie's magic was her own. Her power was her own. She would be damned if she would let anyone control her.

Chapter Seventeen

Prue Clermont

MARK AND PRUE HAD BARELY SPOKEN since she had turned up on the doorstep, tearstained and bedraggled. She had not wanted to talk then, the revelations about what she was weighing too heavy upon her shoulders. Yet in the days that passed since, Mark's concern remained etched across his face and written in his eyes. She might not love her husband, but there was comfort and familiarity associated with him. In the strange world of magic, where she was their worst nightmare, no such peace existed.

She possessed the power to rip out magical essences. A Scourge hadn't existed in centuries, Sadie had said. Was that the tug she felt in the pit of her stomach, the impulse to tear out the very thing that gave mages their power? Prue considered herself a fairly gentle and soft-spoken person, so the thought of being capable of such violence was appalling to her. What good was her power when she could only ever use it for harm?

Did the magical elite know what she was? Was that why the man had come looking for her? She brushed the idea off, uneasy that they could know what she was even before she had. Yet they did not know her as Sadie did. If Sadie was horrified by the revelation of Prue's abilities, what would the rest of them think?

Prue's hands trembled over dinner preparations, and her conversations with Mark were civil, discussions of the weather and how work had been. She would set the table and do the laundry and run through the mundane day-to-day of how her life had been before she'd met Sadie and discovered the Carnival. She could not find respite in it, for knowledge was a burden, and she bore it alone.

"I wish you'd talk to me, Prue." Mark heaved a sigh over their evening meal, setting down his knife and fork, examining his silent wife. "I know that things have been…difficult between us. You left. I called the police and everything, but they had nothing. Now you come back with barely a word spoken of what happened."

How could she explain to Mark, a man who found peace in the mundane and the factory he worked in, what she had discovered? How would he understand the gravity of the situation and the horror and disgust she'd felt ever since the truth had come to light? She supposed that she owed it to him to try, since he'd approached her return with dignity and patience.

She sighed. "I found out that I'm what the magical community calls a Scourge." Prue's legs jiggled beneath the table. "I have…I have the ability to rip out essences. I can, apparently, negate people's magic, permanently."

They sat with the revelation a moment, Prue stewing in the heaviness of it while Mark's expression was one of first surprise, and then realisation. They may be worlds apart, so different from the young man and woman who'd gotten married a decade before, but he wanted to comprehend her, a miracle in itself when he was so against magic and the Carnival.

"Oh." Mark nodded slowly, words failing him. "That is…well, that certainly isn't good."

"I think that…" Misery scratched at Prue's throat, tears blurring her vision. "I think I'm a danger to everyone around me, and that includes you." The words stuck in her throat like cobwebs. "I think that we're too different for things to work between us anymore."

Hurt and irritation chased each other through his eyes, his hands clenching against the meaning of her words. "Why did you come back, then?"

"Because I wanted to try." Prue's voice rose in volume, and she reached up to wipe her eyes. "After I found out I was a Scourge, I thought that I could push it aside, come back here and live a normal life. It just isn't the same. We can't go back, Mark."

Mark stared down at his plate, and Prue's stomach twisted at being the cause of his pain. Whether by her Scourge power or not, all she ever did was harm other people. She was tired of it, so tired. When Mark looked up again, his eyes were bloodshot, lips pressed together in a firm line.

"I see the way that you look at Sadie."

Alarm coursed through Prue, a searing cold washing over her. Silence descended over them like an ominous cloud, any denial dying on Prue's lips. It would be a lie to feign ignorance, but the truth would be sharper and cut deeper than any knife in their modest apartment.

"It's the way I once hoped you'd look at me." A bitter smile crossed Mark's lips as he tilted his head to the side. "You never did, though. Whatever you feel for her, it's more than what you feel for me."

"Mark…" She cracked over the word, like waves crashing over jagged rocks. "I wanted to love you, so desperately. I really did."

Mark buried his face in his hands, and Prue choked back a sob. The stability they had was crumbling down around them. They'd both clung on to their marriage like it was an anchor, but it had just dragged them under instead of keeping them afloat. A chill ghosted over Prue's arms, and she sniffed back more tears. The guilt ate away at her, but she hadn't been the only one who had pulled back. Their marriage had been over the moment Mark returned from war, it just took them some time to catch on.

"What happens now?" Mark raised his face from his hands, eyes red-rimmed.

"I move out, I suppose." Prue murmured.

Where would she go? Back to stay with Ethel, potentially further endangering her aunt? She was a ticking bomb, waiting to go off. There was nowhere she was safe, and no one was safe with her. It was her problem to solve, not Mark's. He had his own inner demons to fight, ones he'd struggled with ever since coming home. Prue would not lay her burdens upon a man who already had too many.

* * *

Prue had almost finished packing her bags when she was interrupted by a sharp rap on the door. Her stomach contorted into knots, hands curling into ready fists. If it was someone hellbent on taking her down, did she stand much chance? Could she call upon her Scourge ability at will? With Mark out at work, she may need to.

"Prue, it's Sadie." The familiar voice, though more tired than usual, had relief flooding through Prue's body and the tension holding her limbs released. "I just want to talk. May I come in?"

Prue walked over and slowly unlatched the door. She hadn't seen or heard from Sadie since the revelation of what she was, and whilst she had appreciated being given space to process it, she had found herself missing her. What would she see when she opened the door? Disgust? Horror? She struggled to erase the shock that washed over Sadie's face when Syl had come to the conclusion she was a Scourge. Prue's clammy fingers tightened on the doorknob before she reluctantly pulled it open.

Although dressed as immaculately as ever, Sadie's appearance was dishevelled, eyes tired and red-rimmed. Prue wanted nothing more than to pull her into a close embrace, yet she remained where she was, leaning in the doorway with little idea how to approach the situation and how the dynamic had shifted between them.

"You're packing." Sadie's eyes slid over the bags on the lounge room floor as she entered the apartment, a furrow in her brow when she glanced back at Prue. "You're leaving Mark?"

"It's for the best." Prue did not wish to speak of it. The decision hurt both her and Mark, felt devastating in ways she had not realized were possible, yet what future did they have together? Prue couldn't give what he wanted, what he deserved. "I'm not sure where to go. Perhaps back to stay with Ethel. If not, then I'd leave the city to go back to my parents."

"Don't be ridiculous," Sadie stated with little room for argument as she shook her head slowly, perfectly coiffed auburn hair swinging from side to side. "You must come stay with me."

"Sadie…" Prue sucked in a sharp breath. "I saw how you looked at me when you found out what I was."

"It was a surprise, yes." Sadie clasped her hands together, and when Prue searched her expression, she saw none of the things she'd been afraid of. Instead there was compassion and warmth, a glimmer in her eyes. "You're special. You're rare. I'm not afraid of you, Prue."

"I could suck the magic from you in a heartbeat!" Prue exclaimed, her frustration boiling over as she threw her arms up. "I don't even understand my power, I don't know if I can control it. You're a mage, and the idea that I could rip your magic from you…how could I live with something like that?"

"Yet you haven't," Sadie pointed out, walking over to rest a comforting hand on Prue's shoulder. "You've been a Scourge since long before you knew what it meant, and you haven't torn the magic from me, or anyone else. You have a degree of control, even if subconsciously."

"How can you not be afraid?" Prue demanded, lost in the depths of Sadie's eyes. "I am."

Sadie's smile was so bright it could light up even the darkest room, light up the frightened depths of Prue's heart. The scent of citrus and honey was a soothing balm, making Prue's breath catch in her throat. "Because, Prudence Clermont, you are a *marvel*."

Sadie's lips brushed against Prue's, a momentary hesitation holding her back, before her cool fingers gripped Prue's shoulder tighter and she kissed her with desperation. Prue caught Sadie's face in her hands and kissed back with fervour. There had always been a tension between them, a bridge not crossed. Kissing Sadie set Prue's soul on fire in the most glorious way, a heat brewing in the pit of her stomach as her fingers caressed Sadie's silky hair.

It had never been like that with Mark. Things hadn't felt *bad*, but this was on a level Prue hadn't experienced. Sadie's lips were soft and tasted like cherries. Her fingers were smooth against Prue's skin. The familiar hunger uncoiled within her, an appetite she now recognised as her Scourge ability tugging at her, begging to be fed. She shoved it back down and boxed it up, caught up in the feeling of Sadie.

When Sadie drew back, her cheeks were flushed and her eyes sparkled in a way they hadn't when she'd first arrived. A small smile lingered about her lips as she raked her fingers through her hair.

"I was actually wondering…there's a Midsummer Ball coming up, hosted by the Seasonal Lords. I was hoping you might come with me."

As Prue's heartbeat slowed to a more appropriate tempo, she couldn't help but question how Sadie merited an invitation. Of course, she doubted that the Lords were aware that Sadie was part of a magical rebellion, though it still begged the question: who *was* Sadie to the magical elite? Not wishing to burst the merry bubble that had formed around them in the wake of their first kiss, Prue maintained a firm hold on her curiosity.

"You want me to come to a ball?" It was decidedly far more glamorous than anything Prue had done. Just thinking of it made her feel like a little girl playing dress-up in her mother's clothing. There was also the matter of her fresh, terrifying abilities. Would she be able to stomach being around that many mages? When her arcane hunger had risen in the past, she had been able to subdue it. Would she continue to do so, or was there a chance it could take hold of her? "We'd be surrounded by mages. Are you sure none of them would know what I am?"

Sadie shook her head vigorously. "Syl is the only other person that knows. Even with him, it took a ritual for him to unearth the truth. We'd know if they suspected something unusual about you."

Though Sadie's words placated Prue, she could not help the disquiet swirling within her. She could not hide her true nature forever. Once the truth came to light, what then? Would Sadie continue to protect her? Would mages seek to use her for their own gain, or would they simply want her dead?

"Prue." Sadie's voice was calming against her frayed nerves. Her pale eyes raked over Prue, fingers reaching out to caress her cheek. "It's going to be alright. You have me."

Prue hoped that she would have Sadie forever, but she contented herself with a streak of daring in the moment, leaning forward to press her lips to Sadie's again. She didn't want to get the taste of cherries off her tongue, and her desire became desperation, fingers curling in Sadie's hair. Sadie gasped against her lips, her arm sliding around Prue's waist as she steered them over to tumble onto the couch.

The lust she had never felt for Mark burned deep within Prue when she touched Sadie, hands traversing the curve of her waist. Sadie shifted on top of her, a wicked grin on her face as the silky strands of her hair tickled Prue's cheek. Any thoughts of propriety were thrown aside as Sadie's deft fingers slipped up Prue's skirt, hands ghosting over her thighs.

All Prue could think about was her heart hammering in her chest, Sadie's lips on her neck, the way she finally understood the sparks that people always talked about when it came to intimacy.

"Just let go," Sadie whispered against her shoulder, her voice trembling and husky, "Let's have this moment, just the two of us."

So Prue let Sadie bring her to dizzying heights she'd never reached before, not on her own nor with Mark, and she rode the high before she had to come crashing back down to reality.

Chapter Eighteen

Ursula Delavane

Ursula sat on the periphery of the Lords' meeting, a distant planet in orbit of a sun whose warmth she could barely feel. Today, she was not the only woman present; Cyril's third wife, Dorothy, perched on the edge of her husband's couch, toying with the ends of her long blonde hair. Perhaps the Lords surmised that if Larkin's mother could be present, so too could other women associated with the inner circle.

It made her bristle with indignation. Dot had been married to Cyril barely two years, still shy of thirty with no opinions of her own and a giggle that inflamed Ursula's every nerve. What would happen next? Would Larkin demand that Andie come along? Considering the insufferable girl was the topic of conversation once again, it would hardly astonish her. At least Sterling and Desmond, widowed and unmarried, respectively, posed little problem in that regard.

"It's been almost forty years since a woman was allowed access to soul magic," Sterling grumbled, taking a puff of his cigar and blowing out a plume of smoke. "Now you intend to grant that privilege to a scrap of a girl? She has a questionable past, no wealth to speak of, and is nothing but a mere showgirl."

"Andie will be my wife one day." Larkin crossed one leg over another, and the certainty in his tone made Ursula wonder if he'd already discussed the matter with Andie. "As I recall, your wife, Penelope, was given access to soul magic and powered you like a globe to a light, is that not correct?"

Ursula stiffened at Larkin's blatant disrespect. Sterling was a doddering fool to be sure, but she at least had the grace to respect the authority that came with generations of power and influence. The man's cheeks reddened and he gritted his teeth; Penelope was a sore subject for Sterling, her passing a decade ago still grating against old wounds when mentioned.

"You will learn some respect, *boy*. You've thrown insults and given no actual reason why this whore of yours deserves the privilege of soul magic."

Larkin's jaw ticked at the derogatory reference to Andie, but he displayed an unusual wisdom in holding his tongue.

Ursula remembered Penelope, a warm and affectionate woman who had been one of the few to get genuine merriment from Sterling. She'd undergone the soul magic ritual early in her marriage, and it had cost her ever since. Over the years, she had deteriorated, eaten away by the magic she was tirelessly producing and handing over for her husband's use. Ursula wondered if she had resented Sterling in her final moments, if Penelope had ever wanted some of her power for herself.

"I think this is a decision best made in private." Desmond's dark eyes flicked between Ursula and Dot. "Perhaps the ladies can fix some drinks and snacks while we hear the merits of Larkin's proposal."

Seething at being dismissed so easily, Ursula hoisted a sweet smile across her lips like one might fly a peace flag.

"Of course, Desmond. Dot, won't you come and help me?"

Dot eased herself off the arm of the chair, pressing a kiss to Cyril's cheek before flouncing out after Ursula. She had once been an aspiring actress until she caught Cyril's eye. She was sweet and pretty, a vexing creature at times, yet she lacked the razor-sharp cleverness that Ursula found most troubling in Andie.

Ursula navigated Cyril's kitchen with ease, setting up crystal glasses and fetching the champagne as Dot leaned against the bench and lit up a cigarette. She examined Ursula with her head tilted to the side.

"Doesn't it ever bother you, Mrs Delavane? Being left out of it all?"

Annoyance slithered across Ursula's skin as she looked up at Dot, taking in her warm brown eyes and cheerful round face. Another idealistic youth, no doubt. What was it with the younger generation of the present and having the audacity to think they should amount to something more? The world did not owe them a thing, especially not upstart airheads like Dot.

"Why should it? This is what happens with all of the women, Dorothy."

"Cyril's been telling me all about the Magical Freedoms Brigade." Dot tapped out her cigarette into the soil of a kitchen plant by the window, eyes wide and eager. "That young man who died on Carnival grounds, he was part of it, wasn't he? Is that why no one really cares who killed him?"

Ursula's fingers tightened around the bottle of champagne. It was one thing to know the Lords' business, but another entirely to be prattling away about it. The shine would rub off Dot eventually, as it had with Cyril's previous wives. Once the rust started to show, he wouldn't find her nearly as appealing. Especially if she ran her mouth the way she was now.

"Yes, Patrick Rhodes was part of this…resistance." The word tasted like the ash of Dot's cigarette on Ursula's tongue. "He was also associated with bootleggers and, from what I understand, in a fair amount of debt. Are you implying that the Lords had something to do with his murder? That they would involve themselves, or actually take seriously, some nobody from Hell's Kitchen?"

"I…" Dot stumbled over her words, the quiet menace in Ursula's voice not completely lost on her. She paused, twirling her cigarette between her fingers. "Of course not, Mrs Delavane. I only thought, because no one ever said, and usually something like a murder is quite serious, no matter who it is."

"You should do less thinking, my dear."

The fact that Patrick's murder remained unsolved did not perturb Ursula in the least. He was not the first person to die on Carnival grounds, and most likely would not be the last. Most of these murders were petty squabbles and while occasionally the Lords would sully their hands, it could certainly not have been Larkin.

Ursula held comfort in the fact that it would never be Larkin, for despite the machinations of the Lords, they were bound by blood to refrain from killing one another. The consequences for going against this oath, as she'd heard from the histories, were extremely severe.

As frustrating as it was to be on the outside of such an important meeting, it was Ursula's place, and she needed Dot to understand that it was hers, too. Wives and mothers were not an integral part of the way things were run. In time, Andie may have the unpleasant surprise of discovering that for herself, if Larkin was as serious as he claimed.

Besides, with the Midsummer Ball approaching, Ursula had bigger concerns than whether one girl was allowed magic. The event had to be precise, it had to be perfect. It was one of the biggest networking events of the year, with the Alderidges and many of their prominent associates in attendance.

The door to the lounge creaked open, and Ursula paused from where she was laying out various cheeses and biscuits on a platter. Larkin swaggered into the kitchen with a spring in his step and a dazzling smile across his lips, and she found her heart sinking, knowing without a word what the verdict had been. He crossed over to kiss Ursula's cheek, swiping a piece of cheese and tossing it into his mouth.

"Has the meeting finished?" Dot practically bounced on the balls of her feet. "Are we allowed back in?"

"Yes, you can go back in." Larkin grabbed one of the glasses of champagne, raising it in toast. His giddy excitement might have thrilled Ursula, who wanted nothing more than for her son to be happy, if she did not know it was giving Andie another foothold to tug herself up the rungs of power. "We can celebrate later. Andie's been given permission to undergo the soul magic ritual."

Dot beamed and clapped her hands, her bubbliness like nails down a chalkboard.

"Oh, how wonderful!"

"Are you off now, darling?" Ursula watched as Larkin tossed back his champagne, downing it like it was water, before setting the crystal glass down with a chime that resonated through the kitchen.

"I've got a lot to attend to before the Midsummer Ball, Mother."

Ursula picked up the tray of appetisers, gesturing for Dot to bring in the champagne. When she re-entered Cyril's lounge, the scent of musk washed over her, mingling with the scent of wood burning over the hearth. She strode over and carefully set the platter down on the glass table, Dot scurrying over and almost spilling the champagne in her haste.

"Larkin is thrilled. I'm glad that you all came to a conclusion."

"Yes, well." Sterling's lip curled. "I can't say I'm pleased that a showgirl is gaining access to one of our most sought-after resources."

"Oh, come now, Sterling." Cyril caught hold of Dot's waist, tugging her into his lap while she gave a little shriek of surprise. "We all know how brutal the ritual can be. In all likelihood, Miss Fairley may not even survive it."

A cold chill travelled down the back of Ursula's neck. She disliked Andie, and thought the young woman was more trouble than she was worth, but the idea of so casually discussing whether she might die did not sit well with her.

"I disagree," Desmond said, more quietly than the others. He had a presence that made everyone stop talking to listen. He lacked Sterling's bluster and Cyril's fanfare, but perhaps it was his simple and practical way of speaking that caught their attention. "I think she's stronger than you give her credit for."

Cyril laughed. "Your son is like a little dog, Ursula. Always yapping until he's given a treat. Sometimes, it's easier to simply placate him. In any case, he mentions that he plans to propose marriage to her, should the ritual be successful."

"Dogs need to be kept on a leash." Sterling's cool gaze swept over to Ursula. "You would do well to remember that. He has been spoiled and allowed to do as he pleases for far too long. He is aware of the conditions of Miss Fairley undergoing the ritual, but my patience with his impulsiveness has limits."

Ursula pushed down her distaste at the comparisons of her son to a hyperactive puppy. It was true that Larkin, much like his father, could act on impulse rather than thinking things through. However, he was more intelligent than men like Sterling gave him credit for. He may be besotted with Andie, but Larkin was the only one of the Lords who dreamed of bigger things than the Carnival and the stale assortment of esteemed company they liked keeping.

Dot leaned forward to whisper something in Cyril's ear. Whatever she said elicited a wicked smile, and he rose from the couch, taking her hand. The smirk on Dot's face made Ursula roll her eyes, leaving little to her imagination.

"I must take my leave, but please feel free to have as much champagne as you like."

The couple departed without another word to the others, caught up in their own whispers and laughter. Sterling's brow relaxed as he watched them go, and Ursula wondered if he was thinking about what his own marriage had been like, back in the days when he had been young and the weight of lordship hadn't yet settled onto his shoulders.

"Why did you agree to it?" Ursula's words rose above the crackle of the fire, penetrating the silence that Cyril's absence had created.

"I didn't," Sterling said primly, the chandelier overhead illuminating the contempt on his face. "I was the only one who voted against it. It's a foolish decision."

Desmond's sigh was riddled with impatience. "Your own wife went through the ritual, Sterling, don't be a hypocrite."

Sterling's eyes dropped to his empty glass of champagne. The truth remained unspoken, though they all felt its malevolent presence, an ashen taste on the tip of the tongue. Undergoing the soul magic ritual had destroyed Penelope. From Ursula's experience, everyone who had indulged in the desire for the power it would give them came out… changed. Yet, she doubted that Sterling's adamant refusal came back of any real concern about what the ritual might do to Andie.

"Alexandra is hardly of the same calibre as Penelope."

"Now you're just being a snob." Desmond picked up the bottle of champagne, watching the golden liquid fizz to the top of his glass. "I went through the ritual, and I'm from humble beginnings just like her."

"She has known associates in the Magical Freedoms Brigade," Sterling snapped, all teeth and impotent anger, and Ursula was left to wonder if this was what truly bothered him about the idea of Andie gaining soul magic. "I understand Larkin is fond of her, but the girl cannot be trusted. We already had the issue with Rhodes…"

Ursula leaned forward. "What issue? I thought none of you cared much for his death."

"We don't." Desmond flopped back, carding fingers through his ruffled dark hair. "The Magical Freedoms Brigade does. Word has it that he was close to the leader, and whoever they are, they're pissed."

"Oh?" Ursula arched an eyebrow. "Word from who?"

"We have an informant." There was a smugness to Sterling's tone as he looked over at her. "Someone who's gaining ground amongst this resistance. Unfortunately, they still don't know who the leader is."

The Magical Freedoms Brigade hadn't actively done anything as yet. They heavily campaigned for the free use of magic, there were scuffles here and there, but they had been oddly silent since the death of Patrick Rhodes. It unnerved Ursula, for the silence couldn't mean anything good.

"Who is this informant?"

"It's classified, Ursula." Sterling snapped, setting his crystal glass down on the table and easing himself to his feet. "It's late. I should be going. I will see both of you at the Midsummer Ball."

When Franklin had been one of the Lords, Ursula had been in the loop about everything. Since his death and Larkin replacing him, she was kept more at a distance than ever before. She wondered how long it would be before she was ousted entirely. As Sterling marched out of the room, Ursula noted that Desmond made no move to leave. At her questioning glance, he held up his glass.

"Can't waste such lovely champagne." Desmond took another sip, dark eyes gleaming as he observed her. "It rattles you, doesn't it? This informant. If it makes you feel any better, I don't know either. It's something Sterling came up with all by himself."

"Do we know anything else about the Brigade?" A hint of desperation tinged Ursula's voice. If Sterling didn't underestimate the threat this resistance posed, she was certain the rest of them shouldn't either.

"Troubling rumours, but nothing concrete." Desmond's lips quirked into a half-smile. "Either this informant isn't doing a good job, or the Brigade keeps its information watertight. Concerning, that they know far more about us than we know about them."

"What rumours?" Ursula pressed. While Sterling might disdain her for being a woman and Cyril simply didn't wish to share, she could trust Desmond to be practical. Keeping her informed was in their best interest.

"The word going around within our circles is that the Brigade might have found Excalibur."

Horror consumed Ursula in icy waves, chains of dread holding her immobile. Excalibur had been lost for centuries, a relic of a time long past. The idea that the resistance, outside of their control, could have one of two of the most powerful magical items in the world was nothing less than deeply disturbing.

If they did have Excalibur, what was to stop them there? Clarent remained quiet within its stone prison, unyielding to the touch of any who had sought it out. With one sword inactive and the other missing, there was no one alive who knew what either of them could actually *do*, and Ursula feared their untold power.

"Do you think it's true? Do you think one of them might be the Born Again?"

A tense silence descended over the pair, Desmond drumming his fingers against the crystal glass in his hand. His expression slackened, thoughtful, before he fixed a serene look upon her.

"You value honesty more than most, so I won't lie to you. Yes, I think if none of our own have managed to pull the sword from the stone, it's incredibly likely that one of the Brigade could do so."

CHAPTER NINETEEN

Andie Fairley

Everything at the Midsummer Ball sparkled like the sun. Andie moved through the crowd post-performance, a shimmer of sweat glossing her limbs as she pushed from *Camelot's* stage down to the dancefloor. In the season of Lord Summer's domain, she was the main attraction, and nothing could steal her glory. A tiara of golden stars adorned her brown curls, a perfect match for the gold glitter that covered her eyelids, the blue of her eyes catching the stray sparkles. Her fringed flapper dress glittered underneath the chandelier like a thousand golden mirror shards.

"Just look at you, darling." Larkin crossed over in a slim fit white suit, adorned with a golden tie. His eyes hungrily roamed her body, his grin widening as he met her gaze. "You were absolutely spectacular. Would you care to dance with me?"

Andie was breathless and a little dizzy from the magic she'd used, her own—with Larkin's permission. Nonetheless, she nodded and let Larkin take her hand, kissing the back of it before leading her over to where some of the others were dancing. He caught her by the waist and tugged her close.

It had been some time since Andie danced with a partner. Typically, she danced on her own, spinning on her toes like a top. Yet there was something soothing about Larkin's hand on the small of her back, the scent of jasmine and patchouli wafting under her nose. She wondered if it was an expensive cologne.

"I have good news. The Lords approved you gaining soul magic."

"Really?" Andie could hardly contain her delight, her beaming smile as radiant as the sun. She had been tiptoeing across a tightrope, and now the other side was in sight. She would *finally* accomplish what she wanted.

"There are strict rules, of course." Larkin caught her hand and twirled her, pulling her back to him. "It's been almost four decades since a woman was allowed to undergo the ritual. I've been allowing you to use your magic at your discretion, but we need to be careful. If the other Lords found out it wasn't gifted, they may not be too pleased."

It irritated Andie that she couldn't perform magic the same way that men could. That there were so many regulations and restrictions that only applied to women. Nonetheless, there was no denying she was more privileged in this aspect than most, and she would do well to recognise that. Joy bubbled up through her entire being, a happiness she hadn't experienced since she'd lost Claire.

"You've done so much for me." Andie pressed her lips to his cheek, leaving a scarlet stain in her wake. "Thank you, Larkin."

"I have something else for you." Larkin drew back, arching an eyebrow. "Something I hoped to give you in private."

Curiosity and suspicion mingled in Andie's mind, but she linked her fingers through Larkin's and led him away from the blinding lights of the dancefloor and into the refuge of the shadows. Over the past few months, she had become accustomed to the layout of *Camelot*, and led Larkin into one of the powder rooms. It boasted luxury, a red velvet couch in the corner opposite the sink and marble tiles adorning the floor. Andie's heels clicked as she paused in front of the ornate mirror.

"Is this private enough?"

Larkin reached into the pocket of his jacket and for a moment, Andie tensed, hoping that he wasn't about to take out what she thought he was. When he turned over his hand to reveal a golden sun pendant, bedazzled with tiny diamonds, the sudden knot that had formed in her stomach loosened, and she breathed out a relieved sigh.

"It's stunning, Larkin."

"Did you want me to put it on you?" Larkin asked, and Andie nodded vehemently. She turned to face the mirror, Larkin's fingers brushing against her skin and sending pleasant shivers down her spine as he fastened the pendant around her neck. She reached up to touch it, perhaps the most beautiful and expensive thing she'd ever owned.

She examined the pair of them in the reflection, glowing and golden like gods. Larkin put his hands on her hips and pressed a kiss to her neck, eliciting a soft smile from her. He had given her everything she could have dreamed of, and more. Maybe she had been wrong to have her suspicions about Larkin, to doubt that he wanted anything other than to make her happy.

Swivelling to face him, Andie stared up into his pale eyes, enthralled by the pride and desire she saw gleaming there. Sliding her arms around his neck, she kissed him slowly, sensually. Larkin had given her everything, and so she planned to do the same. She pressed close against him, revelling in the feeling of the muscles of his body. Larkin's hands tightened on her hips and he surged forward, pressing her back against the marble benchtop.

Andie propped herself up on it, heels dangling off the floor. When she tilted her head back, she saw the feral lust that slackened Larkin's face, something wild and dark that he barely had a hold of lingering in his eyes. She was used to men looking at her with hungry eyes, but she delighted in seeing it in this particular man. She would tear down that last semblance of control, and she would make him hers. She tugged him close against her, loosening his tie and unbuttoning his shirt with nimble fingers.

Larkin's lips found purchase along her neck and collarbone, teeth grazing against her skin, leaving marks in his wake. Andie couldn't quite suppress a sharp gasp at the feeling, as the fire burned hotter within her. Her hands traced down his chest, smugness emboldening her at his sharp intake of breath.

"Andie…" Larkin's voice was husky, hands trembling at her waist. "You don't want to stop?"

"That's the opposite of what I want." Her voice was cool and calm, her expression steady as she leaned in, kissing him and slowly biting down on his bottom lip. "I want you to fuck me until I see stars."

Larkin's strangled groan assured her that she had him right where she wanted him. His hands were warm against her skin as they slid up her thighs, tugging up the hem of her gold dress. She could feel his erection pressed against her leg, and she reached out to rub it through the fabric of his pants, making him hiss in surprise. He yanked her underwear down her legs, and she kicked them off completely when they caught on her heel.

Larkin's hands crept higher, slipping a finger into her as she wrapped her heels around his waist to pull him closer. Andie gasped at the contact, a wicked smile curving the corners of Larkin's lips as he added another finger, his thumb dancing in circles on her clit. Andie's moan resonated through the powder room, head tilting back against the mirror behind her as the warmth coiling inside her intensified. Larkin's other hand drifted up to fondle her breasts through the thin fabric of her dress.

Andie melted into him, her body arching into his touch as the curling of his fingers inside her made her tremble.

"You seem to be enjoying this," Larkin mused, another flick of his thumb drawing Andie dangerously close to the precipice. His lips returned to her neck, teeth and tongue working in unison to draw another long gasp from her. His other hand remained on her breast, teasing the hardened nipple, the brush of her dress against them a delicious ache.

"Larkin…" Andie's fingers dug into his bicep as the movement of his fingers made her toes curl, her body shaking as a wave of pleasure crested over her. A high-pitched moan escaped her, the intense heat of her orgasm cascading over her.

Andie blew a curl from her face as Larkin withdrew his fingers, pale eyes sparkling with deviousness. She may have gained a moment's ecstasy, yet she wanted more. She always wanted more, her need for it reaching out with taloned fingers to claw its way upwards. She seized a hold of Larkin's belt buckle and undid it with ease, unzipping his pants and tugging him hard against her.

"I fucking want you," Larkin groaned against her neck, his breath coming in ragged pants as he battled with his desire. "I've never wanted anything the way I want you."

Andie reached between them to slowly stroke his cock, Larkin releasing a choked gasp. She shifted on the bench, positioning him between her legs and helping guide his cock inside her. There was a momentary stretch, and Andie licked her lips and wrapped her legs around his waist. Larkin sank deeper into her, fingers reaching behind her to fist in her curls.

She let her head arch back as Larkin's hips snapped against hers. She rocked against him, legs wrapping tighter around his waist. One of her hands gripped the bench beneath her for leverage. Larkin's pants combined with his deep thrusts made that pleasant buzz surge within Andie, her loud moans echoing through the small room.

He had wanted this for months, the sharpness of her mind a promise of the bliss of her body. Patrick had made love to her, slow and sweet and uncertain, their youth and inexperience making for a tenderness that Larkin lacked. No, Larkin fucked her, driving into her over and again, all the pretty words that had been on his lips for the past months fading away into the guttural groans of a man chasing his own high.

Power and pleasure mingled within the pit of Andie's stomach, an intoxicating combination that made her lust swelter. She would be a goddess amongst men. She would have everything she craved. She ran her hands up Larkin's back, beneath the softness of his shirt, her nails breaking the skin as she dragged them down. Larkin groaned loudly, the fingers wound in her hair shifting to grip her chin.

"You're going to be my undoing, Andie Fairley."

"I certainly hope so," she purred, arching up as his thrusts became harder and faster. Her fingers clutched at Larkin's shoulders as his lips found their way to her collarbone. This was her future: decadence and desire, all tied into one delicious package. She had worked hard for it, and now it was hers for the taking.

Larkin's hands shifted to her ass, tugging her close against him as he plunged deeper, making her moans ascend into ecstatic cries as he reached a place that made her giddy, her whole body tingling and building up toward a crescendo of fireworks. Hearing the change in the pitch of her moans, Larkin laughed breathlessly against her skin.

"Good girl."

The gravelly murmur of the words combined with Larkin pumping into her at an angle that made her head spin caused the knot coiling within Andie to tug free. She dug her nails into Larkin's shoulders, legs shuddering as her second orgasm rippled through her more intensely than the first. Larkin smirked, but his composure slipped and he groaned, his thrusts becoming sloppy as he climaxed, pressing forward against her.

The powder room was quiet for a moment, the silence broken only by their slowing breath. Andie's body was covered in a light sheen of sweat, her curls undoubtedly tangled. When Larkin pulled out of her, she found herself sticky, and fought the urge to scowl. She should have been more careful, for the risk of bearing a child was one she could not afford. Sliding off the bench, Andie wiped herself off with a towel and fixed her dress, smoothing it out before turning to help Larkin button his shirt and do up his tie.

The door to the powder room burst open, making them both start. It was Flo, dressed in shining silver. Her placid expression shifted as she examined the pair of them, inhaling the scent of sex in the air. Her mouth opened slightly, brow pinching—not in annoyance, but hurt.

"Good to see you, Florence." Larkin's dismissive tone cut through the tension like a knife, and he strode out of the powder room without a backward glance. When Andie traipsed after him, Flo's cool fingers closed around her wrist. When she jerked to face the younger girl, she noted the tense set of her jaw.

"Be careful, Andie." Her voice was low and ominous.

Andie scoffed, wrenching her hand free. "Jealousy is an ugly thing, Flo."

Flo opened her mouth again, but Andie sauntered out before she could say another word. She was still buzzing with the high of great sex, and no one was going to ruin the moment for her. She'd undergo the ritual soon, and even Flo's bitter envy couldn't take that away from her. Yet as she thought of Flo's fingers catching hold of her, the upset twist of her lips, she wondered if there was something she'd missed.

∗ ∗ ∗

Andie was bathed in a halo of light as she stepped back onto the dancefloor. She accepted a glass of champagne from a waiter, a bold move from organiser and sponsors who considered themselves above Prohibition. She let the golden liquid fizz in her mouth before swallowing, casting a look around the room. Her lip curled as she observed the show surrounding her, the trill of false laughter and the empty smiles haunting vacant expressions.

Her performance within the realm of the elite was both far more important and insidious than anything she put on the stage. She was constantly in the spotlight, her every step and word dissected by those who would give anything to tear her down. She would give them no excuse to dig in their talons. Once she underwent the ritual, none of their insipid opinions would be of any value, save those of the Lords.

A low chuckle by her shoulder made Andie spin around to Desmond's amused smile and the dark gleam of his eyes.

"You could spend your time pretending you want to be here. Isn't this everything you worked so hard for?"

"I do want to be here." Andie crossed her arms over her chest, annoyance prickling along her skin.

"Yet you seem…bored." Desmond tilted his head to the side and examined her curiously. The idea that he might see through her pretences, that his discerning look might strip her down to the bone, made Andie's spine straighten and chin tilt up to defy her growing unease.

"Quite the contrary, Lord Winter. I've had a *very* enjoyable evening." She let the words that mattered linger like the sweet taste of honey. What did it matter if she confirmed what the Lords already suspected? She'd heard the rumours about her and Larkin. Tonight had simply cemented them as fact.

"I assure you, the Soul Ritual will be far less enjoyable." His smile became strained, eyes darting over the crowd. The bob of his Adam's apple betrayed his apprehension. "It's a brutal process, Andie."

She scoffed. "I'm not afraid."

"You will be." The words were cool and matter-of-fact, fingers tightening on the stem of his crystal champagne glass. "I have seen true horrors in my lifetime, as have you. There are some things that stay with you, no matter how hard you try to fight them off. The Soul Ritual is one of them."

What ghosts haunted him? Andie wondered. Desmond was an enigma even amongst the Lords. His humble beginnings were well spoken of, yet none could quite piece together the story of his past and how he had come to power. One day, perhaps Andie would solve that mystery herself. For now, she was suspicious of his apparent concern. The Lords had been reluctant for her to undertake the ritual, though she believed that to be more reliant on her gender than any danger involved.

"I hate to interrupt." The familiar voice sent shivers coursing down Andie's spine, dread coiling in the pit of her stomach. "But I hoped I might borrow Miss Fairley."

Andie's dress swished around her knees as she spun on her heel to stare down Noel Alderidge, wary of the cold smile that adorned his lips like a medal of honour. His cruel eyes latched onto her and the smile widened. Whatever he wanted her for, nothing good would come of it, but she would be damned if she'd show a moment's hesitation in his presence.

Instead, she countered his soulless smile with a dazzling one of her own, a savage dawn to counter his darkness.

"But of course."

Noel offered his arm, a thick white scar cording down his forearm briefly catching the light of the chandeliers and making Andie's stomach twist. She accepted his arm, though the brush of his skin against hers was enough to make her nauseous. Her trepidation morphed into confusion as he steered them toward the dancefloor, her shoulders relaxing. Whatever his nefarious intentions, he wouldn't lay a hand on her in front of a room full of people.

"I thought this would give us some privacy." Noel stepped in front of her, the heavy musk of his expensive cologne making her resist the urge to wrinkle her nose. "People overhear things far too easily in the shadows, but no one cares for the idle chatter of those on the dancefloor."

He offered his hand, and Andie's confusion stunned her into stillness, before clarity washed over. Noel intended to use a dance as a distraction from whatever he wanted to discuss, and the current foxtrot was certainly rigorous enough that most would be paying attention to their feet, not whatever the Governor's brother was saying to the Carnival's star performer.

Andie had danced the foxtrot with Patrick on a handful of occasions, more often than not with alcohol pumping through her blood and fumbling her typically perfect steps. She could not be anything less than perfect now, with one of Noel's hands gripping hers in a vice and his other hand on the small of her back.

"I thought I'd take this delightful opportunity to remind you of the bargain we struck the night Claire died."

"What of it?" Andie's voice hitched, a betrayal of the nonchalant expression on her face. Only Syl and Warren knew the reality of what had happened that night, of the way Noel and Andie had both shown their true colours. Though she wouldn't have referred to what took place as a 'bargain'.

"Time is a fickle thing." Noel spun with her around the dancefloor, the champagne in Andie's veins lending a golden sheen to their surroundings. "Everything comes to an end, my daughter's life sooner than most. I need you to be aware that, whilst you might content yourself to dance to whatever tune the Lords play, *your* time will come to an end."

Andie laughed mirthlessly. If only Noel was aware of the power she stood to gain, he may not think so little of her. His hand on her back was uncomfortably warm through the fabric of her dress, and she wished for nothing more than to wrench away from him, but she would never give him the satisfaction.

"So you think whispering empty threats in my ear will frighten me?"

"We both keep our promises." Noel pulled her into a hard spin, making Andie teeter on her heels with a sharp gasp. For a breathless moment, she thought she might lose balance, but she found her footing again. When he caught her again, his grip on her hand tightened enough that she winced, feeling her bones grind together beneath his fingers. In one twist, he could easily break her wrist.

Andie lifted her chin brazenly, staring right into his eyes, devoid of anything but hatred. A malicious smile sliced across Noel's lips and he reached up to sweep her hair behind her ear in what some might mistake for a mockery of affection. "Then you remember my warning."

"You *do* look like your mother sometimes."

"I am nothing like that woman," Andie spat the words, boiling with contempt for the mother she had barely known, the mother who had abandoned her and Syl, forsaking her marriage with their father in search of greener pastures. She reached up and batted Noel's hand aside, stepping away from him.

She could handle his veiled threats, the dark promise that she was doomed. What she could not stomach was the mention of the woman who had never loved her, whose absence had sharpened any soft edges that Andie possessed. Sarah might have given birth to her, but in every real sense, Andie never had a mother.

Triumph sparked in Noel's eyes as he found the weakness in Andie's armour.

"Have a good night, Miss Fairley."

Inclining his head, he turned and strode away into the crowd, leaving Andie to fume with her hands curling into fists. The bright lights and the promises of grandeur were overshadowed by the cloud of Noel's vengeance, and the ominous form it took. She could not say what his intentions were, and that worried her all the more.

She would not have to worry long. The Soul Ritual would be her avenue to liberty. Noel Alderidge would be nothing but a thorn in her side, a thorn she would ultimately find a way to pluck out.

Chapter Twenty

Prue Clermont

If Prue thought the Carnival was decadent, she'd seen nothing until she entered Camelot with her arm linked through Sadie's. The entire venue was a display of obscene wealth and splendour, and Prue scratched at her arms, feeling as though the emerald green silk dress and strings of pearls she'd borrowed from Sadie didn't quite fit her. Could they tell her humble origins just by looking at her? Did she stand out, or was Sadie's effortless glamour, accentuated by a dusky pink dress and gold jewellery, enough to help her blend in?

The scent of rose and sandalwood was thick in the air, and for a moment, Prue forgot how to breathe.

"Relax." Sadie gave her arm a reassuring squeeze, the soft smile on rose-coloured lips sending pleasant chills along Prue's skin. "We're here for a nice night. You don't have to look so frightened."

"Not frightened, just overwhelmed." If anyone questioned who Sadie's friend was, they made no mention of it, intentions and opinions hidden behind polite smiles. Although Sadie exchanged a few brief greetings with many of the others, Prue noted that she didn't stop for conversation. Her gaze kept drifting to Sadie, wondering what the other woman's place was in the colourful spectacle of the magical community.

A waiter offered Prue a glass of champagne, and she regarded him in stunned silence before politely declining. No one here was afraid of the law, as if they knew they were above it. She even glimpsed the Governor of New York, Garrett Aldridge, along with another man she assumed to be his brother, Noel. She recalled a family tragedy upon Garrett's election, a niece's suicide or something of the sort. It had caused a ripple, but not enough to mar Garrett's popularity.

"Sadie."

A handsome man with black hair and brown eyes, about their age, approached with a pleasant smile and an offered glass of champagne.

"Thank you, Desmond." Sadie accepted the glass, her eyes darting to the other man who had trailed over with him. He was a few years younger, with a shock of wavy brown hair and eyes the same cold, hard blue as sapphire. He clenched his jaw as he observed Sadie, the curl of his lip leaving Prue in little doubt his opinion of Sadie was not high.

"What are you doing here?" he demanded.

"I was invited, Felix." Sadie's cool indifference gave the impression she had dealt with this attitude before. A suspicion crept over Prue, itching at the back of her neck, that Sadie's heritage was no secret amongst those gathered.

"I'm Prudence," she stammered, as though by turning the attention upon her, it would distract Felix from his contempt for Sadie. "A friend of Sadie's. It's nice to meet you, Mr…?"

"Desmond Bellisario." Desmond took Sadie's hand and kissed the back of it, a boyish smile crossing his lips that she found charming. "A pleasure to meet you, Prudence. Forgive my friend, he seems to have forgotten his manners amongst the champagne and cocaine."

"Felix Templeton." Felix's response was stiff, uncertain gaze raking over Prue. "Lord Spring's youngest son."

Desmond rolled his eyes. "You don't need to rub in your family connections. Everyone here knows who Sterling is."

Felix sneered. "Well, forgive me, *Lord Winter*."

Desmond was one of the four Seasonal Lords. Prue masked her surprise; she had expected them to be more…well, intimidating and snobby. She'd briefly seen Lord Summer on a few occasions, but never the other Lords, who Sadie had mentioned all had several years on Lord Summer. She'd never pictured that she may be directly introduced to any of them, and Desmond's familiarity with Sadie raised several questions.

"I'm not here to antagonise you, Felix." Sadie took another sip of her champagne. "I was asked to come, and so here I am."

Felix's brow furrowed and he looked as though he had more he wished to say, however Desmond placed a hand on the younger man's shoulder. That simple action drove Felix to silence, and left no doubts as to whom the power truly rested with. Desmond offered his arm to Sadie.

"A word in private?"

Sadie flashed Prue an apologetic look, and panic surged through Prue as she realised she was going to be left on her own. As Desmond escorted Sadie across the hall, Prue remained in uncomfortable silence with Felix, wishing she could press herself into the wall and disappear. Felix tugged his fingers through his wavy hair, before hoisting an unconvincing smile across his face.

"So. A friend of Sadie's. Where did you two meet?"

"At the grocery store," Prue blurted out without thinking, before cringing at how mundane that must seem to a pampered heir like Felix. Everything about this place overwhelmed her: the lights too bright, the temperature suddenly too warm, her hands clammy as she wiped them on the green dress that didn't belong to her.

Something collided with her shoulder, sending her stumbling. Not something, someone. As Prue reeled from the impact, a firm hand gripped her arm, holding her upright. She found herself staring up into the bright blue eyes of none other than the Sun Carnival's most magnetic showgirl, Andie Fairley.

"I'm so sorry, I didn't see you there."

Prue didn't know what to say in response, too awestruck and intimidated by the younger woman's presence. Andie's curls were a tangled mess, and Prue caught sight of bite marks on her neck before she brushed her hair to hide them. Fortunately, Felix was all too delighted to fill in Prue's awkward silence.

"Miss Fairley, isn't it? My father said a lot about you, but he never mentioned how lovely you are."

Prue fought back a grimace at Felix's shameless flirtation, though in truth she was grateful that being in the presence of such a stunning and charismatic woman made her invisible. She had no desire to be seen, lest someone take a closer look and see the truth of what she was.

"Did he now?" Andie scoffed, arching an eyebrow coolly, undeterred by Felix's eyes travelling the length of her body. "Well, he's said nothing of you, though I know Sterling has several children. Three, from memory. Which are you?"

"Four," Felix corrected, stepping into Andie's space despite her clear disinterest. "I'm the youngest. Felix, but you can call me anything you want, darling."

"Oh, the west coast connoisseur." Andie indulged him with a saccharine smile, but Prue could feel the barbed wire beneath it. "Come to think of it, Larkin did tell me all about the Vegas incident."

Prue had no idea what the reference was, but it was enough for Felix's expression to go cold. He took a step back, jaw clenched as he spun on his heel and marched off. Once he'd left, Andie shook her head slowly, turning her attention back to Prue, who felt her temporary invisibility wearing off.

"Spoiled little rich boys. They're all the same. Was he bothering you?"

"No, he was just talking to me while I waited for my friend." The words flooded out of Prue without restraint. She wished she had something witty or clever to share, something that would make Andie laugh. Instead she felt a loss for words, the painful reminder that she did not belong amongst these elegant, glamorous people.

What did Lord Winter want from Sadie? Prue had been promised safety, and yet she never knew what to expect from Sadie. Although it was true that the other woman had protected her in the past, taught her more about magic, she could not help but wonder at the pieces of the puzzle she was missing. More pieces had fallen in her lap tonight: Felix's blatant disdain, Sadie being on a first-name basis with Lord Winter himself.

"What friend?" Andie cast around, curls whipping from side to side.

"That would be me." Sadie appeared by Prue's side, making her start, not having seen her slip back through the crowd. "Thank you for scaring Felix away, he can be either utterly annoying or extremely boring, and I can never tell which is worse."

Andie frowned slightly, but before she could say anything, Sadie had tucked her arm in Prue's and steered her firmly toward the frosted glass double doors leading to the balcony. She nudged them open, and the warm summer air washed over Prue's face as they stepped out into the respite the darkness promised. Away from the blinding lights and too-watchful eyes, Prue's shoulders relaxed.

The doors swung closed behind them, the music and laughter fading as though trapped inside a bubble. Over the steel railing, the city was in a state of constant movement, colourful lights and the cacophony of late-night traffic serving as a soothing backdrop. There was a sprinkle of light rain, though Sadie welcomed it, tilting her head back and letting the drops caress her face. Prue watched her with fascination, the woman she cared so much for and yet knew hardly anything about.

"You know everything about me, Sadie." The words were soft, yet accusatory. "My husband, my aunt, the fact that I'm a Scourge. Yet in return I get shards of you, and I struggle to put together a full picture."

The beginnings of a smile tugged at Sadie's lips. "Was there something particular you wanted to know?"

Prue braced herself. "Well, who your father is, for a start."

Sadie's face closed off, like a door had shut between them, and Prue's stomach plunged into freefall as she realised it had been the wrong thing to say. Shadows passed across Sadie's face in the darkness the balcony offered, and Prue wondered if this was always how she would see her: never fully revealed, never fully in the light. She feared the shadows were such an integral part of who Sadie was that she feared forsaking them.

"I can't tell you that. I can tell you he's the reason I was invited tonight."

Intrigue pulsed beneath Prue's skin, but she pushed it down. It was more than Sadie typically disclosed, and Prue worried a further nudge toward the truth would result in Sadie taking another step back. In being close to Sadie, she acknowledged the tragedy that part of Sadie would always be locked to her.

"Are you always going to keep secrets from me?" Prue asked, unable to fully extract the sting of bitterness in her voice.

Hurt contorted Sadie's eyebrows. "No, not always. Just…there are some things I'm processing. Especially with knowing what you can do. I want to protect you, and there are people in this community who would do almost anything to get their hands on you. So yes, it means there are things I hide."

Prue prickled with irritation, the feeling like electricity flooding her veins. Perhaps when she had been a normal woman with no inkling of what she was, she would agree with Sadie. Things were different. There was a hunger in her that she may not fully comprehend, but knew to be her Scourge power, yearning for magic. She welcomed it like an old friend, half-familiar but with a basic understanding of what it was. She could pull the magic out of anyone who came for her, so why was Sadie coddling her?

"I'm tired of hiding from things." Prue's voice cracked with exhaustion, the light rain slipping down her cheeks like tears.

Her true nature was more than the immense power that dwelled in the pit of her being, waiting to be unleashed. It was also a woman who craved things she shouldn't, like the sweetness of Sadie's lips against hers. She wanted freedom in every sense, yet still she was snagging upon the expectations of polite society.

"You never have to hide from me," Sadie said softly, catching Prue's hands in her own, the soft brush of her skin sending pleasant shivers chasing up Prue's spine. "I want you exactly as you are. Dangerous Scourge powers and all."

The pitter-patter of the rain had increased to a steady volume, Prue's hair damp as she slicked it back from her face. Droplets cascaded down the windows, obscuring the assembly inside to blurred figures and lights. Concealed from curious eyes, Prue cupped Sadie's face and kissed her. The muggy summer air and fresh rain dancing across their skin were an unholy combination, and yet she had never felt more alive.

Her heart thrummed a steady beat in her chest, the silk of the jade green dress she'd borrowed sticking against her back. With Sadie's mouth on hers, she could conquer the world. With the light caress of Sadie's auburn hair against her cheek, fireworks exploded in the pit of her stomach.

Together, they could accomplish anything. So why was Prue still so unsatisfied with the shadows lingering over Sadie?

* * *

The warmth of the hearth was slow to dry Prue's hair and dress, and her cheeks flared with heat at how much of a fright she must appear. She wanted to belong among these people, and yet she trudged inside looking like a wet dog. Prue sighed and carded her fingers through her damp hair, watching as Sadie moved gracefully around the room, her expression becoming terse as she encountered a smirking woman with ringlets pinned atop her head.

"Get caught in the rain, did you?"

The man's voice was pleasant and amused, and Prue cursed her ill fortune as she found herself face to face with the Governor of New

York, Garrett Alderidge. She recognised him from the pictures plastered all through the newspapers. His presence at this event, an event within the magical community, made her pause.

"Governor…Mr Alderidge." She stumbled over her words, attempting to regain some sense of decorum by smoothing out her dress.

"I believe you came with Miss Crawford, though I don't think I've ever seen you before."

An unspoken question lingered in the air, and Prue latched onto it quickly.

"Prudence Clermont. I'm a good friend of Sadie's."

"I admit, I don't know Miss Crawford well, but I can't recall meeting many of her friends." The implication hung over them like a dark cloud, and Prue's stomach churned at the thought that someone may have seen her and Sadie, or else guessed what they were to each other. Her apprehension lent her boldness, and she couldn't help but frown.

"Perhaps if you knew her better, Mr Alderidge, then you would."

Garrett laughed, the mirth stretching from his mouth to his eyes. "That's very true. I apologise if I have overstepped myself."

Prue shook her head fervently. It was odd to be in a room full of influential people, to have the Governor of New York himself speaking to her in such a familiar manner. She had once believed she'd give anything to be seen by these people, and now all she wanted was to get away from them. She didn't want to hide who and what she was, and yet their cruel tongues and prying eyes gave her reason to be nervous.

"You don't owe me any apologies, Governor."

There was no pull to him, no magic that called her very bones. Whatever Garrett Alderidge was, magic had no part in it. A soothing balm in a room full of energy that gnawed at her. The easygoing smile on his face dropped, his gaze locked on something beyond Prue. When she turned to glance over her shoulder, she saw Garrett's younger brother on the dancefloor with Andie Fairley, spinning so fast she thought they might both topple over.

"Unbelievable," Garrett muttered, shaking his head slowly. The tightness of his jaw over a foxtrot puzzled Prue, but unlike him, she was not in a position to be asking questions. When he realised Prue was observing him curiously, Garrett flashed her a smile that didn't quite reach his eyes. "It's been a pleasure, Prudence. I hope Sadie brings you to these sorts of events more often."

The Governor swept off toward the dancefloor with determination in his step. Unease rippled across Prue's skin, accompanied by a sear of warmth from the flames crackling in the hearth, the snap of the logs making her flinch.

She felt as though she had dived into shark-infested waters without questioning what manner of creatures she was swimming with. Politicians, celebrities…who else was involved in this magical community? If they were like Garrett and didn't possess an ounce of magic, then what was in it for them?

Chapter Twenty-One

Ursula Delavane

Ursula had experienced enough Midsummer Balls that this year's failed to thrill her. She smoothed her hands down her silk navy dress and tried to drown out the thick plumes of smoke from old men's cigars, the tinkle of champagne glasses clinking together for a toast. It was the event of the season, and yet restlessness plagued her, beads of sweat pearling across her forehead as she kept her gaze locked firmly on Larkin.

If the Brigade wanted to do damage, the Midsummer Ball was precisely the sort of event they would seek to infiltrate. Yet the Brigade was not exactly notorious for violence, and they had kept their plans well under wraps. The silence was more frightening than threats, like stepping out into a winter morning and not being able to see through the thick fog.

She was being absurd. Ursula drew in a deep breath, gathered the oxygen into her lungs as though it was its own kind of ammunition. She picked up a glass of champagne and took a sip, a patient smile her armour as Sterling Templeton approached. The ruddiness of his cheeks indicated he too had been partaking in the champagne.

"Ursula." He took her hand in his clammy palm, kissing the back of it. "A pleasure to see you, as always."

"I can see your children are in attendance." Her gaze flicked between Sterling's three children, none of whom eased the apprehension coiled in the pit of her stomach.

Charles, the eldest and heir apparent, rumoured to be as cruel as he was powerful. Abigail, the middle child, sharp as a knife with an unsettling smile. Felix, the youngest, whose decadence was well known amongst the elite. Perhaps there was less for her to be concerned about when it came to Larkin than she had anticipated, especially taking Sterling's offspring into account.

"Ah, yes. I've been meaning to talk to you about them, actually."

Ursula raised an eyebrow coolly. "About your children?"

"I must admit, I am not as young as I once was." Sterling offered his arm, and Ursula begrudgingly took it, his skin warm through his merle grey and white pinstripe suit coat. "I have been considering my retirement, and though it's a few years before I consider such a concept, the weariness in my bones pesters me of its inevitability."

"So you're talking about naming your successor." Ursula latched onto this information greedily, revelling at gaining an insight she was certain the others were not yet privy to.

"Oh, it would be Charles, naturally." Sterling waved a dismissive hand, and Ursula conceded he would never have considered another option. He was a man of staunch tradition, and Charles was his first-born son. "I don't see it should be too much of a bother. He and Desmond are close in age."

Age was the only thing Desmond and Charles had in common. Desmond was careful in his speech and movement, yet Charles possessed the reckless abandon of one born wealthy enough that a misstep would not matter.

"Forgive me, Sterling, but I'm afraid I don't understand why this is a discussion if you've already made your mind up." She hoisted a thin smile across her lips as Sterling's eyes locked onto her. There it was, the same sharpness that Abigail possessed, not yet dulled by his advancing years.

"Charles is not as forgiving as I am." Cold steel entered his voice, causing Ursula's hand to slip off his arm. "We may have indulged Larkin's behaviour, and even allowed Miss Fairley to undergo the Soul Ritual, but if either of them were to step out of line…"

Andie may dig her own grave with her bare hands, but Larkin was a Lord, part of their ruling elite. Ursula stepped closer, her smile sharpening as she rested a hand on Sterling's shoulder. A sour taste coated her tongue, a bitterness that made her long for more champagne to drown it out.

"You wouldn't be threatening my son, would you, Mr Templeton?"

Ursula was not the sort to take joy in defying the Lords, or speaking out of turn, but when it came to her son, there were no boundaries she would not cross and no rules she would not break. Her words were gentle enough that anyone near them may assume they were speaking civilly, but cold enough to chill Sterling's blood.

"I would never dream of it, Ursula." Sterling pressed a hand over his heart, eyes widening into a caricature of shock. "I know the boy will come to heel, as he always does. You know, I blame the war for a great deal of things, but mostly for encouraging this fantasy within young women such as Andie that they are no longer in need of men."

"She needs Larkin, and she knows that." Ursula planted her hands on her hips, the silk of her dress smooth beneath her fingers.

"For now." Sterling's eyes glazed over as they scanned the room, and she wondered if he was remembering his own late wife, whose power had eclipsed his own. A pity for her, a triumph for him, in the end.

There was a greater threat that lay beyond the Carnival. The Lords were not foolish enough to invest their energy into hating Andie when the Brigade was becoming so prominent. Snakes in the grass, wolves at their door. Friends and foes, all with bright eyes and charming smiles.

They would feel teeth snapping at their throats, sooner rather than later. Sterling may fear women's independence post-war, but Ursula's opinion was different. The greatest threat to them following the war was something far more dangerous still: hope. A hope that all ambitions were equal, that anyone could reach up and touch the stars.

A hope they needed to crush.

* * *

The greenhouse situated at the back of the Templeton residence was unbearably muggy as Ursula stepped inside, the glass windows dripping with condensation. A warm sheen of sweat beaded across her brow, the back of her champagne-coloured silk shirt clinging to her skin. She lifted her head high and feigned indifference, pumps clicking across the pavement that separated the multitude of green plants into various pathways. Moisture clung to the emerald leaves, as if they too were perspiring.

Ursula had only attended two Soul Rituals before: Franklin's and Desmond's. On both occasions she had come along to the Templeton greenhouse to bear witness. She had perhaps forgotten about the humidity, or else wiped it from her mind.

In the centre of the greenhouse, beneath the warm glow of the hanging lights, was a steel bathtub. It was at odds with the bathtubs in the Delavane home, porcelain white with clawed feet. It resembled a laundry basin in its mundanity, but Ursula had witnessed miracles emerge from the depths of the steel tub.

The four Lords stood around the tub, and when she peered down into its depths, she saw ice strewn through the water. It was tempting, with the greenhouse's heat, to skim her fingers across its surface and delight in its cold bite. Disregarding the urge, she stepped beside Larkin and rested a comforting hand on his arm, squeezing lightly. His grim expression didn't shift, brows tugging together.

"She'll be just fine," Ursula assured him, though she had nothing to justify her words, merely a mother's desire to soothe her restless son.

To the left of the bath, Desmond leaned against a small wooden table, rickety with age and marred by scratches across a once-polished surface. Between his nimble fingers, he tossed a brass stopwatch. A small silver machine also sat atop the table, with a set of numbers, one to ten, and a single hand to read the measurement. The Templeton Scale, an ageing relic used to read a person's magic level once they emerged from the ritual.

Andie walked into the greenhouse with her head held high. Her arm was linked through Dot's, and Ursula wryly noted what a wise decision having Cyril's wife present was. She would see what a beautiful and horrific thing the Soul Ritual was, and make her choice as to whether she would ever embark upon such an ordeal, just as Ursula had done when witnessing Larkin's.

Andie wore a simple black dress and though her feet were bare, her eyes glittered with Sun Carnival gold, the same colour as the hoops that adorned her ears. It gave her a fierce impression, one Ursula feared may not last the night. When Dot hurried to Cyril's side, Larkin strode over to Andie, terse whispers exchanged as his brow furrowed further. Andie took his hands in hers, and Larkin kissed the top of her head. Whatever transpired between them, Larkin accepted it, exhaling deeply as he walked back over to stand beside Ursula.

"You're certain about this?" Sterling arched an eyebrow, arms folded across his chest to indicate his disapproval. "There is no going back from this, nor will we be held accountable for how it turns out."

Andie drew herself up to her full height like a puppet straightening out its own strings, standing almost as tall as Sterling. Her blue eyes burned with determination, and Ursula was certain that nothing those present said would deter Andie from her goal. The young woman possessed the same raw hunger that lived within Desmond, and nothing would stand in her way.

"I have never been more certain about anything in my life." Her voice rang clear and strong.

"Very well." Sterling gestured toward the tub, taking a step back. When he spoke again, the opening words of the ritual resonated with untold power. "May the water claim you. May it take or give, may it steal the breath from your lungs or breathe into them anew."

Andie hiked her dress up to her thighs and clambered into the tub without hesitation.

'Bold girl, foolish girl.'

She paused, sucking in a deep breath as the chill of the water made its presence known. Larkin reached out to grip Ursula's hand, and she rubbed her thumb against the back of his in soothing circles even as his fingers crushed hers.

Andie sank into the water, sliding down deeper until only her head remained above the surface. Desmond clicked the stopwatch, sitting on the edge of the table as it creaked in protest. Andie stared straight ahead of her, her crystalline eyes colder than the ice that must be biting away beneath her skin.

"What happens now?" Dot murmured from beside Cyril. She clung onto his arm and stared up at him with fearful brown eyes, wide like a doe's.

"The cold water slows down her heart rate, to the brink of death," Cyril whispered as he swept a strand of hair behind Dot's ear, his gaze focused on Andie. "Either she pulls back from it, or she succumbs to it. If she survives it, her soul magic will activate."

Larkin had been only eighteen when he had undergone the ritual, and Ursula had protested with every bone in her body. Yet Franklin's cool dismissal was clear: Larkin was an adult, and could undergo the ritual if he chose. Those twenty minutes would be etched in Ursula's mind as long as she lived, the moment of limbo in which she did not know if her only child would die.

When she glanced at Larkin, she saw that same terror reflected in his pale blue eyes. Months ago, she had dismissed his feelings for Andie as infatuation, but the genuine dread that held Larkin's body rigid told a different story. He was in love with her, and if she did not survive the ritual, it would break him.

Andie's teeth chattered, her brown skin losing its colour. Yet she gripped the edges of the steel tub with both hands, fingers curling tight around the metal. When Ursula glanced at Desmond, he checked the stopwatch and inclined his head slightly. Over twenty minutes.

The safe period had eclipsed, leaving Andie floundering in the void of uncertainty. If she didn't pull through soon, she would sink beneath the ice, as so many had before her.

Cyril reached into his pocket and pulled out a flask, taking a sip before handing it to Dot. Dot's eyes were fixed upon Andie, wide as saucers as she took a gulp from the flask. A slow smile started to creep across Sterling's lips as Andie's breath struggled in ragged gasps, fingers slackening on the sides of the tub. Her neck craned back and her eyes fluttered closed.

She had reached it. The point between life and death. Ursula recognised the signs from Larkin's own ritual.

Overhead, the hanging lights flickered on and off, drawing Dot's nervous attention elsewhere.

"Is that supposed to happen?"

Uneasy silence enveloped the congregation. Ursula didn't recall the lights flickering when Larkin had gained soul magic, though every ritual was different. One by one, the bulbs blew, a cascade of glass raining down on them and plunging the greenhouse into darkness. The only light filtered through the windows, and Ursula went rigid as a shadow ascended from the tub with fluid grace.

The lights flashed on in unison, casting their warm glow over Andie vaulting over the side of the tub. Her black dress was soaking wet, dribbling icy water that the soil beneath her bare feet consumed greedily. Her curls were lank and her skin had yet to return to its full colour, but there was a stark presence about Andie now. She'd always exuded confidence and charm; this was something more. Something *powerful.*

Dot scurried forward and kindly placed a coat around Andie. The showgirl reached up and rested a hand over Dot's, holding it in place on her shoulder. The lightbulbs flickered again, a golden gleam shining eerily in Andie's eyes for a moment. A serene smile spread across her lips, sending a chill tingling down Ursula's spine.

"What's the reading?" She turned her attention to Desmond, whose expression was unreadable as he examined the dial. When he addressed the others, dark eyebrows coolly arched, there was no trace of alarm as he read the number aloud.

"Nine."

It was as though Ursula was shocked with a bolt of electricity. Most of the others sat between four and five, the exception being Cyril at seven. A reading as high as nine hadn't been recorded in living memory, not for at least a century. She cast around for the reactions of the others. Horror on Sterling's face, greed on Cyril's. Curiosity lit up Desmond's eyes, while a bright smile dawned across Larkin's lips and he swept over to pull Andie close and kiss her cheek.

A vicious, smug smile pulled across Andie's face. Ursula inhaled a deep breath, Larkin ignorant of the fact that his joy was far from infectious. Sterling bustled over to check the scale as though the number was wrong. Desmond clicked the stopwatch closed and wrestled it into the pocket of his waistcoat. Yet none of the activity mattered in the face of Andie's silent, complacent victory.

What had they created in the Templeton greenhouse? What horrors had they unleashed? They had endeavoured upon the ritual to appease Larkin, but it had gone horribly wrong. How could they now anticipate Larkin would make a docile wife of a young woman who ranked at nine?

They hadn't seen what Andie could even do yet, though Ursula remembered Larkin's soul magic had taken a little while to master. As the lights flickered again overhead like a warning, she couldn't help but wonder what the cost of their mistake would be.

Chapter Twenty-Two

Andie Fairley

Magic had always coursed through Andie's veins, a steady flow that bent to her will and swept to her fingers with ease. Now, it flooded around her body with the force of a raging river, caressing her in its delicious power. Soul magic had a taste to it, like cherries on the tip of her tongue, and she couldn't get enough.

As the Lords left the greenhouse, Ursula and Dot trailing obediently after them, Andie flexed her fingers beneath the lights. *Nine.* A number that, without asking, she knew was higher than any of the others. A delighted giggle burst from her lips, a relief sinking through her shoulders even as the chill of the icy water wore off.

Death had reached out to her with cruel fingers in that tub. She felt its pull against her ribcage, as though attempting to carve out her heart. Once, she would have welcomed its grasp, back when she held death in her hands, and Syl's voice had been the only thing that ripped her away from its dark beauty. It would have been so easy to accept, to succumb to the soothing lullaby of the void.

Death offered her forgiveness for her sins, to cleanse the agony of Claire. It offered a reprieve from the guilt and pain that haunted her since. She had flirted with Death often enough, yet it was only beneath the ice that it showed an interest in her.

Death promised her relief, a respite from a world that had been unfair to her, and yet magic promised more. It was that revelation that kept Andie clinging to life, that brought her back from the brink with power sizzling through her veins. She would no longer welcome Death's embrace, but fight it.

"How do you feel?" Larkin slid an arm around her shoulders, Dot's donated coat the only warmth against Andie's skin.

"Different." It was the only word Andie could settle upon. Her mind magic was not like Warren's. Her heart magic was riddled with the guilt of how she had obtained it. The new form of magic she had obtained was something raw, the appealing shine of its newness making Andie cling to it.

"Once we gain soul magic, we gain...a particular gift." Larkin strode over to plunge his hand into the soil of one of the flowerbeds, fingers burrowing beneath the earth. "It may not necessarily be unique, but it will become your calling."

The daisies perked up and bloomed, brightening to life at Larkin's coaxing. A soft smile spread across Andie's face, yet her wonder at Larkin's gift of life and growth was overshadowed by her curiosity of precisely what the other Lords could do. What were they hiding from her? Why did they keep their abilities so private?

'Because they did not want others to know what they could do.' The answer was a harrowing whisper in the back of her mind, a stark realisation. No matter how much had been disclosed to her about magic, no matter how much she had been allowed to become part of their inner circle, insidious secrets remained locked in their closets, hidden in the shadows where she couldn't find them.

"How will I know what it is?" Andie asked as Larkin dusted his fingers off against his trousers.

"It will come to you. The magic is fresh now, but once it settles in, you'll know."

Andie took his face in her hands and kissed him fiercely. Larkin may not have directly been the one to give her this gift, but he had opened the door to let it inside. She saw the way the others looked at her, the mixture of admiration and dread on their faces as her true power hung over them like a dark cloud. Larkin looked at her the same way: with wonder and desire, as though she was a goddess born anew from the cold bite of the water.

"You believed in me." Andie drew back, tracing her fingers down his cheek. "When no one else did, you thought I would survive this."

"How could I think otherwise?" He looped his arms around her waist, tugging her close. "Forget the Sun Carnival, you're what shines the brightest, Andie Fairley."

Warmth enveloped her whole body, like she'd stepped into the sunlight—like the dampness of her dress and the ends of her curls didn't matter. She beamed, swelling with power and pride at his praise, the lightbulbs overhead flickering on and off as though someone was toying with the switch.

To hell with what the other Lords thought. To hell with their snide insinuations and baseless assumptions about the sort of woman she was, about what they thought she would be now she'd obtained the ultimate magic. Larkin believed in her, and that was all she needed. As long as he was by her side, they were on top of the world.

* * *

The quiet darkness of the early hours of the morning didn't perturb Andie. Back in Hell's Kitchen, there had been all manner of crooks scurrying through the alley like rats. She'd kept her Colt Derringer in her purse, fingers clutched around it in case she needed to fire it. Fortunately, she'd typically also had Syl with her as well, a natural deterrent to anyone who might think to accost a young woman in the dead of night.

She possessed more than firearms these days. The magic that surged through her was a weapon in itself, and so she strode back through Central Park to her trailer without a hint of fear. No, what held her heart in its vice-like grip was the memory that Patrick had died in the shadows, in the darkness where no one had heard him. Despite her glorious victory, tears bloomed in her eyes at the memory of her best friend, his murder still unsolved and casting shadows over her newfound power.

She quickly wiped them away, composing herself. The grim truth was that many violent crimes went unsolved, but that had been in the murky depths of Hell's Kitchen. She had thought herself safe from such horrors in her decadent new world. Patrick's death haunted her, not the product of mugging gone wrong, but a carefully calculated crime. Someone wanted him silenced. What, exactly, had he known?

"Well, don't you look nice!"

The exuberant exclamation made Andie heave a sigh, mentally bracing herself for the unpredictability of drunk Syl. Her brother stumbled through the rainbow of trailers. Someone peered out through the curtain, the glow of yellow light brief before they pulled it closed again. Andie rolled her eyes, tucking her hair behind her ear as she searched Syl's expression for any sign of impending malice.

"What do you want?"

It occurred to Andie that perhaps he hadn't come to see her at all. Syl and Flo lacked any subtlety, and Andie's suspicions around who Flo was stepping out with were dispelled by the sly looks the pair exchanged, the backstage flirting, the cheap lilies in a plastic vase on Flo's side of the trailer. She could not fathom a more strange pairing.

"Bit late coming home," Syl snickered as he leaned against a yellow trailer, examining his sister. "You were with Lord Summer again, weren't you?"

"I went through the Soul Ritual, Sylvester." Andie's tone was cold and clipped, the intensity of the night and Syl's irritable presence grating against her nerves and forcing bitter truth from her lips. "Now, may I go to bed, or is there something you actually need?"

"*What?*" The lazy smile dropped from Syl's face, and he seized her arm in a vice-like grip that made her wince. "Andie, what have you done?"

"Become something more powerful," Andie snarled as she twisted in his grasp, attempting to pull free.

"Don't you understand?" Syl's speech was no longer slurred, his bloodshot eyes wide as he examined her with a growing terror. "There is *always* a cost to magic like that. We've both heard the tales of King Arthur. He went mad with it, all the magic flowing through him that he couldn't control."

"Well, thankfully I'm not King Arthur," Andie snapped, wrenching away and stepping back. "Why do you care anyway? I thought it didn't matter to you whether I lived or died."

Syl reeled as though she'd slapped him. "Don't say that. Don't you *ever* fucking say that."

"Isn't it the truth?" She spat the words, the venom pushing beneath her skin, bleeding free as tears spilled down Syl's cheeks and he flinched, turning his face. "Isn't that what you want?"

"I didn't want any of this!" Syl shouted, pointing an accusatory finger at her. "You made the choice, and we both had to live with it. That's what I said, that you needed to *live* with it. Don't you dare say that I wanted you to die."

Andie lapsed into stunned silence, unexpected tears blurring her vision. Her conviction that Syl had hated her for what happened to Claire had been like iron, impenetrable and unbreakable. It occurred to her that perhaps the person who loathed her the most for everything that happened on that fateful night was herself.

Syl raised an arm to wipe his face on his sleeve. In his green eyes, the truth shone more clearly than any of her delusions. The concept of wanting her dead was a knife twisted between Syl's ribs, a cruelty she had shoved on him without stopping to wonder who had their hand on the blade.

She wanted nothing more than to purge the poison between them, the ugly tension that had marred their relationship for years following

Claire's death. This was the closest Syl had come to reaching out a hand to offer her that chance. Perhaps not forgiveness, but a chance to make amends, to fix things.

"But I did." The words were a whisper on the wind, a shameful reminder of the dark thoughts that lingered in Andie's mind.

Once upon a time, standing over the Harlem River and watching the water settle as it claimed Claire's body, Andie had taken a deep breath and contemplated throwing herself in as well. Yet as her mind had lingered on Syl, on his knees and sobbing into his hands behind her, she couldn't do it. It was for Syl and Warren that she'd made the choices she had that night, decisions that may as well have pushed her over that edge, if she had not stayed alive out of pure spite.

In the steel tub in the Templeton greenhouse, with the icy water eating away at her, she could have slipped under. She felt death beckoning, and yet she resisted. She wanted to live. She wanted to stay, with the prospect that things would get better. Death was no longer an enticing prospect or a welcome escape. She had smiled in death's face, and chosen life.

The scars and the shame of her past were washed away within that chilly water, and the Andie that had emerged was ready to put it behind her.

Syl wrapped his arms around her and pulled her in tight. For a moment, Andie's breath caught in her lungs, before she hugged him back. The stench of stale beer lingered on his clothes, the jasmine and patchouli scent of Larkin's cologne clinging to her hair and coat. They clung to one another the way they had as children, when Syl held Andie's hand quietly as Warren shut himself in his room once again.

In her hunger for power, in her ambition to become something more, Andie had very nearly forsaken her brother. Now, burying her face in his shoulder with her tears seeping into the fabric of his shirt, she acknowledged that perhaps it had never been a choice. Perhaps there was a chance she could have both.

* * *

Andie's sleep was callously interrupted by Flo stomping moodily about the trailer, the accompanying annoyed huffs indicating that the younger girl was in a surly mood. It had become more commonplace of late, though Andie's frequent absences in spending time with Larkin meant she and Flo crossed paths little, two ships in the night with the lights off. There would come a day when Andie was not restricted to sharing a trailer with bratty younger showgirls, but unfortunately being Larkin's lover and obtaining soul magic did not bring about instant prosperity.

"What is it now, Flo?" Andie mumbled sleepily, kicking off the blankets and pinching the bridge of her nose as she pushed her body into a seated position. Rubbing her eyes, she observed the blonde girl in a blue cotton dressing gown, shoving through her racks of clothes with a frantic edge to her movements.

"Nothing fits!" Flo exclaimed, throwing one of her dresses down for good measure.

Her lip curling over Flo's histrionics, Andie sauntered over to the overstuffed clothing rack and sifted through the clothes. Casting a sideways look at the younger girl, she admitted to herself that Flo had indeed gained weight. There was nothing particularly wrong with it, and on someone as thin as Flo it may well be a good thing, but it would explain why none of the dresses fit.

"Here." Andie carelessly tossed one of her own dresses, a black and silver one, to Flo. She was a good bit taller than Flo, so it would sit differently on her. "Try this."

Flo fumbled the catch, almost dropping the dress, turning it over in her hands and staring at the ground. Her fidgety behaviour made Andie's eyes narrow as she gestured impatiently to the dress.

"Will you just try it on?"

"I can't." Flo shook her head fervently, voice cracking over the words. Though her dithering made Andie's annoyance flare, an undercurrent of concern slithered through her. Flo was unusually agitated for what appeared to be a bit of weight gain.

"Florence." Andie blew a curl out of her face, reining in her temper. "You need to explain to me what's going on with you."

Flo reached up to wipe her eyes, setting the dress down over the back of a wooden chair. She tugged off her dressing gown, and Andie's breath caught in her throat at the gentle swell of Flo's stomach. How had she missed it? She supposed there had been signs she'd ignored: Flo retching into a bucket before a performance, Flo not waking up until midday on her days off despite being an early riser.

Disappointment, disdain, and pity mingled within Andie, the combination making her groan loudly. Flo was barely twenty. She couldn't believe that the younger girl was so careless, though unfortunately she could not say such behaviour from Syl shocked her.

"Flo, are you fucking serious?"

"I know," Flo wailed miserably, pressing her hands over her face. "I know it's bad. I could just never bring myself to say anything."

"Didn't you think of solutions?" Andie began to pace, bare feet tapping back and forth across the brown linoleum floor. "You could have seen someone, had this dealt with. Did you even tell Syl?"

"What?" Flo's brow furrowed in confusion, before understanding dawned across her face and she nodded. "Yes, he knows."

"So what now, Flo?" Andie threw her hands up in disbelief. "How do you and Syl plan to go about this?"

The idea of finding herself pregnant was like nails clawing their way down a chalkboard. She did not have a maternal bone in her body, and was fully aware motherhood was not something she was cut out for. Flo, however…she had never questioned what Flo thought of bearing and raising a child, because she had not thought to be in the younger girl's vicinity if and when that came to pass.

"He'll take care of the baby and I." Flo nodded fervently, though her voice wobbled as if she wasn't truly certain. "We'll get married. I'll have to stop performing, but that won't matter. I can stay home and look after the baby."

"And where is home, Flo?" Andie's words were gentler than usual, for the truth was that Flo had no home outside of the Carnival. She'd been an orphan, and then worked in a brothel.

"We're still sorting that out." The younger girl looked down at her hands, chewing anxiously at her lip. When she looked up, there was a sour smile on her lips. "It's odd, isn't it? For so long, I wanted to be like you. Seasonal Lords eating out of the palm of your hand, the most well-known performer in the whole Carnival."

A rare sympathy gnawed its way into Andie. Flo was a fool for getting herself into these circumstances, and yet women so often had little control of their own fortunes. It had taken Andie years of climbing up the social ladder to get where she was, and she still shared a pink trailer that reeked of rose perfume with a pregnant younger showgirl.

How could she blame Flo for wanting to be like her? How often were women pitted against each other, like gladiators in an arena forced to fight their way to glory?

"Sit." Andie steered Flo over to the wooden chair, gripping her shoulders and making her plop down onto it. "How many months are you?"

Flo considered the question a moment. "Five, I think."

"Well, you can't keep performing." It was a statement, cool and matter-of-fact. Andie picked up her brush and raked it none too gently through Flo's tangled blonde hair. "If people haven't already noticed, they will soon. You and Syl need to find a place. You can probably stay with Warren, but he…won't be able to sustain you there forever."

"So I just up and quit?" Flo demanded, frustration colouring her tone and her nose wrinkling at the idea.

"You had the opportunity to take care of matters, and you didn't." Andie paused before reaching over to her dresser and picking up the sparkling silver ribbon she had once ripped from Flo's hair. "If you are so determined to be a mother, fine. But you're too far along to continue performing, and I think you already know that."

Flo sighed quietly, examining their reflections in the spotted mirror by their makeup desk as Andie tied the ribbon in Flo's hair, pulling it out of her face.

"I thought you didn't want me wearing this ribbon."

"I didn't." Andie examined how nicely it glittered in Flo's hair. There was no good hanging onto the memory of a dead girl. Flo could have the ribbon now, a gift for the girl who would apparently be the mother of Andie's niece or nephew. "But I've since changed my mind."

A small smile lit up Flo's face as she turned in the chair to glance over her shoulder at Andie. The moment between them was devoid in the animosity they'd shared in the past, and Andie found herself oddly grateful for it. Flo's fingers reached out to pick up her blue dressing gown.

"Maybe you aren't so terrible after all, Alexandra."

Chapter Twenty-Three

Prue Clermont

The presence of the Alderidge brothers at the Midsummer Ball was an itch that Prue couldn't quite scratch, a troubling happenance that grated against her for days before she could fathom the reason. The magical community within New York ran deep, and she wondered when her presence as a Scourge would prick a vein and make the hidden members bleed out of the open wound. Garrett Alderidge was the Governor.

Back when Prue had first attended the Carnival with Sadie, the magic existed within a bubble. She could freely move between the colourless grey of reality and the rainbow beauty of the magical world. Now the lines had blurred, both worlds blending into one, and Prue could no longer see the boundaries. If the Alderidges were aware of the community, certainly other important officials had to be as well.

When she brought it up over breakfast, Sadie's expression closed off in the way that Prue recognised when she had pushed too far in a direction Sadie didn't wish to go. Frustration at Sadie's secrecy emboldened Prue as she cleared the porcelain plates from the table.

"Do you know of other people involved in the community who are important public figures?"

"Prue." The single syllable was weary, Sadie's fingers pinching at the bridge of her nose. When she drew her hand away from her face, her expression was pleading. "What you need to understand is that the people who are part of the magical community don't broadcast it to the public. People like the Alderidges are dangerous."

"Garrett Alderidge is dangerous?" Prue found that difficult to believe. The Governor's public persona was so down to earth, a friendly man who was always smiling. Even at the Midsummer Ball, that affable smile did not slip for an instant.

"Noel is." Sadie leaned forward, hands pressed palms down on the table. "I don't know what he can do, but he has magic of his own."

Prue remembered Noel from the ball, far more unnerving than his older brother. He hadn't even attempted to smile, his serious expression and intense gaze falling upon Andie Fairley more often than not. Not in a lecherous sort of way, but with a hatred that twisted his lips and burned in his eyes.

A thought crept into Prue's mind, taking root like an insidious weed. Whatever power these people had, whatever Sadie feared about them…she could take it away. She may not yet be practised in the use of her terrifying ability, but once she was, she and Sadie would be safe. She wouldn't have to watch her lover make herself smaller every time they were in the room with powerful people, hiding the shame of her heritage behind tight smiles.

"Is that why you're so determined to hide what I am?" Prue demanded, setting the plates in the sink with a clatter. "Because you're afraid of them?"

Sadie's eyes burned like the fire she wielded. "I am *not* afraid of them."

"Then why?" Prue leaned against the sink, folding her arms over her chest. "I told you, I'm tired of hiding who and what I am."

She shed the layers of the woman she'd once been like a snake shed its skin. She had no use for the meek, mild-mannered woman who had accepted her role as a housewife. That woman would never survive in the cutthroat world of magic. The lines between worlds may be blurred, but Prue was certain which one she wanted to be a part of.

She wanted Sadie. Her hunger to be a part of whatever Sadie was involved with gnawed at her stomach like her Scourge ache. Prue was past being careful, tiptoeing around in cautious steps to ensure she wasn't seen or heard. There was a fire that burned within Sadie, and something darker still within Prue.

"I don't want you to *hide*." The word dripped like venom off Sadie's lips. "We need to be careful, though. People like the Seasonal Lords and the Alderidges, they are very good at these kinds of games."

Prue sighed. "What games?"

Sadie rose to her feet. "You met Andie Fairley. Do you think a woman like that gets involved with the inner circle simply by being powerful, or being herself? The reality is, Prue, men don't want women like us there. They will do whatever they can to push us out. That's why you shouldn't reveal what you can do, at least, not yet."

"So when is a good time?" Prue looked around, as if anticipating the exact date and time to bowl her over. "It's been months. You rub shoulders with people like Lord Winter, yet all you can give me is 'not yet'. Don't you realise how frustrating that is, Sadie?"

"Because I need my father's favour!" The words burst from Sadie in a tide of frustration, rendering Prue mute with the painful honesty of them. Bitter shame washed over the auburn-haired woman's face, her pretty face twisting with it and her eyes dropping down to stare at her feet. "He has the power to protect us, offer us the sort of freedom you so desperately desire."

What was left unsaid, but what Prue read between the lines, was that Sadie's father's favour needed to be earned. The idea that Sadie must grovel for it, down on bended knees to beg because she was illegitimate, filled Prue with hot anger. How dare anyone treat Sadie differently because she was born out of wedlock. How dare her father demand more from her, when he was the one to blame.

"Prue." Her fury must have reflected on her face, because Sadie crossed over to catch her hands, fingers linking them together. "I know you don't like this, but this is what the magical world is like. If you want to be a part of it, you need to realise that."

Prue had to accept it. What other choice did she have? She accepted it as it was, with the simmering intention of changing it in the future. She may not be of old magical blood, she may not quite understand the nuances as Sadie did, but she was the first Scourge in centuries. Syl and Sadie's shock bit deep as a knife, but their reactions told her what words did not: Prue had power, and with that power, she hoped to find leverage.

* * *

An insistent hammering upon the front door launched Sadie from her comfortable position on the couch and roused Prue from the romance novel she'd been reading. Carefully marking her page, she let the ache in the pit of her stomach churn, containing her Scourge hunger as best she could. Typically, she realised it only reared up in situations where she was in danger, but she'd felt it on other occasions too. Her greatest fear was that she would snatch power from someone she cared for, like Sadie.

Sadie wrenched open the door, heaving an exasperated sigh and raking her fingers through her auburn hair.

"You can't just turn up whenever you feel like it, Syl."

"I need somewhere safe where she can stay for now." Syl's words made Prue crane her neck for a look at who 'she' was. When Syl's eyes locked onto her, he grinned and waved. "How's it going, Prudence?"

The cheerful greeting made Prue lapse into stunned silence, for the last time she had seen Syl was when he had announced her Scourge abilities. His companion, a young blonde woman of perhaps nineteen or twenty, peered inside. Prue's gaze dropped to the obvious swell of her stomach, where both of her hands rested.

"Come in, then." Sadie waved the pair inside, lips pursed in irritation. By the way Syl's hand rested on the small of the blonde girl's back, Prue suspected she must be his girlfriend.

"Word in private?" Syl asked Sadie, arching an eyebrow. The blonde scowled at them, echoing Prue's sentiment of dissatisfaction with being excluded. It was astounding how many private conversations Sadie had with members connected to the magical community, even if Syl wasn't necessarily amongst the elite.

"Annoying, isn't it?" The blonde remarked, shaking her head slowly as Sadie gestured for Syl to follow her out of the sitting room. Her gaze locked on Prue, and she hoisted a small smile on her features. She was pretty, in a delicate sort of way. "Florence Rafferty. Most people call me Flo."

"Prudence Clermont, but most people call me Prue."

"They really all live like this, don't they?" Flo's contemptuous gaze raked over the sitting room, and Prue could hardly blame her for her disdain for Sadie's well-furnished space. There was dirt beneath Flo's nails, a rough edge to her that made Prue certain she came from a more impoverished background.

"I suppose so." Prue hadn't entered the homes of the members of the magical elite, though she had long suspected that Sadie's father was one of the top tier considering how well-off Sadie was.

"Most of them are liars and charlatans," Flo said, her lip curled in derision as she scoffed, leaning back in her chair and folding her arms over her chest, accentuating the bump of her stomach. "Can't be trusted. Syl's different, though. Andie, too."

Prue was half admiring and half repulsed by Flo's boldness. The younger woman said whatever was on her mind, with a lack of manners or gratitude for where she found herself. She had seen Flo at the Carnival once or twice, but recalled that the young woman lacked the charm and polish that made Andie shine so brightly.

"Is Andie really that different?" Prue questioned, part curiosity and part disbelief. She would have thought a brash young showgirl such as Flo would envy Andie, not speak of her with such approval.

Flo's annoyance shifted into menace, a nasty glint entering her brown eyes and poison lacing her words. "Is Sadie?"

Unease crawled across Prue's skin. Sadie had always seemed different, but was Prue only seeing what she wanted to? Sadie was clearly from wealth, and there were skeletons hidden in closets Prue was scared to open. There was more she didn't know about Sadie than she did, and the shift in her expression made Flo's mean little smile broaden as the doubts Prue had cast over her were returned in kind.

"Good news!" Syl clapped his hands before rubbing them together, the loud sound making Prue start and Flo twist to face him. "Sadie has agreed that you can stay here for a time."

Prue's brow furrowed. Though it was not her place to condone who Sadie allowed to stay, especially considering she had taken Prue in, she could not help but wonder at the oddity of the situation. Were Flo and Syl not together? Why would Flo be staying, and not Syl?

"Thank you, Sadie." Relief lit up Flo's face. "It won't be for long, I promise. Just until Syl finds us a place."

"Of course." There was a tightness to Sadie's smile, her eyes sharp as the bite to Flo's question about whether she was really different. Whatever she and Syl had discussed, the rigidity of her posture indicated she was not entirely thrilled about the arrangement. Her silence on the matter dismayed Prue, who pondered whether Sadie would open a further discussion later, or whether it would be yet another secret locked away in her vault.

'*What are you hiding now, Sadie Crawford?*'

Chapter Twenty-Four

Ursula Delavane

Dot had begun appearing at the Lords' meetings, which Ursula found thoroughly vexing. Cyril tolerated it, of course, but none of them realised the reason for Ursula's presence amongst the absence of the other women in the families. Larkin had been Lord Summer for a small amount of time, still acclimating to the position his father abandoned barely two years ago. Ursula was there to provide guidance. Dot had no place in such meetings, giggling as she perched on the edge of Cyril's chair.

The latest object of contention sat on the Templetons' polished coffee table: the Grimoire. Considered the oldest occult magical volume in existence, the Grimoire was a patchwork of old spells and rituals, ancient magical knowledge, and several baffling pages written in a dead language none of them could decipher. Over the past decades, the Lords had called in all manner of arcane linguistic experts, but all had been left scratching their heads.

"I want Andie to be able to access the Grimoire." Larkin paced back and forth as he spoke, the top few buttons of his shirt undone and his hair ruffled. He had just come from seeing Andie, which left little to Ursula's imagination. No doubt, she had put him up to this.

"No." Sterling's response was swift but firm, and would have cut through any further argument had Larkin not possessed a talent for pushing forward regardless.

"She is the most powerful of us, Sterling. Why doesn't she deserve the opportunity to learn about our history, as we did?"

Desmond remained silent, arms folded over his chest as he leaned back in his chair and observed the oldest and youngest among them bickering. Cyril was too engaged in flirting with Dot to even pay attention.

"The Grimoire is a relic that belongs to the Templeton family." Sterling's eyebrows drew together in a frown. "I am the one who has the final say, and it's a no, Larkin. We have granted Andie privileges beyond what most women of her position are ever able to attain. She still lives in a performers' trailer."

"She can move in with me," Larkin insisted, causing Ursula to grit her teeth. Though she had been the one to push the matter of marriage, she was yet to see a ring on Andie's finger, and did not think it wise to move the girl in with them prematurely.

"Move her where you will. The Grimoire is granted to the Lords alone. Do you see Ursula and Dot pestering to read it?"

A sly smile crossed Ursula's lips as Larkin fumed, lapsing into sullen silence. As grating as Dot's personality could be, she knew her place, as Ursula did. Neither of the women fell for illusions of their own grandeur, or believed they had the same importance as the men within their circle.

Larkin's sharp gaze cut to his mother, but Ursula shook her head. Her son barged out of the room, taking care to slam the door on his way out.

"Andie has that boy wrapped around her little finger." Sterling eased up from the couch with a reproachful look at Ursula. "He is becoming erratic."

Shame burned in Ursula's cheeks as she accepted the fact that some blame belonged to her. As her only child, Larkin had grown up spoiled, never wanting for anything. It was little wonder he now thought he could continue to stamp his foot and get his way. Cyril and Sterling were also from prestigious families, but she had imagined they had settled into their positions with more grace and dignity.

"I do miss Frankie." Cyril removed a tin of cigars from the pocket of his jacket, lighting one up and taking a deep inhale, before blowing out a thick plume of smoke. "He knew how to get things done, you know? I could never see him being so wound up panting after some showgirl. He knew the order of things."

"Cyril!" Dot nudged him sharply, tossing back her hair. "I happen to like Andie."

"I'm sure you do, darling. She's a lovely girl." Cyril handed Dot the cigar, eyes swivelling to Ursula. "But there are wives and there are distractions. Andie has a lot to learn if she wants to be a wife."

Ursula's attention was drawn to the Grimoire, the fading lettering etched onto its cover, the curl of its spine and the yellowed pages within. A strange pull tugged at her fingers, urging her to open it and examine its contents. She dismissed the sudden yearning as a rash curiosity, shaking off the urge and flexing her hands as if to banish it. There was nothing written within the pages of that book she needed to know.

"I miss Frankie too," she murmured. When he'd been alive, there were no whispers of the Magical Freedoms Brigade, no concern that they possessed Excalibur. There was no wilful young woman trying to push her way into the inner circle. There was order, and though the cost was often violence, it had *worked*.

"Well, I'd like some champagne." Cyril leapt up from the couch, swatting Dot on the backside and making her squeak. "Would anyone like to join me?"

"I'd love some champagne!" she piped up, to no one's surprise.

"Alright." Desmond drummed his fingers on the arms of his chair before rising to follow Cyril and Dot into the kitchen.

Ursula waited for their voices to fade into the background, exhaling slowly. She didn't know how long her reckless son could get away with pushing the boundaries with the other Lords. It was different when he'd been a boy with no power or influence throwing his weight around, but after two years, the others didn't fully trust him.

Her gaze latched onto the Grimoire again, the desire to take a look like an itch that needed scratching. Ursula was not typically a slave to her curiosity, but there was something different about this, like the book was calling to her. There was a pull at her navel, a hunger like she'd never experienced before. Staring at the Grimoire made her mouth water, as if she was starved and it was a lush banquet.

An absurd notion, yet one that made her cast around to make sure no one was watching before she picked up the Grimoire and slid it into her lap, flicking through its aged pages. When her hands touched the book, it was as if a bolt of electricity zapped through her, setting her alight with energy.

Her fingers perused the volume of their own accord, mindlessly flipping pages until it came to rest upon the first of the part that baffled the Lords. The ancient scrawl that no linguistic expert had been able to translate—Ursula could read it perfectly, as though it was written in modern English.

What she read horrified her.

There was no single Born Again. There never had been.

The truth was…more complex. Two swords, two destined to wield them. The Morning Star, able to wield the lost Excalibur. The Evening Star, who would be able to pull Clarent from the stone. Their destiny was not one of peace and prosperity, but destruction and disorder of the magical world. An upheaval, an inevitable change.

With his dying breath, Mordred had driven Clarent into the stone, cementing it there until the Evening Star could wield it. Excalibur had been stolen by Guinevere the Scourge, who had fled along with the essences of Arthur, Lancelot and Mordred. She ran to the shore and entered a dark bargain with the Lady of the Lake. The details of the bargain were unclear, though it was said that Excalibur re-entered the Lady of the Lake's keeping.

The Grimoire snapped closed, and Ursula stared down at her shaking hands, her breath emerging in rapid gasps as horror twisted its fingers in the pit of her stomach.

She should never have read it. She should never have been able to read it. There was nothing special about Ursula, nor did she want there to be. She was content with her lot, until the bizarre urge to peer into the Grimoire overcame her. It had been a *prophecy* written in that ancient language, a twisted tale of a Morning Star and Evening Star.

Did any of the others know? She suspected not, since none before her had been able to transcribe the text. It begged so many questions, the most prominent being: why her? Why was she able to read the passages, when so many others had tried and failed? It filled her with a sense of disquiet, making her set the Grimoire back down on the coffee table and steady her trembling hands.

She sat uneasily with the knowledge, trying her best to stop it from consuming her like a tidal wave. There was no good in panicking over centuries-old words, not when she wasn't certain what it all meant. She focused on what she did know, the details she didn't have to overthink, the warning clear on old paper.

Morning Star. Evening Star.
They will destroy us.

Chapter Twenty-Five

Andie Fairley

Mid-September brought about cooler weather, stormy skies, and Andie's twenty-second birthday. Though insistent she didn't want much to acknowledge the occasion, Larkin was resolute upon a grand lunch with the Lords and their families. Despite knowing the gesture was made of kindness, unease gnawed at the pit of Andie's stomach at the thought of more judgemental eyes than usual.

Traipsing into the Delavane residence with more confidence than she felt, Andie smoothed her hands down her blue silk dress, a gift from Larkin that paired beautifully with the pearls around her neck and sparkling silver makeup she'd adorned her eyes with. Dot shrieked when she saw her, running over to throw her arms around Andie.

"Happy birthday, darling!"

"Thank you, Dot." Of those present, Dot was one of the few whose presence neither grated harshly against Andie, nor raised her temper. The women linked arms and strode into the sitting room, where several small children Andie had never seen quarrelled over toys on the floor. A man and woman in their mid-thirties argued in the corner, and a brunette woman of about Dot's age took a drag of her cigarette as she watched the children with utter disinterest.

"These are Sterling's grandchildren." Dot gestured vaguely, leaning in to murmur conspiratorially. "I'd tell you their names, but to be frank, I can't recall. There are so many of them."

There were five in total, none much older than ten. Andie resisted the urge to wrinkle her nose, following Dot through into the dining room. Leaving the yelling of the children behind was a weight lifted off Andie's shoulders, for she had dreaded the idea of attempting to appeal to them.

"Don't you look stunning?" Larkin strode over, examining Andie with a wide grin. "Give us a twirl."

She spun like a top on her toes, briefly reminded of the awful days in the streets of Hell's Kitchen when she'd danced for money. Larkin caught her arms and steadied her, toying with the string of pearls around her neck.

"Happy birthday, Andie."

"There are so many people." She lowered her voice. "Why are Sterling's grandchildren here?"

"Well, you're practically part of the family now." Larkin pressed a kiss to her cheek, taking her hand in hers. The aroma of rosemary roast lingered in the air, mingling with spiced vegetables. In another room, she heard the cork pop of a champagne bottle. The cacophony mingling with the various scents made Andie's head spin. She was used to crowds, but she hadn't anticipated everyone bringing their whole family for lunch.

"Come sit, dear girl!" Sterling's ruddy complexion spoke to an abundance of alcohol as Larkin and Andie entered the dining room. Desmond sat beside the eldest of the Lords, a fizzing glass of champagne in his hand. Jane hurried in with more crystal glasses bubbling to the brim, and Larkin took one each for him and Andie.

She raised the glass to her lips and took a deep gulp, knowing she would need several more if she was to tolerate the presence of a drunk Sterling and screaming children.

"Happy birthday, Andie." Desmond finished his glass of champagne, leaning back in his seat. "A little loud, isn't it?"

"I admit, I'm not used to so many children." Andie lowered her glass, tucking a curl behind her ear.

"Well, it would be a good experience," Sterling said, wagging a finger as though she was a naughty little girl.

"Pardon?" Andie's brow furrowed as she struggled to interpret the meaning of his words.

"For when you have your own, of course."

The bold assumption made Andie want to throw the rest of her champagne in Sterling's smug face, but she valiantly resisted the urge and tossed her hair back, laughing like he'd said something funny.

"Oh! That's not…that's something I don't…"

"It will be your role." Sterling studied Andie with growing confusion, eyes flicking to Larkin who merely shrugged his shoulders. "Why do you think we agreed to let you obtain soul magic? Certainly some day soon, Larkin will pop the question. You'd do well to follow Ursula and Dot's example, they're both excellent housewives."

"Excuse me?" There was steel in Andie's words and spine as she stared down the arrogant old man before her. Unfortunately, Sterling prattled on as though he hadn't heard her, or perhaps he simply ignored her.

"That's what the women do, girl. Maintain the household, continue the family line, and in your case, gift your future husband magic, since yours is so much more powerful than his."

Larkin tensed beside Andie, and when she rested her hand on his arm, he brushed her off. His pale blue eyes were fixed on Sterling, a sneer contorting his lips. There was venom coating his tongue, and he was ready to unleash it upon the oldest of the Seasonal Lords, whose own tongue apparently never knew silence.

Sterling's words caused as much damage as a car crash, not only infuriating Andie but wounding Larkin's pride in the same instance. The old fool had said aloud what all of them had only ever thought in private: that Andie's magic far surpassed Larkin's, something they'd never considered when they'd agreed for her to undergo the ritual.

"What about Penelope?" Larkin's answering words were cold as December and soft as silk, the undercurrent of sheer malice making Andie's stomach coil with trepidation. "She was more powerful than you, wasn't she? It hardly stopped you from bleeding her dry, sucking down every drop of magic you could squeeze from her."

Panic defeated Andie's cool, calm facade in a moment. It caught her in a vice-like grip, dragging her under and making her stumble from the room before the others could see it in her face. Moving quickly down the corridor, she pushed into a powder room and gripped the edges of the sink, staring down at the drain as her breath came in ragged pants and her vision spun like a merry-go-round.

The taps squeaked in protest as she turned them on, splashing cool water over her face, the moisture a soothing balm on her skin. A rap on the door made her spin around, Larkin lounging in the doorway with raised eyebrows and a cold expression that didn't suit his handsome face.

"What are you doing, Andie?"

"I needed a break." She waved an accusatory hand in the general direction of the others. "You heard Sterling, rambling on about matrimony and motherhood. Just because that's all some women care about…"

"That's what society is." Frustration coloured Larkin's tone, fingers reaching up to tug through his blonde hair. "You've been granted more power than most people dream of, and you're complaining about having to fit into your role?"

"My role?" Disbelief laced Andie's voice, sharp anger searing through her with the burning heat of a fireworks display. Larkin loved her, and he respected her, enough that he'd ensured she could undergo the Soul Ritual. Why was she only just realising now, when she should have before, that his love would come with a cost?

Larkin moved into the powder room, closing the door behind him. Andie took an involuntary step backward, pain racing up her side as she bumped her hip hard against the sink. The disappointment in her lover's eyes made her wish the floor would swallow her whole, but she violently shoved the feeling away. What did she have to be ashamed of, or guilty for?

"You've been honest with me about a lot.," Larkin admitted, reaching up to cup her face in his hands, thumbs gently caressing her cheeks. "The others questioned your worth, but I never did. Not even when you told me about what happened with Claire."

"Murderer." Noel's sneers ricocheted through Andie's mind, and her stomach twisted with the sick shame of what she had done. No matter how much she tried, there was never any escaping it, not even with all this new power.

"So, I want to be honest with you in return." Larkin's eyes were bright and hard as cold steel. "You've probably heard the others talking about my father, Franklin. How it was such a shame he died during the war, and likely a shock too since he was a ranking officer by virtue of his birth. It wasn't a shame, and it wasn't a shock. My father was an abusive piece of shit."

Venom and violence brewed in Larkin's words. Andie didn't think she had ever heard him speak with such hatred, a loathing that stiffened his shoulders and made his fingers tighten on her face.

"In October 1918, Franklin Delavane arrived in New York on the 2am train, where I met him at the station and shot him in the head."

There was nothing but savage triumph in the words, no lingering guilt, no remorse. Larkin had truly *hated* his father.

"It wasn't easy. It goes against our laws for Lords to murder each other, or for an heir to murder a current Lord. Cyril sensed a chance for a new beginning, though. He helped me cover my tracks, and paid for a telegram to be sent to my dear mother. There were no witnesses to the murder, so disposing of the body wasn't difficult."

"Why…" Andie's voice cracked with dread. She grimaced at the tightness of his grip on her face. "Why are you telling me this?"

"So that we understand one another." A chilling smile spread across Larkin's lips, the hollowness of his eyes sending shivers up Andie's spine. "We're both killers, Andie. We both have heart magic, so we've both betrayed people. We have to rely on each other, and trust each other. That means we *both* need to follow the rules."

Once, Andie could see Larkin's intentions written out plain as day, but truth and lies mingled until she no longer knew which was which. Had he really told her about Franklin to gain her trust, or to gain her fear and compliance? Maybe it was a combination of both, a dangerous mix designed to keep her close, a puppeteer tying strings back onto her hands and feet just as she'd sliced them free.

She had been arrogant, too self-assured of Larkin's feelings and absorbed in her own ambitions. She had stepped on the shattered edges of his own fragile ego without wondering what was cutting her. Too focused on attaining her own goals, Andie never considered the price tag.

"Freshen up," Larkin commanded as he pressed a chaste kiss to her forehead. "They're almost ready to eat."

He let go of her face and strode from the powder room, the door clicking shut behind him. The chatter and laughter filtered in from outside, reminding Andie that while time seemed to stand still for her, the world continued to spin.

When Andie thought of Claire's death, nausea bubbled in the pit of her stomach. Shame washed hot over her body, and guilt was a bitter taste underneath her tongue. When Larkin had mentioned his father's death, there was *pride* in his voice, as though the event was a banner of victory he could only wave in secret.

Tears pricked at Andie's eyes, and she pressed a hand over her mouth to muffle a sob. The Lords wanted her to put on a mask, to be someone she was not, to accept the poisoned chalice of matrimony and motherhood. Larkin…she had believed he was different, that he valued her freedom as fiercely as she did.

Now, there was a single question that echoed in her head, repeated over and over again: what *did* Larkin want?

* * *

The Vault was spoken of with reverence amongst the Lords, so expectation weighed heavily upon Andie's shoulders when Larkin announced they would visit, a magnificent end to a less than ideal birthday. The walk through Central Park was unnervingly silent, the weight of Larkin's confession bearing down heavily upon them both. Andie shrugged her thick grey coat tighter around herself as Larkin took her down a hidden passage behind Belvedere Castle, the descent into shadow making anxiety gnaw at her fingers and toes.

"I wanted you to see Clarent in person." Larkin seized Andie's hand, leading her into a circular stone basement with gas-lit lamps. It was cold in the basement, so cold that Andie's breath misted in front of her as the saturation of magic washed over her. It tingled across her skin and tugged at her navel, urging her closer to the sword that gleamed in the low golden light.

"I can feel it.," Andie whispered, wonder and horror harmonising within her as she stared hungrily at Clarent. It was a plain sword, lacking the ornamental beauty of those Cyril Fordyce liked to display in his sitting room. Whispers in the dark prickled up the back of her neck, though she could not hear what they were saying.

"They call it the Traitor's Blade." Larkin's voice resonated through the basement. When he grinned at Andie, the dancing light gave his teeth a feral gleam. "Mordred used this sword to slay King Arthur."

"This is the one they say the Born Again will pull from the stone?" Andie asked, shifting closer to examine it. She held little stock in the devout beliefs of the Arthurian legends that the Lords clung to, but this sword was something real. Power, ancient and dark, rolled off it in waves. It coiled over her skin, like an invisible snake waiting to bear fangs.

"You should try it." Larkin gestured to Clarent. The delight in his expression shifted into solemnness. Andie did not have to ask to know why: Larkin had attempted to pull Clarent from the stone, and he had failed. A question and an answer, both lingering in the darkness, untouched.

Andie's body resisted, her feet dragging as warning bells pulsed through her. Disregarding the oddity of the sensation, she stubbornly nudged such thoughts aside and strode forward, determination pushing her into gear. If she was the Born Again, none of them would ever challenge her again. What was a wife and mother, in comparison to Clarent's chosen?

'*Didn't you think that before the Soul Ritual?'* A nasty little voice in her head asked.

Stealing in a deep breath, Andie's fingers fluttered over the hilt of the sword, before closing around it.

The soft whispers that lingered on the periphery of Andie's consciousness ascended into screams. Her fingers clutched around the hilt of the sword as though glued there by an invisible force. Agony seared through her veins, a harsh punishment for her unbridled greed. An ancient evil stirred in the shadows, faceless, nameless. Its presence was all around her, suffocating her until she forgot how to breathe.

Sheer terror caught hold of Andie, the *wrongness* of Clarent beneath her fingers. She reeled back, stumbling away from the sword until she collided with something solid. Larkin gripped her arms, spinning her to face him. As her panic faded, the rawness of her throat made her realise she had been screaming, too.

"Andie, are you alright?" He swept her hair back from her face, concern etching his features as he looked her over. "That was…I've never seen that happen when someone tries to touch Clarent."

"That sword is cursed," Andie choked out, jabbing a trembling finger at it. She couldn't explain what had come over her, a surge of powerful magic that wanted to drag her into oblivion. The moment she had touched Clarent, it converged on her, thousands of blades tearing into her without leaving a scratch.

"I hoped it was you." There was no mistaking the dismay in Larkin's voice, agitating Andie as she tugged away from him. Larkin could find no glory of his own, so he wanted to attain it through her. How marvellous it would be for him, to have a wife with a nine on the Templeton Scale and the sword Clarent.

"Well, I don't know who your *Born Again* is, but it's not me.," Andie snarled, fingers curling into fists. "I will never touch that fucking sword again."

Anger boiled through her, along with the bitter disappointment that it wasn't her. What was she destined for, if not greatness? Why would she have such powerful magic, if not to become something more? Yet Clarent had rejected her, violently and permanently. The flames of the lamps flickered, and died as one, plunging The Vault into darkness.

"Andie…" Larkin's voice was barely more than a whisper, but it brought her back to where she was and the fact that a soft glow permeated the shadows. When she gazed down at her trembling hands, she realised the light was coming from her, radiating off her and growing stronger and warmer by the moment like she was the sun.

Her gift. Her calling. The unique power she had obtained along with her soul magic. Larkin always told her how bright she burned, and now it was literal. He shielded his eyes from the strength of her light. The heat of it thrummed away within Andie, and she had no doubt that if she reached out to touch him, she would sizzle him to slivers.

"*This is what I am, Larkin Delavane,*" she wanted to tell him, "*not a wife or a mother, but divinity.*"

There were monsters in the darkness. She felt them when she touched Clarent, and saw them in Noel's cold eyes. Yet she was the light, and she would devour them whole.

Chapter Twenty-Six

Prue Clermont

Flo proved an interesting house guest, and through her, Prue learned more of the Carnival. Though vexed by the growing physical limitations she faced due to her growing pregnancy, Flo was all too eager to help out around the place with cooking and cleaning. She would often sing as she did so, her voice a pretty trill that carried through Sadie's apartment and breathed fresh life into it.

Sadie had offered no more insight into the reason for Flo's stay other than that the young woman needed a temporary refuge while Syl found a more appropriate place for them. Syl visited every few days, a whirlwind of charm and colour, occasionally accompanied by the scent of alcohol. He fussed over Flo, which resulted in her scowling and attempting to bat him away as though she found him overbearing.

A sharp rap on the door made Prue and Flo look up. They had been turning over the sheets on Flo's bed set up in what had once been Sadie's office but now functioned as a spare bedroom. The younger woman rolled her eyes, though a smile tweaked at the corners of her lips in anticipation of her lover showing up. Footsteps creaked across the floor as Sadie went to answer the door. Instead of Syl's boisterous tone, there were quiet murmurs that prompted Prue to peer out from the spare bedroom.

"...want to know what she can do. This isn't a request, Miss Crawford."

"How do the Alderidges know anything?" Sadie hissed, tensing when she realised that Prue and Flo were listening from the doorway. She heaved a sigh, tilting her head back so that her auburn hair spilled down her back. "You two can come out. These are some associates of mine."

A pair of men dressed in tweed coats, button-up shirts and bracers lingered in the doorway. Their expressions were pleasant enough, though Prue could not shake the feeling that they rather looked like gangsters with their caps pulled low over their heads. Sadie ushered them inside, closing the door behind them.

"This is Nigel and Lachlan."

Nigel, the one with the ginger handlebar moustache, smiled slightly.

"We're here to see Mrs Clermont. Governor Alderidge and his brother want a word."

Prue paused, her fingers tightening around the door handle to the spare room. The Governor wanted to speak with her? When her eyes locked onto Sadie, her partner would not meet her gaze, and Prue's jaw set as the truth spelled itself out.

"You've told people about what I am."

Hurt roiled like acid in Prue's stomach. She'd trusted Sadie. It had been Sadie who'd urged her to be cautious in the first place, and now it turned out that her secret was no longer a secret at all.

"I only told some close friends of mine." Sadie threw Nigel a poisonous look. "Certainly not the Alderidge brothers."

He shrugged, undeterred. "Word gets around, Miss Crawford. You of all people should know that."

Lachlan moved swiftly as a striking snake, seizing hold of Sadie's wrists. She cried out as he latched something metallic around them, yanking back to examine what appeared to be a thick set of steel handcuffs. Prue nudged Flo behind her, the younger woman's fingers tightly gripping at Prue's sleeve.

"We have to take precautions, you see." Nigel's tone was calm as Sadie gritted her teeth and struggled with the restraints. "Your fire magic isn't going to push through iron that thick."

It had never occurred to Prue that there was anything that could suppress magic. Was there something else in the restraints, or was it simply being bound by iron that prevented Sadie using her abilities. Once, she would have cowered away from these men in fear, but she moved forward despite Flo hissing at her not to.

"Gentlemen, what's the meaning of this?"

"We know what you are, Scourge." Nigel strode toward her, and the threat of imminent violence made Prue flinch but stand her ground. The familiar hunger reared up within her, a craving begging to be indulged. Flo yelped as Lachlan approached her, and she backed against the kitchen bench. Sadie snarled as she wrestled with her restraints, eyes flaring with anger.

"I don't intend to hurt anyone." Prue held her hands high in surrender. She could hear Flo sobbing behind her, and glanced over her shoulder to see Flo had one arm flung in front of her, hand out-stretched as if to ward Lachlan off.

Nigel sighed deeply. "Well, that's a shame, because we do."

He reached for Prue, but she was faster. Instead of fighting her arcane hunger, she set it free, reaching out to grip Nigel's arm in a vice-like grasp. Horror twisted his expression, and the hunger shifted to a tugging feeling, like she was reaching inside him and pulling out his organs. His face paled and a high, thin scream tore from his throat.

Nigel sank to his knees, but Prue kept a tight hold on the power she stole from him. It coursed through her like wildfire, setting her alight and sating the ache she had ignored for so long. It danced across her fingers and tingled against the palm of her hand. She could hold onto it, store it away within her to save. Instead, she dug into it and tore it apart, the magic fading and dying as it was ripped to shreds, discarded like invisible paper.

"*No!*" Nigel howled, the despair jarring Prue and pulling her hard into reality, where the dread of having extinguished someone's magic settled into her bones. She staggered back, shocked, as Nigel doubled over as though she'd landed a punch to the gut.

With a roar of rage, Lachlan whirled on Prue, seizing hold of her and slamming her against the wall so hard her head ricocheted off the plaster. Prue's vision blurred in and out, her head spinning as she tried desperately to reach back into her relentless power. Nigel crawled across the floor toward the hearth, where Sadie crouched to heat the metal on her wrists over the flames.

The crack of a gunshot sliced through the apartment. Prue flinched and screwed her eyes shut as something warm and wet splattered across her face, and in panic, she pushed past the adrenaline to pick at any sources of pain. None, except the throbbing in the back of her head. Opening her eyes, Prue stared down at Lachlan's body slumped at her feet, a jagged wound passing through his skull.

Pressing a hand over her mouth to quell the rising bile, her eyes flicked to Flo, whose calm demeanour and tear-stained face were in strict opposition to each other as she lowered the Colt Derringer in her hand.

A strangled cry by the hearth made Prue spin on her heel. Sadie had a knee pressed into Nigel's back on the carpet, metal restraints looped around his neck. Nigel's fingers fumbled around in the pocket of his trousers, before he extracted a key and slid it to her. With a relieved smile, Sadie scooped up the key and set about undoing her restraints.

"Where did you get the gun?" Prue asked, carefully avoiding looking at Lachlan as she observed Flo. The younger woman kicked off the kitchen bench, shrugging her shoulders and stowing the Colt Derringer back in the second drawer.

"It was Andie's. She doesn't seem to need it anymore, so I brought it with me."

With a click, Sadie freed her wrists and grabbed hold of Nigel's bracers, hauling him to his feet. Her eyes burned with disdain and lips twisted in disgust as she marched him over to the front door and wrenched it open.

"Get the fuck out of my sight."

Nigel scurried out without another word or backwards glance, though Prue's brow furrowed at how lightly he got off when Lachlan's corpse still bled crimson through the carpet.

"Is that smart?"

"Oh, he'll tell everyone what happened." Sadie slammed the door shut, locking it with more force than was necessary. "He has no magic, and a Scourge stole it from him. I doubt others like him will be eager to hunt down a woman who can not only take their magic from them, but wipe it from existence."

The metallic odour of blood clogged Prue's nostrils, and she stumbled over to vomit in the kitchen sink. Her fingers clutched tight at the steel rim, as tight as they'd fastened on Nigel's essence. The stench of death and destruction permeated the apartment. Prue wiped her mouth on the back of her hand, turning the tap on to clear out the sink.

"You want to tell us what the fuck is going on?" Flo demanded, echoing the sentiments Prue had yet to voice. "You knew those men, and they knew the Alderidges."

Sadie sank into a couch in front of the fire, the flames illuminating the tiredness in her pale complexion. Her eyes locked onto Lachlan and she clicked her fingers, fire rising up on his clothes and greedily consuming his corpse before winking from existence in a puff of smoke. The ashes remained, wafting in the air, mingling with the blood all over the carpet. Sadie may dispose of the body in a moment, but the stains of what they had done were harder to remove.

"I mentioned Prue to a handful of people I trusted. As I said, I have no idea how the Alderidges got word of it, but it's not good."

"So the entire magical community could know about me now?" Prue asked. Her stomach lurched again, though free from any contents it might wish to discard. Trepidation traced cool fingers up her arms, raising the hairs there.

"I don't know." Sadie pinched her brow. When she dropped her hand from her face, determination gave her expression a grim cast. "We've been on the back foot this whole time, trying to hide what Prue is. There's no hiding it anymore, not now Prue's destroyed someone's essence."

Prue waited for the guilt to squirm within her, to make her feel small and ashamed. It never did. Realisation reached out to her, like the whisper of cool winter wind. She didn't regret what she had done, because deep down, there was the awareness that Nigel deserved what had happened to him. The man had come into Sadie's home with the intention of harm, and Prue had removed any power he had and left him an empty shell.

The strength of her ability was a warm cloak around her shoulders, a confident notion that the elite didn't despise her, but *feared* her. Many amongst them had powerful magic, but Prue could render it null and void in moments. Her ability was taking power, in both their magic and the influence that went with it, and the weight of what that meant made Prue's head spin and her knees tremble.

"So, what do we do?" Prue's voice was hoarse as she asked, but more serene than she felt.

"The Alderidges wanted a word." A sly smile crossed Sadie's lips as she leaped up from the couch. "I say we oblige them."

The danger dancing in Sadie's eyes made Prue's heart flutter, but beneath the surface, unease took root and began to grow like a weed. What had Sadie said about her, and to who? How did Prue know for a fact that she could trust her, no matter how much her heart yearned for her? The truth came in a dissonant whisper in the back of her mind.

"You can't."

Chapter Twenty-Seven
Ursula Delavane

Ursula had not seen the Alderidge brothers since the Midsummer Ball, and even then, their interactions were civil and scarce. When Noel Alderidge invited her out for high tea, Ursula was pleased, though guarded. Noel was not the sort of man to engage in social pleasantries unless it had meaning. He lacked Garrett's easy charm and smooth tongue, far more prone to seriousness and blunt words. It was that knowledge that pushed Ursula to certainty that the high tea was a guise for a deeper endeavour.

Taylor's Tea Parlour was situated overlooking most of Manhattan, a breathtaking view only eclipsed by the quality of floral tea and cream cakes served. Ursula offered gracious smiles and thanked the staff, while Noel mumbled a word of thanks under his breath as he sipped at his earl grey.

"The food here is lovely." She helped herself to a scone with clotted cream and jam, prising it apart neatly with her knife and fork. "Do you frequent such places often, Mr Alderidge?"

"Not particularly." Noel set down his white china mug unceremoniously. "I wanted to speak with you about something Garrett and I have learned."

Ursula arched an eyebrow, fork pausing over her cake. The Lords kept the Alderidge brothers close, but did not involve them directly in their business. If Noel was seeking a loose-lipped woman who would eagerly spill the Lords' secrets, he would have been better off asking Dot. Yet Noel was clever, and he hadn't asked Dot, which meant it was Ursula's word he trusted.

"What might that be?"

Noel picked up one of the strawberry tarts. "We have heard word of a Scourge living in New York City."

Ursula's skin crawled, the same way as it had when she had interpreted the prophecy in the Grimoire. Unease rippled up her spine. There hadn't been a Scourge for centuries, and if one existed now, it was her first time hearing of it. Though she schooled her features into a neutral expression, the tug at the corner of Noel's lips told her the momentary shock on her face had been noted.

"Ah. You were not aware either."

Irritation seared through Ursula, hotter than the cherry blossom tea she took a sip from.

"What is it you want to know, Mr Alderidge?"

"Noel." A placid smile crossed his mouth. "Please, call me Noel."

"Noel, then." The familiarity of using his given name felt odd on her tongue, a sour taste that contrasted with the sweetness of the cakes. "What do you think I can tell you about this Scourge?"

"Nothing, apparently." Noel leaned back in his chair. "Though I am curious to know your opinion."

Ursula paused, brows creasing. Men didn't ask for her opinions, for they were mostly unwarranted. Being asked specifically what she thought made her uneasy, suspicion slithering up her spine like a worm through the dirt. Why would Noel want her opinion, when he could ask for that of the Lords?

"A Scourge could be a useful weapon," she mused. It had been some time since any amongst the elite had been stripped of their magic through a Scourge Ritual, a punishment reserved for only the most severe of crimes. With a Scourge, the ritual itself could be bypassed, magic taken without the intricacies.

"Hmm." Noel picked up one of the tarts. "Well, I believe there's only one good sort of Scourge. A dead one."

The hardness in his eyes and the venom in his words gave Ursula pause. Rumours often swirled about the nature of Noel's magic, and the whispers crept close to the truth of it. A man who had little to offer magically would not be so concerned about a Scourge. A man who possessed a great deal of it? Well, he would have every right to be terrified.

"Your daughter, Claire…" Noel's eyes sliced to her, sharp and ready to cut. "I heard your brother saying she was talented with mind magic."

Ursula did not mention that it was improper for a young lady to be practising magic, especially when that magic should have been reserved for more important matters. Then again, who amongst them had not engaged in teenage rebellion? Unfortunately for Claire, hers had ended in tragedy.

"She was." The words were guarded, Noel's fingers curling tiger around his cup. She could not imagine the pain of losing one's only child in such a brutal manner. It was an agony that Noel carried as an open wound. Impulsively, she reached over and rested her fingers lightly over his.

"Which I assume she inherited from you."

Noel glanced down at her hand, raising a brow. "An interesting assumption. If you want answers about my magic, you might simply ask. Too many people speak in whispers without bothering to pose the question."

Cheeks flashing with heat, Ursula drew her fingers away as though they'd been scalded. She did not enjoy feeling foolish, nor did she like being treated as a curious child. Nonetheless, she folded her arms and examined him with a frown.

"So why don't you enlighten me on what you can do, then?"

"Telepathy." Noel finished his cake, expression turning thoughtful. "Particularly mind control. You can see why people would be wary, and why it's not something I openly share. It leads to assumptions about me, and about Garrett, that I'd rather avoid."

The Governor of New York, whose younger brother had the ability to control people's minds. Yes, Ursula could see how that would be viewed as problematic. Her eyes flicked to an ugly white scar cording down Noel's lower arm, before he fixed his sleeves to cover it. How could she judge Noel's magic, when she had so recently discovered her own ability to read the Grimoire? They all had their secrets, after all, some darker than others.

"So you want to get rid of the Scourge because you're afraid?"

The words pricked at his pride the way she had intended, judging by the scowl that crossed his lips. Men considered fear a weakness, as though they'd never stared fear in the eye before. Ursula considered it a tool, useful for wielding at one's discretion. To claim one never experienced fear was to lie.

"Not afraid," he snapped. "She's a threat, and I prefer threats eliminated, rather than left to run around until they can do the eliminating."

The twist of Ursula's lips became smug. "Does your concern about this Scourge eclipse your disdain for Andie?"

"Everyone knows what she is now." Noel scratched his arm, poison biting into his words. "Perhaps not the whole truth, since she's clearly told a different version. Enough to know that she's a murderer."

"You expected them to cast her aside for it?" Ursula set her napkin down on the table, incredulous at how a man with so much worldly experience could be so naive. "We all have blood on our hands, Noel. Casting Andie aside for it would mean exploring parts of ourselves we'd rather leave in the shadows."

"Oh, I never thought they'd cast her aside." A dark gleam entered Noel's eyes, his fingers curling into fists. "Not when your darling boy Larkin is so utterly charmed by her. But our charming little Miss Fairley has a darker heart than even he realises. One day, she will suffer for it."

"By your hand?" Ursula recognised a man possessed, so utterly consumed that it may destroy him. Vengeance twisted Noel, the disinterested Governor's brother morphing into a creature far more dangerous whenever Andie's name fell from someone's lips.

"I certainly hope so." The intensity of Noel's stare made Ursula want to sink into her seat, but instead she mustered up a tight smile. "I would hate for anyone to get in my way, Ursula."

Monsters roamed New York City in pretty dresses and tailored suits. Most of their names Ursula was familiar with: Andie Fairley, Noel Alderidge. Once you knew something's true nature, it failed to be unpredictable and lost the element of surprise. The monsters that did frighten Ursula were the ones lingering in the darkness. Faceless, nameless.

The Scourge.

∗ ∗ ∗

With the whirlwind success of Andie undergoing the Soul Ritual, Larkin was kept busy. Most nights he crept into the house in the early hours of the morning, the floorboards creaking as he slipped into his room as if he was a mischievous child avoiding curfew and not the man of the house. Sometimes, he brought Andie home with him, their laughter seeping through the walls, mocking the silence Ursula valued so highly.

Drinks, parties, drugs. Had Frankie been any different when he was twenty-six? Ursula supposed she had been, because Larkin was a toddler at that point. Her wild days didn't exactly end once she became a mother, but having a child did impede them. Frankie had come and gone as he pleased, reeking of tobacco and brandy. It had been up to Ursula to mind Larkin, or else make sure there was someone else who could. Whatever responsibilities Frankie had as Lord Summer, he had very few as a parent.

When Larkin swaggered in with a waft of lilac perfume, earlier than usual at 10pm, Ursula was in a mind to put her foot down. Setting down the embroidery she had been working on, she practically launched herself from the couch, critically assessing Larkin's dishevelled shirt and red-rimmed eyes.

"When are you going to start acting in a respectable manner?" She demanded as he tossed his jacket onto the coat rack with a loud sigh. "You are Lord Summer. You can't be out partying every night…"

"Mother, you are so unaware of my business that it's ridiculous." Larkin raised his voice slightly to drown her out, folding his arms over his chest and staring contemptuously at her. "You know for a fact that Cyril and Dot are out all over town until the early hours of the morning, more often than I am."

"Larkin, I only mean…" Ursula stole in a deep breath, wondering how to phrase her thoughts tactfully. "You need to settle down. Take things seriously."

Larkin rolled his eyes. "Desmond is thirty-three and unwed, I don't see you hounding on him."

"Yes, well, I'm hardly *Desmond's* mother."

"I went out after a business meeting." Larkin fished around in his pocket until he pulled out a tin of cigars. "That's all."

"What business?" Apprehension bit at Ursula's steely demeanour, uncertainty creeping in through the cracks. When it was Lords' business, she was invited to attend. If it was something else, she wondered what Larkin was getting himself into.

"We were discussing the Magical Freedoms Brigade, if you must know." Larkin struck a match and lit up his cigar, taking a puff. "It hardly involves you. Haven't you realised by now? They've stopped inviting you, Mother."

His voice took on a malicious tone that set Ursula on edge. A mocking smile crossed Larkin's lips as he pushed his cigar back between his lips, confident in the knowledge he'd successfully rattled her.

Trepidation prickled along Ursula's scalp. Since Larkin had succeeded his father, she'd accompanied him to the meetings. No longer being invited was disquieting, to say the least. Panic seized her as she wondered whether one of them knew about the Grimoire. If they knew she could read the prophecies, she'd never be invited back again. Perhaps they'd drag her along just to have her interpret for them.

"We know who the spy is now." Larkin put out his cigar in an ashtray, his nonchalant tone defying the deliberateness of his actions. "Sterling told us all about his contact. An interesting choice, but I suppose that's what makes sense about it."

"What of the leader?" Ursula demanded, clutching at any information she could. "What of Excalibur?"

Larkin merely shrugged his shoulders. He was toying with her, dangling his authority like a cat would a mouse. What had Larkin done, Ursula wondered, to prove that he no longer needed his mother there? It was only a matter of time before Ursula was cut out, but she wondered when the final incision had been made.

"Nothing yet."

Instead of Ursula's input, they wanted an idealistic boy. Could things be changing so much that Larkin's word was considered valuable? She inhaled the ash of the cigar, and wondered if she had underestimated her son after all. If any of them had pushed to shut her out, it would have been him.

"Do smile, Mother." Larkin flashed her a triumphant grin laden with spite. "We will have much to celebrate soon."

"Such as?" Ursula demanded, her irritability tangible in the hostility of her words.

"An engagement." Larkin paused halfway up the staircase. "I'm proposing to Andie."

Relief coursed through Ursula, as warm and welcome as a relaxing bath, soothing the muscles of her body. At last, Larkin was embarking on a sensible endeavour. Though she could not say how she would cope with Andie as a daughter-in-law, the young woman would be surrounded on all sides. She would learn to survive, or she would suffocate.

Chapter Twenty-Eight

Andie Fairley

One thing Andie missed since she'd gained soul magic was her days as a showgirl. She was still certainly paid as one, as she was adamant that even if she was conducting fewer performances, she would still be getting her usual pay or else she'd simply take it back up. However, it seemed that the elite frowned upon a young woman who was essentially one of them donning sparkly costumes and beguiling smiles for large crowds. They were not, she noticed, averse to her still living in her trailer. The emptiness now that Flo had moved out was palpable, a silence that stretched on and made Andie brim with anxious energy.

She thought she may even *miss* Flo. At least with the younger girl around, there had been banter between them, sharp thought it might have been on her part. Without the shows to look forward to or Flo to vex, the loneliness crept its way in and coiled up in her heart, nesting there with all its malevolent intentions. Though she may keep company with New York's finest, the critical looks and contemptuous smiles made Andie wonder if she would ever feel that she fit in.

Not that she would ever let them see it. As she bounded around the Carnival with her arm firmly linked through Dot's, onlookers would see Andie's radiant smile and hear her gleeful giggles. They would see the confident set of her shoulders and believe she owned the world. Andie had put on performances for years, what difference was a new one? None of them would ever guess at the frantic hammering of her heart and the way her breath caught in her throat, her head spinning like she was dizzy.

Andie nibbled at her pink cotton candy as she and Dot strode over to the Ferris wheel, glimmering with multicoloured lights. When she craned her neck back, she could see beyond the lights of the Carnival to the stars above. She had wanted so desperately to be one of the elite, so why did she dream of dancing?

"Andie, there you are!" Larkin sauntered over to the pair with a bright smile on his lips and a sparkle in his eye. Andie released Dot and threw her arms around him, shrieking as he picked her up and spun her around. Another show, of course. The sort that made people around them gush adoringly, while Andie saw how he burned with resentment at the strength of her magic.

Since Andie's birthday dinner, there was a shadow behind Larkin's eyes. Since being reminded that she was more powerful than him, his smile was more strained, his fingers just a little too tight when he caught hold of her. It was truly astounding, just how much mere words could shatter Larkin's confidence and cause jealousy to take root deep within him.

Larkin always said she shone bright as the sun. He was right, he had just become envious of her time in the spotlight.

Of course he cared about her. Of course he brought her flowers and expensive clothes. Yet beneath that love for her was an insidious undercurrent she found it hard to look at too closely. Larkin fell for her when she was beholden to him, and their dynamic had shifted when she gained her own soul magic.

"Have you and Dot been enjoying your adventures?" Larkin asked, pressing a kiss to her forehead when she nodded fervently. "Good. I was hoping that I could borrow you for a moment."

"Always." Andie beamed, her magic washing over her skin like warm water. She let it bathe her in its tingling sensation, her body taking on the slightest hint of a golden glow. Larkin's smile faded a fraction, before he clasped her hands in his. His thumbs rubbed her palms in soothing circles, and for a moment, there was a peaceful silence between them. For a moment, she could pretend things were the same as they were when Larkin had first taken an interest in her.

Then Larkin was getting down on a bent knee, releasing one of her hands to reach into his breast pocket, and Andie's breath caught in her throat. Beside her, Dot gasped loudly, serving to draw more attention to them. Andie froze to the spot as Larkin opened a small box and produced a glittering diamond ring. As people crowded together to watch the spectacle, all eyes upon them, Larkin held the ring up.

"Alexandra Fairley, will you marry me?"

Earnestness shone on Larkin's face, and Andie searched his eyes for a flicker of malice, and found none. Yet she had expressed to him, in the powder room at her birthday dinner, that this was not the future she wanted. The lights of the Ferris wheel were blinding, the scent of the cotton candy sickly sweet beneath her nose. Her breathing quickened, and the panic welled up within her, waiting to consume her.

Andie was trapped, a deer in the headlights unable to escape the oncoming collision. If she rejected Larkin in front of everyone, it would ruin him. It would ruin her. It would destroy what she had worked so hard to build. Had Larkin somehow misunderstood her? Did he believe she'd change her mind if he spontaneously proposed?

The tears that bloomed in Andie's eyes were from overwhelming anxiety, but the crowd would believe they were tears of joy. She leaned into the act, pressing a hand to her mouth as if in surprise. She forced herself into motion, nodding her head vehemently.

"Yes, of course."

What else was she meant to say? It was a situation with only one outcome: Larkin getting what he wanted. Whatever he felt for her, whether he truly believed she had changed her mind or just wanted to push her in the direction he needed her to go, she could hardly bear to look at him. A brief spark of hatred flashed through her, a feeling that only accentuated the panic rising within her. She shouldn't *hate* Larkin, not even for a moment.

Larkin slid the diamond baguette cut ring onto her finger, the yellow gold inlaid with several smaller diamonds, and the crowd applauded as he got to his feet. A smug satisfaction smoothed out his handsome features. His shoulders were straighter, chin tilted triumphantly upwards.

Andie flashed a charming smile, letting Dot squeal and examine the ring, riding out the horrible moment by standing still and allowing everything to pass her by. The anxiety wasn't going away, her knees trembling violently and threatening to give out beneath her.

"If you'll all excuse me. This has all been very exciting, I don't know if it's good for my nerves."

Catching Larkin's hand, Andie marched towards the hall of mirrors. Pulling in a deep breath, she loosed the air from her lungs as they stepped into the dim lighting. Larkin frowned as he pulled the curtain to the entrance closed behind them, confusion furrowing his brow as he surveyed Andie. She stepped back until the bare skin of her shoulders brushed against the cool glass of one of the mirrors.

"What the fuck was that about?" she demanded, her voice hoarse as distress rubbed her throat raw.

"What are you talking about?" Larkin threw up his hands in disbelief. "It was a proposal, Andie. I would have thought you'd be happy. I love you, and I want to spend the rest of my life with you. Isn't that what you want?"

"No!" She blurted the word out thoughtlessly. Larkin flinched as though she'd slapped him. Pushing her anger down and rubbing her damp hands on her dress, she shook her head slowly. "I thought…I thought we were on the same page about this. I don't know how much plainer I can be. I have no desire to get married, or have children."

Larkin raked both hands through his hair in frustration. "You said yes. Out there, in front of all of those people, you said *yes*."

"What choice did I have?" Andie snarled, her fury snapping like an elastic band as she pushed herself off the mirror to glare at him. "You put that pressure on me because that was the answer you wanted, and the answer you knew I would give you in front of a crowd. It was a performance, Larkin. The real answer is *no*."

The frustration slowly faded from Larkin's face at her words, until all that was left was a dark anger that turned his eyes cold. Without warning, he lunged forward, gripping her by the neck and slamming her back against the mirror. Andie's panic escalated into sheer terror as his fingers tightened around her throat. A sneer crossed Larkin's face as he examined her with raw rage.

"I have done everything for you." Larkin's words were dangerously soft, dripping with venom. "I have given you power beyond your wildest dreams. I have never once tried to quell your ambitions. Yet you would spit it back in my face and humiliate me. Have you ever considered how difficult you are to love?"

He may as well have punched her in the gut, for she was sure it would have hurt less. Andie was self-aware enough to realise she was not easy to get along with, but "*difficult to love*" clawed its way beneath her skin and tore open a new cut on her heart.

He sounded the same as when he'd confronted her in the powder room and revealed the truth about Franklin's death. The quick flash of hatred she felt for Larkin in the moment of his proposal was reflected tenfold in the loathing that tightened his jaw. His fingers on her throat pressed her immobile against the mirror. She didn't know what to say, or if she was even meant to speak at all.

"Larkin...," she choked out.

"No, you're going to listen to me." He moved closer, his breath warm against her cheek. "If you take back your answer, you are going to regret it. I'm not pushing for a hasty wedding. I'm not pushing a timeline at all. But we are engaged now, and it suits us both best for it to stay that way. Do you understand?"

Andie wanted nothing more than to spit in his face. Anger mingled with her fear, a combustible combination that would surely explode.

How *dare* he treat her in such a manner. She pushed beneath her soul magic to the depths, something deep and dark she hadn't touched in years. She could make him release her, and go out to the public and announce he withdrew the engagement. She could make him do cartwheels, if she wanted. Yet she had forsaken her telepathy the night Claire died for good reason, and if she broke that vow…Syl would never speak to her again.

She had decided to play a dangerous game, and now she was out of moves. Larkin had her at a checkmate, and she had to concede defeat. It stung at her pride, but it was the only move she had left.

"Do you understand?" Larkin repeated, enunciating each word, fingers moving up to grip her face. In the dim reflection of the other mirrors, she saw him for what he was.

"Yes." The word was a tired rasp, tears welling in Andie's eyes even as she struggled to blink them away.

"Good." Larkin released her, and the lack of pressure on her neck made her gasp for air. He straightened his jacket. "Pull yourself together, and then come back outside. It would be a shame to miss the chance to ride the Ferris wheel."

Larkin strode from the hall of mirrors, the curtain flapping closed after him. Andie's legs buckled beneath her and she collapsed to the ground, desperate sobs pushing from her lips. Larkin's resentment had brewed quietly and exploded with the force of a grenade. She had pushed him too hard, and seen what really waited when she pricked at the last of his restraint.

Andie had power. It radiated out from her in waves, obvious to those around her. Yet Larkin was the one who possessed the influence, and in a moment, he could destroy her. She had been so arrogant, wrapped in the cocoon of his obsession with her, that she hadn't anticipated what might happen should she fail to meet his expectations. The answers were spelled out clear as day, and Andie pressed her face into her hands and cried as her worst nightmares caressed the corners of her mind.

No matter what she was, no matter how powerful or charming, she would always belong to Lord Summer.

* * *

Andie returned to Warren's home in a fancy silk dress with her engagement ring sparkling on her finger. She strode boldly through the shadows of the streets with her head held high. A handful of pickpockets watched her with curious eyes, and she half hoped and half dared them to steal the ring from her. All of them shrank away, and she acknowledged her power radiated off her even in the inky dark of Hell's Kitchen..

"Andie." Warren greeted his daughter with his typical warm enthusiasm, but the gentle smile on his lips froze when he inspected her, noting the finger-shaped bruises on her neck. Before she could be condemned to pity, Andie nudged past him and moved inside. By the clashing and banging in the kitchen, Syl was visiting too. She did her best to adjust her hair to cover her neck.

"Heard about Larkin's proposal." There was a swill of dishwater as Syl removed one of the mugs from the sink to dry. When he turned to Andie, a mischievous grin graced his lips. "How about we see that rock?"

Andie sat down at the dining table, nudging aside her father's tarot cards. The ring on her finger sparkled in the dim light, though she wanted nothing more than to tear it off and toss it into the sink with Syl's dishes. Syl dried his hands on a tea towel and strode over, but the impish gleam in his eyes faded when he drank in Andie's silence.

"What happened?" Warren asked as he trailed into the dining room, crossing over to Andie and brushing her hair back from her neck. Syl inhaled sharply as he took in the bruises. Irritated, Andie batted him away. She had no desire to be fussed over and questioned. She had no stomach for their sympathy.

"You wanted to see the ring." Andie extended her hand, flexing her fingers so the diamond glittered in the sliver of light that filtered through the dusty curtains.

"Did Larkin do this?" Syl's green eyes narrowed, a nerve ticking in his jaw.

"Just shut up about it, Syl."

"You want to marry him?" Syl gripped the edge of the table, leaning forward to assess her. When his gaze raked over the bruises, a fire lit behind his eyes. "This isn't you, Andie. The girl I know didn't cower away from men like that, she pushed back against that sort of behaviour."

"I did!" Andie snapped, lurching up from her chair and rocking the table in the process. "I did push back. That's the problem here. I pushed too hard."

Her brother bared his teeth, his concern nearly suffocating in that moment. "I'm going to…"

"Going to do what?" Andie pressed, raising her eyebrows. "You realise you're talking about Lord Summer."

Syl's eyes fluttered closed in defeat, and he reached up to pinch the bridge of his nose. For a few moments, uncomfortable silence washed over the table. In the quiet, Andie gathered her composure around her like a cloak. She could not afford to dwell on this. She could not let the tears fall, because if they did, she wasn't certain when they'd stop. The show must go on, and she would keep performing, just as she had done as a girl when she'd danced until her feet bled.

When Andie spoke again, her tone was calm and collected. "I have this under control. I don't need you running around making a fuss, Syl. I can handle Larkin."

Syl snorted disbelievingly, shaking his head as he strode from the room. She heard the door to his bedroom creak and then click shut. With the most combative of her family members sequestered, Andie's attention turned to Warren. His pity scorched like fire, and she pushed off the chafing feeling.

"I understand the appeal of the Carnival." Warren pulled a chair back and sat down, steepling his fingers in front of him. "When I was about your age, I felt the same way. It was…addictive, seeing that kind of magic, envisioning yourself with that sort of power. It's only ever belonged to the elite, and I am so proud of you for pushing your way to the top. Not many people achieve what you have, Andie."

She sank back into her seat. "There's a 'but' coming, isn't there?"

"But," Warren's smile was thin as he continued, "for every marvel, there is also a horror. For every use of magic, there is a price that's paid. After what happened with Claire, you know better than most some of the costs associated with magic. I learned that after some time at the Carnival, and when I finally managed to leave, my hands were stained with sin."

Andie frowned. Warren rarely spoke of the years he'd spent at the Carnival, in a similar position to Syl. All she knew was he had left with a bad taste in his mouth. She'd never questioned what mages who weren't associated with the Carnival actually did, though she supposed they were all similar to Warren: keeping to themselves, their magic kept quiet. Only the elite were permitted to use theirs in public. She ruefully thought that perhaps she understood where the Magical Freedoms Brigade was coming from.

"Larkin wants to marry you because you're of use to him, Andie. I'm not denying he might care for you, but you need to be careful. He will chew you up and spit you out. It's what people like that always do."

"You're wrong." Andie shook her head vigorously. "You said it yourself, not many people achieve what I have. Larkin has his flaws, but it's thanks to him I've gotten this far. It's my magic, yes, but I've needed his connections."

"Andie." Warren rested a hand over hers, dark eyes boring into her. "You don't owe him, or any of them, a damn thing. This magic you have, that's all you."

Andie ran a hand down the length of her face. She acknowledged what Larkin had done for her, but Warren was right: the magic was *hers*. Not Larkin's, not anyone else's. She was responsible for what she had become. Whether she had a glittering ring on her finger or not, she made it on her own merit, no matter how much credit others would claim.

"Do you really want to marry him?" Warren asked softly, the words as comforting as a hot cocoa on a winter's night.

"No," Andie admitted. Marriage to Larkin would be shackles upon her wrists, locking herself in a cage and handing him the key. She had not yet decided what she wanted, moving forward. Until she did, she had to play the game the way they wanted her to. "But I'll take on the role he wants me to, for now."

CHAPTER TWENTY-NINE

Prue Clermont

It was Sadie who suggested the meeting place, a speakeasy in Brooklyn that Noel unofficially owned. A public space, she claimed, was the best way to meet the Alderidges. The moment Prue stepped into the dimly-lit space, she was accosted with the scent of musk and leather. The lights hung low and the room was full of shadows, perfect for bootleggers and gangsters who wished to do their business unseen. The whole space was in wooden tones, oak browns through to deep mahogany.

Sadie tucked her arm firmly through Prue's and marched over to one of the booths. Seated within was Governor Alderidge's brother, sharp eyes latching onto Prue as she and Sadie slid into the seat across from him. The other was the handsome dark-haired man from the Midsummer Ball, Lord Winter.

Sitting on the table in front of them was a tattered old book, which Lord Winter drummed his fingers on as he observed the women. There was also a bottle of whiskey, which Noel had poured himself a shot of.

"Prudence Clermont." Noel knocked back the shot in greeting, leaning back to observe her. "So, you're the Scourge. You were at the Midsummer Ball, were you not?"

"She was my companion." Sadie spoke before Prue had the chance to open her mouth. "I can vouch for her."

"I am not interested in your opinion, Miss Crawford." Noel's lips curled in contempt, and at the same time, a hard gleam lit up Sadie's eyes. "I'm interested in speaking with Mrs Clermont."

Six months ago, in a bar with two powerful men, Prue would have wanted to shrink into the seat and wish the ground swallowed her whole. Since the revelation of her power, she had changed. She would no longer be bullied into submission by men who wanted to throw their weight around. She reached for the bottle of whiskey and one of the empty shot glasses, pouring herself some. The whiskey burned its way down her throat as she swallowed the shot.

"I'm not sure what's been said about me, Mr Alderidge, but I have no intention of stealing anyone's magic, if that's your concern."

"Yet you did." Triumph dawned in Noel's expression. "Poor Nigel. He hasn't been the same since."

Prue scowled. "Perhaps Nigel shouldn't attack people if he doesn't want them to respond in kind."

Beside Noel, Lord Winter threw back his head and laughed, flashing pearly white teeth. "I like her."

Noel wasn't amused. "Regardless, I think you can see why people in our community would be concerned. Magic is precious, and often difficult to obtain. It's been centuries since a Scourge existed, and it's got people on edge."

Beneath the table, Sadie's fingers brushed against Prue's. She gave her lover's hand a light squeeze. Once, Sadie fought her battles for her. It was time that Prue stood up for herself.

"I can see why they would be. I don't know what you want me to do to prove that I'm not a threat."

Noel responded by opening the ancient tome on the table. He impatiently flicked through to a specific section, before turning the book to face Prue and examining her expectantly.

"Can you read this for me, please?"

Prue stared at the text on the page, dumbfounded. It appeared to be written in another language. She wondered if this was some sort of test, and what precisely it was designed to prove. After studying the page for a few moments, she shook her head slowly. Dread seeped into her, dread of what might happen now that she wasn't able to accomplish whatever they wanted of her.

"I have no idea what it says."

Noel and Lord Winter exchanged a sharp look, before Noel nodded.

"She's telling the truth."

"Excuse me?" Sadie's tone was scathing, eyes narrowing as she stared Noel down. "You're using your magic to read her mind, and yet you're worried about her stealing your essence?"

"I'm just taking precautions." Noel closed the book, sliding it back across the table to Lord Winter. "The passages on prophecies are written in a language we've never been able to decode."

"Only one person alive knows, and he's not generally willing to share," Lord Winter mused.

"Two," Noel corrected curtly, causing Lord Winter to arch an eyebrow, expression shifting to avid interest.

"Oh really? Who's the second?" When Noel remained silent, Lord Winter's curiosity morphed into irritation. "Keeping secrets from the Lords isn't generally a wise idea, Noel, not even for the brother of the Governor."

"Well, now that you two have your own business to sort out." Sadie slid from the booth, planting her hands on her hips. "This has been fascinating, but we should be going."

"We aren't done here." Noel's cold eyes snapped to Sadie. "Sit down."

"Please," Lord Winter added, gesturing for her to rejoin the booth. He displayed all the manners and patience that Noel lacked, which warmed Prue to him. She wondered if perhaps that was the intention. Distaste pursed Sadie's lips, though she sank back down into the booth.

Sadie's agitation pricked at Prue's inquisitiveness. She was not the one being interrogated, and whilst it could be that she was simply protective of Prue, she had the suspicion there was an undercurrent of resentment. That would be a discussion for later, as Prue's attention was focused on the two dangerous, powerful men who sat on the other side of the table.

"You sent men after Prue to have her killed." Sadie's fingers tightened around her shot glass, although Prue couldn't tell if she intended to pour herself whiskey or smash it over Noel's head. "She doesn't owe you anything after that."

"Ah. Yes." Noel smiled ruefully. "An overreaction on my part, admittedly."

Prue could feel the pull of his magic, the way it called to her. It would be so easy to rip it from him, just as she had done with Nigel. Would it taste as bittersweet on her tongue? Would it tingle across the tip of her fingers? She yearned to tug, if only as a warning to Noel of what she was capable of, but she pushed aside the urge.

"We think you could be an asset to us." Lord Winter leaned across the table, dark eyes gleaming and a charming smile lighting up his face. "You have an incredible gift, Mrs Clermont. Perhaps we could all work together to our mutual benefit."

Unease sloshed in the pit of Prue's stomach and tightened her shoulders. Lord Winter may be more affable than Noel, but she recognised that even the sweetness of honey couldn't disguise poison. Lord Winter was the salve to Noel's sting. That did not mean he was worthy of trust.

"What's in it for me?" Prue was astounded at her own boldness, yet she understood her own worth. What price would they put on her? What did they think she was worth?

Noel and Lord Winter exchanged a startled look, as though such a simple question had caught them off-guard. Lord Winter recovered from his shock first, schooling his features into that same benevolent, neutral expression.

"Our protection."

"No." Prue's answer was resolute. She barely knew these people, how could she trust them to have her best interest at heart? What need did she, a Scourge, have of their protection? They wanted to utilise her power, yet offered nothing in return.

The firm response caused Lord Winter and Noel to exchange another look. Lord Winter merely shrugged his shoulders, though Noel's brow furrowed into a frown. Prue had the distinct impression that the elite weren't told 'no' very often.

"You may want to reconsider, Mrs Clermont."

"I do not." Prue nudged Sadie with her foot, and the pair slipped out of the booth. "I heard what you have to say. I am not a danger or a threat, unless you treat me like one. Regardless, I am not beholden to the Lords, and I don't intend to start being so now."

Her heart thundered in her chest, adrenaline coursing through her at her boldness. Noel had sent people to kill her, and she wasn't taking him at his word when he claimed it was simply an 'overreaction'. As for Lord Winter, his polite silence was more frightening still, a quiet uncertainty that gnawed at the frayed edges of Prue's nerves.

They had expected her to come to this speakeasy and be thrilled with their offer, the chance to join such a prestigious order. Instead, Prue found her voice. *She* was the Scourge. *She* was the one they were afraid of. She held power at her fingertips, both figuratively and literally, and so she was the one whose say had the most weight.

It absolutely terrified her, and yet utterly enthralled her at the same time.

* * *

"You said no?" Flo's voice escalated in pitch, brown eyes like saucers as she stared at Prue and Sadie. The fragrant aroma of garlic simmered over the apartment as Flo set the spoon down where she had been stirring vegetables over the cooktop.

"It was the right decision." Sadie curled up on the couch like a cat, kicking her shoes off and nestling amongst the cushions. "You can't trust Noel or Desmond."

Once, the statement wouldn't have cut beneath Prue's skin with such talons. Once, she would simply have agreed with Sadie. That was before she grew a spine of her own and stopped taking Sadie's word as law. She no longer doubted herself and her potential, for she had witnessed her power in all of its horrifying glory.

"You mean like I can't trust you?"

Sadie pinched the bridge of her nose. "Prue…"

"You want me to, but how can I when you are constantly keeping secrets?" She planted her hands on her hips, frustration giving her tone an edge. "It seems you're comfortable telling your friends about *my* secrets, but you never want to talk about your own."

She had pushed down her irritation with her lover during the meeting because there had been larger issues at hand. Now, back in the apartment with only Flo as a witness, she had little shame in calling it how she saw it. A sour taste lingered in her mouth, and it wouldn't wash away until she had some answers.

"What is it you want to know?" Exasperation slithered across Sadie's expression as she bit back. "Is it because I spoke to Syl in private about why Flo is staying here instead of with him?"

"Sadie." Flo's eyes were hard as marble as she stared the older woman down, gripping the wooden spoon in her hand so tightly that her knuckles gleamed white. Whatever her reasons for staying with them, it was clear she had no desire to discuss them, and Prue had no intention of pushing her.

"Stop doing that, Sadie." Prue shook her head slowly. She held no animosity for Flo, who seemed caught in the middle of everything. A pattern was emerging, the pieces of a puzzle in Sadie's behaviour that Prue had now put together.

Sadie's nose crinkled in confusion. "Doing what?"

"Leveraging everyone else's secrets to protect your own!" Prue snapped. Her patience had worn thin, once something soft and gentle but now brittle and fragile. Neither her Scourge powers nor Flo's reasons for being there should be the sacrificial lambs that Sadie placed on the altar to hide the truth she was so desperate to conceal. "Who is your father, Sadie?"

The shadow of an old hurt haunted Sadie's eyes. "I can't tell you that."

"Then you cannot expect me to trust you, when you can't trust me."

Prue strode into the kitchen, taking the wooden spoon from Flo and stirring the vegetables. Cooking was a comfort, a dose of nostalgia. She had left the life of a housewife behind her, yet that didn't mean she couldn't indulge in things that reminded her of the woman she'd been then.

Sadie was a delightful enigma there, but the mystery grew tiring, grating against Prue like nails against a chalkboard. She cared deeply for the woman in the other room. She wanted more than anything for Sadie to open up to her, and she didn't know how much longer things would last between them if Sadie continued to hold all the cards to her chest.

Prue just needed to find out how to prise the box of secrets open.

CHAPTER THIRTY

Ursula Delavane

LARKIN HAD BEEN ON EDGE SINCE he'd proposed to Andie at the Carnival, perplexing Ursula. Hadn't this been what he'd wanted, what they had all wanted? On the nights since, she had come into the lounge room to find him nursing a glass of brandy as he stared into the hearth, eyes glistening with emotion as they reflected the flames. Despairing of his melancholy and concerned for his wellbeing, after a week of such behaviour, Ursula had to intervene.

"You barely touched your dinner tonight. Again." Ursula sank onto the velvet couch, removing the bottle of brandy from her son and lifting it to her lips to take a swig. Larkin glanced at her, arching an eyebrow at such uncharacteristic behaviour.

In truth, there was more than simply Larkin's moodiness that occupied Ursula's attention. The day would no doubt dawn when the Lords realised what she could do. They all had their own gifts of perception, none more so than Desmond. He could sense fear like a wolf seeking out its prey.

"The night I proposed to Andie…" Larkin's words were soft, barely audible over the crackle of logs in the hearth. "I did something unsavoury."

"What do you mean?" Ursula had witnessed plenty of her son's unsavoury behaviour; the years before Andie, where there was a tireless parade of various girls, the increasing habit of his cocaine usage. Yet, her stomach coiled, for had she not always sensed there was the same darkness in Larkin that she refused to acknowledge lingered in her?

"I lashed out at her." Larkin inhaled sharply, the clench of his jaw laden with guilt. "She and I argued in the hall of mirrors. I grabbed her by the neck, quite hard. She had bruises."

An icy sensation spread across Ursula's limbs, rooting her to the spot. Vivid reminders of Franklin's fists and the damage they could do replayed in her mind, causing her breath to catch in her throat. Larkin had loathed his father, despised the abuse that Franklin put both him and Ursula through. Yet he carried on the same vicious cycle, the same regrets following a bout of violence.

"Larkin…what were you thinking?" Her voice was softer than she expected, laden with concern she had not realised she held.

"Andie said she didn't want to marry me," Larkin spat, misery blooming in his eyes. "That she'd only said yes to spare me humiliation. My anger got the better of me and…I lost control."

"*I lost control.*" For all Larkin's waxing poetic about giving Andie the same rights as the rest of them, the truth was a gun that had been loaded and now fired. With all her burgeoning power, he anticipated that she would slide, however reluctantly, into the expected role of being his wife. He had lost his patience with her when she refused to.

Larkin pretended that he had longed for Andie to be his equal, but he wanted to control her. He paraded around with words like "independence" and "freedom" dripping like diamonds from lips, designed to entice a woman as ambitious as Andie, when it couldn't be further from the truth. He wanted her to know that he had the upper hand, that *he* was the reason for her rise. When Andie pushed back, Larkin's temper had snapped. Her refusal to comply was more than stubbornness; it was heresy.

"Do you love her?" Ursula asked.

"Of course I do." Larkin sounded scandalised that she would question it, his eyes snapping across to hers. "I've been patient with her. I gave her so much freedom, maybe too much. I love her, but she'd be nothing without what I've done for her."

His fingers clenched around his glass, eyes ablaze with fury as he turned back to the hearth. Love mixed with rage was an unstable combination, like setting a match to fireworks and expecting they wouldn't explode. Ursula knew better than anyone what love like that could do, how utterly it could consume and how terribly it could destroy.

"Then what happens now?" she persisted.

Larkin tilted his head back dramatically and rolled his eyes as if she'd asked something immensely stupid.

"I marry her, Mother. Eventually, I have a Delavane heir. That's the way it goes."

The brandy burned its way back up Ursula's throat, and she suppressed the sudden urge to vomit. The words were a cold echo of everything she had pressed upon him, the expectations of his role as Lord Summer. The ring that Andie rebelled against, put on her finger at Ursula's insistence, would be the girl's prison.

Her son was no longer Larkin Delavane, the darling boy she had raised. He was Lord Summer, cool and calculating, determined that no one would stand in his way. The worst part was that Ursula was the one who had created him. All the sacrifices she had made, the unspoken sins that never came to her lips that she had committed to protect Larkin, had culminated in him becoming exactly what she had hoped.

He was a son Franklin would be proud of, and somehow, that horrified her.

✳ ✳ ✳

An invitation to Garrett Alderidge's apartment for drinks would typically have delighted Ursula, but when the mention of her specifically bringing the Grimoire came up, dread settled like a brick in the pit of her stomach. She would pretend it was an odd coincidence, as she had no intention of digging her own grave. Usually she would ask permission to borrow the book, stored in the Templeton library, but impatience and anticipation wore down her politeness, and she took it without posing the question.

Ursula plastered on a gracious smile as she entered the apartment, kissing Garrett's cheek as they greeted one another before being shown into the lounge room. Keeping her smile firmly intact, she set the Grimoire on the coffee table, perching on the edge of the cream couch. Noel strode into the room, quiet as a whisper, and dropped on another of the couches.

"You moved the iron maiden." Her eyes cast around for the metal contraption, but it was nowhere in sight. Privately, she was relieved—as a brutal memento of the past of magic, it had rather unnerved her.

"Yes, we moved it to Noel's." Garrett waved a dismissive hand, eyes locked onto the ancient volume on the table. "So this is the Grimoire. What a treasure. Noel told me it was old, but even still…"

"Is that so?" Ursula's eyebrows sketched upward. "When was it that Noel saw the Grimoire?"

"Lord Winter and I took it when we met with the Scourge," Noel said, leaning back in his seat, arms draping around the back of the couch. He was far too pleased with himself for her liking. "We thought given the odd nature of her magic, she may be able to interpret the prophecies, but we were wrong."

"How unfortunate." Clasping her hands demurely in her lap, she hoped that the movement would disguise how much they trembled. She could feel Noel's intense gaze locked on her, and avoided looking at him.

"Fortunately, we have an alternative." Garrett's smile was riddled with a hunger she hadn't seen in him before. She had often wondered how a man as pleasant as Garrett entered a dirty business like politics. Now, she thought perhaps she might have an understanding.

"What alternative?"

"You, Mrs Delavane."

She scoffed. "What a ridiculous notion."

"Mouths lie, but minds don't." Noel eased himself forward on the couch. "Yours is so *loud*. Scrambling with thoughts of prophecy, of the Grimoire. The Morning and Evening Star, I believe?"

A wave of red-hot anger surged through Ursula. "Get out of my head. You have no business being there."

"Please, Ursula." Noel held his hands up as if in surrender. "We all know that the magical elite are full of underhanded tricks, don't get offended when I match that."

Ursula seethed in silence, fingers twisting tight in the fabric of her dress. She had been backed into a corner like a frightened rabbit, and it sent hot shame coursing like molten lava throughout her body. She was a member of the magical elite, not some dog Noel could whistle up when he wanted some prophetic answer.

"Please." Garrett slid the book across the table to Ursula. "Will you translate it for us?"

Civility, to soothe the sting of his brother's callousness. A tingle spread up the nape of Ursula's neck, a hard pull toward the Grimoire. Licking at her lips, Ursula flicked through until she reached the first page on the prophecies. It would be easy to let lies fall smoothly from her lips, but Noel would ascertain the truth.

So she told them everything. The Morning Star, who would wield Excalibur. The Evening Star, who would pull Clarent from the stone. The dark destiny that the pair possessed. Noel sank back in his seat, rubbing his chin in thought. Garrett's attention remained on Ursula, enraptured by her recount.

"Fascinating. Are there other prophecies as well?"

"Not written in the Grimoire." She shook her head fervently. It wasn't technically a lie, though she could not have said what lay in the pages of the magical tomes kept in Sterling's library.

"We could use your help, Ursula." There was a shift behind Noel's eyes, like the sun eclipsed by clouds on a rainy day. "You aren't one of the Lords, but you're still within their circle. I see no reason why we can't come to a mutually beneficial agreement."

The silence that settled over the group was like spiderwebs, tangling around Ursula, suffocating her as if she had breathed them in. She swallowed hard and retained her mask of composure. The Alderidge brothers may gain information from her, but she might also learn how this uneasy alliance best suited her. Garrett was the Governor of New York, Noel his most trusted spy.

"You want me to serve as a spy?" The words were sour behind her teeth, the mere thought an affront. She had been loyal to the Lords since she'd married Franklin, and continued that loyalty after his death.

"Oh, don't be absurd." Garrett waved a nonchalant hand, eyes widening in affront at her accusatory tone. "We would never ask you to do something so clearly against your conscience. What my brother is trying to say is that…you see things the others don't. The Lords have a focus on growing their own power and influence, and while you assist them, you don't share that vision."

She pushed her mind away from Larkin's sins. The idea that her thoughts were not safe, even locked in her own head, was disturbing to her. When she glanced across at Noel, his expression was unreadable.

"So then what do the two of you want?" Ursula asked, fingers skimming over the fading surface of the Grimoire. Her voice was sweet as two sugars in a nighttime tea, saccharine smile disguising the sharp edges of her question.

"The Morning and the Evening Stars." Noel's eyes lit up with greed like the Ferris wheel of the Dusk Carnival. She understood now how Garrett had come to power, and how he retained it.

"Unfortunately, I don't know who they are." Ursula swivelled to face Noel, her pleasant smile twisting like a razor. "Go on. Am I telling the truth?"

"I am not prying constantly in your thoughts, Ursula," Noel snapped with a scowl, and she remembered their conversation over high tea, the way he despised the insinuation that he used his magic against others at a whim. Yet, had that not been what he'd done when he invaded her thoughts and revealed she could read the Grimoire?

"You both know of the Magical Freedoms Brigade. I'm certain that, by now, you've heard the rumours that they may be in possession of Excalibur."

"The Brigade doesn't have the sword," Noel drawled, crossing one leg over the other and reclining in his seat.

Ursula frowned at his cool certainty. "Then who does?"

"Isn't it obvious?" Noel's smugness made her itch to rip the smile off his lips. "It's still with the Lady of the Lake."

PART THREE
QUEEN OF WANDS

Chapter Thirty-One

Andie Fairley

The Templeton residence was awash with colour on the night of Halloween, laughter bubbling as freely as champagne when Andie strode into the entrance hall. The scent of sandalwood incense was heavy on the air, the hall crowded with party-goers eager to experience the prestige of a Templeton Halloween party.

She spotted a number of clown costumes, a good deal of cackling witches, and a handful of masks including what appeared to be someone dressed as a plague doctor. As Andie shrugged off her coat and hung it on the rack, an audible gasp coaxed a smirk from her. She had dressed to make an impression, after all.

Drawing her chin up high, Andie nudged her way through the guests, attempting to spot a familiar face. Though she did enjoy the attention, it lasted a fleeting amount of time before the press of the crowd weighed heavily on her lungs and made her knee tremble. Pushing aside her anxiety, she let the jazz crackling on the record player wash over her like a calm breeze. She wriggled her toes in her shoes, fighting the urge to dance.

"What exactly are you supposed to be?" Beneath the heavy layers of red and white makeup caked onto the man's face, the shock of hair gave him away as Felix Templeton, pausing mid-conversation with another clown to examine her.

"A dead bride," Andie said with a smirk as she gathered the fabric of the vintage wedding dress she'd acquired from a small Harlem shop in her hands and did a twirl, the curls she'd pinned to her head threatening to tug loose at the action. The berry juice smeared across the white fabric wouldn't rinse out, but thankfully, Andie had no intention of re-wearing the dress.

"How utterly charming." Felix grinned, pearly white teeth slicing through the intense red make-up. The praise caused Andie to sink a curtsy, mischief sizzling through her veins as she strode past into the lounge room.

In truth, she had believed Sterling too old and uptight to allow such an event, though it made for a good networking opportunity. There would be political figures amongst the rabble, cleverly concealed in costumes so as not to reveal their identities. Andie seized a glass of champagne from one of the silver serving platters set down on a table, the golden liquid bubbling down her throat and giving her a pleasant buzz.

A shrill of laughter made her crane her neck and cast across the other side of the room to see what, precisely, was so amusing. A man dressed as a scarecrow leaned against the mantelpiece, a dazzling grin aimed at a young woman dressed as a witch. It was only when he reached out to tuck a strand of hair behind the woman's ear that recognition surged through Andie, her fingers tightening on her empty champagne glass.

Larkin.

Confusion and chaos brewed into a deadly concoction that poisoned Andie from the inside as she set down the glass with a clunk, stepping toward her fiance. Before she could open her mouth to utter a word, the plague doctor swept across like a dark shadow and caught her by the arm. Andie twisted angrily, but the unknown assailant dragged her to the back door, wrenching it open and pulling her outside.

"What the fuck?" Andie demanded, staggering back as the plague doctor pushed the door shut behind him. The back porch was adorned with dozens of golden lanterns, and she could see the dim lights of the greenhouse glowing in the dark.

The figure removed his mask, revealing the raised eyebrows of Desmond Bellisario. Andie loosed a dramatic sigh and pinched her brow, not entirely certain why Lord Winter had brought her out onto the back porch when she'd been ready to dig her heel down into Larkin's foot.

"You were about to cause a scene." Despite the obvious reprimand, there was amusement in Desmond's tone, reflected in the shine of his brown eyes. "Considering how you're dressed…"

"What about how I'm dressed?" Andie snapped, planting her hands on her hips. The irritation of seeing Larkin flirting rubbed her patience raw, until the barest threads remained. Fortunately, the wait staff had the sense to place some glasses of champagne on the table outside, along with a bottle of Dom Perignon sitting on ice in a metal tub. She picked up a glass and knocked the liquid back, savouring how her muscles loosened, how the delightful haze intensified.

Desmond held up his hands. "I didn't mean to offend you. I simply meant that I think you and I both know how Larkin would see you dressed in a bloodied wedding gown."

There was no hiding from Desmond, no concealing her intentions behind a pretty smile and a sweet lie. He recognised her costume for what it was: a spiteful dig to Larkin's ribs. They were cut from the same cloth, two street rats from the dregs of New York who had somehow managed to find a place for themselves amongst high society. Andie's eyes locked onto his, daring him to chastise her.

"Am I meant to apologise?"

He chuckled. "You wouldn't mean it, and I don't believe you owe me one, in any case."

Andie refilled the glass, watching the champagne bubble to the surface, much like her temper. Why was Desmond so easy to get along with? Not just with her, but with everyone. She couldn't think of anyone who had a bad word to say about the man. He was honest without being harsh, firm without being cruel.

"You are insufferably likeable," she snipped.

"I'll drink to that." Desmond picked up a glass of his own, raising it in toast before bringing it to his lips.

For a few moments, there was a tranquil silence between the two of them. A slight breeze made the golden lanterns bob around before stilling. When Andie glanced at Desmond, his expression was thoughtful as his gaze locked onto the greenhouse. Was he remembering his own venture into the ice bath, or thinking on hers?

"How did you do it?" The softly asked question caused Desmond to lurch from his reverie, looking at her intently. "Make the others accept you, I mean. You're from the gutter like me. You wouldn't even know it now, with the way they treat you."

"It took time." Desmond swirled the liquid around in his glass, watching it hiss and churn. "A long time, and a lot of work. I had to prove myself, over and over again. You want to stand out, but first, you need to learn to fit in and play by their rules. They will never let you shine if they can't share in your glow."

Andie scoffed. Lately, all the light had fizzled out of her. Since the incident in the hall of mirrors, the raging inferno had simmered down into a smouldering flame, barely kept alight. The spark in her was fading, and it terrified her. She never had to dull herself down before, and the idea that she was doing it now to appease Larkin, to slot into a role she never wanted, replaced that fire with an anger that was older and colder.

The anger that pushed forth the night Claire died, an anger that scared her.

"So I shine?"

"Oh, you *shine*." Desmond's adamant assurance evoked a surprised smile from Andie, her eyes raking over the strong set of his jaw, the way his mouth dimpled when he grinned.

Danger danced along the back porch as Andie stepped closer, a champagne-laced edge to her confidence as she tilted her face up and examined Desmond. She had never been afraid to dare, and the memory of Larkin flirting with the woman by the mantelpiece was a kick to the sternum.

"Watch." Andie took Desmond's hand, slipping her fingers through his. Her magic bloomed to life like a flower in spring, the warm glow of her light wrapping around their joined hands. The tickle of it against her skin made Andie's smile widen, and she saw the light reflected in the golden glow in Desmond's eyes. He stared down at their joined hands as if in a trance, the warmth of it a soft caress along her bare arm.

"See?" Desmond's gaze tore from their hands to latch onto her face, wonder burning bright in his eyes that couldn't be hidden by his attempt at a stoic expression. "There's still light in you."

After a heartbeat, he drew his hand away from hers. The sunlight aura around them flickered and faded. Andie couldn't help the disappointment that mingled with guilt in the pit of her stomach, especially when Desmond wouldn't look her in the eye. The shameful swirl mixed with the champagne, though it no longer gave her the same buzz.

"We should go back inside. At some point, Larkin is bound to question where you are."

* * *

Larkin's reaction tasted as delicious as chocolate ice cream on a summer's day, melting in the heat across her fingertips. Fury darkened his pale eyes as he pushed himself away from the mantelpiece. When he crossed the room, he seized Andie's arm, much as Desmond had done. Unlike Desmond, he dug his fingers in until she grimaced, marching her upstairs into the empty Templeton library and slamming the door shut behind them.

It was the heavy desk that situated near the door that Larkin pushed her up against, newspaper stacked high across its surface. He had little care for the fountain pens that skittered across the floorboards, anger pulsing in his temple and the clench of his jaw.

"Is this punishment, Andie?" he demanded, drinking in the white fabric stained with crimson. "Is this to spite me for the hall of mirrors?"

Andie sneered, the desk digging into her lower back uncomfortably. To deny it would have been to lie, and though it was tempting, the truth was so much more delightful. When had she liked watching him seethe? When had their dynamic twisted into something with an undercurrent of violence always simmering beneath the surface?

"Well, I wouldn't have thought it mattered, since your attention has been otherwise occupied tonight."

Larkin laughed hoarsely. "Are you jealous?"

"Why would I be jealous?" Andie's voice pitched sugar-sweet, a saccharine mask for the viciousness beneath. "I was out on the back porch showing Desmond my light magic."

"Desmond." Larkin shook his head slowly, his blonde hair falling across his face. "You know his power is empathy, don't you? All he has to do is touch you, and he gets snatches of your emotions, sometimes flashes of memory if he concentrates enough. He can twist them to his advantage too, but I bet he never told you that."

Andie tilted her head back so that he could see her smirk in the moonlight.

"Now who's jealous?"

"Why should I be jealous?" Larkin planted his hands either side of her, leaning forward. "You're my fiancé, after all."

She made a disgusted noise. "So you now see me as some property that belongs to you now. How utterly charming."

"You aren't property," Larkin admitted, fingers surging up to catch in her hair, startling a gasp of surprise from her.

He pressed his lips hungrily to hers, pinning her to the desk with his body. It wasn't the same way he'd first kissed her in the bathroom of Camelot, desperate for the taste of her on his lips, the way he'd kissed her so many times since. His kiss was harder now, as though he sought to devour her. She reciprocated with equal ferocity, arms reaching up to hook around his neck, tugging him tight against her.

They'd had sex several times since the Midsummer Ball, as was only natural for a young couple drunk on the euphoria of their power and their lust for one another. Yet tonight was different, a shift in the way that Larkin touched her, possession instead of reverence. His lips descended on her neck, leaving a series of harsh bites along the tender skin. She dug her nails into his shoulders until he hissed at the sting.

When Larkin drew back to look at her, there was an unhinged light gleaming in his eyes, like an uninhabited cabin in the woods that she wasn't sure if she should enter. There was something horribly empty in his expression, a vacancy where once there had been passion, hard anger where once there had been admiration.

Larkin tugged hard at the hem of her dress, pulling it up her legs, but Andie swatted his hands away. Grabbing the front of his shirt, she pushed herself off the desk and propelled him backwards until he stumbled into a seat on one of the emerald velvet couches. A smug smile curved her lips as she swung a leg over him, straddling his lap. She gripped his chin and kissed him, his teeth sinking into her lip hard enough so they both had the metallic tang of blood on their tongues.

Larkin's hands roamed her breasts, as she made short work of unbuckling his belt. Whatever passion they'd shared in the past, tonight was different. It was waging war, a battle of nails and teeth on skin. It was hard and angry, each of them striving for control. Andie shifted to slide her underwear down her legs, Larkin's breath coming in ragged pants as he pushed his pants down.

Andie lowered herself onto his cock, a soft hum of pleasure escaping her at the feeling of being filled by him. She let her head tilt back, curls brushing against the back of her neck. Gripping the back of the couch, she snapped her hips against him, a long groan tearing from

Larkin's throat. His hands slid up beneath her dress to rest on her ass, surging up to rock against her.

For Andie, sex had been about pleasure until she'd met Larkin. Now there was an undercurrent of power too, the knowledge that in rolling her hips the right way, or gripping a handful of his fine blonde hair, she had him at his weakest. If she had a knife, if she wanted to, she could just as easily kill him as she could bring him to climax.

A familiar coil of heat wound up within Andie as she rode him, his uneven breathing and occasional groans making a wicked grin split across her face. She could tell by the bright shine in his eyes and the guttural sounds that each roll of her hips dragged from his chest he was close. He might believe she belonged to him, that he owned her, but in that moment *she* was the one who had the control.

Her hips stuttered against him, her pace faltering as the heat blazed into an inferno. Andie dragged her nails down Larkin's chest, a dizzy ecstasy washing over her and a cry of pleasure bubbling from her lips as her climax rocked through her body.

Triumph flared in Larkin's eyes and he burst upwards, rolling them so Andie was pinned beneath him on the couch. He caught hold of her wrists and pinned them either side of her head, his thrusts hard and fast as her shaking legs wrapped around his waist. Despite a momentary flash of annoyance with him, Andie found soft moans emanating from her mouth despite herself.

"Good girl." Larkin's teeth flashed in a deranged smile, fingers tightening on her wrists in a way that made Andie wonder if he meant to break them. His thrusts grew rough and sloppy, hips rocking against a few more times before he groaned loudly, climaxing in her as his body shuddered and he collapsed on top of her.

The scent of pine and old books wafted over Andie, encouraging her to take a deep breath. Every wall of the room was lined with bookshelves that stretched from floor to ceiling, stacked with a number of books. She supposed money was not an issue when you were a member of the magical elite. She longed to trace her fingers along the books' spines, a hunger for arcane knowledge accompanying her steely certainty that there would be more on magic in some of the volumes.

The pale light of the moon, along with that of the glittering stars, filtered through the arched window, its luminescent white glow spilling across the wooden floorboards.

Andie watched the way the shadows of the trees outside mingled with the moonlight, light and darkness dancing across the ceiling. Her breathing began to even out, though as she sat up, she grimaced at the sticky sensation she so despised after sex. Nudging Larkin off her, she strode over to the desk and seized a few tissues, wiping herself clean before tossing them in a trash can near the door.

Larkin eased himself up, buckling up his pants. Walking over to Andie, he caught her by the chin, tilting her face up to examine the hard gleam in her blue eyes.

"Next time you wear a wedding dress, you'll be the bride."

A thought that had circulated in Andie's mind for months bloomed to life, and she threw caution to the wind as she asked the question that she had bitten back for so long.

"Did you kill Patrick?"

The young man she had loved, buried in the ground without a name to who had murdered him. What did the elite of the Carnival care for a boy from the slums of Hell's Kitchen? Yet Andie cared. Months after she first felt the chill of dread seep into her bones, an anguish that continued to snap at her heels, she still cared.

"Andie." Larkin's lack of astonishment at the question made nausea rise in her throat. He arched an eyebrow at her accusing glare. "What reason did I have to kill Patrick? We both know you would always have chosen me."

Releasing her, he marched from the library, the door creaking closed behind him. The fury that held Andie rigid dissipated in his absence, and she exhaled sharply. His last words lashed against her harder than a slap to the face, biting all the deeper because they were a horrific truth she hadn't wished to confront.

Andie had pushed aside whatever she had with Patrick because she wanted power. She wanted more, she *always* wanted more. Patrick had been buried in the dirt knowing that he would never be her first choice, not when her ambition held her in such tight claws.

Angry, self-loathing tears pricked at Andie's eyes, but she quickly brushed them away. Instead, her gaze cast around the rows of books, content in the knowledge that she had been left alone with a magical arsenal at her disposal.

A decadent delight nestled within her, taking root and growing like a weed. Her fingers swept over the desk until they reached the stack of newspapers, the ones dating back to 1918 beginning to yellow and fade. Her eyes greedily roamed the stacks of books, gilded spines gleaming softly in the moonlight.

Andie exhaled anger, and inhaled power.

Chapter Thirty-Two

Prue Clermont

Flo was mere weeks away from giving birth, and the idea of having to sit around and rest until such time as she had the baby clearly did not appeal to her. The young woman's complaints resonated from the couch as she offered to cook, to clean, to do anything that might occupy her boredom. In a way, Prue pitied her, trapped in the confines of impending motherhood. She didn't see Syl resting, after all. He bounded around Sadie's apartment in that ever-exuberant way of his, all broad smiles and effortless charm.

"I found a place for Flo and I!" he declared, sitting on the couch to sling an arm around the girl's shoulders. In his free hand, he nursed a bottle of beer. "So we shouldn't be a bother for you now, especially with Flo's due date coming up."

"It's been nice having her stay." Prue honestly had enjoyed the younger woman's company. It made for a relief from the brewing tension between her and Sadie, since Flo was blunt and open about most matters.

"I've been thinking about your Scourge powers." Syl's brow furrowed as he spoke, a deep thoughtfulness settling over him. "You worry that they're harmful, but what if they could be useful?"

The heavy rock of suspicion settled in Prue's stomach. "What do you mean?"

Syl's breath trembled as he sucked it in, eyes squeezing shut. His arm tightened around Flo's shoulders, and she threw him a bewildered glance. Syl opened his eyes and raised the bottle of beer to his lips and took a chug.

"You could remove the essence of people who are dangerous. To others. To themselves." Syl's jaw set, resolute. His green eyes flicked up, fierce and intense. "You could take away Andie's essence."

"What the fuck?" Flo lurched away from him as though his fingers had grown talons. The horror on her face was echoed in the hard twist in Prue's chest, a sheen of cold sweat settling over her limbs.

"She's your sister." Prue stared him down, waiting until shame caused Syl to lower his gaze. "Why would you want to take that away from her?"

"You have no idea, either of you." An urgency crept into his tone, a sharpness uncharacteristic of his easygoing personality seeping into his expression. "When she gained soul magic, Andie was ranked a nine. I don't know exactly what she can do, but she has always been powerful. Even her mind magic alone…I can't even begin to fathom what her heart and soul magic are like."

His voice rasped, grating over an emotional wound that none of them could see. Syl was typically unbothered by danger or gore. He had scrubbed the bloodstains out of Sadie's carpet without flinching. Yet when he spoke of Andie's mind magic, terror lingered in his eyes. There were ghosts in his past, and they haunted him still.

"So you think Prue should remove Andie's magic because what, you're jealous?" Flo snapped, the words cutting as deep as she'd meant to and making him flinch.

"This isn't about jealousy. When we were teenagers, I saw her do things that…she *is* dangerous. Beyond that, do you really think the Lords would allow someone with that kind of strength to exist without wanting to control her?"

"They would." Sadie strode into the room, arms folded over her chest and a grimness pulling tight at her features. "They would do what they've done for centuries, to the women they deem worthy of undergoing the soul ritual. They would use her as a battery, her magic to power her husband's."

"But Andie doesn't have a…" Syl paused, an eerie silence descending over the group. The beer bottle slackened between his fingers, before he raised it to his lips and drained the rest of it.

"How do you know that?" Flo asked Sadie, eyes wide with dread.

"It's what they did to Penelope Templeton, Lord Spring's wife." She shrugged her shoulders as though brushing off the matter, but there was a rigid set to her body, an uncomfortable hunch to her spine, as though she was trying to shrink in on herself. "She was powerful, and she spent her life gifting her magic to her husband. It's what they'll expect of Andie."

Prue's eyes locked onto Syl, watching as he shifted uncomfortably in his seat at her beratement. "It's a thought I won't entertain. I'm not taking magic from your sister because you think she might be a threat."

It was odd, to think the glamorous woman she felt she'd never have anything in common with suddenly became relatable. Prue understood the feeling of people perceiving someone as a threat before the danger had come to pass. Why should someone be judged for what they might do, instead of what they had done? Why should they be held accountable for their power, but not what they'd accomplished with it?

"It's not just me." Syl set down his empty bottle on the coffee table, crossing one leg over the other. "The Magical Freedoms Brigade is getting restless. First the death of someone they'd planted in the Carnival, now a Scourge and a powerful female mage? It's not looking too great."

"Syl." Prue's voice was gentle on the word. "What was Patrick doing at the Carnival?"

Grief tightened his jaw, and she was reminded of how close the two men had been. The loss of Patrick went beyond whatever he'd been to the Brigade, and what he'd meant to Syl.

"Only the leader of the Brigade knows the specifics, but from what he discussed with me, he was getting in position to steal their book of magic, the Grimoire. Patrick was also one of two operatives powerful enough to attempt the Scourge ritual."

"How many people do you need for the ritual?" Prue recalled Sadie had mentioned it. Though the ritual was nowhere near as hard-hitting as a Scourge, it still possessed the ability to remove a person's essence. Not destroy, though; only a Scourge was capable of that. A sour film coated her tongue.

"At least two or three, depending on the power of the mage." Syl leaned forward, hands steepled together in his lap. "With Patrick dead, it rendered the ritual impossible. There was no way a single mage could do it on their own."

Trepidation trailed cruel hands down the back of Prue's neck. Syl had specifically mentioned Patrick was one of two people capable of completing the Scourge ritual, which implied that there was a target in mind. The Brigade had intended to steal an essence, a plan that Patrick's death had foiled.

"I need you to be honest with me." Prue sank onto the couch beside Syl, resting a hand on his shoulder and feeling the tension of his body beneath her gentle touch. "Whose essence was Patrick meant to steal?"

The question hung in the air like a dark cloud promising rain. An uncomfortable revelation made itself known to Prue: the mission had failed because Patrick was killed. Yet now the Brigade had the perfect solution. A Scourge that didn't need to rely on the magic of another person, a Scourge who could not only take an essence, but obliterate it. A thrill of fear rippled up her spine.

"Larkin Delavane."

The words were spoken quietly, barely above a whisper. Flo pressed a hand over her mouth in shock. Across the room, Sadie leaned against the kitchen bench with worry lining the downward turn of her mouth.

There was a puzzle forming before them, the pieces of which they'd been supplied over a long period of time. Only a few were missing now, enough to conceal the whole picture from view.

"How did Patrick get found out? Did the other operative betray him?"

"She wouldn't have." Syl shook his head, adamant despite Prue's own misgivings. "All it would have taken is for one of the elite to push into his mind. He was good at holding up his mental guard, but a skilled mind mage would've been able to pull down the barriers."

"Why did the Brigade want Larkin's essence?" Prue asked.

"I don't know," he sighed and ran a tired hand down the length of his face. "A threat. A warning. It was the leader's plan. All I know is that it was a stupid plan, because it got Patrick killed."

"They'd want Prue now," Flo murmured, inquisitive brown eyes shifting from her lover to Prue. "A Scourge is a lot more powerful than a Scourge ritual."

Syl held up his hands. "Now, hang on…"

"No, she's right." She'd heard an offer from the elite, and turned it down. She needed to know what her other options were, and it sounded like the Brigade had a need for her. There was much more for her to learn, and only one way forward. "I need to meet with the leader of the Brigade."

* * *

Mark remembered how she liked her tea; black with no sugar and only the slightest dash of milk. Prue stirred the tea, staring down into its murky depths and watching the liquid swirl together in a watercolour splash of dark and light. The mundanity of everyday life had been her shackles—until she had broken free. Now, Prue could not help but wonder if she missed the dullness, if those shackles had not been to protect her but to protect others from her.

"I confess, I didn't think you'd ever want to see me again." Mark slurped at his tea, setting the cup down in the saucer. "When you wanted to leave our marriage behind, it felt like that meant everything in your old life. That I wouldn't be part of the new one at all."

In truth, Prue had not been certain what role Mark would play following their separation. She had known him since they were young, and the idea of cutting him out completely stung like salt in a fresh wound. She drummed her fingers against the sides of her cup.

"I know what we have may not be love," she said, navigating her words carefully around the shards she'd broken his heart into. "Mark, you are the one thing I can trust. I know exactly who you are, no secrets, no lies."

"This world of magic doesn't offer that." A wry smile crossed Mark's lips, and he shook his head slowly. His disappointment in her involvement in the arcane world was palpable, and yet she would not give it up.

"It provides opportunity." Prue clasped her hands together, fingers intertwining. "Opportunity for me, to be something other than a housewife. Our life was…comfortable. I'm beginning to realise perhaps I am not made for simply 'comfortable'."

"Where do I fit into that, then?" He leaned back in his chair. Dark shadows circled under his eyes, as though he hadn't slept in days.

"I was hoping…as a friend," she hedged, her voice caught somewhere in her throat with the vulnerability of the words. Would it have been easier to simply cut him off entirely, than to offer him such a foreign role to fill in her life? Was it a slap in the face, to hold out the hand of friendship when she had spat love out? The silence stretched on between them, fraying at Prue's nerves like a blunt knife.

"It might take some time, but…" Mark nodded. "I think I could do that. You are a remarkable woman, Prue. I'm sorry I saw it too late. I'm sorry if I was the reason you…"

"Mark." Prue raised a hand, pleading for him to stop. The blame rested on her, for pretending she could continue to occupy a space she had outgrown. War had changed him, and magic had changed her. "Please don't be sorry. You were a good husband, and I often find myself missing your company. In some ways, I think we were always more friends than we ever were lovers."

Perhaps it was selfish of her, to yearn for some stability within a life that was constantly changing, and expecting Mark to be the one to be that steadfast rock. Yet the more Prue thought about it, the more certain she was that she wanted him to have some place in her life. Despite their differences, Mark had only ever been kind, and tried to understand what it was she wanted.

"Friends, then." Mark reached out and placed a hand atop hers, his skin rough but his touch warm. It didn't make her heart skip or shivers course up her arms the way Sadie's touch did. Instead, it was like a warm blanket on a bitterly cold winter's evening, a sense of comfort and security.

Prue smiled, squeezing Mark's hands in hers. "Friends."

CHAPTER THIRTY-THREE

Ursula Delavane

URSULA HAD NEVER BEEN TO HELL'S Kitchen in her life. She had frequented the streets of Brooklyn and Manhattan, where high society mingled, where the air was fresh with promise and power. Hell's Kitchen was a poison in comparison, the streets littered with low-level criminals and hopelessness. She cringed as a rat scampered over her boot, but didn't protest as Noel continued down the lane with his hands stuffed in the pockets of his grey coat.

"You get used to it." He turned to glance over his shoulder at her. "When Claire was a girl, she used to visit her half-siblings here. It wasn't ideal, but I hoped that she would grow up with companions. Garrett and I were close, and it was something I wanted for her."

Thanks to Andie Fairley, Claire had never grown up at all. She wondered how sharp that cut must sting, how deep the wound went. Perhaps it was part of who Noel was now; sharp to the point of cruelty, blunt and unforgiving. The reek of mould permeated Ursula's nostrils, making her crinkle her nose. The place was rotten to the core.

Noel rapped his fist against the wooden front door, and a tall, handsome man opened it. Ursula had seen Warren Fairley a handful of times during his Carnival employ, though she could not say she was overly familiar with the man. Warren's blue eyes flicked between the pair of them, unease shifting across his face, before his gaze settled on Noel.

"It's been a while, Mr Alderidge."

"I hoped that Mrs Delavane and I might come inside." Noel's smile held no warmth, and his eyes were cold as chips of ice. Nonetheless, Warren nodded and gestured for them both to enter the house.

It was cramped and small, the floorboards scuffed and aged, the curtains punctured with holes from moths and possibly other creatures. The damp smell lingered over the sandalwood incense burning on the dining table. Ursula hugged her coat more tightly around herself. She had agreed to accompany Noel to speak with Warren, though the specifics of their line of interrogation eluded her, as did the reason why she needed to be present.

"Have you come for a reading?" Warren took a seat at the dining table, the chair creaking beneath his weight as he leaned forward to shuffle a deck of tarot cards. When he looked up expectantly, Noel shook his head slowly, sitting across from Warren. Ursula remained standing, hovering uncertainly.

"No." Noel removed his flat cap, setting it in front of him. "I'm here to speak with you about the prophecy."

Alarm flashed through Warren's eyes, and Ursula's breath caught in her throat. She recalled Noel mentioning that there was one other who could read the prophecies in the Grimoire, and she had assumed it was someone who had flown under the Lords' radar since they were unaware. She hadn't imagined it would be Andie's father.

Noel's cool, pleasant smile didn't waver in the face of their astonishment.

"Now, I'd prefer we didn't lie to one another, since I'll know the truth. There's a lot I know about you, Warren. Sarah did a lot of talking during our marriage."

The other man flinched as if Noel had struck him. Sarah—mother of Syl, Andie, and the late Claire. Ursula didn't know much about Noel's late wife, though it seemed she had left her first husband and two young children not long after Andie was born. She had seen Noel's wounds, and now it seemed they'd rubbed salt in Warren's.

"Alright then. Yes, I read the Grimoire. I know about the prophecies."

"Wonderful." Noel clasped his hands in front of him. "So then, what does your daughter know of it?"

Warren's fingers tightened on the edge of the table, a sudden iciness stealing all the warmth from his features. When he glowered across at Noel, Ursula could feel the fury simmering off him.

"Don't you *dare* bring my children into whatever insidious game you're playing."

Noel's mouth twisted sharply, his eyes brightening with hatred. Warren gritted his teeth and clutched at his head. Ursula stifled a gasp at the realisation that Noel was using his mind magic to hurt Warren. Whatever she had agreed to, it hadn't been to barge into a man's house and torture him.

"I had hoped you'd cooperate, Warren. Do they know about the Morning and Evening Stars?"

"You can read minds." Warren's voice was taunting, though ragged with pain. "I'd have thought you could decipher that for yourself."

"Your daughter's head is a cesspit, regardless of the fact it's difficult to get into it," Noel snarled before waving a dismissive hand, malice thinning his smile. "Your son doesn't have anything approaching a useful thought in his skull, since he's drunk or high most of the time anyway."

"I don't think they know anything," Warren rasped out. "At least, nothing that I've told them."

"Good." Noel released his hold on Warren and the other man slumped in relief. He glanced over his shoulder at Ursula, who took a tentative step forward. "Mrs. Delavane here is also able to read the prophecies in the Grimoire. We're trying to determine the connection, since apparently, no one else can."

"Bloodline." Warren's response was immediate, his suspicious gaze shifting to Ursula. "It's been at least a thousand years since the time of Arthur Pendragon, so I couldn't tell you precisely what descent that gives you unless you have a very detailed family tree. There are books that claim bloodline is—"

"What books?" Ursula interrupted, confusion clouding her ability to think. "The Grimoire made no mention of bloodline."

Warren lapsed into silence, eyes dropping to his lap. Noel's smirk grew serrated as he observed the other man's visible discomfort.

"Warren left the Carnival's employ in quite the hurry, after stealing some books from the Templeton library. Ancient tomes, almost as old as the Grimoire itself. That's where you learned about bloodlines, isn't it?"

Ursula had never heard of such volumes, though she supposed this would have been over two decades ago, and Sterling was the sort of man loath to discuss his own failings. By the sound of it, the books had never been returned to the Templeton library. Perhaps they were still in Warren's possession.

"I lost them years ago, if that's your next question." Warren's hands remained clenched on the edge of the table. "After everything that happened with Sarah, and then Claire…I lost days. I couldn't tell you what happened. The depression took a hold of me and it wouldn't let go. When I pushed through, I could no longer find the books."

Noel was silent a moment, nostrils flaring, before he nodded curtly.

"So, the bloodlines," Warren inhaled deeply. "The tomes claimed that only those of a magical bloodline—Merlin, Arthur, Lancelot, any among them—were able to claim the language of their forebears. I assume it would work in a similar way to magic. Not everyone would have it, but you and I are descendents, likely from different bloodlines, that possess that gift."

If Ursula was descended from an ancient bloodline, it meant that Larkin was too, that he may also have inherited such a gift. Families such as the Templetons stemmed from centuries before, but it amused her to realise that this was a magic inherited through *her*, unrelated to Franklin's prestigious Delavane line.

"Well, we have Clarent," she murmured, more to herself than Warren, before raising her voice. "What about Excalibur? The prophecy claims that the Morning Star would wield it, but no one knows if it's still with the Lady of the Lake."

"It is." There was a cold certainty about Warren's voice, a shadow of deep contemplation crossing his face. "Bear in mind, there is a misconception that the Lady of the Lake is in a specific location. That isn't true. She is in the water, wherever she needs to be. The boundaries of space and distance don't apply to a creature of pure magic."

"Is this written in the tomes as well?" Noel drawled, leaning back in his chair as though this conversation bored him, though Ursula could see the ravenous gleam in his hazel eyes.

"No." Warren paused for a moment, long enough for Ursula to hear the giggles of children in the street. "I know because twenty-six years ago, the Lady of the Lake appeared to me and offered Excalibur to me."

Noel's face shifted, growing hard as marble, and Warren hissed and keeled forward again. Ursula leaned across to grip Noel's arm, shaking her head. His mental torture of Warren left a sick feeling in the pit of her stomach. There had been no lie in Warren's words, not in the defeated way he'd said them, nor in the shame that crept into his blue eyes.

"You're telling the truth." His voice was barely above a whisper, a mixture of astonishment and horror.

"My children never knew. Neither did Sarah." Warren's voice was strong despite the latest bout of magical torment Noel had heaped upon him. "I never told anyone, because of the same way you reacted. I'd be shunned and called a liar. She offered me the sword, and I refused."

A wave of frustration prickled at Ursula, itching along her skin. There were so many who would give anything for greatness and glory to be bestowed upon them, and Warren had turned his back on it.

"Why? Why would you refuse such a gift?"

"Because it wasn't a gift," Warren spat, alarm tightening his limbs and an old dread burning deep in his eyes. "Nothing of such power is ever offered for free. I didn't want to pay the price, and so I declined."

The question of the price lay on the tip of Ursula's tongue, but she swallowed it whole. Warren had already given up enough information, shared parts of himself that no one else had ever got to see. It was just a shame those parts had been coerced out of him by the nature of Noel's magic.

"You know, Warren, you're a good man." Noel picked up his flat cap, placing it back on his head and easing himself to his feet. "It's such a shame that your daughter is a poison."

A nerve ticked in Warren's cheek. "Don't talk about Andie like that."

"Noel." Ursula's voice was a soft warning. What parent would not be protective of their child? Noel had valid reason to hate Andie, but that didn't make the young woman a monster. They all saw in different shades, their children with rose-coloured glasses and the people they'd made up their minds to hate in bleak grey.

Warren plucked a card from the tarot deck and set it face up on the table, a grim smile twisting at his lips. "Seven of Swords. It seems you have an interesting time ahead of you, Noel."

Noel stared at the card, colour draining from his face. Ursula was not familiar with tarot symbolism, though Noel's shocked expression told her it was nothing good.

"Thank you for your time." Shrugging his coat tighter around him, Noel marched from the Fairley residence without a backward glance. Ursula strode out after him, craning her neck up to the sky to see that gunmetal grey clouds had gathered overhead, threatening to spill rain.

"Did you really have to hurt him?" Annoyance coloured her tone as she fell into step beside Noel on the street. She could appreciate wanting answers, but Warren had done nothing to earn such a volatile attack on his mind.

Noel stuffed his hands in his coat pockets. "Some people need a push, Ursula. Warren is one of them."

Ursula wondered if part of Noel's hatred of Andie stemmed from a dislike of her father. The two men had, after all, been married to the same woman at different times. Whatever his reasoning, it was apparent that Noel held Warren in contempt. Warren was certainly not innocent, but it did make Ursula question Noel's motives.

"So what now? We know that Excalibur is still with the Lady of the Lake, at least as of twenty-six years ago."

"Which is more than anyone else knows." He tossed Ursula a thoughtful look. "If Warren stole those volumes from Sterling, there may be more with information that could be useful to us."

Ursula stopped abruptly, boots scuffing against the sidewalk. The scent of rotten fruit carried on the breeze, and thunder rumbled overhead along with a brief flash of lightning.

"Are you asking me to steal from Lord Spring?"

"No." Noel's tone was steady, as if speaking to a child throwing a tantrum. It only made her more vexed with him. "I'm asking if you can have a look and see what else only you can read. I doubt Sterling's perused many of them, he doesn't seem like much of a reader."

It was a tempting prospect. Ursula did not consider herself rebellious, but there was a delicious irony in having knowledge that the Lords did not. Perhaps then they would be forced to consider her usefulness, instead of shutting her out of meetings because Larkin requested it. She did her best to prevent a smile from slipping onto her lips, for she didn't want Noel thinking she approved of his actions.

"I can look. I can't promise more than that."

Chapter Thirty-Four

Andie Fairley

Andie's trailer was a glittery chaos of shoes, dresses, and old costumes as she unceremoniously dumped the contents of her life into boxes. As Larkin's fiancé, it was expected that she would be moving into the Delavane residence with him. The trailer that Andie once despaired of had become a safe haven, if only for a few more days until she was expected to have her things ready.

She almost missed sharing it with Flo. At least with her present, there had been a flow of conversation, regardless of the layers of snark. It had not been so utterly quiet, feathers and sequins staring silently back at Andie from the bed. She heaved a sigh and tugged her fingers through her curls, nails catching in the coils. The Delavane residence had plenty of space, yet it would feel claustrophobic in comparison to the trailer.

A sharp rap on the door made Andie blow out a sigh. She was not in the mood for interruptions, not when she wanted the whole thing over and done with. When she threw open the door, she paused to see Flo standing with her hands on her prominent stomach. Surely she had to be due within a week or two. Large bump aside, it was Flo's red-rimmed eyes that caught Andie's attention.

"May I come in?" Flo asked.

"Alright." Andie stepped back to give Flo a wide berth, allowing her into the trailer unimpeded, a dozen questions on her mind as the heavily pregnant blonde sank down on the bed amidst the clothes.

"I miss living here sometimes." A soft smile crossed Flo's face as she trailed her fingers over the red velvet of one of Andie's dresses. "It was nice to have my own space."

Andie arched an eyebrow. "Have you and Syl quarrelled?"

"No, not at all." She shook her head fervently, shuffling herself forward so she perched on the edge of the bed. When she stared up at Andie, bitter guilt shone in her chestnut eyes before she averted them. "There's something I've been meaning to tell you for a while now. I kept trying to pluck up the courage to do it, but…"

"Just spit it out, Flo." There had never been any beating around the bush between the pair of them. Had she damaged one of Andie's prized dresses? If so, Andie hadn't noticed while taking stock of them for the move.

"The baby, it…" Flo closed her eyes and inhaled deeply, tears slipping out from beneath her lashes and cascading down her cheeks. When she opened her eyes again, her bottom lip trembled. "It's not Syl's, Andie. It's Larkin's."

The words snatched Andie's breath away, holding it prisoner in her chest. Horror stiffened her limbs, followed by the hot sting of betrayal injected in her veins. Surprise never registered, for she had seen Larkin flirt with other women. She had simply assumed that he was too absorbed in her to follow thought with action. Though she had never wanted to have Larkin's children, suddenly Andie could hardly stand to look at Flo's bump.

Once, it would have been Flo's banner of victory, one she would have waved tauntingly in Andie's face. Yet Flo couldn't look Andie in the eye, misery and shame etched across her pale features as she hung her head and awaited Andie's verdict.

Andie pinched the bridge of her nose, warding off the pounding that had begun in her head. What use was anger when she only had part of the truth? What use was fury at Flo when she had far better places to direct it?

"Explain." The single word was curt, a cold command that had Flo stammering to obey.

"It happened in February, not long before the Valentine's Day performance. You and Larkin…he said you quarrelled over a former lover of yours. He said that things were over between the two of you. He invited me to come and have a drink at his place, and then we did some cocaine and had sex."

"Just once?"

"Only once." Flo nodded vehemently, choking back a sob. "Andie, I didn't know until later that he was lying. I know you and I didn't always get on, but I would *never* have done it if I knew he still intended on pursuing you."

Guilt riddled Flo's body, making her hunch in on herself. Her words dripped with shameful earnestness. The truth was written there plain as day for anyone looking for it, and so Andie believed her. A starstruck young woman, giddy over attention from a powerful man… of course Flo had fucked him.

"Does Larkin know?"

"No." Flo chewed at her lip, picked at her nails. "Syl and I started stepping out together not long after, and when I found out, he was the first person I told. He promised to tell people the baby was his, and treat the child as his own once it's born."

"Flo." Andie rested a hand lightly on her shoulder. "I'm not angry with you. Larkin told you there was nothing between him and I at the time to get you into bed. Men fucking lie, all the time."

"I know that." Flo pressed her face into her hands, cheeks reddening with embarrassment. "I used to work in a brothel. I know that men say anything to get what they want, and I just…I wanted to believe him, Andie. I wanted to believe I meant something, and then he ignored me afterwards and I knew it was nothing."

Humiliation rolled off the girl in waves. Andie sat down beside her and pulled the younger woman into a hug, letting Flo cry into her shoulder. She had never much liked Flo, though perhaps she'd become more bearable lately. It didn't mean Flo deserved to be used and discarded, simply because Larkin hadn't had sex with Andie.

In this, they were bonded. In being mistreated, in different ways by the same man, they shared a unique pain. She slipped her hand into Flo's, offering a lifeline to anchor her. When Flo squeezed her fingers with a weak smile, she knew it had been accepted.

Since Larkin had seized her by the neck and pushed her into accepting his proposal in the hall of mirrors, Andie believed she only had one choice: accept the role she found herself forced into. She realised the folly of that, for when had she ever meekly resigned herself to the box others attempted to put a lid on?

She deserved better. Flo deserved better. Andie had power now, glowing at her fingertips, causing the Lords to scurry around in trepidation of what she might do. In truth, Andie's magic was a formidable weapon, but her greatest had always been her mind. The cogs of it turned like clockwork, ticking over until they found a solution.

Larkin once said he thought she'd be his undoing, and he was right. Andie wouldn't be his bride. She would be his reckoning.

* * *

When Andie had organised a cocktail night with Dot, she hadn't intended for Felix to be present, and found herself vexed that he was. When she'd first heard of Felix through Sterling's complaints, she had found him rather fascinating. There had been an incident in Las Vegas where Felix was caught in bed with a married couple, leading Sterling to bemoan his youngest son's decadent lifestyle. Andie had been impressed, until he'd arrived in New York and attempted to flirt with her, clumsy overtures souring her to his previous acts of daring.

"I can't help but admire your ring." Dot took Andie's hand in her own as Felix stirred some honey mead in with some lemon juice across the kitchen. "It positively sparkles, doesn't it?"

"Well, show me yours." Andie hadn't paid close attention to Dot's own ring, for how much Dot fawned over hers.

Dot proudly extended her delicate long fingers. Her ring was not a typical diamond, but rather a pink stone that Andie didn't recognise.

"That's incredibly unique, Dot."

"Isn't it?" Dot beamed, tossing her hair back. "It's rose quartz. Cyril says that it represents true and unconditional love. He made the ring himself, you see. His soul magic is to do with minerals or rocks, or something of the sort."

Dot shrugged a nonchalant shoulder, and Andie bit her tongue from reminding the older woman that she was Cyril's third wife. Nonetheless, she processed this new information in contemplative silence. The Lords didn't like to give her inklings of what they could do, though she was now aware of what three of them could do. Magic that could manipulate rocks and minerals…it was an interesting gift.

Andie's mind drifted back to the newspapers she'd read in Sterling's library, including an incident that occurred on October 15 in 1918 when there had been a cave-in at 93rd Street Station in the early hours of the morning. There had been no casualties, but it lined up with what Larkin had mentioned off-hand regarding when he had killed his father.

"I call this one the Nectar of Life, ladies." Felix presented each of them with a pale yellow cocktail in a crystal glass. Dot and Andie chimed glasses, before all three of them went quiet to let the alcohol burn its way down their throats. The mixture of honey mead and lemon juice ran smooth over Andie's tongue.

"That was actually divine, Felix."

"Yes, well, it's your turn to make one now." He caught her by the shoulders and steered her into the kitchen.

Andie's gaze raked over the myriad ingredients and alcohol options present on the kitchen bench. Should the police call upon them, they'd have enough evidence to cast them in jail, though Andie supposed considering the influence of men like Cyril, that would likely not come to pass. She'd seen how subtle the bootleggers were in many of the bars and clubs, working under the radar to sell their wares. The magical elite had no such restrictions.

"What about a lavender one?" Andie picked up a sprig of rosemary, waving it back and forth and indicating the lavender gin with her free hand. When Dot grinned and Felix nodded fervently, she started putting the ingredients together, selecting an elderflower juice to add to the mix.

"Felix is quite the natural at this." Dot nudged him slyly. "He worked at bars in Las Vegas for a while before Prohibition."

"Oh, what about your days on the acting circuit?" Felix leaned against the glass cabinet housing Cyril's liqueurs, arching a mischievous eyebrow. "You certainly had some wild days before you settled down with Cyril."

Dot giggled and blushed but made no further comment. Andie busied herself mixing the lavender gin and elderflower juice, adding sprigs of rosemary to each of their glasses as a garnish.

"You don't act anymore, Dot?"

"Oh, goodness no." She waved a dismissive hand, taking a pack of cigarettes off the kitchen bench and lighting one up. "Not since I married Cyril."

"What was that last one you were in?" Felix cast a discerning look at her. "Railway Road or something, wasn't it?"

"The worst performance of my career!" Dot wailed, pressing her free hand over her face in embarrassment. Andie could certainly see how she was an actress, with her flair for the dramatic.

"Did you film that one on an actual train?" Andie asked as she distributed the cocktails across the bench.

Dot's cigarette bloomed cherry-red as she took a puff, exhaling smoke as she nodded vigorously.

"Yes, at 91st Street Station. I heard they were awfully cross with having to shut down for filming several hours a day."

"Oh, isn't that close to where the cave-in happened in 1918?" Andie latched onto the connection with relish, raising her cocktail to her lips and letting the lavender flavour sit in her mouth a moment before swallowing.

"Yes, that was 93rd Street Station." Dot propped herself up so she was sitting on the bench, swinging her legs, none the wiser to Andie's line of questioning. "What a miracle no one was hurt! Can you imagine if such a thing had happened in the middle of the day?"

In the middle of the day, Franklin's murder and the cave-in would have drawn in too much suspicion. Yet if it was the middle of the night, and no one was around, why would the cave-in be needed at all? Considering what Dot had mentioned, Andie was certain the cave-in would have been Cyril's doing.

Andie mulled over the point with frustration coursing through her alongside the lavender gin. The only murder she had committed, which she reflected on with no shortage of sick guilt burning like bile up her throat, she had been so scared she had immediately gone to dispose of the body. She should have done better by Claire, allowing her sister to be buried, in a grave where her loved ones could have placed flowers. Instead, she had dumped her body in the Harlem River like a stone.

"Andie?" Dot's brow furrowed. "Are you alright? You look a little…distant."

"I think I just need to sit down." She sank down to the polished kitchen tiles with her half-drunk cocktail, letting the coolness of the marble seep into her skin. She supposed even if Claire's body was fished from Harlem River, it would have been obvious that it hadn't been the water that claimed her, but the bullet in her head.

Cause of death.

Andie inhaled sharply as realisation shook her with triumphant hands. The cave-in meant that Franklin's corpse would have been horribly disfigured, to the point where any mortician could not have questioned that the falling rocks were the cause of death. The cave-in was intended to absolve Larkin of any blame.

No one had any reason to suspect Cyril of causing the cave-in, not when there had been apparently nothing to gain for it. No one had any reason to suspect Larkin had shot and killed his father, not when Ursula had received a telegram to say he'd died in the war. Only someone with all of the facts could put together the puzzle.

Only someone who knew Larkin from the inside out could destroy him.

Chapter Thirty-Five

Prue Clermont

In the depths of late autumn, Central Park was an array of red and yellow hues, the leaves rustling down from the trees to trek across the grass. They stuck to the soles of Prue's boots as she and Sadie took a turn about Belvedere Castle. The sun crept beneath the trees, trailing pale orange and purple across the sky. The brightness of the evening was a stark contrast to the colourless grey of Prue's coat, and the nerves that tangled up within her.

After Prue had mentioned meeting the leader of the Brigade, Sadie's reluctance had been palpable. It was evident that Sadie herself was a part of it, considering her friendships with Syl and the late Patrick. Nonetheless, Prue had no idea how deep that connection ran. Sadie proposed they walk in Central Park, and claimed she would offer Prue some of the answers she'd sought for some time.

"Are you the leader of the Brigade?" Prue blurted out, stopping in her tracks and extricating her arm from Sadie's. The thought had weighed upon her mind since they'd ventured out. Sadie had the resources and the connections. She was secretive and held her cards close to her chest. The idea was not entirely impossible.

Sadie glanced sharply at Prue, surprise flaring in her eyes, before a laugh bubbled up from her lips. "No, I'm not. I can see why you might think that, though."

"Was that your idea from the beginning?" Bitterness tinged Prue's words, the rosy haze of their shared memories dulling as she wondered whether she'd been used. "Get to know me and gain my trust so that the Brigade could use me?"

"Prue, I didn't even know what you were in the beginning." Hurt hardened Sadie's voice as she levelled a shocked stare at her.

"So then tell me the truth." Prue folded her arms over her chest, staring at the splendour of Belvedere Castle over Sadie's shoulder. She'd never been inside, for in truth she typically frequented Central Park to attend the Carnival. Even those days seemed long past her.

"This is truth." Sadie gestured to the castle, and a hungry gleam shifted into her eyes as they raked over the castle. "This is where it's hidden, Prue. Clarent, the sword in the stone. There are secret crypts beneath this castle, and Clarent lies within its depths."

"Clarent?" she repeated blankly.

Sadie pitched a sigh. "Legend says that all magic stems from the time of King Arthur. Guinevere was a Scourge like you, and she removed the essences of Lancelot, Arthur, and Mordred and stored them away. The same legend also says that Arthur's sword, Excalibur, and Mordred's sword, Clarent, were separated, with Clarent being returned to the stone from which it came."

Prue blinked a few times. "You're telling me...there's a magical sword buried beneath Belvedere Castle?"

She'd heard whispers of Arthurian legend, snatches of names or phrases, never quite enough to piece together a connection. If Guinevere was a Scourge and stole so many essences, it made sense as to why the magical community would be so worried about Prue. Annoyance crept over her like a cobweb, the irritation that knowledge had once again been kept from her when she may have benefitted from it.

"The Brigade wants the sword." A soft smile crossed Sadie's lips, a dreamy expression flitting over her face. "It would give them enough power to challenge the status quo. So far, none of the magical elite have been able to draw it from the stone. Perhaps it doesn't belong to them, after all."

"Does the Brigade still want to use my abilities?" Prue pushed, realising that despite Sadie's adamant insistence that she hadn't used Prue, she had never answered whether the Brigade still sought her out.

"Yes." The truth from Sadie's lips was running water over a fresh burn, soothing and comforting. "The second operative who was meant to work with Patrick to perform the Scourge Ritual on Larkin…it was me, Prue."

Cool discomfort slithered along Prue's skin, tingling at her scalp and along the back of her neck. She chided herself on not having suspected as much, knowing already that Sadie was a powerful mage. The regret that tugged down at the corners of Sadie's lips and the sheen of tears in her eyes betrayed her true feelings about Patrick's death. They had been closer than Prue realised, and it was obvious how important they both were to the Brigade.

"They still don't know who killed Patrick?"

"Whoever it is, they've covered their tracks exceptionally well." Hatred and grudging respect fused in Sadie's turn, and she reached up to wipe at her eyes. "No leads yet, and it's been months."

"Tell me more about the swords." Prue reached out to take Sadie's hand, squeezing lightly. Their eyes met, a bolt of lightning searing through Prue's stomach at the electricity of their combined gaze. "Why are they so important?"

"The leader of the Brigade has some old tomes." Sadie's brow furrowed in thought as she continued. "From what they can tell and who they've spoken to, it seems there's some prophecy on the Born Again drawing one of the swords. There's definitely more to it, but some parts of the tomes are indecipherable."

"Why?"

Sadie shrugged. "They're written in the ancient language of magic. Few can interpret this, it died out centuries ago. Even the best linguists couldn't solve it. The leader thinks there's someone who can, though."

"You aren't going to tell me who the leader is?" Prue asked, despising the pleading note that entered her tone.

"They'll reveal themselves soon, I promise." Sadie closed her eyes and tilted her face back, illuminated by the dying light of the sun and Prue thought she'd never looked so beautiful as she did right now. The quiet was broken only by the trill of birdsong, and Prue couldn't see anyone else around. She wondered if, like the Carnival, this was another space that kept magic hidden unless you wanted to see it. For the first time, she wondered who created those sort of magical barriers, for they were only really seen infrequently.

"Enjoying a brisk sunset walk?"

A sardonic man's voice made Prue whirl around, heart hammering like a drum as she realised they were not alone after all. A man and a woman approached them with matching hawkish smiles, which combined with the similarity of their features, made Prue certain they were related. They shared the same mousy brown hair and grey eyes, not to mention fine clothing that rivalled anything Sadie owned. The man carried a burlap sack in one hand, and there was a dark stain across his black trousers that made Prue's stomach twist.

"Charles. Abigail." Sadie's eyes flicked between them, but her body had gone rigid. This was not like when her apartment had been invaded by some Alderidge associated gangsters. Fear held her rigid, lit up her eyes and sank into the downward turn of her mouth.

"Sadie." The woman's voice was low and sweet, reminding Prue of molten honey. There was something oddly familiar about the pair, as if she'd seen them before. "Well, this is all rather unpleasant."

"Did your daddy dearest send you to do his dirty work?" Sadie sneered, and the fear bled from her as contempt took its place. The disdain that contorted her features cleared any doubt that she was familiar with the pair. "I can't imagine why he'd send you, Abigail. Aren't you forbidden from doing magic, like the rest of the women?"

Abigail clenched her jaw. "I was given an exception, just for this."

Violence loomed in the air like a dark cloud. Abigail and Sadie glared daggers at one another, and Prue could feel the heat radiating from Sadie. She would morph into a blaze of flaming glory with the slightest provocation from Abigail.

"This is about the Scourge," Charles drawled, an air of perpetual boredom surrounding him as he rummaged around in the burlap sack. "Father thinks perhaps your meeting with Lord Winter and Noel Alderidge wasn't enough to convince you, and that you may need further prompting."

Charles tossed something that hit the ground with a thud, rolled, and landed at Prue's feet with a squelch, and it took a moment for her to process what she was staring down at.

Mark's head. Her husband's head. Eyes screwed tight shut as if he'd died in agony.

Prue's scream ripped through Central Park and startled the birds from the trees. A sound drenched with anguish and horror…but above all, an incandescent rage. She reached for Charles with no hesitation, murder thrumming in her heart. She and Mark had never been perfect, but he had been a good husband, a good man, and this rich asshole had *killed* him to prove a point. She would prove hers too: that no amount of money on this earth would save Charles from her fury.

"*No!*" Sadie pushed herself between Charles and Prue, arms lighting up with flames as she held one out to each to separate them further. Confusion jolted through Prue, but her anger won out.

"Get out of my way, Sadie. I'm going to rip him apart."

There was more she wanted to say. There was more she wanted to scream. Yet when she opened her mouth, the words died on her lips. She sucked in a deep breath as the air was pulled from her lungs, and the triumphant smirk on Abigail's lips as she twisted her fingers made Prue certain she was responsible.

Her vision blurred, swimming in and out of focus. Sadie, still aflame, was shouting curses at the siblings. Charles's mocking laughter. Abigail's cruel smile.

The last thing that came into focus was Mark's pale face, the grimace forever etched on there, as everything went dark.

Chapter Thirty-Six

Ursula Delavane

Larkin and Andie's arguments filtered through the upstairs floorboards, seeping down to where Ursula nursed a glass of tempranillo by the fireplace. She couldn't quite decide if it was better or worse than listening to the rhythmic thumping of the headboard against the wall. Ursula couldn't tell what was being said, but Larkin's voice was low and ominous, Andie's hard and angry in response.

After a few moments of tense silence, the door to the bedroom swung open and slammed closed, the thud of feet quickly descending the stairs. When Ursula glanced over, Andie rifled through the coat rack. Shadows in the shape of finger marks lingered on her wrists. Ursula's stomach coiled and she set down the glass of tempranillo, the taste sour on her tongue.

"Where are you going at this hour?"

"To see my family." The girl looked over at Ursula with resolute blue eyes and the sort of charming smile painted on her lips that she would adorn back in her performing days. "You needn't worry, Mrs Delavane. I'll be perfectly fine."

Before Ursula could say anything more, Andie wrenched open the front door, a gust of cool wind sweeping through the house as she stepped outside, tugging the door closed behind her. Only once her footsteps receded did Ursula hear another pair of feet on the staircase. This time, the wine was a requirement, no matter how it tasted, as Larkin joined her in the sitting room.

Mention of the bruises on Andie's wrists died on Ursula's tongue. By the set of his jaw and the hard gleam of his eyes, he'd not want to hear what she had to chastise him about. Larkin sank into the couch, fingers gliding through his unkempt blonde hair.

"When's the wedding?"

"What?" Larkin's head jerked toward his mother, tense expression slackening in astonishment.

"Do you think dragging this out will make matters easier?" Ursula arched an eyebrow, setting down her empty glass. "Larkin, things are tense between you, and you aren't even married yet."

Larkin tilted his head back, rolling his eyes. "So a quick wedding would resolve that?"

"A child would resolve that."

The words settled between them, cold as the first snow of winter. Larkin had never much struck Ursula as paternal, but neither had Franklin. There had been a shift in Franklin and Ursula's dynamic when Larkin was born. Some things they'd never get back, some things they'd gained. Being a parent was a tumultuous experience, yet Ursula would not have given it up for the world.

"She doesn't want children, Mother." There was a frosty edge to his tone that made Ursula ponder what *he* wanted. "We've had that conversation."

They lapsed into uncomfortable silence, the snap of the logs in the hearth the only respite to an uneasy quiet. Larkin had invested too much in Andie to give her up. His utter obsession with her had twisted, growing thorns and drawing blood. She practically glowed with power now. The only way through was forward, and yet Larkin struggled to see the path.

"What is it about her that vexes you?" Ursula questioned, picking up the bottle of tempranillo and refilling her glass, the red liquid sloshing against the sides of the bottle. Andie was certainly not always easy to get on with, but her razor-sharp wit was paired with an effortless charm that made her almost palatable.

Larkin inhaled sharply through his nostrils, staring into the fire. As a child, he had always told Ursula that he would gain control over the flames. When Franklin had sharply informed Larkin of the cost, gripping the small boy's shoulders and shaking hard until he trembled, such fantasies faded from Larkin's mind. Yet somewhere over the years, the elements factored into Larkin's inventory. The wine went bitter in Ursula's mouth as she pondered when he had gained heart magic.

Who had he betrayed for it? What had he done for it?

"She wants freedom, and I want more than anything to give it to her." Larkin released the breath he'd been holding. "It's not real though, is it? The illusion that we can be free. The rules of society apply to all of us. She's just stubborn. She thinks she's above them."

The melancholy in his voice proved his affection for Andie was no lie. Yet love made fools of them all, as it had once done to Ursula. She would have done anything for Franklin, and he wielded her loyalty as brutally as a knife. Did Larkin feel the sting of being the one who did the loving, instead of the one who was loved?

"If she cares about you, she will compromise." Ursula had compromised so many times over the years, if not deserted her wants completely to prioritise Franklin's. If Andie did not bend, then she would break.

A rueful smile tugged at the corners of Larkin's lips, cynicism spelled out in the shake of his head.

"She'll fall into line. She just needs a bit of convincing."

Nausea swirled in the pit of Ursula's stomach as she stared down at the last dregs of the tempranillo bottle. She had seen the methods of Larkin's attempt at conviction, the black and blue it left behind, so familiar to the long-faded bruises she once bore. He may not have raised a hand to strike her across the face as his father might, yet Franklin's ghost lingered in the Delavane residence, breathing down their necks.

* * *

Being invited to spend time with the Alderidge brothers was becoming a frequent occurrence, though Ursula was surprised when she had afternoon tea with Garrett alone. Noel's absence was both cause for comfort and concern. He was an intense and intimidating presence, yet she could not help but wonder what Garrett wanted from her without Noel around.

He buttered his scones with precision, sipping from his porcelain cup with precision, made small talk with precision. Unlike Noel, who despised chatter and pointless social interactions, Garrett thrived on it. He was, after all, the Governor of New York. When he set his cup down to nestle in its saucer, he fixed Ursula with a warm smile.

"You know, I'm pleased that Noel has found a friend in you. He has few enough."

"I'm glad he feels he can confide in me." Ursula's fingers drummed across the rim of her own cup as she swallowed the barbed notion of friendship with Noel Alderidge.

"I thought we might discuss something." Garrett set the spoon back in the jam. "This is my second term as Governor of New York, and more than anything, what I want is to create change. After the war, there's a lot of hopelessness. Prohibition has been more of a hindrance than a help."

"I'm afraid I'm no political advisor, Mr Alderidge." Ursula's shoulders tensed, for she had stated a fact they were both aware of. "So I must ask, what is it you think that I can do for you?"

"Magic," Garrett said as he clicked his fingers, delight widening his smile. "So enthralling. When I found out about its existence, I must admit, hope stirred in me. I wondered what we could use it for, so you can imagine my disappointment when I learned that it existed for parlour tricks and shows behind closed doors."

'*He sounds like Larkin.*' Unease rippled up Ursula's spine at the realisation that Garrett and Larkin expressed the same desire: for magic to become more widely used. Was that not also the same thing the Brigade were fighting for?

"So you want magic without boundaries?" The contempt dripped into her voice despite her best efforts to suppress it.

"Oh, goodness, no." Garrett's eyes widened with horror at the thought, and she was struck by how theatric he was. "Rules exist for a reason. I can completely appreciate what the Lords have done, and how they have maintained order. I think magic could be…let's say, regulated."

So not quite the same as the Brigade, then. Whatever Garrett thought magic could accomplish, he didn't believe it should be a free-for-all. Strict administration was the only way forward in such an outlandish endeavour. Ursula sighed, clasping her hands together in her lap and leaning forward.

"Mr Alderidge," she said, bringing her hands together in her lap, "I can appreciate your zeal. Magic is used by the elite, just quietly. Think of it as Prohibition. On the books, alcohol is illegal and not in distribution. Off the books…well, there's quite a lot happening there."

"Imagine a world where mages could use their magic for the betterment of society!" Garrett spread his arms wide. "The advancements we could make medically, the way magic could become a part of everyday life."

"Imagine the horrors, Mr Alderidge." Ursula's voice pitched soft, yet firm. "We have just experienced a war like no other. What sort of damage do you think may have been done if magic was used to fight it? There are many reasons why magic is kept hidden."

The reason for her summoning was clear now. Garrett wished her to be his advocate in approaching the Lords for a magical expansion. The Alderidge brothers had become a vital part of the inner circle, and yet if their ambition exceeded their influence, Ursula feared what would become of them.

"I can understand your reluctance." Garrett added a teaspoon of sugar to his tea. His movements were careful, methodical. "I don't intend to upset you, Mrs Delavane. I simply wanted to share my ideals, and I know that Noel has come to think you are a person worthy of sharing them with."

Ursula wasn't certain whether she should be flattered or alarmed. "That's very kind of him."

Had Noel shared Warren's revelations with Garrett? The brothers were close, so it was difficult to imagine he hadn't. Cool discomfort blew like a breeze over Ursula. Noel was deliberately drawing her in, making her feel a part of whatever he and Garrett were planning. She had no idea what the brothers were up to, yet they weren't content with their lot. Noel's digging for Excalibur *meant* something.

What made Ursula so disturbed was not the fact that the Alderidge brothers were plotting, for wasn't everyone? Didn't everyone have their own agendas? No, what chilled her to the bone was that, for whatever reason, they believed she was someone they wanted to include in their schemes. She just did not yet know why.

Chapter Thirty-Seven

Andie Fairley

CALLING A MEETING WOULD HAVE RAISED suspicions, set the Lords on edge, and thrown Andie's carefully curated plan to the wind. Not to mention the fact that Sterling would have sneered and said it wasn't her place to demand such a thing. Instead, Andie waited until an opportunity presented itself, like a flower unfurling into bloom. She sweetly asked to go with Larkin to the latest meeting. After all, didn't Dot attend them too now? Desperate to please, or perhaps desperate to fill the growing cracks in their relationship, Larkin agreed.

Andie waited with a glass of champagne in hand and nervousness eating away at the pit of her stomach. Her hands were clammy and she jiggled her legs, trying to dispel her anxious energy. Fortunately, the Lords were too preoccupied with discussion of the Brigade and a fugitive they'd captured to notice. Despite her own agenda, she paid attention, noting that the information they tossed around nonchalantly in front of her may be beneficial later.

What she was about to do was horrific, and yet it was also just. She deserved independence, to break free from the shackles Larkin had fastened upon her. Every bruise on her wrists was another tally to the score, another addition to the myriad reasons why Larkin needed to be removed from a position of power. What happened to that position, Andie also had ideas on.

"I wondered if I might contribute something." Her words were gentle and soft, a stark difference from her usual boldness, as if to coax them in with honeyed bait instead of demanding they walk into the trap.

"What sort of something?" Sterling appeared disgruntled by her interruption, as he was most of the time when she spoke. He was a problem she could deal with later on, but for now, she had one primary focus.

"I wanted to discuss the events of October 15, 1918."

Larkin stiffened, pupils blown wide with panic. Across the room, Cyril's fingers tightened around his cigar, shoulders tensing as he continued to peer out the window as though the entire conversation was beneath him. Emboldened by their guilty reactions, Andie pasted on a dazzling smile as she continued on.

"From my understanding, at least, it's illegal for an heir to kill one of the Lords. Is that true?"

"It is." Desmond's brow furrowed, though keen interest gleamed in his dark eyes. "What are you implying?"

"So, are there consequences for that crime?" Andie asked as she leaned back in her chair, crossing one leg over the other, enjoying the way all eyes focused uneasily on her. "Or is it like Prohibition, where it happens behind closed doors but no one really cares?"

"It's a serious offence, young lady." Sterling scowled at her, causing Andie's smile to widen. "Punishable by being stripped of rank and magic, and potentially even exile. Why would you even mention such a thing?"

"Because someone here has done just that." Andie's gaze locked onto Larkin. She let the implications settle over the others, an accusation without mention of a name. Standing behind Cyril's chair, Dot pressed a hand over her mouth.

She would never have been able to bring Larkin down of her own accord. So she did the one thing he wouldn't anticipate: played by the rules instead of lashing against them. She hardly needed to ruin Larkin, when he had done as much to himself.

"Andie…" There was a warning in Larkin's voice, a shocked glint to his pale eyes.

"What are you saying?" Sterling's words hitched with astonishment. "Are you claiming that Larkin murdered his own father?"

"Well, there is someone who could clarify for us all, if you doubt my word." Andie glanced expectantly at Desmond, recalling what she'd been told about his ability to see fragments of memory. "On October 15 1918, Larkin shot his father dead at a railway station upon his return from war. He covered up the incident and organised for a telegram to be sent to Ursula to state that Franklin had died in war. It does sound much more heroic, I'll admit."

"*You fucking bitch!*" Larkin's temper snapped like an elastic band, fury contorting his face as he lunged at her with a snarl. Desmond caught his arm and held him back, and Andie arched an eyebrow. His outburst was condemnation enough, and the horrified silence that crept into every corner of the room proved it. Desmond glanced at the others, his mouth set in a grim line as he gave a single curt nod.

Larkin's death sentence.

Sterling settled back in his chair, face blanching as he ran a hand over his beard. Cyril's reaction was more measured, eyes darting continually to Larkin as he reached behind him to clasp Dot's hand.

"We all know the punishment for the crime." Sterling cleared his throat and eased himself from his chair, looking expectantly to Cyril and Desmond. "It will take all three of us. We can discuss how to proceed afterwards."

"What are you talking about?" Larkin examined the group with blatant dread, his fear intensifying when no one spoke up for him. "You're really going to strip me of my magic? To take my essence out of me? Most of you hated Franklin!"

"The Scourge would have been useful about now," Desmond muttered, fingers raking through his dark hair.

The Scourge Ritual. Andie heard the others speak of it in hushed whispers, a punishment for only the most severe crimes. Larkin's magic would be ripped from him, his essence stored in a jar and kept with the other known essences in the Templeton wine cellar. He would no longer be Lord Summer. Whoever and whatever he became, it would be entirely ordinary.

A fate worse than death.

The other three Lords rose and escorted Larkin from the room. His pleas were audible all the way down the corridor. Dot scurried across the sitting room and sank into the chair beside Andie.

Freedom tasted like ash on Andie's tongue. She slid the ring from her finger, closing a fist around it until the hard edges cut into her skin. Dot rested a soft hand over hers, thumb rubbing over the back of Andie's hand in soothing motions.

Larkin deserved it. For what he had done to Andie, for what he had done to Flo. He deserved to become nothing, a cautionary tale that the others told their children. Yet had Andie done it because she thought it was justice, or because there were things she hungered for that Larkin stood in the way of? Did it matter? She held herself resolute, adamant that she had made the right choice.

Larkin's screams echoed up from the wine cellar, and despite the anger and resentment she held toward him, tears welled in Andie's eyes and slipped silently down her cheeks. Noel had called her a monster, and after all this time, he was right.

✳ ✳ ✳

Larkin's demise held a cold chill over the evening that had little to do with impending winter. The other three Lords returned exhausted, with no sign of Larkin. Desmond set about fixing himself a drink, while Sterling excused himself to putter around upstairs. Andie didn't quite know what he was doing, but she could hear his steps thumping about as if he was pacing. Cyril excused himself to the yard, and another opportunity presented itself to Andie. Leaving Dot curled on the couch with her glass of champagne and putting the ring back on her finger, Andie strode outside.

"I know that can't have been easy." She leaned against the wall, watching as Cyril straightened up from where he'd been inhaling a line of cocaine. "What you did to Larkin. He is alive, isn't he?"

"Of course he is." Cyril assessed her with a guarded expression. "I wouldn't lean too heavily into the sympathetic act, sweetheart. You wouldn't have said a word if you'd cared about his fate."

Andie took the pack of cigars and box of matches from his pocket, lighting one up and taking a puff. She blew out a smoke ring, watching it fade into the cool night air, before turning her attention back to Cyril.

"Dot showed me her ring. Rose quartz, beautiful craftsmanship. You did well on it. Mineral magic, wasn't it?"

Cyril remained silent, a nerve ticking in his jaw. Andie smiled calmly, twirling her cigar around between steady fingers.

"I read in the papers about a cave-in at one of the railway stations. The same station that Larkin met his father at on the night he killed him. The cave-in happened that same night. I thought that was rather odd."

"What are you going to do?" Cyril raised his eyebrows, a nasty gleam brightening his eyes. "Report me to the others as well? I had my own reasons for helping Larkin that night. I think if you were going to turn me in for my assistance, you'd already have done so. Yet you kept that information for yourself."

"Leverage." The word was sweet as honey on Andie's lips. "With Larkin gone, what happens now, with Lord Summer?"

"We induct someone else." Cyril raised a hand to wipe away the sheen of sweat that had gathered on his brow. "Desmond's predecessor had no heir, either. It was how he came to power. Not ideal, but desperate times call for desperate measures."

She smiled humourlessly and held her silence on Flo's unborn baby.

"Oh, Larkin has an heir." Andie held out her hand, letting her engagement ring gleam in the low light, the shimmer of the diamond catching Cyril's eye. "He and I were to be married, before everything that happened."

Cyril's eyes darted between her and the ring, before harsh laughter burst from his mouth. Andie's lips pressed into a thin line as she let him have his moment of mirth. It would not last long.

"Darling, you can't be serious. You think because you were engaged to Larkin, you'd merit a spot amongst the Lords? There has never been a Lady. It's simply not done. Women are hardly permitted to use their own magic…"

"I was," Andie reminded him, folding her arms over her chest. "You have few options. Who else would you induct? I am more powerful than any of the Lords, more powerful even than you. You need a replacement for Larkin, and I stand here ready and offering you one."

"Leverage," Cyril repeated the word, though it was sour. "Let me guess: I advocate for you, or you tell Sterling and Desmond about my involvement in Franklin's murder."

"It's illegal for a Lord to murder another, so…" Andie let the threat linger on the night air. There was every chance that Cyril could brush her off, and yet she doubted it. He had far more to lose than her.

"It's a vote." Cyril said curtly. "I can't ensure anything, you must know that. Sterling will push against it."

Andie flashed a saccharine smile. "Desmond won't."

* * *

The drop in temperature in the wine cellar made Andie shiver and wrap her coat tighter around herself as she descended the stairs. Low lights illuminated the space, a blonde figure curled up on the ground, surrounded by dozens of bottles of wine. He raised his head at the click of her boots, expression hardening. There was not a single scratch on Larkin's body, but his red-rimmed eyes sharpened with an agony beyond her comprehension.

"Are you happy now?" His voice was hoarse, petered out from screaming, and brimming with hatred. "Was this what you wanted, Andie?"

It had never been about what she wanted, and that was entirely the problem. Larkin masqueraded as her liberator to win her over so she would let down her barriers, and then he had wanted to devour her. She wondered, in his attempts to consume her, if the taste of her had become acidic.

"I know about Flo." She planted her hands on her hips, staring down at him. Once he had been a spectacle to behold, Lord Summer himself. Now he was a broken man, and she was the one who had made him so small. "She told me what happened between the two of you. I wonder, how many others have there been since?"

"Is this about another woman?" Larkin eased himself to his feet, hands balled into fists. Once she may have feared his wrath, but now he had nothing left. The power had been ripped from him. "I would have thought you above petty jealousy. It was only Flo, and she meant nothing to me."

"Stop." Andie raised a hand to silence him. Flo had cried over Larkin, over knowing she was just a placeholder, and hearing Larkin confirm that only made Andie's heart harden toward him. "Don't talk about her like that. This isn't about Flo. It's about you and I, and what you wanted us to become."

"I wanted to marry you!" he shouted, baring his teeth as he strode over to her. Andie dropped her hands to her sides, letting the soft glow of light at her fingertips serve as a warning. "I gave you everything, and you bled me dry. I offered you my fucking *heart*, and you ripped it to pieces."

"You never loved me." The words cracked as they left Andie's lips, illusion giving way to reality. "You were obsessed with me. You loved the idea of what we could become. The moment I gained soul magic, you realised you wanted to be the one who held the power. You might have married me, but you wanted me on a leash."

Larkin's jaw clenched. "I offered you freedoms no other woman has, and you spat them back in my face."

"You offered me a golden cage." The silence that extended between them, the resentment that burned in Larkin's pale eyes, told Andie she was right. "You just wanted it to look like freedom."

She turned away from him, eyes raking over the bottles of wine. Each one had a subtle shine, as though the liquid inside held a shimmer. Frowning, Andie picked up one of the bottles and turned it over. The label didn't boast the wine type and region, simply a person's name scrawled across the bottle. Brendan Smith.

"They already took mine upstairs, if you're looking for it." Larkin's voice dripped with malice, and there was a cruel glint to his bright eyes when she whirled back to face him, fingers tightening around the bottle.

"What are you talking about? What is this?"

Larkin's smile stretched across sharp teeth. "I think you already know the answer."

There was no wine in the bottle at all, but instead a soft silvery sheen, like liquid glitter. Andie's body trembled as she realised the 'wine cellar' didn't hold wine at all, but essences. Dozens of them, perhaps hundreds. This was what it looked like to have the magic torn from you and stored away. Andie shoved the bottle back, staggering away.

"I want you to know that I will always remember you did this to me." Larkin strode over to Andie, his quiet loathing cutting in beneath her skin. "You truly are heartless. Remember this: magic or no magic, there is no escaping me. I will always find you, Andie. When I next see you, you will bitterly regret this day."

Andie sneered at his hollow threats, the last taunts of a doomed man. What future did Larkin have outside of the Carnival? How could he possibly hurt her now, when she was the one with the power?

"You don't frighten me, Larkin."

His response was a cold smile, empty eyes raking over her before he marched from the cellar. Alone amidst the dozens of stored essences, Andie's breath misted out in front of her, and she rubbed her arms to ward off an even deeper cold.

*   *   *

Lady Summer.

The words were as bright and warm as a summer's morning. A sense of achievement settled on Andie's head like a crown, even as she settled back into the trailer she had started off in. She did not dare show her face at the Delavane residence, knowing that even if Larkin had deserted it, Ursula would be there. While she planned her next move, and her next living situation, the familiarity of the trailer comforted Andie like a blanket and a hot cocoa.

Desmond and Cyril had voted for her, and Sterling against. It was precisely the outcome she had counted upon, and so victorious, Andie had departed the Templeton residence with the Grimoire tucked under her arm. Sterling had shoved it at her, claiming she would need to read it if she was ever to become one of them. She had only got a few pages in before someone knocked on the door.

"It's Flo," the familiar voice called out, causing Andie's shoulders to slump with relief. The last thing she needed was a heated confrontation, though she somehow doubted she had banished Larkin from her life completely. He'd want revenge, and she'd be ready when he came to claim it.

"Come in," she called as she set the Grimoire on her bedside table. She was surprised that Flo hadn't gone into labour yet, for she was certainly due any day, if not past her due date. "I have good news."

"Really?" Flo winced as she sat down on Andie's bed, strewn with clothes she had yet to unpack.

"Larkin's gone. He's no longer Lord Summer." Her voice alluded to smug satisfaction, but betrayed none of the hidden guilt and dread that mixed in her veins. Guilt was nothing new to her. "It was a process, but…they agreed to make me Lady Summer."

Instead of being pleased, Flo's soft eyes widened with horror and she rested a hand over her stomach. Andie wondered if it was to do with the fate of the father of her child, and that perhaps Flo had a shred of compassion left for Larkin.

"Andie, you've put yourself in danger."

"What are you talking about?" She laughed off Flo's trepidation. "I'm the most influential woman in New York, Flo. Once I figure out where I'm going to live, once I adjust to my position…"

"You think they'll accept you?" Flo's tone was sharp. "Haven't you realised that these people don't want women in power? If you are, that's because they're going to watch your every move, waiting for you to fall."

"I won't fall," Andie assured her, with as much conviction as she should muster. "Listen, Flo. You don't have to think I've made a smart move. I've made the best move for me, and you need to accept that."

Flo sighed heavily, tilting her head back so her blonde hair cascaded down her back. Some women, like Flo, wanted a simpler life. She wanted a family, and she'd gained that with Syl and the baby she was due to have any day. Andie wanted power, and she'd gained that in making Larkin her sacrifice.

"Look, I should go." Flo pushed herself to her feet with some effort. "I just wanted to say if you do need to stay somewhere, Syl and I have a place now. You could stay with us, until you find your own."

Andie shook her head. "I don't think that's a good idea."

"Alright." Flo's jaw clenched at the rejection, but she made her way to the door and stepped out of the trailer into the darkening sky of the evening. "Just be careful, Andie."

"Goodbye, Flo." Andie closed the door and latched it, striding over to flop on her bed, amongst the clothes she desperately needed to sort through. No matter the trailer she lived in, and no matter her murky past, she was Lady Summer. The other Lords couldn't touch her, not after they'd destroyed Larkin for his actions.

She let a few moments pass as she closed her eyes, absorbing what this meant to her. As Cyril had said, there had never been a Lady amongst them. She was the first. She was the exception. A giddy smile crossed her lips, despite the horrors she'd both endured and committed to rise to such an exalted station.

Rolling onto her side, Andie reached out for the Grimoire, only to find that it was gone. She sat bolt upright, casting around to see where she could have thrown it. Yet despite the chaos of her clothes, Andie knew with absolute certainty that she'd set the Grimoire down on her bedside table. The only reason it would be missing completely...

Flo. Andie's jaw clenched as the pieces of the puzzle slotted together. It had been a brief visit, but of course it would be if Flo was only there for one thing. The only question was *why*. Flo had never shown much of an interest in the history of magic, and to Andie's knowledge only dabbled with verbal magic during her tenure as a showgirl. If she'd just wanted to read over the Grimoire, she'd have asked.

It hadn't been Flo's idea, that she was now sure of. Cold certainty of that settled over Andie, as well as apprehension. If the Lords found out she'd had the Grimoire stolen from her, she couldn't imagine the sort of trouble she would be in. Especially since they were all aware of how desperately the Brigade hunted for any scrap of magical arsenal they could obtain. Rumour had it that the Brigade was closing on in Excalibur, if they had the Grimoire...

A sudden gasp tore from Andie's mouth as utter horror and the sharp sting of betrayal seared at her skin.

There was only one person Flo was that devoted to. Only one person she would risk crossing Andie for, risk stealing the Grimoire for. After all, what was duplicity if you were committing it in the name of someone you loved?

It was Syl. It was fucking Syl, and somehow Andie had missed it.

Andie thought herself capable of convincing performances, but she had been eclipsed by her brother. Who would ever suspect the perpetually drunk employee? Who would think the enigmatic leader of the Brigade was a man who stumbled about the place, lacking conviction and clarity? It was the perfect ruse, and Andie had fallen for it spectacularly.

Shoving open the door to her trailer, Andie steeled herself to confront her brother, to give him the push that may damage their newly repaired relationship. Sharp pain exploded at the back of Andie's head, the force of the blow knocking her forward onto the ground. Her vision swam in and out of focus, blurred figures emerging from the shadows. A dull ache throbbed in her skull, and though she fought against the darkness, it closed in around her and dragged her under.

Chapter Thirty-Eight

Prue Clermont

When Prue woke, it was to a soft pillow and a warm blanket. Baffled by her surroundings and alarmed when the memory of Mark's decapitated head resurfaced, she struggled against the silk sheets, prying them off and examining her surroundings with rapid breaths. A large room, a chandelier hanging overhead, velvet curtains draping the windows. It didn't look to be a prison, though she wondered if the handle would turn if she tried the door.

As if summoned by her thoughts, the door burst open, a man entering with a silver tray that he set on the dresser with some force, sloshing liquid from a teapot. Prue recognised his unruly brown hair and the swagger to his step from the Midsummer Ball. Felix Templeton glanced over his shoulder with a raised eyebrow.

"Look, if you're going to attack me and steal my essence, I'd rather you got it over with."

"What is that?" Prue gestured to the tray, though the scent of herbal tea and buttered scones wafted over. Her stomach grumbled in complaint, and she wondered how long she had been unconscious.

Felix sighed. "Breakfast. It's not poisoned."

She wondered why Felix was bringing her food instead of a servant, for she was absolutely certain the Templeton family had them. She sat down on the edge of the bed, gripping the blanket with clammy fingers as she glowered at Felix. He sighed and leaned against the door, clicking it shut behind him.

"This isn't exactly how I wanted to spend my morning either." Felix began to tick off his fingers, noting answers to questions she had not yet asked. "You're in the Fordyce residence. You've been here three days. My psychotic siblings seemed to think it was smart to get me to watch you as the Lords conducted some important business, but they needn't have worried since you only just woke up."

"Charles and Abigail are your siblings?" Prue's mind worked sluggishly to catch up as she crossed over to pour herself some tea. "The three of you are Sterling Templeton's children."

Felix clapped slowly. "There we are. You're caught up. Now, my father and the other Lords wish to have a meeting with you downstairs. They sent me up because frankly, I don't think Father cares what you do with my essence."

Prue couldn't trust him, couldn't trust any of them. Yet it had been Charles and Abigail who had attacked her and Sadie, not Felix. Smarmy though he may be, smugness was not enough of a crime for Prue to warrant attacking him. The tea scalded Prue's tongue as she took a sip, and she hurriedly set the cup and saucer down.

"I don't think I'm hungry," she murmured, her stomach churning as she looked over the scones.

Examining herself, she realised she was in the same clothes she'd been wearing when she'd met Sadie in Central Park. Where was Sadie? She hoped that the other woman was alright, though perhaps by merit of knowing Charles and Abigail, she was receiving treatment befitting a guest rather than a prisoner.

"Alright, then you should accompany me downstairs." Felix offered his arm, and Prue reluctantly took it. Her hair was a mess, oily at the roots, and she didn't even want to consider whether her clothes smelled stale after three days of unconsciousness. Brushing aside thoughts of her bedraggled appearance, Prue followed Felix down the corridor, voices carrying upstairs from the living room.

"Charles and Abigail need to control themselves." A man's reproachful voice, one Prue didn't recognise, chided. "Magical wards aside, what were they thinking carrying around a man's head in broad daylight?"

Prue's feet shuffled to a stop. They were talking about Mark, as if he was nothing. To the Lords, her husband was a mild irritation, a vexing obstacle that Charles and Abigail had attended to without discretion. The familiar arcane hunger clawed at the pit of her stomach, and it took considerable effort to push it back down. Felix examined her, sympathy pinching his brows, before he gave her arm a gentle tug.

"Come along now."

Prue's eyes blurred with tears and a lump itched in her throat as she pushed forward. She would dwell on Mark later, when she could handle her grief privately. These bastards did not deserve to see her cry. They wouldn't know the damage they'd done to her until she was ready to display it.

"Ah, Felix. Finally." The oldest of the men, Lord Spring, reclined in a couch by the window with a mug of tea steaming in his hands. "I'm glad to see that the Scourge is finally awake."

Felix rolled his eyes. "She has a name, Father. Try to use it."

Prue's eyes raked over the trio of men. Odd that one was missing, since she knew there were four Seasonal Lords. The only one she recognised was Lord Winter, whose lips were pressed together in a distasteful line as he glanced at Lord Spring. When he turned his attention to Prue, his expression softened.

"I was truly sorry to hear about your husband, Mrs Clermont. Charles and Abigail stepped outside their jurisdiction, and they will be punished for it."

Lord Spring's eyes narrowed at the clear contempt aimed at his oldest children, though he remained silent.

"Punished?" Once, Prue may have held her tongue, but that was before she had grown a spine of steel and learned to stand on her own two feet. "What good is punishment? My husband is dead. There is no coming back from that. Whatever message you were trying to send, trust me, it was received."

"Now, I think we can save that conversation for later." Lord Autumn, the man whose voice Prue had heard from the landing, waved a dismissive hand. Hot fury surged through Prue's veins, but she bit down on her lip. "We know what you are capable of, Mrs Clermont. We also know you're aware of the Brigade, and what they're trying to do. In fact, I daresay we know more about you than you might think."

Trepidation danced along her arms, raising the hair on her skin. For months, she slipped into the comfort of being invisible to the elite, only to face the unsettling awareness that her anonymity was an illusion.

"What do you mean? You've had someone spying on me?"

The shuffle of footsteps on carpet caught Prue's attention, and she looked over her shoulder as Sadie moved into the room. Her eyes were red-rimmed as though she'd been crying, and Prue went cold all over at the idea that the Lords had hurt her. When she stepped toward her, Sadie's gaze dropped to the ground.

"Miss Crawford has done a wonderful job in keeping us informed of your progress." There was no denying the smug glee in Lord Spring's voice, the way his smile broadened as guilt tightened the set of Sadie's jaw.

Icy betrayal seared through Prue's gut, puncturing her heart like a blade. Part of her had known not to trust Sadie, known that there was more to her even as Sadie had unravelled one secret after another. Yet…Prue's mind buzzed with confusion. Sadie revealed things about the Brigade that only an insider would know. Her role there was no lie, unless…

Bile rose in Prue's throat. She was not the only person Sadie had betrayed, not the only person whose trust was manipulated. Sadie was a double agent the whole time. A cold, dark shard of Prue wondered if perhaps Sadie was the one who had murdered Patrick after all. She didn't even know who the woman she fell for was anymore, because it certainly wasn't this silent stranger.

"Why?" Prue choked out the word, feeling it catch in her mouth. Tears stung at her eyes, but she blinked them away. "*Why?*"

Sadie hated elitists like the Lords. She had constantly spoken of them with disdain dripping from her tongue, her zeal for the Brigade's ideals what had made it all so convincing. What purpose could it possibly serve her in being beholden to the Lords?

"You've done well, Sadie." Lord Spring set down his mug and rose from the couch. There was an oddness to the familiarity with which he addressed Sadie, the affection in his tone. Prue's gaze flicked between the pair and her stomach twisted painfully, horror tightening the knot. How had she not seen it before? The pale eyes, the line of the jaw…

"Thank you." Sadie's eyes wrenched up from the carpet, bright with hatred. "*Father.*"

Chapter Thirty-Nine

Ursula Delavane

Rain pattered down the windows of the sitting room as the front door lurched open, startling Ursula from her seat on the couch and causing the tea in her mug to jostle and slosh into the saucer. Her alarmed heart beat a frantic pace in her chest as thunder rumbled ominously in from the open front door, a gust of wind whirling in on Larkin's heels.

She paused in the hallway, a sliver of moonlight illuminating her face. Her son was completely drenched, his blonde hair beading with droplets of water. His shirt was half-unbuttoned, the sheer misery on his face making her body stiffen. Larkin looked as though he had been tortured. A sob choked from his lips as he fell to his knees, and Ursula hastened to close the front door.

"Where have you been, Larkin? I haven't seen you in days, and now you turn up in such a state…"

"They didn't tell you." Larkin looked up at her, raising his hand to sweep his hair back from his face. "No, I suppose they wouldn't."

Concern quickened Ursula's movements as she grabbed a towel from the hallway cupboard, draping it around her son's shoulders.

"Have you had cocaine again?"

"They took it from me," Larkin spat, wrenching away from her, the towel fluttering to the floor as he scrambled to his feet. "They took *everything*."

In the daylight with the sun dazzling his hair, as Lord Summer, Larkin exuded power and charm. In the corridor, drenched with rain and stumbling over himself, despair written across every muscle of his face, he was like a scared child hiding from the thunder. His tall frame shook, perhaps with fear but perhaps with rage.

"Who took what?" Ursula planted her hands on her hips, impatience pushing through her worry.

"The other Lords." Larkin's bloodshot eyes flicked up. "They performed the Scourge Ritual on me. Banished me."

Terror stole the breath from Ursula's lungs. She had been part of the elite long enough to know that such a punishment was only bestowed upon those who had committed the most heinous of crimes. Her heart ached for the loss of her son's power, snatched away from him, and yet the question that left her lips was tinged with dread.

"What did you do?" When Larkin's jaw worked and he stared at the ground, her trepidation pulsed into panic. "What did you *do*, Larkin?"

"I did us all a fucking favour!" Larkin barked, his eyes wild and a snarl on his lips as he finally met her gaze. "Franklin was a monster. He hurt me, he hurt you. He destroyed everything around him."

Ursula's brow furrowed. She'd received a telegram that Franklin had died during the War, and yet…she stared at her son in utter horror. It had never been a secret that Larkin had loathed his father, but Ursula never expected him to resort to murder. Not when the cost, should his crime be discovered, would always have been severe.

"You killed him." The accusatory whisper was followed by an unhinged, mirthless laugh from her son.

"You never would have known. I kept it to myself for years. Then that fucking little bitch decided to betray me."

Andie. Who else could Larkin be speaking of? For months, her name was uttered with admiration, like dreams dancing off Larkin's lips. This time, hatred burned in her son's pale blue eyes, lips twisted with the venom of which he spoke her name.

Ursula took a step back, shaking her head. She had worked for years to protect her son, to propel him into being the sort of man who would do the Delavane name proud. Instead he had become this, a creature who spat his lover's name with murder in his heart, murder that he was certainly capable of. The raindrops spilled from Larkin's hair and shirt onto the floorboards along with his sins.

Her husband. His father. A monster though he was, Franklin had been *theirs*.

"You've doomed yourself." The words cracked with sorrow at what he had become. "You did this to yourself, Larkin. I can't help you now."

"*Help* me?" Larkin sneered, examining her with contempt. "When did you ever help me? When did you do anything other than what benefited you? I should hardly be surprised that you'd choose to save your own skin over mine."

"You have no idea what I have done for you!" Ursula exploded with indignation, her hands balling into fists by her sides as Larkin lapsed into shocked silence at her outburst. "You couldn't have a clue about the sacrifices I have made to get you to where you are now."

Lightning flashed outside the sitting room window, briefly lighting up Ursula's determined expression. Something dark lingered between them, a secret to which Ursula dangled the key, a lock she had concealed up until then. She didn't know whether she was relieved or dismayed when Larkin let the moment pass, the lock remaining untouched.

"So you won't defend me."

"No." How could a single syllable be so painful, like reaching into her chest and ripping out her own heart? Anguish settled in her chest at the hurt that flashed through Larkin's eyes. She loved her son, since the moment she had first held him in her arms, since his first word and his first step. Yet he was a grown man now, and she was no longer holding herself accountable for his transgressions.

A hollow smile pulled at Larkin's lips, a light leaving his eyes.

"I see."

He trudged back down the hallway and wrenched the door open to the howl of the wind, stepping out into the night without a backward glance. When the door slammed shut behind him, Ursula felt in her bones that she had lost him. Leaning against the front door, she pressed her face against her arms and sobbed.

* * *

Ursula did not consider herself ready for visitors, not after Larkin's abrupt departure, from the house and from her life. Yet when the Lords called upon someone, they were not to be left waiting. So when Cyril arrived, Ursula silently let him inside and called upon Jane to prepare them some tea and biscuits. The quiet extended between them as Ursula sat on the lounge, huddled up with a coat wrapped around her.

"I take it Larkin came back, after the ritual." Regret weighed heavily on Cyril's voice as he reached across to pick up a biscuit. "I want you to know that I am truly sorry, Ursula. None of us wanted it to come to that."

"I suppose you'll need to elect a new Lord Summer." Ursula's voice was stiff and matter-of-fact as she picked up her mug of tea. It wouldn't do to sit in Cyril's presence and sob. They both knew how harsh the fall could be, after a meteoric rise.

"Well, we already have someone." Cyril became intent on examining the biscuit in his fingers. "Lady Summer, rather."

Ursula's entire body tensed. After all that had happened, surely not. The Lords shut the women out, they didn't accept them amongst their own ranks. The grim set of Cyril's mouth told her everything she needed to know.

"You made *Andie Fairley* the new Lady Summer?"

Desmond would have voted for her, of course. He was modern and tended toward progress, not to mention he seemed to have a soft spot for Andie. Sterling would have railed against it, a stickler for tradition and a man who believed Andie's rightful place was as a wife and mother. Which meant, if the vote had succeeded, Cyril would have had to vote for Andie as well. Ursula could not fathom why.

There had to be a motive, and she could not find one, which made her suddenly wary of Cyril. The man never did anything unless it benefitted him, so how did having Andie as Lady Summer do so? She regarded him with blatant suspicion over the rim of her mug as she took a sip, but thankfully he was too busy chewing at his biscuit to notice.

"It won't be easy for her. The first woman, amongst all of you men."

"It wasn't easy for Desmond," Cyril pointed out, dusting crumbs off his lap. "He managed quite well in the end."

"Well, there are other reasons, too." Ursula twisted her hands in the hem of her blouse, debating the morality of what she intended to say. Yet, what harm could come of it? Her son had disgraced himself with his own behaviour. What more was another crime they may well have suspected him of?

"Whatever do you mean?" Cyril's brow furrowed.

"I imagine she would be devastated once she learns that Larkin murdered poor Patrick Rhodes." Ursula feigned astonishment at Cyril's mouth dropping into a gape. "Oh, didn't you know?"

"I…no, we didn't." Cyril's fingers raked through his hair, eyes wide with shock. "I mean, I assume a few of us suspected, but we believed Larkin was beyond some petty jealousy over some young man that Andie was friends with."

"A past lover." Ursula nodded slowly, guilt chewing away at her from the inside out. "He didn't like the idea that Andie might choose Rhodes, so…"

Larkin was exiled, stripped of power, for a far greater crime than the one Ursula insinuated he was responsible for. What harm could it do to lay another one at his feet, if only to neatly tie Patrick's murder up? There was a motive. There was certainly evidence he was capable of it. Besides, it had almost been a year since the young man's death, and nothing had ever been discovered.

After all, who would suspect that Ursula could have been the one to drag a knife across his throat and leave him to bleed out? The visceral memory made her shudder, blood staining her fingertips that she had never quite been able to wipe clean. She had come so close to the truth with Larkin.

"You have no idea what I have done for you!"

He never would. Ursula's own horrific crime was a secret she would take to her grave. The same place Patrick had taken his plans to steal Larkin's essence.

CHAPTER FORTY

Andie Fairley

Andie awoke to the taste of ash in her mouth and dim light flickering down over her. Wincing at its brightness, she was too disorientated to struggle as she was dragged from wherever she'd been curled up. Her feet fumbled and she collapsed to her knees, bitumen digging into her skin, scratching at her bare legs. As her eyes adjusted, she squinted around her and breathed in her surroundings. The damp odour of water. The strong scent of petrol invading her nostrils.

Andie glanced behind her to see several cars, one which had its sleek trunk opened, from where she must have been dragged out onto the road. Ahead of her stood the Harlem River Lift Bridge, dim lights glowing in the thick blanket of night that stretched around them. Apprehension surged through Andie, twinging at the sore spot where someone had hit her in the back of her head.

This was the place where she had tossed Claire's body into the Harlem River. This was the place where she and Noel had their tense confrontation. A whisper of death floated on the night sky.

"Awake at last." Noel strode over, gloved hands clasped behind his back and a thick coat flapping about his heels as he approached Andie.

A cool shiver raced up her arms that had little to do with the winter chill in the air.

"How long was I unconscious?" Andie barked, pushing herself up off the road and drawing herself up to full height. "What the fuck do you think you're doing? I'm Lady Summer now, you can't just…"

"Not for long" Noel replied enigmatically. Triumph gleamed bright in his hazel eyes. "You think your title means anything to me? You think you're something now, just because some rich men told you that you are?"

The late night air caressed Andie's curls, sweeping them back from her face. She could hear the swell of water lapping against the sides of the bridge. At her contemplative silence, Noel's wicked smile broadened. He seized a hold of her arm and tugged her away from the cars toward the bridge. Panic swelled within Andie, despite her best attempts to push it down. Her breathing quickened and her legs trembled beneath her.

"I never forgot what happened that night." Noel released her as they stood at the edge of the bridge, staring down into the liquid black abyss beneath. "I never forgot what you did."

He rolled up his sleeves, exposing the thick white scar along his left arm. Andie flinched and turned her face, memories burning behind her eyes.

The metallic tang of blood as it splattered all over the ground. Noel's fingers shaking as they gripped the knife. Syl screaming at her to stop. Andie, sobbing and laughing, as she pushed her magic harder than ever before, as she tried to save her family by condemning herself.

"I want you to look!" Noel seized hold of her chin in a bruising grip, dark hatred in the narrowing of his eyes and the flash of his teeth.

"I never meant to hurt Claire." Andie's voice shook as truth settled over her bones. The truth of why Noel had brought her to the same place his daughter had been thrown into a watery grave. "Neither of us could save her, so I made it quick. I should never have thrown her body into the Harlem River, I know that now…"

Noel's cruel laughter rang in her ears as his grasp on her chin tightened like a vice.

"Too late."

"You expect me to regret what I did to you?" Hoarse mockery filled Andie's voice. "You made me turn that knife on my brother and you promised me that my father was next!"

For so long, Andie had guarded the darkest truths of that horrific evening, a truth only she, Noel, and Syl fully understood. As she had fallen to her knees and sobbed, begging for forgiveness for what she had done to Claire, Noel had pressed both a knife and the might of his mind magic upon her.

"Your brother is next. I want you to tell him it's alright, like you did with Claire. I want you to comfort him in his final moments, knowing you're going to use this knife to slit his throat."

Andie had cried so hard she couldn't get the words out. The knife had quivered violently between her fingers as she had dragged herself, one step after another, toward a horrified Syl.

"Then I'll take you home to your father, and you'll do the same to him."

Warren, who was the only parent Andie had. Warren, who Noel had already taken enough from. Her fear and grief was eclipsed by sheer rage, and it was the anger that burned through Noel's control. She had turned, knife in hand, and asserted her will instead. She had mind magic too, and Noel had no idea how powerful it was.

"No," she had growled. *"You take the knife. You can carve your arms open."*

She remembered his horror vividly, as he had taken the knife and pressed it to his arm, dragging the point through his skin. Her own laughter, mingling with hysterical tears of rage and terror and relief.

"Stop, Andie! Stop!"

It was Syl's screams that made her relinquish her hold, and when she turned to face her brother, his green eyes alight with dread, she realised what she had almost become. She watched him take a staggering step back, the bond between them yawning further apart, and realised he saw a monster. She would have killed Noel if not for Syl, and that knowledge had weighed them down for years.

She had never used mind control magic since, ashamed of what she had almost done with it, of what it had cost when it came to Syl.

"You will never touch my family. You want people knowing about this when Garrett is running for office? I don't think you do. Tell them whatever story you want, but if you implicate my family, I will destroy everything you love. Starting with Garrett."

Syl's devastated silence had been louder than Noel's roar of rage. Yet when Andie lifted her chin high and stood her ground, Noel made no move to attack her. The hatred that twisted his face, the blood that poured down his slashed arm, said more than any cutting words he could have hurled her way.

"I waited until you ascended." Noel's whisper made her skin crawl. "I waited until you had everything, so I could take it all away from you."

His eyes flicked to something over her shoulder, the scrape of metal over asphalt grating against Andie's ears. When she pivoted to follow his gaze, her panic crescendoed into absolute terror. Two men dragged over an iron maiden, the front yawning open like it was waiting for someone to step inside.

She would die encased in iron. She would die powerless.

Noel seized her by the arms and shoved hard, sending her staggering into the iron maiden. The front slammed close with a clang of finality, encasing her with only an eye-level slit for her to peer out of. The lack of spikes that would typically embed the interior of such a horrific torture device was little comfort to her, for the iron maiden served a different purpose entirely.

"Noel," her voice rasped as tears welled in her eyes. "Noel, *please.* I'm begging you. Let me out!"

"Nine on the Templeton Scale," he taunted, folding his arms over his chest. "What a fucking waste."

Andie beat her fists against the metal. She ignored the pain that throbbed in her hands, or the way her knuckles split and bled. Blind horror overwhelmed every other sense, until she was reduced to a hollow shell of Lady Summer, a terrified woman sobbing and screaming as she desperately tried to claw her way to freedom. She screamed until her throat burned raw.

The iron maiden shook as it was dragged further across the road, toward the edge of the bridge. Andie alternated between hurling curses and begging for her life, but neither made any difference. Sadistic glee lit up Noel's face as the iron maiden teetered on the edge, the water rushing beneath her and the wind whistling through the small slit.

She reached for the spark of magic within her, but it was nowhere to be found. So the rumours about being encased in iron were true. She had nothing left to fight back with, no words, no weapons. Her impending doom was compounded with her sheer helplessness, a cruel punch in the gut.

"Goodbye, Miss Fairley," Noel called, the malicious taunt in his tone sending her into a renewed frenzy of pounding on the metal. "May you rot."

The iron maiden tilted over the edge and hit the water with a splash, before sinking beneath the churning surface.

* * *

Under the water, it was peaceful. The serene quiet was a stark contrast to the brutality of Andie's body fighting inevitable death, water invading her lungs and choking her slowly. She had no strength left to kick or punch at the metal. The struggle left her, pulled out of her as callously as the air from her body. Her eyes fluttered and closed, hair drifting in a sluggish halo around her head.

The cold hands of death reached for Andie, brushing over her with eager fingers. A lost girl beneath the bravado. A wreck beneath the confidence. A heartless creature that Larkin never would have loved. Her voice, always too loud, forever silenced.

Until light burst through Andie's closed eyelids and she found herself gasping for air. When she reached around her, there was no metal beneath her fingertips. Prying open her eyes, she found herself nestled on the sand, and when she looked around, what appeared to be a glass dome separated her from the water. Moonlight from above the surface cast reflections and fragments of pale light through the dome.

Was she dead? Was she in some sort of afterlife? As questions whirled through her mind, a shape shifted through the water and materialised into the form of a beautiful golden-haired woman in the dome.

"Where am I?" Andie demanded.

"Everywhere and nowhere," the woman replied cryptically, her voice as sweet as birdsong on a spring morning. "In a realm that exists beyond space and time."

"Who are you?" Andie examined her warily. The woman was garbed in a simple white dress that appeared to be made of pure light, glimmering as it shifted in the sand as she approached Andie.

"My dear girl, do you not know?" The woman laughed lightly, tilting her head to the side. "I have many names. Most would simply call me the Lady of the Lake, but I was someone else before that. You may call me Guinevere."

The Lady of the Lake. Guinevere the Scourge. They were the same person. Andie's brow furrowed. It didn't make sense, considering the fact that the Lady of the Lake had existed when Guinevere was the wife of King Arthur. Sensing her confusion, Guinevere approached, setting her hands on Andie's shoulders. Warmth flooded through her, like the first sip of tea on a cold winter evening.

"When I stole the swords of power, Excalibur was the last I returned to its watery grave. I made a deal with the Lady of the Lake, and I took her place beneath the water, with Excalibur in my keeping. I serve now as its guardian, as the new Lady of the Lake."

Andie's mouth went dry. Whatever bargain Guinevere struck with her predecessor, it meant she'd spent a thousand years with Excalibur in her protection. Andie cast around, but could see no sign of the fabled sword.

"Why am I here?"

"To make a deal," she said plainly. A shark's smile graced Guinevere's lips, a hungry glint in her eyes. Andie saw the Scourge, the dark creature that had stolen magic from Arthur and his knights. "You are a dead woman, Alexandra. Your enemy threw you into the water to drown, but I can give you life. I can give you power. I can give you Excalibur."

Andie's heart hammered against her ribcage. "For what price?"

"Replacing me." Guinevere shrugged her dainty shoulders. "Not today, not tomorrow. But one day, you will feel the call, and you will answer it. You will become the new Lady of the Lake, cursed to wait until you can bestow Excalibur on someone worthy."

"You think I'm worthy?" Amusement coloured Andie's words, a laugh bubbling up from her lips.

"Sweet girl." Guinevere moved closer, her lips brushing against Andie's forehead, the ghost of maternal affection. "You have always been worthy. You have always suspected that you were destined for something greater. You are the Morning Star, wielder of Excalibur."

She was not the first person this honour had been offered this to. Of that much, Andie was certain. Yet the fact that Excalibur remained buried beneath the water meant that others had refused, the price too steep. Andie had no other option. She could choose life, and the sword of a long-dead king, or she could drown in Harlem River.

The woman before her waited patiently, hands clasped demurely in front of her. Patience was an art form, to someone who had waited a thousand years for this moment. She wore grace as her cloak, wielded kindness as her shield. Andie saw her for what she was beneath the armour of courtesy: a kindred spirit.

"I accept." Andie's voice was resolute. She would have a power like no other, a power that extended beyond being a nine on the Templeton Scale. They would kneel before her, as they should have from the beginning. They would recognise what she was, or they would bleed.

"Then take Excalibur and air in your lungs as my blessing." Guinevere's fingers caressed Andie's face, moving down to press hard against her ribs. As Andie winced, the dome around her popped like a bubble, water crashing in around her once again. Guinevere vanished, a heavy weight digging into Andie's right hand, the iron maiden no longer trapping her inside its metal shell.

Struggling against the pressure of the water, she kicked hard, launching herself upwards. When she broke the surface, she gasped in lungfuls of air. The cars were gone, Harlem River Lift Bridge deserted. How long had she been beneath the water, breathing by Guinevere's mercy? A dark blanket of stars glimmered overhead, and Andie dragged herself from the river and onto the shore.

Looking down, her fingers were clasped around the most beautiful sword she'd ever seen. The power hummed from it, a soothing pulse of magic in contrast to the horror she'd experienced holding Clarent. A golden rose was embedded in the hilt, the blade reflecting the silvery moonlight as she turned it over in her hand. The balance was perfect, the weight even, as if it had been made for her.

The legendary Excalibur. The sword of Mad King Arthur, and it belonged to her. She had no inkling of what Guinevere meant when she had called her the 'Morning Star', though perhaps it was a name for the one who wielded such a sword. She knew without a doubt what wielding such a sword meant: glory.

She choked out a sob, pain and paradise reconciling within her as tears mingled with the water on her cheeks. The attempt on her life was fresh and agonising, an open wound she refused to acknowledge. Yet beyond that desolation, there was delight. Salt and sorrow laced her smile, tears still tracking down her face.

Andie placed both hands on Excalibur's hilt, magic jolting through her. Pulses of golden light flooded from her, bathing the Harlem River in a warm glow. Brightness pushed out the shadows, light chasing the darkness from the banks of the river. Yet the darkness still existed in Andie's heart, where it thrived.

Noel had tried to kill her, and he had failed. Cold certainty had lined every muscle in his face as the iron maiden had tumbled into the water, the certainty that she would drown in the cold river.

Andie's smile twisted sinister as she gripped Excalibur and strode from the river's edge. Her heart thundered a war drum in her chest. The Lords, the Alderidge brothers, Larkin…they had seen nothing yet. Anyone who dared cross her would wish they had never been born.

The Morning Star marched to the beat of an impending battle, dripping with water and wickedness, Excalibur glowing bright as the sun in her hand.

Chapter Forty-One

Prue Clermont

The wallpaper in the bedroom that Prue was confined to was peeling and faded, pulling back to reveal the beige paint beneath. She had more time to inspect it than do anything else, reeling from the shock of Sadie's betrayal and the truth of her heritage. In truth, she was more angry at herself. How had she not noticed? Sadie was always invited to prestigious events. She had stopped her from ripping Charles and Abigail's essences to shreds, when they had more than earned it.

A knock on the door made Prue start, fists curling in the blankets on her bed. The Lords were still debating what to do with her, as far as she could tell. Sadie had come to her door, attempting to plead with her through the wood, but Prue refused to see her or speak to her. That, at least, Sadie respected. Prue's stomach twisted every time she heard Sadie's soft footsteps padding away, yet she stood her ground.

Sadie had betrayed her. Prue didn't owe her a damn thing, least of all the opportunity to deepen her web of deceit, to further confuse her with secrets and half-truths.

"It's Lord Winter." He paused. "May I come in?"

Prue didn't think she had much choice. She was a prisoner, not a guest.

"Alright."

The door clicked open and he strode into the room, eyes raking over the decor with a humourless smile. If Prue remembered correctly, Lord Winter was the only one of the quartet who was from an impoverished background. He had done well for himself. She wondered if he'd betrayed someone he loved to do it, bitterness settling into the pit of her stomach.

"Lord Spring wants to meet with you, but I hoped we could have a private word first."

The older Lords were candid, but Lord Winter had a quiet demeanour that unsettled Prue. The familiar hunger pulled at her, though she ignored its seductive allure. Lord Winter hadn't done wrong by her yet. She regarded him with suspicion.

"About what?"

"The others are terrified of you." An amused smile tugged at the corners of his lips, dark eyes flicking to her. "I'd be lying if I said I wasn't, too. But fear makes people do stupid things, and I've come too far to let it rule me."

A shadow passed over his face, a door closing behind his eyes. Whatever lay in the depths of his heart, fear had played a part in it. Despite Lord Winter's calm composure, there were broken shards that Prue didn't reach for, lest she cut her fingers on their sharp edges. Instead she watched him with silent anticipation, waiting for the part where he got to the point.

"It may not seem like it, but we have enemies." Lord Winter's smile tightened. "Some of them may be closer to home than we'd like to imagine. In fact, I daresay that the Alderidge brothers are top of that list."

Prue lurched to her feet, startled by his blunt accusation. Noel Alderidge had been the one to accompany Lord Winter when he'd met with Prue and Sadie, and there hadn't appeared to be any animosity between the pair. Though, she supposed wryly, the same could be said of her and Sadie. Had Lord Winter known the truth the whole time?

"Why would you possibly need my help?" Prue demanded. She had too eagerly set her foot into one trap, and had no intention of doing it a second time.

Lord Winter was quiet for a long moment, the silence stretching until Prue wondered if he would respond at all. Then he sighed, shoulders slumping.

"The magical barriers that hide locations such as the Carnival from the public eye…they're failing. We don't know why, but there is something *wrong* at the moment. The other Lords have more urgent matters at hand. I prefer to think in the long-term. If the barriers fail, we risk exposure. We risk more than that, if we can't determine the cause."

Prue tapped her foot impatiently. "Again, what does this have to do with me?"

"Because I believe you're the key." Lord Winter's dark eyes lit up with fervour. "The first Scourge anyone has heard of in centuries. If there's someone I want on my side, I'd like it to be you."

Prue processed this information with no small amount of concern. The magical barriers failing, Lord Winter suspecting the Alderidge brothers had ulterior motives, the sudden and unexplained absence of Lord Summer…there certainly were a lot of troubling things occurring in the magical world.

After Sadie, there was much for Prue to reflect on. There was every chance that Lord Winter simply wished to use and discard her. There was every chance he was lying, and would betray her given the chance. Yet as she assessed his earnest gaze, she couldn't think why. He'd disclosed information that would be treacherous if discovered by the others among the elite, all because he wanted her help.

Prue liked feeling useful, and that people might hinge on her assistance. If Lord Winter betrayed her, then she could destroy every piece of magic within him. Such a dark thought may once have frightened her, but the days were gone when she shrank away from her power. People would want to use her regardless, so why not give them consequences when they did?

"In return?" Boldness pulsed through Prue as she folded her arms over her chest. If she was to assist Lord Winter, she wanted a fair deal.

"Well, freedom from this hellhole for a start." Lord Winter arched an eyebrow as he looked around the room. "Protection, too. I can't promise you'll ever be safe, but I can vow to do my utmost to provide sanctuary."

"I can't promise you'll ever be safe." At least he was honest, she supposed. Nonetheless, the notion of being hunted for the rest of her life left a sour taste beneath her tongue. She tried not to think of Mark, for whenever she did, bile rose in her throat and tears bloomed in her eyes. She would grieve him in private, as he deserved.

Prue considered her options. She could refuse to help Lord Winter, uncertain of where her future lay or whether she would ever be released from the prison that was this damn room. Or she could accept, knowing that she had his promise to free her and give her a safe haven, whatever that may look like. One of the options was certainly more attractive than the other, and she snatched at it while she had the opportunity.

"Alright, Lord Winter. It's a deal."

A grin spread across his face. "Please, call me Desmond."

∗ ∗ ∗

The Templeton library was tranquil as Prue stepped inside to meet with Lord Spring. He was all the more formidable for being Sadie's father, for being the father of those monsters, Charles and Abigail. All scions of a magical dynasty, the Templeton name and blood giving them unprecedented levels of access and privilege. Squaring her shoulders, Prue walked over to the desk where Lord Spring sat, poring over the latest newspaper.

"Your children *murdered* my husband." Prue managed to keep her voice level even as devastation threatened to unbalance it. No matter her conversation with Lord Spring, no matter what he wanted, she would not let Mark's death go unpunished.

"Do you know what collateral damage is, Mrs Clermont?" Lord Spring peered over his glasses, his disdainful expression and derisive words making Prue's hands ball into fists by her side. "Your husband's death was unfortunate, and I can only assure you that Charles and Abigail will be dealt with."

Somehow, she sincerely doubted that.

"What about Sadie?" she pressed, desperate to know how his illegitimate daughter had managed to sink her claws in so deep, what Lord Spring had told her to discover. "You barely even recognise her, and yet…"

"Enough, Mrs Clermont." Lord Spring held up a hand, mouth twisting in contempt. "You are fortunate that the Alderidges' clumsy attempts on your life failed. You are alive and well because of us."

"Because you need something from me." Prue's words were soft but firm, secure in their certainty. If the Lords had intended to murder her, she would be dead.

"Of course." Lord Spring steepled his fingers on the desk as he observed her. "You are a Scourge, an anomaly. Considering the fact that we are currently having a crisis with regards to the Magical Freedoms Brigade, your abilities could be very useful."

He wanted her to steal magic from those who were fighting for their right to use it. Shivers crawled like worms across Prue's skin. What little the resistance had, Lord Spring wanted her to rob them of it. She reined in her disgust and horror, swallowing the insults that lingered on the tip of her tongue.

"To make it easier for you to stamp them out, you mean."

"They are a danger to themselves and everyone around them," Lord Spring snapped, and Prue wondered how often he had people question him, how often people stood their ground instead of merely capitulating. "Magic has been closely guarded for a millennium for a reason. We safeguard these secrets so people cannot use them for something stupid."

Prue only knew what Sadie had told her about the magical community. Perhaps she could utilise her new alliance with Lord Winter, discover more about the things Lord Spring and the rest of the elite were hiding.

"Well, why don't you just have Charles kill them?" Acid bit into Prue's words. "That's what you did to my husband, after all. Your children seem resourceful, and more than up to the task."

"There is no need for theatrics." There was a cold warning in Lord Spring's tone, in the dark gleam in his eyes. "Fortunately, yes, my children have proved relatively competent. At least, the older two. Though I cannot say the same for Felix and the bastard."

Prue flinched as though he'd slapped her. Despite her anger and hurt toward Sadie, the callous words from Lord Spring, the contemptuous twist of his lips, indicated his utter disapproval of his illegitimate daughter. Sadie, whose conflicted expression and the crack in her voice had told Prue she was doing everything in her power to get Lord Spring to notice her, to care about her. The notion Sadie had done any of this to protect Prue herself settled heavier over her shoulders.

"What did you say?" Prue's voice was dangerously soft. A quiet dare, pushing Lord Spring to make a decision: back down in the face of her anger, or continue forward. He barrelled onwards without a moment's hesitation.

Lord Spring scoffed. "Oh, come now. You know by now what Sadie is. An unfortunate mistake. At least my other children have some pride in themselves. Sadie would grovel at my feet like a dog begging for scraps. It's unbecoming, almost as much as her *queer* tendencies."

Prue's blood boiled in her veins, her body beginning to tremble with rage. This old fuck had set his psychotic oldest child on her husband and didn't care a thing about the murder of a wholly innocent, uninvolved man. He watched Sadie pleading for a shred of his affection, and weaponised his paternity against her.

Lord Spring was one of the worst kinds of men: indifferent to anything but his own power, and what he could gain. A scion of an ancient name and an old legacy, believing that his own existence was a contribution to magical society. He treated Sadie like dirt, and so Prue would prove to him that he was less than dirt. That he was nothing.

Cold fury propelled her into motion, and she reached down into the depths of her power and shook it awake, calling it to action. She splayed her fingers on the desk and leaned forward, Lord Spring's startled expression lasting a mere moment before his eyes widened with horror as she plunged her power into his essence and *ripped*.

Lord Spring screamed, the agony-riddled sound echoing through the library as Prue tugged hard, wrenching the essence from his body with all the anger and hatred she could muster. In her grasp, his magic felt different to the first time she'd done this, sharper and more electric. It zapped at her fingers as if pleading to be released. As Lord Spring slumped against the desk, sobbing, Prue's lips twisted in a thin line as she held the essence in both hands and tore it apart.

Let him serve as an example of what she was capable of. Let him show the others that she didn't care for their fancy titles or their influence. If they crossed her, she would take the only thing that mattered in their society: their magic. Now, he was not Lord Spring. Now, he was just a man.

Invigoration swept through her body, and when she loosed a breath, her shoulders relaxed. A warmth spread across her, like she had stepped out into the sunlight. There was a strength to her limbs, like a tree digging its roots deep. She looked down at the pathetic, crying man before her, tucking a strand of brown hair behind her ear.

"Let me be clear, Mr Templeton." Prue's voice contained the same firm politeness that she'd always possessed, with an undercurrent of something older, darker. The undercurrent of Scourge power. "I am not part of the magical community beholden to the Lords, and I have no intention of becoming so. I am a Scourge, and I follow my own instincts, not the whims of frightened old men."

He had no response to that, other than to muffle another sob. He curled over his desk, reeling in the loss of his magic. Prue had taken it apart, scattered it to the wind, with nothing left for him to cling to. She crossed over to the door to the library and threw it open, inhaling the scent of old books and rose potpourri on the landing.

It smelled like freedom.

CHAPTER FORTY-TWO

Ursula Delavane

URSULA HAD REELED IN THE DAYS since Larkin's departure, certain that her heart was broken. How could she grieve someone who was still alive? It hurt as much as the cruel barb that Larkin had been responsible for Franklin's death. Her husband and her son, lost to her. The house echoed with her footsteps, an eerie silence descending upon the Delavane residence. Every noise resonated, leaving behind the quiet certainty that she was alone.

Perhaps it was that loneliness that led Ursula to invite Noel over for tea, or perhaps it was the temptation to see if there was anything more he'd learned since their last discussion. She had nothing new for him, she explained over jam-and-cream laden scones. Considering the state of affairs following Larkin's departure, the Templeton library was not an easy place to simply slip into.

"I imagine they will soon be at work deciding upon a new Lord Summer," Noel said carefully as he sipped at his tea, hazel eyes bright with a zeal Ursula couldn't fathom.

"They already did, or rather, *Lady* Summer." She prickled with irritation. She was Larkin's mother. If they were truly to embark on the foolishness of appointing a woman to the position, it should be her, not the girl Larkin was yet to wed. "Andie Fairley assumed the role, the same day they took Larkin's magic from him."

"Well, I don't see that being a problem." He set his cup down in its saucer, his mild tone betraying the severity of his next words. "Considering the fact that I killed her."

Ursula lapsed into stunned silence, the same sort that had occupied the house for hours at a time. It was no secret that Noel harboured hatred in his heart for Andie, and yet killing her…as he was not one of the Lords, it technically did not go against any of their regulations. She knew what it was like to have blood on one's hands, though Noel never made any attempt to disguise it.

"What? When?"

"I tossed her into the iron maiden and threw it into the Harlem River." Noel shrugged, his utter lack of remorse tracing chills up her arms. "No matter how powerful her magic, she could never use it there."

Ursula's fingers trembled around her own cup as she raised it to her lips, taking a long sip. She had never much liked Andie, but *murdering* her…she realised, with cold dread, exactly what sort of man she was dealing with. Noel was dangerous, a fact she had never considered when she'd unwittingly allied herself with him.

"Regardless." Noel waved a dismissive hand, as if the brutal murder of Lady Summer and the most powerful woman in the city was of little consequence. "I have other matters I wish to discuss with you. We've found the Arthurian essences, in a way."

Ursula's breath halted in her throat, the cup dropping from her fingers and tea spilling across the table, seeping into the white cloth. The Arthurian essences—those of Arthur, Mordred and Lancelot. They'd been lost over the years, and so the claim that Noel had found them was a bold one. If he was lying…

"In a way?" she repeated, ignoring the milky stain spreading across the tablecloth like a disease.

"Arthur and Mordred's were…removed." Distaste curled Noel's lip. "Recently, if the look of the place is anything to judge by. We were only able to retrieve Lancelot, and so Garrett and I have decided to keep it safe to prevent it from meeting the same fate as the others."

Two essences missing. It was far more disturbing than if all three had been found, because it meant someone had stolen the essences. If the Lords hadn't mentioned them, hadn't bragged about discovering them, it was most likely the Brigade. Ursula shuddered to think what they would do with such powerful magical artefacts.

"I need your help with this." Noel reached across the table, resting his hand over Ursula's. The brush of his skin on hers made her start, drawing her back to reality. When she glanced at him, his hazel eyes were beseeching, pupils dilating. "Whoever has the missing essences won't use them for our benefit, I can assure you."

"How can I help?" she demanded, resisting the urge to draw her hand away from his. "Because I can read some of the text written in a long-dead language? What good is that when it comes to real magic?"

"Oh, Ursula." Noel tilted his head to the side, pity crossing his sharp, handsome face. "What you can do is real magic. If the Clermont woman is a Scourge, then you're…a Linguist, I suppose. Someone who can interpret what was written all those years ago."

Unease coursed through Ursula with the force of a raging river, threatening to topple her and drown her. Just as Andie had drowned in the Harlem River. Had it been quick, she wondered, or had she fought it like she had fought everything else in her life? Noel thought she was *useful,* and somehow that was far more terrifying than a lifetime of being simply an accessory to power.

"What is it you're proposing?"

"Well, that's exactly it." A rare smile flashed across Noel's lips, bright and cutting as the steel of a knife. "I'm proposing."

He swept from his chair, crossing over and kneeling before her, taking his hands in hers. Her heart thundered in her chest as she stared down at him, bewilderment holding her rigid in her seat as Noel laid his intentions bare.

"Ursula Delavane, will you marry me?"

There had been love in the eyes of the first man who had proposed to Ursula, when she had been young and naive enough to believe it was the only thing that mattered. There had been determination in Franklin's, much like in Noel's now. Good matches were not about love or affection; they were about weathering the storm together. She had come to care for Franklin in her own way over the years, despite his abuse.

Perhaps she could do the same for Noel. He was a broken creature, wounded by the deaths of his wife and daughter. There were jagged edges to him that had never been allowed to heal. Together, they could bring forth the shattered shards they'd accumulated over the years, and piece them back together again.

"Yes." The answer was easy, leaving Ursula's lips on a single breath. She would be sister-in-law to the Governor of New York, wife to a powerful mage who had the ability to read minds. She would be able to continue living the life of luxury that, since Larkin's rise and fall, looked as though it may leave her behind.

She would be important.

* * *

The lights of the *Jolly Codger* flickered overhead as Ursula sank further into the chair at her booth, the heady scent of sandalwood teeming through the bar. Above the counter were colourful murals of people laughing and dancing, the boldness of the paint indicating they were fresh, not yet tainted by the ravages of time. Behind the counter, jazz music crackled across the record player, the bartender tapping his foot in time as he served drinks.

"I didn't know if you would come," Warren muttered as he slid into the booth across from her, removing his hat as he inspected her. "I'm glad that you did. We have a lot to talk about."

He raised a hand and alarm coursed through Ursula, before she swivelled in her seat to see that he'd summoned one of the waiters to fetch them a drink. She remained silent as the young man approached and set down a bottle of brandy and two glasses. Warren poured himself one, but Ursula shook her head at his inquisitive look.

"I don't know why you wanted to see me, Mr Fairley." Her fist uncurled to reveal the crumpled note she'd clasped in her fingers, the same one she'd found in the letterbox with a location, date and time written down, signed off with the letters 'WF'.

Was it about Andie? Ursula was quite attuned to grief, and saw none of it in Warren's blue eyes, or the tense set of his jaw. Had he not yet found out about his daughter's fate? Ursula's quiet continued, for she would not be the one to break Warren's heart with such horrific news.

"You and I are the only ones who are able to read the ancient language written in the old tomes." Warren clasped his hands in front of him, observing her keenly.

"Linguists," Ursula murmured.

Warren blinked in surprise. "Yes, I…I suppose. When you and Noel visited me, I told you the truth. He could see into my mind, but not even he could see everything. It was true that the old tomes went missing and were lost to me. Fortunately, or unfortunately, depending on how you want to look at it, I happen to know exactly where they went."

Ursula leaned forward, her interest piqued. It was bold of Warren to be telling her this, considering they were not overly familiar. Did his trust stem from desperation, or did he have something to hold over her in exchange for her silence? Her stomach twisted at the idea that he might know about Patrick.

"Where are they now?"

"My son has them."

His son. Syl. Ursula remembered the young man, around Larkin's age, a constant stumble in his step to attest to his drunkenness. Yet there was a sharpness in those green eyes, and the theft of old tomes indicated that they'd vastly underestimated what the boy was capable of. Did he know what Patrick was sent to do? Did he have a part in the plan too?

"There were three magical essences stored in a hidden location. Arthurian essences." Urgency laced Warren's tone, pushing her to take him seriously. "Two of them are gone. The Lords don't even know where they were kept, let alone what's happened. But with two gone…"

Ursula frowned as he shook his head slowly. "Tell me."

Warren raised his glass to his lips and downed the brandy.

"The Arthurian essences served as our protection. The wards that kept the magical community hidden from the everyday world. There is only one essence left now, and those barriers are hanging on by a thread. This is bigger than some power struggle within your little inner circle. This is the fate of the entire magical community."

Had the truth been written in the tomes, or had Warren discovered it another way? Considering how much he was already divulging, Ursula didn't imagine a push for further answers would go well. Had Noel known what the essences did when he informed her about them?

"Where are the essences now?" she demanded, her voice growing stern when she was answered with hesitant silence. "*Warren.* If you want my help, then you need to tell me."

"The essences were stolen in two separate instances, from what I know." He stared down at the table, his eyes burning with a shame she didn't understand. "Mordred's essence, I couldn't say. But Arthur's essence…"

Horror and hope chorused within Ursula. "You know where it is."

"It's too late, Mrs Delavane," Warren's voice cracked over her name, and the misery on his face made an icy shiver ripple up her spine. "It's already done."

Ursula succumbed, pouring herself some brandy. "What are you talking about?"

"I only ever wanted what was best for both of them, and now…" He breathed in deeply, closing his eyes. "Syl has infused himself with Arthur's essence."

Dread trickled from the top of Ursula's head to the pit of her stomach. Everything clicked together, the final pieces of the puzzle slotting into place. Syl was more clever than they'd given him credit for, and he wouldn't have idly consumed something as ancient and powerful as an Arthurian essence unless…unless he was the one who had been running things from the beginning. Unless Syl Fairley was the leader of the Brigade.

"You will never discuss this with anyone else." Warren's deep voice was laced with a power that made her tremble. "Noel will never see this in your mind."

Ursula opened her mouth, wincing at the way the brandy still seemed to burn down her throat. Horrified, she glanced between Warren and the half-finished glass of brandy on the table. He smiled tightly, and she realised the harsh truth: he had never trusted her at all.

"Did you poison me?" she choked out.

Warren shook his head slowly. "A pact. An unbreakable vow. The moment you consumed that brandy, you were bound to it. I would like to think you wouldn't cross me, but deceit is often in the elite's nature. I'm sorry for tricking you, but I had to be certain."

Any thought, any idea of disclosing what Syl was, what he had become, faded from her mind. When her mouth opened, any such words died on her lips, as though she lacked the ability to speak them. She stared down at the magic-infused brandy.

"It's completely up to you whether you choose to help me, Mrs Delavane." Warren pushed himself to his feet, picking up his hat and setting it on his head. "Know this: I have fought long and hard for what is left of my family, and if you endanger them, you will pay the price."

"What do you want me to do?" Ursula demanded, her voice hoarse with anger. "How can I possibly help you if your son has already consumed an essence?"

"The other one, Mordred's." Warren shoved his hands in his pockets, extracting a few coins and counting them out. "You can help me find it."

He strode up to the bar and placed the coins on the counter. Ursula's head spun as the brandy sloshed through her veins, as the jazz music got louder and louder. She gritted her teeth and pressed her hands over her ears, trying to catch her breath as she choked on the air in her lungs.

Death was coming for them all, and it wore Syl Fairley's face.

Chapter Forty-Three

Syl Fairley

The Vault hummed with magic, whispers slipping out through the cracks. As the Magical Freedoms Brigade stormed the underbelly of Belvedere Castle, Syl closed his eyes and let the low buzz lull him, a soothing presence that stroked calm fingers across his scalp. A firm grip on his bicep brought him back to reality, to the darkness illuminated by poor torchlight as the seven members of the Brigade he'd brought with him lit up the way.

"We can't turn back now," Flo hissed in his ear. At nine months pregnant, she and Syl had quarrelled over whether she should have accompanied him, but Flo had insisted she didn't want to miss a moment of their triumph. Nonetheless, guilt gnawed away at her, present in her eyes whenever she looked at the Grimoire in her hands.

Syl supposed he should thank Andie. The Grimoire had gotten them this far, through layers of magical wards that he didn't know if even his new power could surpass. Since he'd infused himself with Arthur's essence, a painful procedure he hadn't even been certain he'd survive, his magic felt…different. Stronger. He could do things he couldn't before, and that knowledge draped over him like a cloak of calm.

"I have no intention of turning back." Syl raised his voice to call out to the others. "Get back!"

They scuttled away from the round stone door that secured the Vault, and Syl concentrated, raising his hands and letting his magic feel out the pulses beyond. They'd been searching for Clarent for over a year now, and when Flo had learned the truth of the Vault, she'd been eager to inform Syl.

The Brigade had once been a drunken idea, a frustration born from too much mead and an angry heart. Yet Patrick shared that determination early on, and in the years since they'd first banded together, the Brigade had grown in numbers and strength. So Syl's thought had become a reality, and a band of disillusioned youths had become the founding members of the Brigade.

Concealing the identity of its leader, as the elite noticed its existence, was paramount. Syl slipped comfortably into the role he was so used to; that of the drunken fool, the bitter young man who used alcohol to drown his grief.

Andie would forgive his treachery, just as he had forgiven her sins. The way she'd killed Claire, the attempted murder of Noel…the darkness within her heart had horrified him once, and he'd turned his back only to face the same within himself. As he had come to terms with her cold ambition, she would have to understand why he'd convinced Flo to steal the Grimoire from her.

Syl inhaled sharply, delving into his magic and focusing it upon the door in front of them. What he possessed now was an odd form of magic he'd never seen before. Not mind, heart or soul. Something unique. The power of Arthur Pendragon. It weighed heavily on his shoulders, and filled him with a solemn delight he frequently suppressed. There was no good in succumbing to the thrill of power, for it would absolutely corrupt him.

Syl raised both of his hands and splayed his fingers. The door to the Vault shimmered as if water disturbed by a thrown rock, before it vanished entirely. A shocked gasp emitted from his lips as the rest of the Brigade cautiously moved through, as if the door had never existed in the first place.

A grin sliced across his face as he moved through into the cool shadows, examining the way the dim lights illuminated the sword in the middle of the room. Mordred's sword, when he possessed Arthur's essence. It would be an irony, to be sure. Yet the whispers around him ascended into cheers at his approach, and elation rose up within him, dangerous as a wildfire.

He was born for this. Everything he had accomplished led him to one moment.

Syl had always loathed the elite. The way they'd treated Warren, casting him aside like garbage the moment he'd left the Carnival burned brightly in his memory. The sneering face of the man who'd convinced their mother she'd lead a better life without them. The bruises on Andie's neck and the sparkling ring on her finger.

They were monsters, all of them. They aspired to ultimate control, and Syl would teach them a lesson they would never forget. They could attempt to hoard magic for themselves, but it was out in the world. The Brigade had weapons at their disposal, including the old tomes Syl had stolen from Warren when his father had been in the midst of a deep depression.

Guilt nipped at his heels, halting his steps. Syl despised lying to his father, stealing from him. The man had done everything in his power to be a good father, to both Syl and Andie. He didn't deserve what Syl had done, and yet with such power, Syl could protect his father. He could even protect Andie, no matter how adamant she was that she didn't need anyone other than herself.

Syl had known Andie far longer than any of the current company she kept. Beyond the confidence and charm, she desperately wanted to be loved. Perhaps that was why she'd put up with Larkin's shit as long as she had, convinced that because she'd gained power, she could also gain his heart. She would have found that with Patrick, but…

Syl swallowed the lump in his throat at the thought of his best friend. He had never imagined, when he'd stationed Patrick and Sadie at the Carnival, what might happen. Patrick was a talented mage in his own right, and his sudden death had almost upended Syl's carefully laid plans. It had broken Andie, and Syl had wondered whether any of it was worth it, if people might die for it.

Yet if he abandoned the Brigade, Patrick's death would be for nothing. Stealing Larkin's essence had paled in comparison to the discovery of the Arthurian essences. There just happened to be a sweet irony in Larkin being stripped of his magic regardless, as if fate had always intended it. They could have taken more than one, but that did not bode well for avoiding discovery, so they had decided upon Arthur's.

"It's beautiful," Flo breathed, and when Syl glanced at her, her wide eyes were fixated upon Clarent. She rested a hand on her stomach, and his gaze followed the movement.

When he had learned about Larkin's child, he'd done everything in his power to protect Flo, dreading the day when the Delavane scion would learn the truth. As it happened, he never had. Regardless, protecting Flo and the baby was of the utmost importance to Syl, Delavane blood or not. He hadn't expected to care so deeply about her when they'd begun stepping out together, but Flo was tenacious with a warm heart, and so Syl's guard had lowered without him meaning it to. The child would not share his blood, would not know what it was like to be treated differently because of the colour of their skin, but he would love them no less fiercely.

Steeling himself and blowing out a deep breath, Syl cautiously approached the sword. The thrum of magic was rich in the air, washing over his skin like warm water. The whispers in the dark grew louder as he stepped up to it, examining the craftsmanship. There was a devastating beauty in it, the weapon that had killed Mad King Arthur.

Syl reached out with cautious fingers and let them close around the sword's hilt. The whispers around him ascended into chants, his name repeated over and over. Bliss trailed over his skin, a soft touch that relaxed his shoulders. From the darkness, something ancient and powerful called to him. He would answer it.

Syl pulled, expecting resistance. Instead, Clarent slid free of the rock that held it prisoner for a thousand years, into the hand of its new bearer.

Flo pressed her hands over her mouth, wonder shining in her dark eyes. The other members of the Brigade fell into an awed silence, the hush extending through the dark depths of the Vault. A cool shiver raced up Syl's spine as he turned Clarent over in his hands, admiring the ruby-encrusted hilt and the way the blade shimmered silver in the dimness. The sword's ancient magic pulsed off him, ripples of it spreading through the Vault, choking every last crevice.

The Evening Star grinned, elation surging through his veins, and raised Clarent to the sky.

CHAPTER FORTY-FOUR

Larkin Delavane

A SPEAKEASY IN BROOKLYN HAD BECOME LARKIN'S haven, a place away from the world of magic where he could drown his sorrows beneath the warm glow of the lights. He still had money, after all. Slamming down his glass on the bar, Larkin signalled the bartender to refill it. The alcohol didn't completely ease his suffering, but it did remove the sting. The burn of whiskey coursing down his throat was far easier to swallow than Andie's betrayal.

Larkin inhaled a deep breath, swilling the whiskey in his glass. Everyone he thought he could trust had turned their backs on him, and for what? None of them had liked Franklin. He had done them a favour by killing him. His father, the bastard, was violent and cruel, and worse than that, he had lacked any insight and ambition. Not that anyone had listened to Larkin's attempts to expand their magic usage beyond the Carnival.

"I heard you've been here every night lately." A familiar drawl made Larkin's fingers tighten on his glass, his jaw clenching as he swivelled on his stool to meet the cool gaze of Cyril Fordyce.

"What the fuck do you want?" he snapped. As Lord Summer, he possessed more patience, more politeness, more charisma. Yet they'd stolen his title from him, along with all of the magic he possessed. He didn't owe Cyril a damn thing, not when the older man had been part of that unforgivable theft.

"To talk to you." Cyril sat on the stool beside Larkin's, ignoring his scoff. "I know you must resent me, but I had to play my part, Larkin. What do you think would have happened if we both took the fall?"

"I thought you may have defended me, at least." Larkin glared at Cyril with bloodshot eyes, noting the genuine remorse on his face. "You, my mother…everyone turned their backs on me because it was *convenient.*"

His voice cracked over the last word, breaking like a wave on the rocks. It had been disturbingly easy for them to cast him aside. His mother, who should have been his first and last supporter, had turned her back because she had valued her reputation more than her son.

"Well, perhaps you should stop killing people, then." Cyril beckoned the bartender over for his own glass of whiskey.

Larkin's brow furrowed. "What are you talking about? The only person I killed was Franklin, and you know that."

Cyril paused with his glass halfway to his mouth. "Your mother said you killed Patrick."

"Why the fuck would I do that?" he demanded, confusion morphing into agitation as he drummed his fingers against his glass. "Why the fuck would she *say* that, unless…"

Unless pushing the blame onto Larkin would solve the mystery of Patrick's death. Unless Ursula, in all her regal elegance, had been the real murderer. The realisation caused unhinged laughter to bubble forth from Larkin's throat, and he shook his head slowly. Betrayed by not one, but two of the women he held dear. His hatred solidified like a rock in his stomach.

"Larkin," Cyril sighed, raking his fingers through his hair, peppered with more grey than Larkin remembered. "I want to help you, but I need to be careful. Surely you can understand that."

"I'm not an idiot," Larkin sneered. His mind drifted to the horrors of the Templeton cellar, the unbearable agony as his essence was ripped from him. He had begged for death instead, had wanted death over powerlessness. "So, who did they pick to replace me?"

The grim set of Cyril's mouth told him that he wouldn't like the answer.

"Andie Fairley became the first Lady Summer."

Larkin went absolutely still, a coldness sweeping over his body. That fucking *bitch*. Not only did she have the audacity to take everything from him, but she'd then assumed his title like she had the right to it. When he thought of Andie, his heartbeat raced, his fingers itching to wrap around her throat and squeeze. He'd choke the life from her with his bare hands for what she'd done to him.

"Was it real?" Cyril asked, a rare sympathy to his tone. "What you felt for her?"

Angry tears welled in Larkin's eyes and a bitter smile bit across his face. He had fallen for Andie with everything he had, determined that he would win her over. How could he ever have loved such a cruel creature? How could he have ever wanted her to give him her heart, knowing now that she had none?

Andie was beautiful and charming, but now he saw she wielded those blessings like a whip. She cut him to the bone with it. He would have made her his wife, and yet she had chosen spite over tradition. He didn't give a fuck how powerful she was now. He would make it his life's mission to destroy her, as she had destroyed him.

"I loved her," Larkin admitted softly, the words acidic on his tongue. "I loved her, and she ruined me."

"I need your help, Larkin." The words made his head whip up. "As you need mine. Maybe we can come to an agreement."

His answering laugh was mirthless. "What could you possibly have to offer me? I have nothing left. Whether you wanted to or not, you helped see to that."

"Come with me," Cyril said as he rose to his feet, draining the last of the whiskey from his glass. Brow furrowed in suspicion, Larkin eased himself from his stool. What was the worst that could happen? He had already been betrayed, already lost everything he cared about. Either Cyril was genuine, or he would be giving Larkin a merciful demise.

He followed the other man away from the warm glow of the bar and into the shadows of the secluded booths, each with a velvet curtain drawn around it for privacy. The two men stepped inside, and when Larkin tugged the curtain shut, something glowed in the darkness. At first he thought Cyril had a torch, but when he looked, it was a silvery light in a jar.

An essence.

Larkin's heart leapt with hope. "Is that…is it mine?"

"No. It's something better." Cyril set the glass jar on the table with a dull thunk, his smile sinister in the cool glow of the essence's light. "There are things happening in this city far beyond you losing your position. Magic is not what it was once, but as one of the Lords, there is only so far I can go."

Clarity settled over Larkin despite the buzz of the whiskey. He was beyond the reach of the elite now, since they had forsaken him. They believed him to be powerless, destitute. Perhaps that was what they wanted of him. He hungrily examined the essence in the jar, the idea of a future where he had magic. The taste of it was sweet on his lips.

"So you want me to do your dirty work. To look in places you can't go."

"You could put it that way." Cyril slid the glass jar across the table, the shine of it illuminating Larkin's face. "In exchange, I will give you Mordred's essence."

Fascinated horror caught the words on Larkin's tongue as he stared down at the unassuming essence in the jar. This was an *Arthurian* essence. This was power beyond anything he could have dreamed of… and Cyril was offering it to *him*. With such cruel, ancient magic in his veins, Larkin would be unstoppable. He could rip Andie Fairley apart, and even she wouldn't be able to stop him.

The temptation was too delicious to ignore, despite knowing that such a mighty boon would come with consequences. He would crawl through the mud, he would bloody his hands for Cyril, if it meant he got his power back. By the triumphant gleam in Cyril's eyes, he knew it, too.

"I accept."

"Sit down." Cyril unscrewed the lid on top of the jar, and the essence began thrashing angrily in its prison. "This is going to hurt."

Acknowledgements

Writing historical fantasy is not an easy process, and I have so many people to thank for helping me make this story what it is today. I have always been fascinated by the Roaring Twenties and so when this idea sparked to life, the setting and time period were obvious to me. Working within the framework of our world instead of one I had created proved difficult, but I am so grateful for the help I've had with creating this story.

To my critique partners: Kellie & Lauren. Thank you for keeping it real with me and giving so much detailed feedback that really made me think. Your comments, both the constructive and the general reactions, fuelled me to push through with this at times when it felt like it was messy or getting too hard.

To my beta readers: Julia, Charlotte, Annie, Abra & Kristy. Thank you for providing your thoughts on this story, and really giving me things to consider when finetuning the aspects of plot and character development. Having additional sets of eyes really helped make this book the best it could possibly be.

To my amazing editors, formatters & designers: Natasha & Alex at Fox & Rabbit Press. Thank you for seeing my vision for this story and helping me develop this into what the book has become today. Your dedication to helping with research, character development and backstory, not to mention attention to detail, has made this truly shine and I cannot thank you both enough for all the work you put into this. Historical fiction can be a struggle, and you made my dream a reality and enriched the story and characters from our first conversation.

To the women reading this: I hope you find something of yourself in this book. Strength and determination comes in so many different forms, and my greatest dream is to inspire others as I myself have been inspired. Never let anyone doubt your strength, and never be afraid to let your voice be heard.

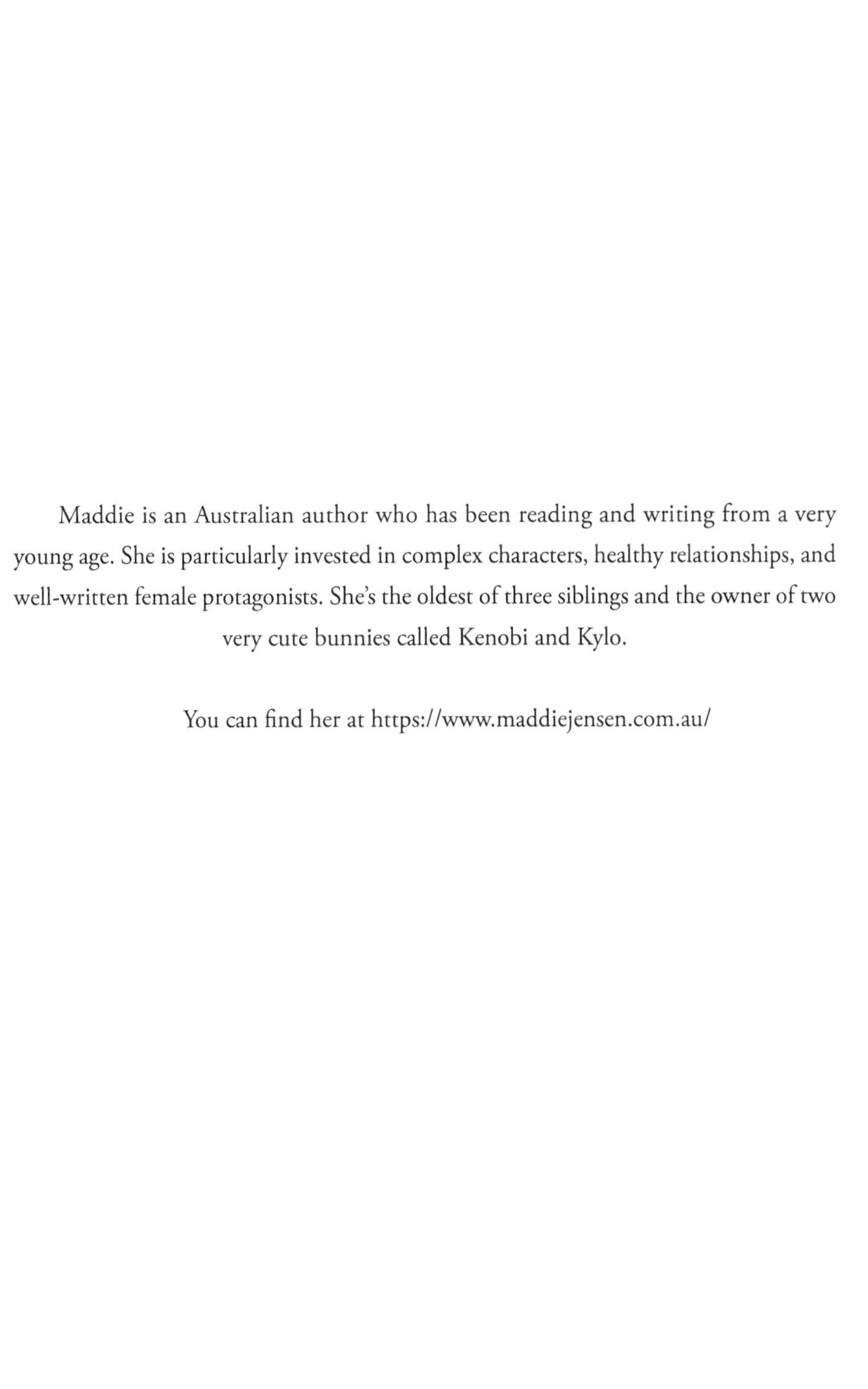

Maddie is an Australian author who has been reading and writing from a very young age. She is particularly invested in complex characters, healthy relationships, and well-written female protagonists. She's the oldest of three siblings and the owner of two very cute bunnies called Kenobi and Kylo.

You can find her at https://www.maddiejensen.com.au/